NIGHT BLIND

For Vic Basile —
your brother is in here
somewhere, & we are
so happy to meet you.

to Peace —
Jan Worth-nelson
9/23/11

Poetry by Jan Worth

Home During a Dry Spell
Ridgeway Press

Moving
Water Brother Publishing

NIGHT BLIND

A NOVEL

JAN WORTH

iUniverse, Inc.

New York Lincoln Shanghai

Night Blind

Copyright © 2006 by Jan Worth

iUniverse books may be ordered through booksellers or by contacting:

iUniverse
2021 Pine Lake Road, Suite 100
Lincoln, NE 68512
www.iuniverse.com
1-800-Authors (1-800-288-4677)

This is a work of fiction. All of the characters, names, incidents, organizations and dialogue in this novel are either the products of the author's imagination or are used fictitiously.

Permission granted by Wesleyan University Press to use excerpts from "The Blessing" and "Lying in a Hammock at William Duffy's Farm in Pine Island, Minnesota" from *The Collected Poems of James Wright*.
Lines quoted in Chapter Twenty-one are from "To My Dear and Loving Husband" by Anne Bradstreet.
Lines quoted in Chapter Twenty-four are from "To His Coy Mistress" by Andrew Marvell.

ISBN-13: 978-0-595-39977-2 (pbk)
ISBN-13: 978-0-595-84365-7 (ebk)
ISBN-10: 0-595-39977-0 (pbk)
ISBN-10: 0-595-84365-4 (ebk)

Printed in the United States of America

For Ted

ACKNOWLEDGMENTS

This book has been a work in progress, in my heart and mind, for thirty years. With such a long gestation, there are inevitably many people to thank, and I am grateful for the support of several significant institutions and for the love and patience of my many friends, family, and literary colleagues. Among them:

The U.S. Peace Corps, which changed my life.

The Ragdale Foundation for two wonderfully fruitful residencies, at which the first serious drafts emerged. I especially include my sister "bluestockings," Sibyl Johnston and Janet St. John.

The Warren Wilson MFA program, which provided an unparalleled and ongoing community of teachers and kindred spirits.

The English Department and the College of Arts and Sciences at the University of Michigan–Flint, which have allowed me the joy of teaching and talking about writing to my heart's content.

The people of the Kingdom of Tonga, in particular Sione and Sivai Osamu and their children, who offered openhearted and unfailing love and good humor during my Tonga years.

All the readers, including Lora Beckwith, Cary Bernstein, Dennis Brown, Helen Blumner, Deborah Clancy, Ellen Dudley, Marla Houghteling, Theodosia Robertson, Art Vinsel, and Rich Wisneski. Also those who listened in various backyards, living rooms, and workshops and kept the red wine flowing: Bob Barnett, Jacob Blumner, Philip Greenfield, Ralph and Audrey Johnson, Josie Kearns, Joe Matuzak, Scott Russell, and D. J. Trela.

Emile Hons, whose continuing, active love for the Kingdom of Tonga is an inspiration.

Shawn Johnson, who helped me trust my path.

Alex "The Blade" Nalbach, gifted editor and friend, who walked with me through the darkest times.

Eileen Pollack, whose feedback reignited my energy for revision.

Lindsay Sagnette, who believed in the book even when it was still an awkward teenager.

Phil Weiss, a generous man whose passionate obsession with the events of 1976–77, both prodded and stimulated my own.

Driftwood Review, under former editors Dave Larsen and Jeff Vande Zande, for publishing an early version of chapter two.

Professor Eric Shumway, for Tongan versions of proverbs in the book that was the Tonga PCVs' Bible in 1976: *An Intensive Course in Tongan* from the University Press of Hawaii. The English versions have been paraphrased to suit the events of the chapters that follow.

Numerous Tonga Peace Corps volunteers and staff from long ago whose memories and friendship helped shape my story, among them Mike Basile, Carolyn Bly, Roger Bowen, Bob Forbes, Kevin Holmes, Lorraine Leiser, the late Ralph Masi, Jim McGivney, Rick Nathanson, Bob Peterson, Doug Peterson, Joe Perrone, Tom Riddle, Bill Stults, Kerry Wilson, Dave Wyler, and Jackie Yakovleff.

Wes and Gail Worth, cherished family, who offered me harbor in California in the months after Peace Corps, when I was still desperately afraid of earthquakes, insisted on going around barefoot, and tried to light the stove with a match. Also my sister Connie Smoke, who helps our family remember and appreciate our shared legacy.

Danny Rendleman, beloved poet and friend for life, who was with me so many miles of the journey, even that kava party one winter night in Flint.

My new California family—Sasha, Bill, Riley, Deborah, Jesse, and Michael—who have done more than they know to make this book a reality.

The terrific editors of iUniverse, whose lively, respectful attention and professionalism made this a far better book.

And most of all, I celebrate the miracle of love from my husband, Ted, whom I always dreamed of meeting again and who is a much better man than Gabriel Bonner.

CHAPTER 1

▼

October 1976

Potopoto 'a niu mui. *The wisdom of a young coconut.*[1]

News of the murder hadn't reached me yet that morning, and my one wish, my only wish, was to sleep off my hangover. But the Kingdom of Tonga wanted me to wake up. It wasn't just the rooster I knew so well by then, his bright orange cape of feathers quivering with every crow, every screech, from the lowest branches of the lemon tree. It wasn't just the tapa makers, pounding rhythmically, patiently, with their wooden mallets at the strips of fiber on an ancient hollow log. It wasn't just the mangoes falling on my tin roof every ten or fifteen minutes. It wasn't just the goat jumping with a clatter onto Tevita's minimoke, the beat-up old dune buggy, and producing a stream of shouted curses from the kids. It wasn't just the family pig rubbing against the outside of my hut and squealing to be let in to get his chin scratched. It wasn't just the church bells of Nuku'alofa. The whole damn country didn't believe in sleeping in.

I rolled over on my metal cot, the iron creaking, and rubbed my eyes. I flicked a mosquito off my arm and stared at my net, rolled up and dangling limply from the lashed beams. I couldn't stand having the net around me, the way everybody told me it should be to protect against filariasis. As a kid, when I thought I'd be an explorer, the idea of a mosquito net over a bed seemed exotic. The first time

---

1. Tongan versions of the proverbs at the start of each chapter are from Eric Shumway's *Intensive Course in Tongan* from the University Press of Hawaii. However, I have taken liberties with some of the English translations, adjusting them to match events of the chapters. Any paraphrases or inaccuracies are the responsibility of the author.

Tevita, my landlord and de facto Tongan father, showed me how to untie the net and let it down, I eagerly climbed into the bed. But within minutes, I felt entombed. The world outside looked gauzed over, fogged. Other than that first night, to make Tevita happy, I never used it.

I nudged at the hurricane window, propping it open an inch or two with a stick for fresh air. Hinged at the top, the push-out windows seemed to be cut into the hut as an afterthought. When the windows were down, my Tongan house was dark, day or night. But when they were open, there was nothing between me and the world outside. I'd developed a habit of pushing the windows open just far enough for a bit of air and light, but not far enough for anyone to see inside. I needed light the way other people needed caffeine, and with a hangover, I really needed air.

The morning air of Polynesia still amazed me. Rich and spicy, not crisp and clean like winter mornings back home in Ohio—the kind of sharp air that makes a person resolve to stand up straight. This air was lavish and damp, luxuriant with the scents of gardenia and salt water. Margarita air.

Not that you could get tequila here, unless some had just come through duty-free from somebody's trip home. Beer, yes. There was always beer.

I was twenty-five that October, about to turn twenty-six. I'd been in college in the '60s and had been a reporter for the first half of the '70s. But I'd never drunk so much beer in my life. The house brew at the Coconut Club was Steinlager, in brown quart bottles, fifty cents each. The bar served little white paper bags of peanuts stapled at the top for another twenty cents. I could make a supper out of that combination, and often did.

Last night, though, the party hadn't been at the Coconut Club. The Peace Corps treated us instead to the country's classiest establishment, the International Dateline Hotel.

The occasion was to honor me and twenty other greenhorns, the trainees of Tonga Group 17. We'd just finished our three months of in-country boot camp, just like sixteen other groups of Americans had done in the ten years before us. We'd spent three hours each morning sitting cross-legged on mats in the humid, two-story training house, struggling to master the vowel-rich language. We'd dozed through endless lectures about kinship systems and the politics of ancient Polynesia. We'd nibbled from canoe-sized platters of cassava and taro, conscientiously chewed octopus and raw fish salad, and bent over, one by one, yelping and bitching at Clark, the Peace Corps doctor, for gamma globulin shots.

And then we got kicked out of our cozy communal quarters, Kalisimasi's Guest House, and into whatever individual Tongan abodes the Peace Corps had been able to wrangle. I moved into a cockroachy, oval lashed-bamboo hut on Tevita's property. Despite its bugs, it was a respectable little place with its own flush toilet, a cold-water shower, and a two-burner hot plate. Other Peace Corps volunteers moved to whitewashed concrete block condos next to the high school or to wood cottages on stilts over the lagoon. And ready or not, last night, we were declared trained and ready to start our jobs. After the feast, the crowd spilled into the hotel's leafy courtyard and danced, flirted, bragged, and sang Tongan songs, Bob Dylan songs, and French folk songs until two or three o'clock. I remembered someone yowling "Five Hundred Miles" and being shouted down.

I remembered wobbling back through the dark on my new black, British one-speed bike, smoking a final cigarette behind the hut, and staring at Orion, bright even to my night-blind eyes, before collapsing here, on my narrow cot.

A bit of cloth dangled from a nail on the windowsill. I smiled. That torn swatch, bright red, matched the shorts Mac Barnett had on when he scrambled through the window.

I hadn't planned it. I'd turned off my one electric light and clicked off my flashlight, too addled by beer to read, when I heard a rough knock at the back window.

"*Salote*," Mac whispered. I loved hearing my Tongan name, which is Charlotte in English. It made me feel *gone*—gone from Ohio, gone from boredom, gone from a lot of things.

I pushed open the window. All I could see were his glinting eyes. He said, "Let me in before Tevita catches me and beats my ass."

He had a rare pint of gin in his back pocket and a lime off a tree behind the house. We sat cross-legged on the floor and drank the gin until it was gone and we were taking off each other's clothes and French kissing. He was stout and sturdy. When he pushed into me, I thought of pop beads, those kid necklaces of the '50s. We laughed. I was crazy about him.

Tevita must have heard the ruckus and knocked on the door. I hurriedly gathered up my underwear and pulled on a green wraparound cloth, what I'd learned was called a *tupenu*. I yelled, "Wait, wait, Tevita. I'll be right there," to give Mac enough time to tumble out the window and make off through the banana patch behind the hut. I paused to breathe and then opened the door to Tevita, whose broad, brown forehead was creased with worry.

"It's okay, Tevita. I'm fine." I articulated the words carefully, trying not to slur them. I was plastered.

"Salote," he said, "I thought I heard something over here." He stood stolidly, looking me over, his feet spread apart, his arms folded over his barrel chest.

"It's nothing, Tevita. I'm fine. Thanks for checking." Tevita frowned and held his ground without saying anything as I flashed him what I imagined to be a dumb-looking, goofy smile.

Everybody swore you could sleep with whomever you liked in Tonga, but they just couldn't come and go through the front door. The middle-of-the-night getaway was supposed to be the Tongan way. Yet Tevita appeared to be upset.

I had no doubt that by the time Mac was gone, Tevita knew I'd had company. If I'd offended him, he didn't show it. If he were amused, he didn't let on. He finally grunted and lumbered away, back to the big house where his wife, Filipa, probably waited with a bowl of boiled plantain to calm him down.

Tevita's monitoring unnerved me. The Peace Corps trainers, Liz and Wade, warned me to expect it. They said to behave with respect. But Tevita acted so pious, and his concern seemed exaggerated. I wasn't sure what to think.

You're wondering about the murder. Here's a clue: the victim was a young woman, a Peace Corps volunteer, lovely and sexually bold and doomed. And this is where it starts—I mean, where it starts to be important who *I* was when it all happened. Point one: I was a preacher's daughter. I'd been monitored all my life, and that was one reason I joined the Peace Corps, to get away. I didn't trust piety or what we used to call *holiness* back in Ohio. Point two: I couldn't read Tevita. Was he secretly entertained and conning me into believing something else, even into being a little afraid of him? I was confused about Tevita, but I was also confused about myself. I wanted to be a good girl, but not by my father's definition. I suppose I wanted to be a good bad girl, like Mae West, but even after being away from Ohio for several years, I was far from solving any of these puzzles.

Tevita probably knew about Mac and me, since he seemed to know everything. He also probably knew that Mac wasn't the first guy I'd gone to bed with in Tonga. But Mac was the first one I courted the Tongan way. I wanted to try it. According to Liz and Wade, that meant feigning disinterest publicly and never, ever making a date in front of others. It was about discretion, they said. Appearances.

I tried so hard to get away from Ohio back then that it makes me tired to remember. Once I escaped from the parsonage, I slid easily into hippie life. Eagerly gave up my virginity in a stuffy attic bedroom in off-campus housing at Kent State. Slept with twenty-seven guys. Kept a list on a legal-sized envelope I took with me everywhere. June 8, 1971, the day after I graduated from college, I spent my commencement gift money to take the bus to Chicago, where I met up with Number Twenty-eight. Together, we hitchhiked to California. We had a few adventures, and then I ditched him and moved to the next guy, and then the next. Hitchhiking in South Laguna, I took a ride from a lecherous geezer, who offered me a job at his newspaper. Karma, I probably sighed, and told him I had a journalism degree. I had enough money left to buy a dented '65 Corvair, red with a black convertible top, and tooled around my news beat in Southern California's beach locales: Corona del Mar, Balboa, Emerald Bay—charmed names, charmed places. During my off hours, I pranced proudly topless at faux-Buddhist retreats and burned my bras at least once (and wished I hadn't the next day, surveying my always inadequate underwear drawer). I believed, I thought, in "free love." Whatever that meant.

Liz and Wade, the sweet and serious couple—a former priest and nun—acted as if sex didn't exist, which was ironic since I figured they left their orders because of it. But for me and most of the other volunteers, coming to Tonga was about the sexiest thing we'd ever done. You could always feel the heat. We found one another in dark corners and at the end of the table at the Coconut Club, and we talked passionately about everything that was going on. Usually somebody'd be feeling somebody else's thigh through it all. We were like cousins, understanding one another's overheated libidos perfectly, as if we'd played "doctor" in our parents' rumpus rooms for years. Yet we found ourselves caught in a web of rules.

Mac had been in the Kingdom for three years. As gregarious as he was, that was enough time to get to know almost everybody. He spoke the language fluently, and, in fact, had lived here on Tevita's property before me. Over beers at the Coconut Club, gently squeezing my thigh, he offered notions of Tongan discretion. It was a catacomb of rituals that anybody could learn, like a dance or a church service. After all, he promised, it wasn't that you couldn't do anything. You just had to make it look like you weren't. That was the difference between good girls and prostitutes, *fokisis* or foxes, as the Tongans called them. I considered his advice. I didn't want to get labeled a *fokisi* when I had work to do, but I couldn't imagine being celibate for two years, either. So I bought him another Steinlager and decided that when the time was right, I'd invite him over. But he didn't wait for an invitation. Last night he had invited himself.

Before Tevita barged in, Mac had sighed loudly and said, "I've lived here three years, and I've found out one thing for sure: I like to fuck." He'd arrived a virgin, and in the States, he said, he felt nerdy and unsure. Here, the Tongans took him under their wing. He said he felt confident now.

"And come to think of it, I have Uncle Sam to thank," he concluded. But now Mac was ready to go home, back to Cedar Rapids to study hydrology. I admired how he'd gotten the Tongans to like him. I liked his flagrantly sloppy, baggy shorts and bony Midwestern legs. I liked his mass of hay-colored hair, pulled back most of the time in a ponytail. I liked his thick glasses and his bawdy wit. I also liked the fact that he was about to go home.

Just then, two brown fingers reached under the hurricane window and began to pull it up.

"Who's that?" I muttered in Tongan.

It was one of Tevita's kids, the six-year-old. I still wasn't sure which was which by name—there were eight to keep track of. Propped against the little girl's hip was another, baby Lupe—I remembered that one. The older girl peered under the window at me but spoke only to the baby. They both craned to get a peek. I tried my fiercest dirty look. The kid was unimpressed. The baby sucked her fingers and stared some more.

"See?" the kid said to the baby. "That's the American. Look at her skin, how funny and white. Daddy gets money for giving her this hut. See? See the American? She's still in bed."

I suddenly realized that in the night's heat I'd thrown off my green *tupenu*, and Tevita's kids were seeing me buck naked, just as I'd been when Mac clambered out the window. I jerked the *tupenu* back around me, but it was too late.

"For chrissake," I spat in English. "Didn't you little bastards ever hear of the word *privacy*?" As a matter of fact, most of the Tongans hadn't. Privacy, I grudgingly remembered from some tiresome lecture, was antisocial in Tonga.

I glared at the older girl and growled in Tongan, "Get lost." Then I made a big show of slamming the window down, careful not to catch her fingers. She shrieked with mock outrage and scurried away, the wide-eyed baby still bouncing on her hip.

"The American's naked! The American's naked!" the kid screamed like a town crier, up and down the coral road.

Actually, Tevita's daughter hadn't used the word "American." She said *palangi*. *Palangi* this, *palangi* that. It was the word for white person. Supposedly, according to our language teacher, Pulu, it came from the word for stick or mast. When the Dutch navigators Schouten and Lemaire (see, I *was* paying attention) came in 1616, and then Tasman in 1643, and later the urgent rush of explorers in the eighteenth century, Wallis and Cook and the infamous Bligh, the Tongans first saw their masts, poking up forebodingly on the horizon. The appearance of those tall sticks came to embody a dazzlingly confusing mix of history on both sides: hospitality, betrayal, curiosity, fear, repulsion, dread, greed, conspiracy, hostility, resignation, envy, gratitude, resentment, hope. Now the word held all the meanings together and was applied to almost every Caucasian. It was dawning on me that I would never *not* be a *palangi* here. Whatever else I was, the word came first, the thing that defined me above all else. I was an outsider.

Finally, I swung my legs onto the damp, woven floor mat and sat up, my head in my hands. Then I stood up, the blood rushing away from my head, and stumbled uncertainly toward the table, looking for an aspirin from my Peace Corps first aid kit. I was going to need it.

CHAPTER 2

▼

Ngali pe tevolo mo e po'ulí. *The devil fits in with the night.*

I finally opened my door and propped up my windows, declaring that visiting hours had begun. Tevita's wife, Filipa, looked up and smiled from the back porch where she did most of the cooking for her rambling, ravenous brood. Unlike many of her countrywomen, Filipa had not ballooned in middle age. She was delicate, the only evidence of her eight pregnancies a slight belly. Soft black hair curled around her face, and she had a perfect Polynesian complexion: honey-colored, not too dark, and not too white. When she smiled, she showed dimples that made her elfin and delightful. Her sparkling almond eyes sometimes watered and squinted. I thought maybe she needed glasses.

She was stirring the contents of an enormous aluminum kettle. I figured it was probably giant blocks of taro.

"*Ha'u*, Salote," Filipa called, "Come on over and share my lunch!"

My Tongan was coming along. I was impatient to speak openly and fluently with Filipa, but in the meantime, she didn't seem to care. She knew enough English to get the main points, and she smiled at everything I tried to say in Tongan. I don't know how I sounded to her. In Tongan I was inarticulate, and I didn't recognize myself that way. In English, I trusted that I could sound facile and slick; my SAT score in language arts had been a healthy 750. I loved that number.

But at the beginning, Filipa and I had to stick to basics, language without subtlety. Our friendship was elemental and comforting, like grade school—primary colors, the ABCs, and the present tense.

"*Malo e lelei*," I said, settling on an upturned stump under the overhang. "Thanks for being well." Filipa handed me a platter of taro. "*Malo*," I said again, picking up a piece with my fingers and taking a bite. It was an acquired taste, heavier and gummier than a potato and richer, like sherry to chardonnay. I'd learned I could make a delicious meal of boiled taro root and *lu*, the dark green leaves of the taro plant cooked in coconut milk.

The baby, Lupe, "little pigeon," freed from her sister's earlier grip, tottered from around the corner and climbed into my lap, begging a snack. She grinned at me and whispered "*pahlangi.*" That word again.

"Hi, sweetie," I said in English. Nuzzling her baby neck, I forgave the embarrassing wake-up call. "Yeah, American. White person. Crazy about you, even though you woke me up in my birthday suit." Lupe looked at me quizzically, nodding to the unfamiliar syllables as if they were a nursery rhyme, and grinned. She held up her pudgy little fingers and said, shyly, "*taha, ua, tolu,*" teaching me to count to three. "*Taha, ua, tolu,*" I complied.

Lupe and her brother Mosesi were the darkest of Filipa's children, as dark as Ghirardelli chocolate, like their father. The rest were a rainbow of honey brown, taupe, and cappuccino. That's why I remembered those two names: their siblings made fun of them, gaily and mercilessly, using a word that had arrived in Tonga, we were told in training, with the American soldiers during World War II: nigger. *Nika,* as they shouted it. No more lovely than at home.

It was clear that not all Americans honored their host country or left behind useful remains. One guy from Louisiana, a former volunteer, was in a Tongan jail right then for growing pot. The soil and weather were perfect for it. And though Tevita said that Tonga appreciated the Americans who protected Nuku'alofa during the bloodbath in the Solomon Islands, the Yanks loved to party and left behind pale and sometimes oddly blond children. But for me, until the events of *this* bad day unfolded, it was the legacy of *nigger,* that shocking, bitter word, which most sourly summed up the Americans who'd been here before.

Lupe's cheeks bulged with taro. She picked up another chunk and pushed it into my mouth. I chewed extravagantly, saying, "Yummy, yummy, yummy!" and making faces until Lupe burst into giggles, half-chewed taro plopping out of her mouth. I managed to plant one last kiss on the back of her neck before she squirmed down and tottered away.

"She like you," Filipa said in English. "You're the favorite *palangi* of her."

"She's so cute," I said. The fat and sociable Tongan babies, healthy and cared for by a flock of aunties, weakened my resolve not to have kids. It was fun cradling babies in my arms; Tongan moms handed me their kids as if they thought I knew what to do. They clucked and smiled when I snuggled their little darlings and cooed sweet nothings in my made-up mix of English and Tongan baby talk.

Filipa reached for a battered aluminum kettle and poured us both a cup of tea. I watched as she dripped creamy condensed milk into a cup, stirred it, and handed it to me with both hands. The tea was excellent. I swallowed it gratefully, feeling the sugar and caffeine rush relief to my dehydrated cells.

We sat there watching the breeze riffle the banana leaves. Kosi, the family goat and lawn mower, awakened from his perch on a junked minimoke and stretched his neck, ogling us. Then he jumped off the car and gamboled away. The moke was supposed to be a taxi, one of Tevita's money-making schemes. He thought his two oldest boys, Siaosi and Touliki, would keep the family in canned mackerel by running the jalopy around town. But the thing kept breaking down, and the boys didn't like tourists, who treated them not like boys but like museum exhibits. Or mules.

"I heard about trouble last night," Filipa said suddenly. "*Pisikoa* trouble." Peace Corps trouble? I caught my breath. Had I gone over the line so badly? I looked quickly at Filipa, but, inscrutably blowing on her tea, she turned away from me toward the banana patch, where Lupe was chasing the goat. Should I 'fess up and admit that Mac had come and gone through the back window?

I lost my train of thought, remembering Mac's sturdy body, remembering how we stripped off our gin-soaked clothes, trying not to laugh for fear of getting caught, and how we kissed madly before getting down to serious business. The lantern burned down, and the moon sent slivers through the lashed bamboo walls and onto his beautiful chest, catching like glints of broken glass in his eyes.

Or was it better to play dumb like the Tongans, admitting nothing, denying everything? I sighed, apparently loudly, and Filipa turned back toward me, looking at me without a smile.

"What kind of trouble?" I finally said, trying to be casual.

"*Pisikoa* woman," Filipa said intensely. "Too many *mafus*."

Mafu was the word for heart—and for boyfriend.

"No good," Filipa said. "Too many *mafus*."

I felt my face go pale. Maybe some of the kids saw Mac slip away. Maybe someone talked to him on the road, knew he was drunk, and complained to Tevita. "I'm sorry," I began.

Just then, the white Peace Corps Land Rover pulled into the coral driveway. The white Rover usually signaled a cheerful event: a chance to gossip, a delivery from home, a visit from an American. I jumped up to see who was driving. But when Mac leaped out, I felt a quick blush come up, and I hesitated. I looked at Filipa, who betrayed nothing.

"Maki," Filipa called out. "Come here and see your Tongan mommy." Mac strode quickly up the drive and made the proper greetings. He looked sharply at me.

"There's some really bad news," he said. "I came to pick you up. We have to go to the Peace Corps office. We have to go to a meeting."

He looked at Filipa. My brain struggled into gear.

"Whatever it is, Mac, I have a feeling she already knows."

He dropped onto the stump and leaned his head into his hands. "Melanie Porter's dead," he said.

The shock stopping everything.

Then my voice, croaking: "Dead? She's dead?"

I stood up. "What the hell happened?"

"They found her stabbed to death in her house."

"*Oiaue, fakapo,*" Filipa interjected, nodding. *Oy-yah-way*, the mournful exclamation. *Fakapo*. Murder.

"Jesus," I said. I paced around the boiling pot, Filipa watching me. "Jesus." I felt my forehead tighten—the hangover attacking. "Who the hell did it?"

"You'll never believe this. They've got Mort Friedman in custody."

"Oh, my god. Mort? But..." I tried to take it in.

Mort was a short, muscled guy from—where? Minnesota? Wisconsin? He looked like a wrestler, broad and burly. I'd met him a few times at training parties, but he hung back and mostly talked to the other guys. I'd always associated the idea of murder with either great brains or great passion. Mort seemed to have neither.

"They say he stabbed her twenty times, and she bled to death."

"Jesus Christ. Why?"

"Say it in Tongan, Maki, speak Tongan," Filipa said urgently.

Mac apologized and quickly translated, then went back to English. But he didn't answer *why*.

"He got her good. Used a fish knife. She lost so much blood so fast, they probably couldn't have saved her, even if..." He paused. "He got her everywhere. Her body was in ribbons."

"You saw her?"

"Yeah."

"*Oiaue*," Filipa said, and keened a long, mournful phrase.

"She's saying an awful thing has happened," Mac said. "You're right, Filipa, you're right."

I lurched over to Mac and put an arm around him, as much to steady myself as to comfort him. Something buzzed at the corners of my eyes—blood, or panic.

There wasn't a single ambulance in the entire Kingdom, and the hospital was ominously called the *falemahaki*, the house of disease. Even if Melanie'd had a chance, she might not have made it.

"Damn," I said.

Mac continued in choppy sentences, half-Tongan, half-English. He'd been home a couple of hours when the police knocked at his door. They'd been rousting Peace Corps staff, one by one. Melanie's body was at Vaiola Hospital, and they took him there in a noisy minimoke.

Her body lay on a table, her eyes still open, her face blue and swollen. He reached to close her eyelids, but a policeman stopped him. She had wounds everywhere: her stomach, her chest, her neck, her face, her temples. A strip of skin hung off her skull, where it looked as if the killer had tried to scalp her. Her arms were bruised, scratched, and slashed, probably when she tried to defend herself. The doctors had hooked her up to a saline drip on both arms, hoping to coax life back, but once it was determined she was officially dead, they unhooked the needles and left the tubes dangling at each side. They had cut off her yellow dress—Mac recognized it from the party—and set it aside, covered with blood, on a metal rack.

Mac got a ride from the hospital to her house and arrived just as Evelyn Henry, the Peace Corps director, arrived. She told him to go home, but he said he wanted to see, that he had to see. He realized he was shouting. A couple of Tongan police shifted from foot to foot. He stepped across the threshold, and as his eyes adjusted to the darkness inside, he saw that everything was as the killer had left it. Blood. On the whitewashed walls, on the pandanus floor mats. On her linoleum table and wooden folding chairs. In the sink. Blood in the doorway, bloody handprints on the door frame, which she'd probably grabbed as she tried to crawl for help.

"Jesus Christ," I said again. Filipa asked a few quick questions and added her own thoughts, too fast for me to understand. Then nobody said anything, and Filipa bowed her head.

"That's what I heard about," she finally said, in English so I would understand. "You better go now. You better go."

Mac jumped in on the driver's side, and I climbed in on the other, dazed and self-conscious, as Filipa stood up and watched. Chickens scattered behind us, clucking wildly. The coral gravel crunched.

I reached across the vinyl seat for Mac's thigh, trying to wrestle down a rising vertigo.

"I can't believe it," I said. "How could this happen?"

"He stalked her after the party," Mac said, staring straight ahead. The Rover bumped and swerved. "Supposedly he went crazy because she didn't want to go to bed with him. They say Mort tried to get her to go back to his place after the party, but she went with Gyorgy instead."

"But murder her? He and Gyorgy were good friends, I thought. How could he murder her? How could he do that?"

"She and Gyorgy stopped by the Coconut Club, but it was closed," Mac said. "I guess Mort followed her back to Gyorgy's place. Gyorgy said they thought they heard something in the bushes, but didn't think much of it. Then they say Mort followed the two of them back to her place when Gyorgy drove her home. Mort must have waited till Gyorgy left, and then he must have gone inside with his knife and attacked her."

"Jesus, Mac. Where's Mort now?"

"In a cell at the police station," Mac said. "When they picked him up, he hadn't bothered cleaning himself off, and he had blood all over him. He'd used the knife to cut open a watermelon, and he was sitting there eating it, with blood all over it, over himself." Mac spat out a sound, half cough, half sob. "He was eating watermelon with her blood on it."

"I didn't really know the guy," I said bleakly.

"People thought Mort was crazy," Mac replied. "But they thought he was harmless."

I felt speechless and cold. Last night, the new single women volunteers (there were only three of us) had sat at a table together, sipping from sweating cans of beer, and watched Melanie Porter dance. That yellow dress was ankle-length, chiffon, cut low at the bosom. We checked her out like jealous old ladies, tut-tutting under our breath.

"Where'd she get a damn dress like that?" I whispered to the other two, Bridget and Diane. "I thought we were supposed to dress modestly down here."

"I know," Bridget whispered back. "And how does she get away with wearing yellow? I look fucking dead in yellow. She looks like some kind of damn angel."

The Peace Corps men noticed, too. Just starting her second year in the Peace Corps, Melanie had been a kindergarten teacher from North Dakota, and the nectar she gave off, her all-American sexiness and grace, attracted men like ants. She'd been a cheerleader, a homecoming queen, and an athlete, and she was buoyantly healthy. But she also had sophistication that went far beyond that of the average cheerleader. Her father, people pointed out, owned a mining company, and he'd moved to Minot from New York. Melanie came from old money. Her parents sent her to Europe, and she'd made the rounds of finishing schools and graduated from one of the Seven Sisters—I couldn't remember which. She just had something. She could smoke a cigarette like Marlena Dietrich and dance like Ginger if she had to.

Last night Melanie was dancing with everybody, letting one guy after another cut in. It was hard to tell whom, if anyone, she liked best.

None of the three of us young crones-by-comparison had been popular in high school. Bridget had been president of the National Honor Society. Diane, an upright but overweight salutatorian, dated boys from Demolay. She went to the prom with the pimply-faced president of the Math Club, and though she hated herself for refusing, she couldn't bring herself to kiss him. Bridget and Diane had both endured braces; at least now they had fine teeth. Worst for Bridget, though, she had curvature of the spine and wore a body cast from ages twelve to seventeen. In those cruel years, she could never make matching sweater sets fit over her horror-movie body. Now her neck was a bit too long, and her chin seemed squashed upwards. She had a jumping gait, almost a canter, as if her body couldn't believe it was free of its restraints. I'd been free of braces (my sister got those, my parents explained, and I got college) and free of body casts, but I was consigned by my sheltering, suspicious parents to Saturday nights without dates and a lonely absorption in *Middlemarch* and *Jane Eyre*. For all of us, the homecoming queen was the enemy, our nemesis, the target of our ridicule and the wellspring of our adolescent envy. Sitting there watching Melanie, we squirmed in shame as old resentments flared up.

"The trouble is, she's *nice*," Bridget said as Gyorgy, a Canadian volunteer, swooped Melanie up for another dance. "I hate it when beautiful women are nice."

For a moment the rest of the dancers stopped to watch, but then, as if not to call too much attention to herself, Melanie glided away into the crowd.

I have to confess that, in my diary, I fussily categorized the Peace Corps volunteers into types. We were such a mix, such a motley group, that I wanted to see whether I could fit us all into any system I could invent or understand. I settled on three groups: the altruists, the adventure seekers, and the lost. The altruists were missionaries, idealistic and eager to help. They were leftovers of the Kennedy kids, I decided, pioneers who couldn't wait to take their youthful American energy to the world. But by the late '70s, I noted like a professor in my mildewy book for the scholarly paper I might write someday, the altruists' ranks had thinned. After Vietnam and Watergate, a more practical bunch emerged—the adventure seekers, who claimed little philosophical reason for volunteering, but who wanted to take advantage of what seemed like the playfulness and good heart of the government's most touchy-feely program. These volunteers, too, often arrived with personal gusto, tried everything, and then had trouble focusing on their work.

The lost were the people who didn't want to join the army and couldn't seem to find a niche at home. Some of the lost found themselves steadied by the demands of new experience, and others sank deeper into trouble, confused and paralyzed by the cultural and physical changes.

I counted myself among the adventure seekers, of course, because it sounded best. I certainly didn't want to be an altruistic missionary, although my father liked to tell people that's what I was. And nobody wanted to be lost.

Bridget and Diane were adventure seekers, to be sure. Melanie was a mellifluous blend of altruism and adventure, like the girl on the cover of *Seventeen*. I didn't know where to put Mort. But I did know, even after only three months, that the volunteers that we heard had cracked—usually dropping out and going home early—were the altruists, outraged by their lack of control, or the lost, sent home for their own good, usually to some benevolent dry-out clinic.

I recalled that Mort was finishing his second year. I couldn't remember whether he'd signed up for a third. The re-uppers were a special class, the Brahmins of Peace Corps, and they intimidated me. Some had jumped the cultural fence and didn't want to hang out with other Americans. It was a badge of honor to speak enough Tongan to hold your own, drink with Tongans, tell dirty jokes. A lot of us tried not to be American for a while. We wanted to be something we'd never been. Some wanted to stay to avoid going home, to avoid fitting in back there, like our boring, unhappy parents. Some were surprised by their luck in Tonga; like Mac, they had been accepted. I didn't get that feeling about Mort, though. He was nobody, another tanned *palangi* in a flowered shirt who drank too much. There were so many single guys that I had trouble keeping them apart.

"He was into black magic—did you know?" Mac said. "Some of the old women knew it. He was always asking them about the old religion. They just thought he was another crazy *palangi*. Now it turns out…"

"What about Gyorgy? Where's he?"

"The British consulate. They said he tried to break into the police station to get at Mort, but when they calmed him down, he said he had to get off the island. They gave him something, a tranquilizer, I guess."

Gyorgy was Mort's opposite: a tall, handsome guy who, despite his six-foot-three height, seemed more interested in finding vermouth for his martinis than threatening anyone. He taught English and philosophy at the high school where, rumor had it, the Tongan kids held him in considerable awe. He had a reputation for being cultivated—the exact word somebody in my group used when we first met him at the Coconut Club. We caught him making some point about Puccini and berating Viliami, the Coconut Club's beloved bartender, for letting the gin run out. Gyorgy was negotiating with his bosses back in Ottawa for a third service year. Greeting the new trainees, he'd been congenial, but more concerned with the liquor shortage than with our newcomers' angst.

Gyorgy, too, had a story, which Mac told me one night at the Coconut Club while Gyorgy stretched himself elegantly over the snooker table. After his father was killed in the Hungarian Revolution in 1956, his mother wheeled Gyorgy across the mountains in winter in a baby carriage. Inside his diaper were three gold coins. Beneath him, wrapped in a ragged baby blanket, was a small, polished icon that had been in Gyorgy's family for three hundred years. He and his mother traveled by night and ate snow. His mother gave one of the gold coins to each family who sheltered them. Eventually they found their way to Canada. In Ottawa, his mother sold the icon for twenty thousand dollars, the grubstake for their new life. Since then, people said in the Coconut Club, no other woman could equal her saintliness. Gyorgy remembered none of the escape from Hungary, but he spoke with a faint lilting accent and seemed happy to be alive. Yet he constantly kept Melanie at his side; her glamour suited him. The other men watched and envied, coveting his panache. Gyorgy and Melanie looked great together, a couple out of *The Great Gatsby*. He intimidated me.

"Poor Gyorgy," I said.

"He'll be messed up over this," Mac said. "It'll tear him up. He's just the kind of guy who'll feel responsible." We considered this in silence.

"So, where's…the body?" I asked.

"I don't know. They took it somewhere. I don't know how these things work down here. Evelyn's taking care of that."

We pulled into the Peace Corps parking lot, a grubby, gravelly expanse already nearly filled with the standard-issue black bikes and a couple of ratty vans and taxis. The concrete block building had only one graceful feature: a second-story balcony that looked out over a reef lagoon lined with stilted mangroves. I'd spent several blissful evenings on that balcony at Peace Corps parties, sipping New Zealand beer and congratulating myself for getting out of Ohio. Sometimes an outrigger canoe would course through the water; sometimes I could see uncountable stars.

On the first floor, the Peace Corps doctor dispensed quick remedies for diarrhea, coral cuts, flu, various bug bites, and boils, which everybody, to their horror, seemed to get. He also ordered the whole bunch of us in for shots, including the aforementioned gamma globulin, which left a knot the size of a golf ball in the butt but protected everybody from hepatitis. Some Tongans regarded the doctor as superfluous, a luxury for the Peace Corps and an insult to the Tongan health care system. He had not been called in last night until it was too late. From what Mac said, though, no one could have saved Melanie's life, not even the Peace Corps doctor.

At the top of the rickety stairs was a large meeting room where the Peace Corps put on parties, showed Marx Brothers movies on a small, tattered screen, and held meetings. On one side were four offices—for the country director, Evelyn Henry, and her two assistants, and the training office where various terminating volunteers, like Mac, worked on contract for extra cash before going home.

Volunteers from all over the island of Tongatapu were gathering. Some, stationed outside Nuku'alofa, had come in by bus or had ridden their bikes. Some, like me, had been informed and picked up by the two Peace Corps Land Rovers, which had been crisscrossing town all morning. It was complicated to get the word out to all the forty volunteers on the island because no one had phones, but by noon, the story had been broadcast on Station A3Z and anyone who hadn't heard knew then. A3Z was turned on everywhere, all the time.

My forehead ached. Oh, this was a nasty hangover.

"I don't want to go up there yet," I said to Mac, watching people slowly navigate the stairs. "Go on. I'll be there in a minute." I sat in the Rover as Mac joined a couple of other volunteers, everybody hugging and going up in two's and three's. Just then, I didn't want to be part of the group. I didn't want to be a Peace Corps volunteer. I wanted to be Charlotte Thornton, independent operator, former Buckeye, good in bed, occasional wit. I didn't want to have to talk about what had happened.

In Kent State dorm rooms in the '60s, it was a free for all and a party. I was proud to have given up my virginity at 1009 Vine, a funny, rhyming Dionysian house, no grownups in sight. Later, in California, I used to crawl into bed with any guy I liked, and it was a private matter between the two of us. In the series of walk-up apartments of my five years on my own, no one cared what I did with men. There was no such thing as a neighborhood, only condo associations that had meetings nobody ever went to. Sex didn't have ramifications. It was a right, like free speech. We had birth control, penicillin, and a seemingly endless supply of willing partners, someone always waiting to be next.

Damn. Tonga was going to be different. In a weird way, the country was beginning to seem more and more like Ohio. Had I been hijacked? Was it fate? For the first time, Tonga felt threatening, its flowery nectars toxic, too sweet in the nose. Perhaps I would come to suspect the hot, black nights that made me want sex whether it was a good idea or not. What was I trading for my supposed escape?

I was proud of my sexual history. It made me feel alive. I thought, no matter what else happened, my cherished memories were proof that I was in the game, that I *had* escaped. I was living my own life, and all those men were my beloved evidence. With my envelope list as a crutch, I could name them all. I could describe them all—a point of honor to me then. I made "free love" with old men and young men, tall and small. I went to bed with a beautiful black man who drove me home in his Jaguar. I slept with a Vietnam vet who had delicately removed his artificial leg. I think it was the left. I slept with a six-foot-eight hippie with two feet of hair; high on mescaline, we did it under a bridge at the Colorado River.

Partial to rivers, I smoked dope in a tiny MG on the Mississippi with a Harvard boy whose father was in politics. That time I got pregnant. I wasn't even on the pill and should have known better. I had to fly to New York for an abortion; it was 1970, pre-Roe. The guy or his ambitious father paid for everything. Also on my list were a poet, a preacher, an ex-con, a wheeler-dealer, and a piano bar roué. Also an architect, a filmmaker, a car dealer. A boss or two. Libertarian, Unitarian, Catholic, Quaker, Jewish, and Ba'hai. Even a Republican: I was ecumenical and nonpartisan. The times were on my side. After a few years on the pill I decided to try an IUD, because I didn't want chemicals in my body. I came to Tonga with a Copper-7 installed, lucky seven in my womb, so simple, good for three years. I could feel the little knot at the end of the thread of it if I ever wanted to check on my protection. Sometimes I couldn't believe the choices I had. It was easy.

I know that sounds crazy nowadays, with rape drugs dropped in drinks and serial killers and AIDS. But back then the worst we had to fear was herpes. Penicillin took care of all the rest. It seems quaint now and unbelievable, like a dream that corresponded with my youth—a brief, amazing time when sex couldn't kill you. I thought it would always be like that. I took it for granted.

It was easy and exhilarating, but had nothing to do with sexual pleasure. I never came, something I noticed but didn't particularly care about back then. It wasn't my goal or my concern. What mattered was experience, stories, conquests. What mattered was anything not Ohio, not my father or my mother, not the innocence I doggedly aimed to shed. Sexual pleasure wasn't easy for me to start with. At a women's lib workshop in Laguna Beach one time, a beautiful lesbian nurse named Rainbow Skye examined me and told me I had a "high clit" and kindly explained I'd need to ask my lovers for special attention. I remember smiling and feeling relieved: so *that's* why. In occasional private moments in my various apartments, I took care of myself, but with men, I had no patience. I didn't want to ask for anything. I just wanted another story.

I was at Kent State trying to be a hippie in May, 1970. It was Saturday night, a party on the hill outside Taylor Hall, everybody smoking pot and cheering as the ROTC building went up in flames after the United States invaded Cambodia. Who lit that damn thing was never clear, but it was just a rickety old wooden Quonset hut, anyway. Who'd have known that fire would lead to all those tanks and soldiers right on campus, all that shooting, all that blood on Monday? I was in class when it happened, but the teacher, blanching at the sound of sirens, let us out of class early. When I got to Taylor Hall, the bodies were gone, but blood remained, a shocking amount of it, blood spattered and pooled and tracked through. People moved in slow motion, paralyzed with horror and confusion.

Like everybody, I'd been seeing bloodshed in Vietnam every day on the news, but Kent State slammed me. None of us could have believed those guns were loaded; how could the National Guard, young guys our own age, keep order at a peace demonstration with loaded guns? How could they shoot *us*, their neighbors, their peers?

That day my boyfriend of the week and I took off for Niagara Falls, the most nonpolitical spot we could think of. We put on black raincoats and rode the Maid of the Mist, bought trinkets at the gift store, drank sloe gin, and fucked wildly in a cheap motel. We went to see "Butch Cassidy and the Sundance Kid" and couldn't take it; we cried for two hours. Kent State, too, was supposedly another reason why I was in Tonga—to get away. But like the rest of Ohio, it followed me here. I brought it with me.

Now Tonga was calling out bedeviling variations on my confusions. Back home I could indulge my grief privately, work things out on my own. Here, somebody was always watching. If it wasn't Tevita worrying about me, it was the Peace Corps staff making judgments. Or the other volunteers, in varying stages of loneliness, horniness, or envy, inevitably starving for gossip. Emotional life in Tonga, along with everything else, was community property.

And now everybody would want to analyze everything. What made Mort crazy? Why Melanie? Did she lead him on? Weren't all the volunteers supposed to be friends about sex? Should Melanie have been dressed like that at the party—bold cleavage, long legs tantalizing through chiffon? Wasn't she playing with the guys, flaunting her wholesome good looks? And what about Gyorgy? Was she playing two guys off against each other? Why did Gyorgy let her go home? Or why, for that matter, did he take her to his place in the first place, late at night, with the neighbors and Mort probably watching?

And what did this mean for me? I was still alive, young, and sexually bold, like Melanie. And now, as I'd been after Kent State, I was half-terrified, full of dread, and depressed.

Spilling out of Mac's backpack on the front seat was a half pack of Golds and a beat-up book of matches. I pulled one out and lit it. Now the moralists would come out of the woodwork. They would say, "We told you so." They would say, "See what comes of a woman like that?"

The avalanche of questions and my hangover depressed me more. I couldn't think straight. And I couldn't get it out of my mind that when Mac and I were making love last night, half-crocked on gin and lime juice, making light of everything including our own pliable bodies, Melanie Porter was getting killed, apparently for refusing to do the same thing. How could that happen?

I finished the cigarette and stubbed it out.

CHAPTER 3

▼

Matangi lelei, to ki he la mahaeha é. *A good wind, but it falls on a torn sail.*

I'm going to leave my young me smoking and miserably clamped to the sweaty passenger side seat of that Peace Corps van for a moment because there are a few more things you need to know.

I've already said that coming to the Kingdom was about the sexiest thing I'd ever done. Now I'll commit myself: at the beginning, it was *the* sexiest. Of course the pungent air, the exotica of palm tree and reef and the Southern Cross and canoes on the lagoon had a lot to do with inciting my hair-trigger Midwestern libido, but the Tongan language itself also took some of the rap.

Most of us in Tonga Group 17 moaned and whined about the three hours a day we spent in language class. But I had a secret. I loved the ribbons of language, the fluid magic of sentence making. I was awestruck by the sensuality of the Polynesian tongue. How could I have grown up not knowing that such a beautiful language existed? It was like a cat, one minute clicking its consonant claws across the floor, the next purring vowels and rolling over on its back in the sun. While I had toiled away, dutifully memorizing staunch Anglo-Saxon verses and astringent Puritan hymns, the Tongans, thousands of miles away, were speaking with honey, ripe moonlight, and salt water.

Every word ended with a vowel, rippling into the ear like a song. My name, as I've noted, became *Salote*. The Peace Corps became *Pisikoa*. And then, there was the provocative prefix *faka*. Dozens of common Tongan words began that way: f-a-k-a. Our textbook, written by a Mormon scholar and missionary, had six pages' worth.

When Group 17 first heard the language spoken—in late August, in the California Hotel in San Francisco during staging—titters erupted when Pulu, who met us there, announced with a straight face, "Volunteers, the word for *beautiful* is *faka'ofa'ofa.*" The word for respect—a key concept in the soberly formal culture—was *faka'apa'apa.* Doing things the Tongan way was *fakatonga.* Even the word murder, which we learned first as merely a curiosity, never dreaming of its hard attack into our lives, was *fakapo*—literally, of the dark. Pulu had no particular explanation. He swore it had no connection with, well, that English word, which out of Tongan courtesy he would not say. *Faka* was just a linguistic quirk, a coincidence. No wonder everybody got horny. I especially enjoyed hearing it come from the mouths of the pious American do-gooders—our trainer Liz, for example, or Evelyn Henry, the sanctimonious country director. If they wanted to communicate, they had to force their lips and tongues to form the "F" word. Even to say please required *fakamolemole.*

For me, in 1976, it felt right, *fuck* being a totemic word in my personal lexicon. For me as a preacher's daughter, swearing carried particular power. I knew well that language said everything about a person. My mother, a former schoolteacher, hated bad grammar. Anyone who said "I seen him," for instance, was scaldingly labeled low-class. The only thing worse was having beer on your breath, my mother said, but swearing wasn't far behind. My parents, professional Christians, foreswore even derivatives like *gee* and *gosh darn.* In moments of extreme emotion, they used *shucks*—or worse, fell stubbornly, ominously silent. When transcripts of the Watergate tapes hit the press, my father was traumatized. It wasn't the cover-up that devastated and disillusioned him. It was Tricky Dick's "expletives deleted."

The first time I heard the "F" word spoken aloud, I was thirteen and was visiting my older brother in Detroit, where he worked for GM. He was driving me around town in his hunter green Corvette and got cut off in traffic. When he yelled, "Fuck you!" to the offending driver, I felt an adult thrill.

Later, I became one of those kids who could work the word *fucking* into every conversation. *That was a fucking great Grateful Dead concert…we had a fucking horrible time…that is fucking good dope…he is a fucking idiot…*and on and on, the word as all-purpose as salt. Eventually, the word lost its novelty, but for me, *fuck*—so satisfying to yell at the world, so biting and defiant—was a word I would always connect with the first, fearless years of my freedom.

So I was greatly amused when, in the fall of 1976 for hours every morning, I was repeating one word after another that sounded like *fuck.* The weather was *faka'ofa'ofa.* The discussions were *fakafiefia,* enjoyable, and when I began to get better at it, I tried to *fakakata,* or make people laugh.

And I wanted to be *fakatonga,* to fold myself into what the locals always called "the Tongan way." I wanted to change the way I looked. In Burns Philp, a dusty general store, I fingered bolts of cloth in bright island patterns from Fiji and from Tahiti and bought enough for three Tongan outfits.

To become *fakatonga,* I needed expert female help. I knew whom to enlist. By lucky happenstance, Kalisimasi was not only the cosmopolitan owner of Kalisi-masi's Guest House, our training home, but also Filipa's sister. It was partly because of Kalisimasi that I'd been sent to Tevita for a place to stay. I trusted her. She had showered us with wonderful food, good humor, and tips on finding our version of the Tongan way, and I got in the habit of joining her in the back yard of the guesthouse for a smoke during afternoon breaks or in the cool dark after dinner.

In her excellent English, honed from the economic practicalities of hosting hundreds of travelers over the years, Kalisimasi explained that she had never married and that at age fifty she had never felt better. Her business was thriving, and she liked being the boss. Her name, I quickly realized, was a Tonganized version of "Christmas." That delighted me.

"My father's name was Pasikala," Kalisimasi told me one time with a grin, "from the English word for bicycle, and I guess my mother thought it would give us a little prestige to have an English name." Another sister, she pointed out, was named Isita, for Easter, of course. But Filipa, one of the youngest children, was simply Filipa.

If names were destiny, the shrewd and energetic Kalisimasi fulfilled hers, bringing merriment and generosity to the trainees' confusing and exciting lives. I needed her now.

So Kalisimasi and Filipa helped me pick a seamstress and hovered encouragingly at my side when I stood self-consciously on an unsteady, three-legged stool outside the seamstress' hut. The old woman crawled around me, wheezing through a mouthful of straight pins. When the pins were all in, she straightened up. "You *Pisikoa* have beautiful ankles," she cooed. "No scars."

I stiffened. Despite my rowdy history, I thought of myself as a plain woman, asymmetrical and always a little overweight. As long as I could remember, I'd assumed I was fat. I'd been on diets on and off all my life. I thought I'd never accomplished "a look," and I thought that I didn't give off a sense of ease, though the occasional man had told me I was shaped like a woman built for love. I had small, solid breasts, hourglass lines, a flat stomach, and round, muscular thighs. I wasn't good at taking compliments back then. I didn't understand what it actually meant to be "built for love," and I would have rolled my eyes, not seeing what he saw. No matter what any man said or thought, I fretted over every pound, rejecting the notion of curves.

It was true I had almost no blemishes, unlike the Tongans who had scars from boils and bush knife cuts and cooking burns. All I had were two tiny chicken pox scars, one at the top of my right leg and the other below my clavicle between my breasts. I had good skin.

"She's right," Kalisimasi said. "See that beautiful spot above your knees, Charlotte?"

"What beautiful spot?" I said, trying to look down while the old woman complained and told Kalisimasi to make me stand up straight.

"This beautiful three or four inches above the knee." Kalisimasi came up and firmly pinched the front of my right thigh. "This is the sexiest part of a woman in Tonga. We call it *ngako.*"

Filipa and the old woman agreed I had promising *ngako*. "*Faka'ofa'ofa,*" the old woman exclaimed, almost swallowing her mouthful of pins. I wasn't convinced. Men tended to call me "interesting." In high school, I'd been the Christian drone who wrote beautiful paragraphs that my teacher read out loud to the class. I read books and daydreamed, waiting. I trusted men who found me funny. My favorite compliment was from a guy I used to give blow jobs to all afternoon in a white-walled room in Costa Mesa—he said I was "inventive." True, some men mentioned my body and seemed surprised when I voiced self-doubt. Some tried whispering praise at intimate moments, noting what they said to the silky insides of my thighs. But I always insisted it was my wit, my brains, that kept my lovers engaged.

And yet, I couldn't help thinking that my new *tupenus* flattered me. One was soft peach cotton that looked gently tie-dyed. Another was a Fijian geometric, black and white. The third was a swirling print of blue, green, and purple hibiscus, palm fronds and pineapples. I loved them all. Each ankle-length, wrap-around skirt tied at the waist, and over the skirt was a loose, matching tunic with billowing sleeves. The *tupenus* were loose, and nothing grabbed at me anywhere. My whole body was covered, but I was rarely hot. Flies and mosquitoes couldn't get to my legs, yet I could move as nimbly as I liked.

Times change, I thought, eying myself in a squiggly mirror at the seamstress' hut. In my teens, some of my bitterest fights with my father were over clothes. First, a prom dress. I had to fight with him even to go because my father disapproved of dancing. My mother took up my cause, and he finally gave in, on one condition: my mother had to make the dress. My father didn't approve of wasting money on "fripperies" that showed a girl's shoulders. My mother found a

McCall's pattern that we could both accept. Then she altered it to show less neck. It was rose floral brocade, and even though the dress had sleeves and there was no visible cleavage, for one night I felt really grown up.

Later, trying to make the most of my hard, flat stomach—all those years of singing from the diaphragm for various church choir directors had given me nice, hard abs—I snuck away to tiny shops and slipped on two-piece swim suits and bare midriff tops. With money hoarded from my part-time job as a library page, I assembled a secret wardrobe.

College freed me, finally, to dress as I liked. Like all the other girls, I got diet pills from an old campus doctor and dropped pound after pound. I could wear miniskirts, and did. I had a pair of red leather, knee-high boots and a blue- and white-striped minidress to die for; I was a walking flag. I had drawers full of hip-hugging bellbottoms that showed skin from my belly button to my braless bosom. Back then, before I knew about *ngako*, when I looked in a full-length mirror, I frowned at my thighs and thought them unacceptably thick. But they had a good shape.

Once, in the summer of my first apartment, my father came to pick me up for the weekend. He was so outraged by my miniskirt that he wouldn't let me in the car. We stood in the street, yelling.

"Hypocrite!"

"Whore!" An epithet so shockingly rare that he pronounced it "hoo-er." My roommates cowered nervously behind the tacky screen door and didn't help.

That time he won. Humiliated, I went back inside and changed while he fumed in his silly Mustang, bright red as always. At least my roommates made me take a hit from the house bong. "He's a bastard," they righteously agreed.

But now I had slipped into Tongan modesty like a familiar shoe, swathed in fabric as if to make myself invisible.

Bridget and Diane were slower to make the switch. Diane dressed primly, like a stenographer. Bridget favored matronly, A-line prints. But some of the male volunteers began to change. If you avoided calling it a "skirt," the wraparound was a masculine look, emphasizing powerful legs and behinds. Supremely confident in his brown-belt manliness, Sam, the curly haired Jewish guy from Los Angeles, was the first to show up at language class in a red flowered *tupenu*. Of the lot, he had the best ass. Before long, the other guys got up their nerve to abandon their sticky khakis, Oxford shirts, and heavy leather sandals for colorful wraparounds, T-shirts, and flip-flops. The men had to learn to arrange the *tupenu* around their crossed legs so as not to show anything. It was rude to stick the knees up in the air, with the arms folded around them. But the proper way to sit came easily to these young Americans from the '60s: it was the lotus position.

So we spent a lot of time thinking about what we wore and how to wear it, and commenting on what everybody else wore. When Melanie showed up in that sexy yellow dress at our end-of-training party, she was wearing more than just fashion. It's hard to prove now, but at the time I believed that even if she hadn't been murdered, none of us would have ever forgotten the way she looked, her Rubens body flushed and exuberantly graceful when Gyorgy swooped her around the dance floor, the chiffon flying around her like wings.

CHAPTER 4

▼

Tangi ke vikia kae 'au e kaingá.
Longing to be praised by others while relatives perish.

Though you first saw me waking up with a hangover, and you are still waiting for me to get out of the Peace Corps van and face the awful details of the murder, I want to delay the inevitable. I want to remember that party before Melanie's dance, before the warm October night turned sinister. Who were we? How had we all converged here, sucked into the vortex around her body?

Melanie died, after all, in a tribe of storytellers. Some stories are so powerful that they change everything. That's the way the murder was: a dark and complicated event that entwined and bound us all. From that day on, any of us who knew Melanie, who had watched her dance, who knew Mort or Gyorgy, or even those who used a fish knife or ate watermelon or said we were proud to be American could hardly look at any of these things the way we had before. But the way the tragedy changed us seemed to depend on what we'd brought to Tonga; we were cornucopias, already filled with potent history. And some of that history came spilling out as we sat, unknowingly about to be struck by tragedy, at the end of training party.

Liz and Wade dictated that for a last ordeal, the graduating volunteers had to provide the entertainment for the party. Bridget confessed that in her years in the cast, she learned a dozen card tricks, so we made her a top hat of banana leaves and installed her as the Great *Pisikoa*. Diane revealed she'd always wanted to be a drum majorette in high school and had learned a few routines. Some Tongan boys made her two wooden batons, and she dropped them only twice. I had no talent that I could think of, so I recited "Thanatopsis." After that, Diane taught Bridget and me a couple of high school cheers, the closest any American girl— especially *we* three squares—ever gets to the splendor of the Tongan dance.

The men's entertainment acts were even more physical. Tony knew how to juggle, and Sam pulled out chukka sticks and kicked karate. Mac, our training leader and my crush, proved again what a good sport he was by doing an Elvis impersonation. He settled on "Hound Dog" because Tongans loved Elvis and hated dogs. With the possible exception of "Thanatopsis," the talent show was a howling success.

Vic and Betty, a gentle couple in their forties, had played coffeehouses in their youth, and after our entertainments, they led us all in folk singing. They were in their element, and here is how they got there: One day they were about to sign a purchase agreement on a fancy new house, about $200 a month out of their range. Shaken by the size of the new mortgage, they bought a bottle of Jack Daniels, sat on the crumbling concrete steps of their comfy old back porch, drank shots, and cursed the rat race. The next day they tore up the mortgage papers and applied to the Peace Corps. They didn't get rid of everything, and Vic brought his sweet acoustic guitar to Tonga. Together these old peaceniks nudged us into the innocent pleasure of harmony on "If I Had a Hammer" and "Michael, Row Your Boat Ashore."

While we sang, the widow Clare sat quietly alone, looking tragically lovely in a sky blue caftan, as elegant and delicate as a bird. She was fifty-one, still mourning her husband, a famous Russian violinist. One Friday the thirteenth, he collapsed as the two of them jumped up and down, hugging each other on their bed and screaming at a mouse. He had bravely traversed the Iron Curtain and played at Carnegie Hall, but he died in fear of a little pest. Clare couldn't get over the dark absurdity. On the thirteenth day of every month, she wore black, got Viliami at the Coconut Club to pour her a shot of vodka, and toasted her one true love. The Tongans, who elaborately mourned the dead, always understood. And the rest of us, even before the murder, accepted her grief.

There was Jeff, sitting at the piano and waiting his turn. Jeff had a Princeton PhD in literature. His dissertation was on Gabriel Garcia Lorca, and he spoke fluent Spanish. His young wife had just dumped him for a professor twice their age, and he wanted to run away. He figured the Peace Corps would assign him to South America, where he could have stepped right in. But they had other ideas. No position opened up where he would have been a natural. He remembered the call: how about the South Pacific? "I told them I didn't know anything about it, but here I am," he said. The only other skill he had to offer was that he could play piano—specifically, ragtime.

Last night for the first time, Jeff installed himself at a scratched black piano in a corner of the courtyard, the oversized rubber plant leaves bending into his line of sight, and played sparkling Scott Joplin and Marvin Hamlisch. His talent was a surprise, yet he looked the part, bespectacled and mustached. As his fingers pranced over the eighty-eights, wisps of thin, blond hair fell onto his forehead. He could have been working a burlesque joint, ignoring the clientele. I almost went over there, imagining myself turning the pages in a feathered boa. Instead, I leaned back to hear what Diane was saying after a few beers.

"I'm innocent," she was saying to Bridget. "But that's the point of being here. A person can be too innocent. I'm tired of being so sweet." I was further along that road than Diane, but I knew what she meant.

A big Swedish blond who was too awkward and thick in the torso to be quite glamorous, Diane was like a milkmaid. She had radiant skin, and she was industrious. Her job would be her first ever at the local house of disease. According to everything she had just learned, she would help hospital administrators get out the word on various sicknesses and ways to prevent them. Her job would take her to the outer islands. She'd never been away from home; in fact, she had never been west of the Mississippi. Her parents were conscientious Lutherans who wanted her to stay home forever.

"You have great instincts, Diane," Bridget said. "You did good." She was a kid from Indiana, who told us she grew up so close to the Indianapolis Speedway that around Memorial Day she could smell exhaust for a week. She'd never been to a single race, not once. It was that body cast for scoliosis that kept her away, and when she got the cast off, she couldn't wait to try out her incredible lightness of being.

"Do you realize what it's like to be in a body cast in Indiana in the summer?" she said. "The one thing I had to have at my side was a long stick that I could push down in the cast to scratch my back. I used to lie there sometimes during the race, listening to the engines rev over and over, and wonder what it would be like to be out of that cast and down on the grass in the infield. Sometimes I could smell the beer and Coppertone."

Diane said her brother went down there once and got so drunk he didn't even know who'd won. "Guys and cars," Bridget sighed. "Some chick in a body cast didn't get much attention in Indianapolis, I can tell you that."

She was an entomologist, paired with a guy from Brooklyn named Tony on a filariasis prevention project. Bridget loved bugs. In her years of confinement, she read voraciously. Natural science was her favorite subject, and bug complications fascinated her more than any other. To be in Polynesia with its giant flying cockroaches, several species of mosquitoes, and stinging centipedes was heaven for her.

Though the scoliosis and the years in the cast had left her with a slightly disfigured body, her eyes were large and bright and wonderful. She looked a little like an interesting giant bug herself. And she was great at singing the alto harmony on "Swing Low, Sweet Chariot."

I decided to try one of my stories on the other volunteers, one I'd been saving, the one about my boyfriend who set his hair on fire.

"I've got a 'how I got to Peace Corps' story for y'all," I shouted. "Vic, listen to this one. It starts with corrupt government, and you'll like it."

"Okay, I'm listening. It better be good."

"Well, I'd already sort of applied to Peace Corps, but I hit all these bureaucratic snags that I didn't understand. I wrote to my congressman for help, but he got convicted of bribery at about the same time and wasn't exactly available..."

"I know about that guy—that jerk in Orange County," Vic said, his energy ignited. "I remember him."

"Well, okay, that's the government part of the story, just for you. Anyway, it's the goddamned Bicentennial, right? It's the Fourth of July, and we go to the beach with a bunch of other people to do our fireworks, and my boyfriend..."

"What was his name?" somebody demanded. Details mattered.

"Maharishi Mike."

"Right on!" A chorus of hoots.

"He was really into transcendental meditation until his teachers disowned him because he wouldn't give up pot. But he had his own system of meditating and eating macrobiotic food, so he kept calling himself Maharishi Mike."

"What about the hair?" someone asked.

I paused for a swig of beer. "Well, Mike's brother was there, with a bottle of Wild Turkey. And Mike and his brother were really close, and when it's time to light the fireworks, they're smashed."

"Bad combination," Vic said.

"No shit," I said. "So Mike decides he's going to be in charge of the Roman candles. He starts doing this wild sort of druid dance in the sand with his hands full of gun powder, swinging his arms around and around, and before we knew it—blammo."

Peals of laughter. "Was he hurt?"

"No, his brother and a couple of other people wrestled him to the ground with a beach blanket and put him out. He was just singed—lost his eyebrows, though. And I decided two things at that moment. One, he was a flaming idiot, and two, I had to get out of the country."

"What happened to the congressman?" Vic asked.

"He went to jail. And I got into Peace Corps."

That really prompted a round of cheers. "A happy ending," Vic yelled.

Jeff's last ragtime riffs tinkled off into the palm trees. The Tongans took it from there. They were born entertainers. Demure girls performed a sitting dance, the *ma'ulu'ulu*, hands and arms choreographed to haunting chants from older women in the back row. Coconut-oiled men leaped and shouted to furious drumming on shiny silver biscuit tins. A single woman danced the *ta'olunga*, her body glistening and sinuous. Tongan boys prowled and jumped around her. A few Peace Corps guys joined the mock-lecherous routine, to screams of hilarity from the Tongans. Tongan and Peace Corps alike reached into back pockets for paper money to stick to the girl's oiled shoulders and legs. She made a good haul.

After the *ta'olunga*, a row of muscular young men with painted faces burst onto the dance floor, shouting and brandishing fake wood swords, their wrists and ankles and waists circled with long green leaves, feathers, and shells. They writhed, turned, hurtled, amazingly in rhythm. And then, from behind the line of warriors, emerged a single dancer. He lit orange flames on two long batons. He twirled them, threw them high, caught them, and did it all again and again while the drums pounded. We all yelled "*malie, malie,*" bravo, bravo.

Then I thought I noticed something. I nudged Diane.

"Do you know who *that* is?"

The fire dancer was Viliami, the young bartender from the Coconut Club. We'd admired him many times at our tastefully disheveled hangout.

"He looks *good*," Diane agreed, spellbound. "I'm ready to stop being innocent."

"*Really* good," Bridget said.

I know that Melanie and Gyorgy and Mort were somewhere during all of this, but we didn't notice. The veteran volunteers had their own clique. Maybe Melanie and Gyorgy had already left, jaded about the Tongan dances and bored with the Peace Corps palaver. Maybe Mort was already malignantly brooding, lying in wait. Maybe the night's ominous drama had already begun.

Oblivious, the rest of us sat down together in a circle on mats under the hotel's outdoor pavilion. Pulu went around the circle, reminding his male students to keep their knees down and the women to settle sidesaddle. A kava ceremony began. An old Tongan woman rested her gifted hands gracefully, palms up, on her lap, in front of a huge wooden bowl. At her right was Simione Feitulu, the oldest chieftain in town.

The ritual was ancient and prescribed. Behind the kava maker, a young man rhythmically pounded the kava root into small pieces on a stone and passed a handful to her. With dexterity wielded since her teens, she swept out a foot of coconut husk to scoop and stir the kava into cold water, poured slowly into the bowl by a man on her left. It was an art: every movement of her hands was ballet, circles within circles. When the kava was ready, the chieftain called out *"kava kuoheka!"* and she dipped the first coconut shell into the beige liquid. She handed it to the chieftain, who handed it to her niece. Gracefully, the girl delivered the cup, holding it forward with both hands, and returned to have it filled, and delivered that one, and returned, until everyone around the circle drank one cup. There was a moment of silence, and then the singing started.

The songs were all about lost love: lovers drowned at sea, lovers stolen by another, the loved who simply didn't love back. Sitting there that night, I decided that kava singing was the most beautiful music in the world. I loved the tight harmony, the high tenors, mournful and romantic. I loved how the singing went on for hours.

The kava helped. It had a bite like cloves, and its mild narcotic effect eventually slowed the songs and heightened their melancholy. Invariably, the lonely lover turned his eyes to the ocean and, with nothing more to seduce, praised the islands, sang to the dolphins, crooned to the moon. Eventually, we struggled up to shake out our legs, spilled into the courtyard, and straggled home. I rode my black bike, alone, even though I am night blind. There was a full moon, and I could see everything.

In Tonga when we told one another stories, we remade ourselves as we went along, so far from home that nobody'd know the difference. There was always more time, another Steinlager, another congenial moon to wander home under, and our stories were like tartans, elaborate patterns woven from a handful of traditional colors: money, unhappy families, and boredom. As to the literal truth, I don't know, and it didn't matter.

I was Example A. I could pick whichever part of my story applied, based on my audience and the circumstances. There was truth in all of it, but the story never stopped there. If I were flirting, I could imply that I'd come to Tonga to explore uncharted erotic territories, with sly references to Margaret Mead and the aphrodisiac effects of the tropics. That usually got the job done. But I cultivated variations. A useful one was that I said I was tired of telling other people's stories. In Southern California, I said more than once, I felt oppressed by rich people who'd already made it and had loaded their autobiographies with adventures, successes, and insights. Californians understood the restless quest for experience, I'd say, for crossing boundaries. That's what the state was there for—to accommodate overachieving dissenters. My editors at the *Daily Anchor-Democrat*, curious old newspapermen, were forever assigning me to interview such people: a woman novelist with a fishing boat in Juneau; the Star Trek writer who'd become a radical environmentalist; the actor who was changed from male to female in one of the first operations in Denmark. I interviewed a furniture store heir with a winning race horse, an Olympic swimmer, a Basque shepherd, a thirteen-year-old cellist who'd won the ear of Andres Segovia, a gorgeous but practically mute college boy who'd appeared in the third Playgirl center fold.

And I'd go home and think, *huh*. I'd fix a weight-conscious smoothie of raw eggs, skim milk, and frozen strawberries in the blender and sip it thoughtfully on the tiny balcony of my apartment, with a view of another tiny apartment and, below, two green dumpsters and a parking lot. I could do better than sit around waiting for other people to make some decrepit editor's heart beat faster. I wanted to do something myself. And see, I *did*, I'd say assertively, thumping the table at the Coconut Club with the palm of my hand before gulping down another swig of beer.

And of course, there was my story about getting away from home. *Home* home, which was Ohio. It's like one of my friends once wrote after we drove Ohio's long swathe of Interstate 80: Why is Ohio so *big*?

Most people, at the very mention of the word "Ohio," immediately understood why I wanted to be somewhere else. I'd say, "I'm from Ohio," and they'd sympathetically say, "Ooohh." They'd think I was trying to get away from carrot Jell-O and roast beef cooked till it was gray, and men in matching white belts and shoes even in February, and the Cuyahoga River catching fire. Of course they were right. If you stayed, it was indictment, and you lacked imagination. If you left, no matter how trivial or mediocre your life turned out to be, at least you could say, "Well, it's not Ohio."

People from Ohio were everywhere. The first day I landed in Tonga, a guy from my hometown was among the crowd at the airport. His mother and my mother had already corresponded, he said, and I recoiled. Fortunately, he was stationed on an outer island and disappeared soon after, but getting away from home was clearly no simple matter.

My Ohio was inextricably intertwined with religion: stained glass windows, Fanny Crosby hymns, tent revivals, stentorian preachers, altar calls, and a list of prohibitions as long as a pew—no dancing, no cards, no makeup, no swearing, no movies (except, of course, grudgingly, *The Sound of Music*), no drinking, no smoking, no revealing clothes. My father's brand of religion prohibited even the sensual possibilities of baptism by dunking. We were "sprinklers," fastidiously flicking a few chaste droplets on barely lowered heads. It was sometimes hard to keep straight what we were saying yes to except homegrown roughage and modest silence.

My father wasn't just a preacher, but a fundamentalist in heart and doctrine. Unfortunately for him, his wife was restless and skeptical. She kept his fanatic leanings somewhat under control by insisting that new experiences could be edifying. Once when they visited me in Southern Cal, my mother, giddy and girlish with the novelty of sitting on the floor in a Japanese restaurant, tried to get him to taste some sake. "Just lick a little off my finger," she said, dipping her pinky into the porcelain cup. "Just try it!" But he'd taken The Temperance Pledge at fourteen, back on the farm, and he refused. My mother and I exchanged exasperated glances. At that moment, we were both bored to death with the reverend and his rectitude.

All through my childhood, my father retained one streak of audacity. He liked fast cars. He favored bright red Mustangs, for example; apparently Protestants could believe in the Ford Motor Company. He fussed over a succession of shiny chassis like prized heifers. He said his cars made people take notice and reconsider their stereotypes about preachers. Men of the cloth didn't have to be milquetoasts, he insisted. He drove wildly and badly and had frequent fender benders, but when his victims found out that he was a minister, they hesitated, slunk away from the debris, and slipped their ID cards back into their wallets. I guess it was bad luck to sue a clergyman.

Later he bought a series of motorcycles and disappeared for long rides in the country. He always went too fast. Once he lost control of his medium-sized Harley on a strip of ice, ran it into a snow bank, and slid a hundred yards on his behind. He came home drenched in slush, the backside of his pants completely scraped away. Even then, my father said that the Lord was one with men and their machines. God had a sense of humor, he claimed without particularly smiling; certainly his wife and daughter's muffled risibility wasn't part of it. God, he revealed, had just given him a little reminder not to take the curves so fast.

If anybody were going to be flamboyant, I learned early, it would be the men. Women were supposed to fluff their plain brown feathers and nestle tidily.

Almost all my relatives were in churchy occupations. Both grandfathers were preachers, one a traveling evangelist and the other a farmer and a math professor who also officiated over a Nazarene flock. On my mother's side were two preacher uncles and a third who was a devout farm implement salesman. On my father's side, the list ran on.

I was part of the family business, a child obediently touting holiness from one parish to another. A lovely, leafy neighborhood in Canton. A grimy downtown church in Akron. A four-church parish in the hills of Coshocton County, where we lived in a town misnamed Blissfield with a sadistic Amish dentist and, on the bright side, a great view of the Northern Lights. I was a dutiful child, exemplary. "Never any trouble," my mother always murmured—until I catapulted myself out of there.

Brothers and sisters, there's no decadence like Puritan decadence. It builds up a ferocious appetite. With each delicious *yes* for a few years after I left, I blazed against authority, gulped wine, sucked in blue tobacco smoke, devoured men, spat curses, and fled to the Tropic of Capricorn.

All that was riding on my back in 1976—all that, and my mother and my mother's misery. My mother lived most of her life in frustration and regret, and I knew it. She had to quit teaching high school French and home economics when she got married because in the '30s in Ohio, that was a rule. There were rumors about her breakdowns—the first in college when she was dumped by some kid named Timmerman, the last when she tried to return to teaching in the '60s but quit after she was mugged in the teachers' lounge. My father was her rebound love, set up for her own good by my grandmother, supposedly a panacea after the cruel Tom Timmerman. In their wedding pictures, my mother looks shocked and slim in an unadorned white satin dress, already wounded by life. My father looks callow and out of his league, his face achingly eager and sweet. But he was a believer, a true believer who would soon develop his love for fast cars. That little bit of wildness didn't yet show on his face in 1936, but that ache for hot cars would appear again and again, an untamed streak he never quite curbed. You wouldn't have thought it would be my dad with the secrets; it was my mom you'd have guessed hid a deep well.

At the breakfast table, for example, my mother never described her dreams. This always spooked me. My dad always related his in excruciating detail, even when they mortified the rest of us with embarrassing specifics about showing up in the pulpit with no pants on or getting diarrhea on a pastoral visit. He acted like every symbol should be soberly considered and etched in stone. I always believed that my mother's dreams, in contrast, were too dark to be repeated. But how could I know? She never explained. I thought it was because if the lid flew off, whatever flew out could never be stuffed back in. How could I know?

I was a late arrival, the last of three, perhaps my mother's last grab at happiness. By the time I was a teenager, my brother and sister were grown and gone, and I was alone in that claustrophobic house with my self-involved, unyielding dad and my melancholy mom. Avidly, I planned to get away, and get away good.

For years I hated everybody and everything from my old life—the endless church services, the quiet, clean sanctuaries with their limpid colored glass, the doleful music, the off-key choirs, and most of all the fierce patriarchs in black suits who hated women, including my mother and, by deduction, me. It was not just that they were uncompromising; they feared and reviled what they called "the world." To such men, the world was deeply dangerous. Evil lurked in every corner, especially the sunny, seductive ones. And evil had to be confessed. Evil had to be fought, and evil would return, again and again, until you were dead.

This was not so much terrifying or infuriating as it was desperately, exhaustingly dull. My father embodied it all. To me in those early years of escape, he was foolish—an anachronism, an old prig. I felt for my mother, though I didn't understand her loyalty. The young are cruel that way. But my father was my target. And I didn't know to pity my poor lovers, taking all that baggage, receiving all that furious, preying energy. In addition to conquest, adventure, and experience, having sex was bittersweet revenge. Every time I captured a new man and *fucked* him, as I would have said it, I proved my father wrong. Sex did not lead to hell any more than the occasional cup of sake. Sex was my personal edification, and nothing bad would come of it.

And of course when I graduated from high school in 1967, the world was ready-made for me. I laced up my hiking boots under a long peasant skirt every morning, soberly reminding myself that the world might blow itself up at any time. I assiduously tackled my new life: lit another joint, put on my embroidered blouses (or took them off), and set out to have some fun.

If my mother had been happy, maybe things would have been different. Maybe I would have ignored the hippies, resisted California, stayed in church, canned green beans, joined the Missionary Society, played the organ at funerals, and married a mild, steady man who wore white shirts to work. Maybe he and I would have driven a Chevy sedan and had a couple of nicely scrubbed Protestant kids. Maybe.

But an unhappy mother is dangerous for a girl, making her wild with guilt and dread. I was determined to prove I was not like my poor mom, that woman with dreams too awful to tell.

But then, all the *palangis* I met in Tonga seemed to have their own Ohios—what they wanted to get away from, what they didn't want to be. Unfortunately, making our escape from our Ohios proved far more complicated than any of us expected.

CHAPTER 5

▼

Faifai malie na'á pe paki'i ha la'i telie.
Take care not to break a telie leaf—or proceed cautiously, according to the protocol.

Eventually I did climb those stairs into the crowded room and wedge myself into a seat in the back row. On my left, a stern-faced Mac. On my right, Bridget and Diane. Evelyn Henry was red-eyed and distraught, but as soon as she started the meeting, I could see that she was also excited by the turn of events. Maybe her forgotten outpost would get some attention.

She was a painfully stylish woman from Arlington, Virginia, divorced and in her fifties. People said she got the job because of politics. What politics, whose politics, I never found out.

Maybe Evelyn Henry thought being country director would be like being an ambassador of some small European country, say, Lichtenstein. Maybe she thought it would be an endless parade of cocktail parties and exotica. Instead, even in the best of times, she had to manage a horde of hippies, half of whom seemed to think getting out of the United States was the crowning achievement of their lives, and the other half of whom seemed to be a bunch of naïve do-gooders.

She lived in a roomy, one-story house in an expatriate, waterfront neighborhood that looked charming, but because of the way Nuku'alofa dumped its sewage, the area had a sickening smell. Her beach was unusable. And even though she had a housekeeper and a cook, she still had to put up with flying cockroaches, unreliable electricity, and scarce hot water like all the rest of us.

At least she had use of one of the white Peace Corps Land Rovers, but how far could she get? Kolovai, fifteen miles to the west, where bats were sacred and fluttered by the hundreds in the trees? Or Niutoua, fifteen miles to the east, where three moss-covered boulders, called the Ha'amonga Trilithon, were among the nation's few official tourist attractions? No, she was as trapped as the rest of us.

Still, she always gamely made herself up (she vacationed in Singapore twice a year and restored her supply of lipstick and perfume), wore high heels with a matching purse, and always tied a wispy, matching scarf around her purse handle. Traversing Nuku'alofa's muddy streets, she looked like a dervish, her scarf flying out with trivial gaiety.

Standing up straight at the front of the room, Evelyn Henry declared the facts. She told us that Melanie Porter's body would be sent back to North Dakota with a U.S. government escort. She said Mort Friedman would be charged with murder and that a Peace Corps lawyer from New Zealand was already en route to represent him. She said the penalty for murder was death by hanging. She stopped talking and looked hard at the floor. The room was silent.

"The potential repercussions of this are enormous, as I'm sure you all understand," she said. "There are worldwide implications for Americans and for the Peace Corps." Her eyebrows arched with importance. I imagined she was rerunning scenes from "Patton" in her mind. I imagined her practicing these lines in front of her wavy mirror.

She told us that a Peace Corps psychologist was on his way to assess Mort Friedman's sanity. She said the psychologist would be available to counsel any volunteer who needed him. She said Mort had confessed. She didn't mention Gyorgy, who was, after all, Canadian.

"Didn't anybody notice anything about Mort?" someone asked. "Some of us were worried about him. Didn't he give off any clues?"

I craned my neck to see who had asked the question. I thought it was Skip, a volunteer who'd re-upped after his first two years and was nearing the end of a third.

"That's a question that will haunt me to my dying day," Evelyn Henry answered dramatically. Her voice had lost some of its confident timbre. "I certainly had not heard of anything, and we'll have to find out a lot more. Obviously, now we know that this is a person who needed help, and we didn't see it in time."

Quiet sobs started up. Evelyn Henry began to lose her audience as one small group and then another broke into distressed, panicky private conversations. Bridget and Diane dabbed at tears with the backs of their hands. Mac looked straight ahead, his mouth set. I tried to concentrate. I watched the director lift her hand vaguely, ineffectually, to regain the crowd's attention.

"Please," she said. "Please."

She told us this was the first murder in the last ten years in the Kingdom. She said it was the first murder of its kind—one volunteer killing another—in Peace Corps history. There'd been one years before in Tanzania, she said, when a husband and wife went off on a picnic, and the wife ended up dead. The husband was acquitted. In Tonga, this was the first murder in memory involving *palangis*.

From training, we all knew the story of one other *palangi* murder—the stoning of John Norton, one of the escapees from the mutiny on the *Bounty*, on the rocky shore of the volcanic island of Tofua. That was two hundred years ago. But in twentieth-century Tonga, a *palangi* murder was also complicated. Evelyn Henry was explaining it now. On one hand, speaking politically, she said, the diplomatic problems would have been worse if a Tongan had killed Melanie or if a volunteer had killed a Tongan.

The room rustled.

"Melanie's dead either way, isn't she?" someone mumbled. This time I knew it was Skip, the front row skeptic.

"I'm sorry. I am truly sorry. But there are some realities we have to face." She paused.

"I have another thing to say," she continued. "Apparently this tragedy was related to…happened because of…" She struggled. "It was a *love triangle*."

Ah, there it was. The words so old-fashioned, so Victorian. I groaned and looked at Mac, who lowered his head and looked back, shrugging helplessly.

"I know where she's going with this," I whispered.

"Volunteers, I beg of you," Evelyn continued. "Be careful with your behavior. You are here as representatives of the U.S. government. You're under a great deal of stress, and this event is going to make it even worse. You must be…careful."

"*We* did not kill Melanie," Skip shouted. "A guy who was obviously going crazy killed Melanie, and you knew about it, and you didn't do anything about it."

In the shock after his outburst, Evelyn Henry looked at Liz and Wade, the training directors, and at her assistants. They hustled over to Skip and tried to put their arms around him, as if they were at a revival meeting. He threw them off. Then he leaped up from his chair and left the room, noisily pounding down the long stairs.

In the air hung a sinister pall. Inside my chest, a time-release dirty bomb was letting off contaminated particles—it was something I hadn't felt for years, but remembered too well from sitting in church, while my dad tried to get people to come forward and accept Jesus Christ as their personal savior while some good woman warbled, "Just as I am, without a plea, but that thy blood was shed for thee…"

Those disagreeable particles were guilt. I must have done something. I must have sinned. I hated the ickiness creeping over me. And when I should have been mourning Melanie and demanding justice, this is the thought that first clogged my mind: I was going to have less fun. Sex, my beloved sex life, the prize and flag of my freedom, would probably have to be lowered off the mast and folded up and mothballed for the next two years.

I looked over at Bridget and Diane, who wouldn't look back. As far as I knew, I was the only one of the three of us who'd had any sex since disembarking on the steamy runway from our Air Pacific jet. I spotted Sam in a nearby corner—the LA boy, my first lover in the Kingdom. He caught my eye and shook his head. We'd sat together on the plane for the long lap between Hawaii and Pago Pago, and before the first real atoll showed up below, he had declared, "I think you're sexy." I shot back something sarcastic, but, addled by vanity, I took the bait. As it turned out, he was an ideal first mate, funny and cynical. A Jewish kid from the Fairfax District, he had taken to the Asian community and had earned a brown belt. He was in Tonga to be a journalistic consultant for the *Tonga Chronicle*. Free labor, they figured, for tough reporting and page layouts. The only thing he believed in was his own body, which he fussed over as if it were an expensive racehorse. To objective eyes, his body wasn't a perfect vessel—he had a pot belly, and his behind stuck out, though a shapely behind it was. We had slipped out of a boring lecture about "Rank in Tonga" and stole back to his house—an overflow place in back of the guesthouse he shared during training with three other volunteers.

It was his first time in the Kingdom, too. Thin brown curtains rustled in the whitewashed room. A rooster crowed. Somewhere someone shouted greetings and laughed. And just as Sam came, a blue skink skittered across the wall. Now I called him Lizard. The name stuck, and without knowing why, everybody else started calling him Lizard Sam. He didn't seem to expect anything from me afterward except the chance to pair off again if the moment favored it.

Tony was there, too, sitting woodenly in the front row. Tony, an entomologist from Brooklyn. My Tongan one-night stand, not as successful. An Aussie expatriate from the World Health Organization had a party. Tony and I drank too much and sneaked into a back room with a little balcony. He was nervous, and it all happened fast, standing up and fumbling on that second-story back porch over an alley lined with trash cans from Nuku'alofa's only Chinese restaurant. We rushed, teetering with booze, the night air flooded with heavy scents.

Afterward, straightening myself up, I wondered why I'd done it. I watched Tony zip up and said, "Know why Baptists never make love standing up? They're afraid somebody'll think they're dancing."

He looked at me oddly. I smiled a crooked smile.

"Preacher's kid joke," I said lamely.

"Ha ha," he said.

"Hey, you wanted to, too. Admit it."

We went back to the living room, where a Tongan hunk and a tiny Aussie woman were doing the jitterbug. Among the expatriates, the dance was all the rage.

That once was enough. Tony'd be deeply scared off sex by the murder, of that I was sure. He was Catholic.

Be careful. Fucking depressing words. Wasn't I part of the first pill generation ever, glorying in its liberation? Hadn't Roe v. Wade just established that my sisters and I finally had the say-so over our own bodies? Hadn't I come of age at the best goddamn time in human history to be a woman?

"Here we go," I whispered, focusing again on Evelyn Henry's pained performance. "Get out the chastity belts."

"She's a Christian, you know," Mac warned. "I bet religion gets into this somehow."

"This is a time for us all to pray for Melanie and for Mort," Evelyn Henry said on cue. "And it wouldn't hurt for more of you to make appearances at the churches during the next few weeks. God will help us all get through." Her syrupy voice droned. I couldn't look at Mac.

"I heard she's having an affair with the regional director," Mac said, loud enough to ripple up a row or two.

"Yeah, but I bet next she'll say something about Jesus," Sam muttered from his corner.

"Jesus Christ exhorted us to forgive," Evelyn Henry said. "Pray for Mort to be forgiven."

"I don't believe what I'm hearing," I whispered. I was about to curse out loud.

Lizard Sam smirked. "Man," he said, "doesn't she know Mort's *Jewish*?"

"Shut up, all of you!" Bridget said.

"Now, while you're all here, I have one more thing for you all to do." Evelyn Henry's voice picked up, sounding relieved to move to another subject. She was almost merry, as if she were about to announce to the kindergartners it was time for milk and cookies.

"We've received the absentee ballots for the presidential election. If anyone wants to vote, this is your chance, and we'll mail all the ballots in together."

The strangeness of the moment took a while to sink in, but eventually we shuffled forward, as if drugged, to pick up our ballots. I got in line. From the incongruous chitchat, I gathered that everybody was going to vote for Jimmy Carter. I said I was going to vote for him, too. For most of us, it was because of Jimmy's mother, Miss Lillian, the ex-Peace Corps volunteer, who was already an old lady when she signed up. Miss Lillian was our idol.

We also voted, en masse, to meet later at the Coconut Club. My head still pounding, I asked Mac to drop me off. I had to get some sleep.

"Would you pick me up at seven?

Mac agreed and screeched off the property, the Peace Corps Rover coughing out a cloud of smoke. I stood there for a moment in the dust, trying to get my bearings. I knew what was bugging me: I didn't want the murder to change me. I wanted everything to be like it was before. But it was too late.

Ma the pig was the first to greet me—the closest thing to a pet on the property, a sweet brown runt who rubbed against me like a dog. His unambiguous affection was a relief. I knew I couldn't get attached to the little guy. His name meant bread, and I knew he was meant to be food. In the meantime, whenever Ma pushed open my door as he had learned to do and came inside like a puppy, he always made me feel at home.

With Ma at my side, I walked wearily toward my hut.

"Salote! Come and say hello!" Filipa sat with Tevita on a tattered mat in a circle of shade. I felt disoriented that she was so cheerful when the last time I'd seen her, just a few hours ago, she'd been moaning loud *oiaues*. Tevita was back from tending taro and manioc in the bush, and Filipa was washing his feet and massaging his ankles in a dented cast-iron basin. The sight of the two of them like that embarrassed me. It looked so intimate, so—married. They signaled me to join them, and Tevita poured me a glass of orange soda from a bottle at his side.

"Here, drink, Salote," he said serenely, as if he had not plunged into my hut last night, as if there'd never been a murder. I plopped down and self-consciously arranged my skirt around my legs, urgently feeling the need for modesty. I focused my attention on the glass of orange soda so that I wouldn't look at Filipa rubbing her husband's feet. They didn't seem in any hurry to talk about what had happened. I forced myself to wait, sipping the cool drink.

One year during Holy Week, my father tried the ritual of foot washing on Maundy Thursday, and the parish was never the same. I figure it was the eroticism of naked feet that did it. For one thing, the women parishioners had to show up for church without their girdles and hose if they wanted to participate. They did. They wanted to savor the sexy freedom of showing up at church without bindings. I think they wanted to enjoy the delicious, conflicting emotions of pleasure and unseemliness. It was Biblical, after all, for the pastor to wash their feet on Maundy Thursday. But their husbands and my mother were suspicious. Like the women parishioners, my father was more enthusiastic about the experiment than my mother thought prudent. Prurient was more like it. And the stolid, stoic men didn't want another man touching their feet, even the pastor. The whole thing proved too controversial even for discussion, and, more disappointed than he could admit, my father never tried it again.

Now here was Filipa stroking Tevita's feet and Tevita leaning back against a tree trunk, the most natural thing in the world. It was their country and their marriage. No angst here, murder or not. I felt stranded and alone.

"Salote, I have a big idea how we can make some money," Tevita said suddenly. I took in my breath and wondered whether I'd heard him correctly. Was there to be no discussion of the murder at all?

"You just listen," he said. "What can we get our hands on cheap that a lot of people want?" Filipa began to shake her head slowly without looking up.

"Cheap?" I said, confused and suddenly exhausted. "I don't know. Coconuts?"

Tevita grinned and shook his head.

"Tomatoes?"

He wagged more vigorously. I found myself intensely irritated. Filipa only frowned and dug her hands like claws into his feet.

"Listen: lime juice!"

He paused and beamed brilliantly, resting his hands in his lap.

"Lime juice?"

"Lime juice!"

Filipa stopped massaging and waved an exasperated hand across the yard. "We have a lime tree right here," she said. "I'm looking at it. Everybody has them!"

"But those limes are bad, small and dry," Tevita persisted.

I'd had an occasional gin and tonic at the Dateline Hotel. There was always a slice of lime with the drink, and of course Mac had plucked a lime from that very tree last night for our hijinks, but I had to admit I'd rarely seen limes in the market.

"Filipa has many aunties in Niautopatapu, and you know what they have all over that beautiful island?"

I bit in spite of myself. "Limes?"

"Yes!" His fervor was boundless. "They grow beautiful limes there, Salote, beautiful lime trees on every lot, beautiful lime trees along the ocean, beautiful lime trees in the bush. Everywhere you look, beautiful lime trees. So many limes Filipa's aunties and uncles can never eat enough. See, they have too many limes!"

It was, he clearly believed, an entrepreneurial masterstroke. They had too much of something, and Nuku'alofa didn't have enough. The concept was so obvious that he couldn't believe he hadn't thought of it before. The rest—the details—seemed trivial.

Tevita, I was learning, was a tireless hustler. He got 30 *pa'anga* a month for renting my hut, my *fale*, a tidy addition to the 150 a month he earned as an accountant for the Ministry of Business and Trade. And Tevita liked being a civil servant to the King, who was another hustler with a head for numbers. Tevita always had some scheme up his sleeve. He'd been talking about building another small hut on the back corner of the property, to rent to another volunteer. He'd build another classic Tongan house. "He knows what you *Pisikoa* want," Filipa smirked, making me feel childish for wanting to live *fakatonga*. He would make it oval in the Tongan style, and he'd put down a concrete pad and roof it with tin, like mine. But unlike mine, which had walls of lashed bamboo, he wanted this one to be made of wood, solid and easy to paint. A spot behind the mango tree, nestled in the banana patch, would be perfect.

Tevita's father was Japanese, a whaler who came through Tonga just long enough to make his mother pregnant. Tevita never knew him or even saw him, but he had his father's last name: Hasimoto. For hundreds of years, Tongans had been making love with everyone who stopped in their remote corner of the South Pacific. Small wonder the Europeans called the area the Friendly Islands. From what I gathered when I wasn't skipping training lectures to jump in the sack with Sam, even before the Europeans arrived, the "pure" Tongans were mixtures. When they weren't killing or being killed by Samoans or Fijians, they were making babies with them. And since this lusty whaler Hasimoto fled the Kingdom soon after the marriage, he had left no fortune for Tevita.

But Tevita's mother achieved respectability of sorts: she became the cook for the Queen and made enough money to clothe and educate her only son and to be grudgingly left alone by the scandal mongers.

Being an only child was a problem. It wasn't the Tongan way. Where would be the family to help his mother live in old age? Where were the sisters to keep Tevita in line? Where was the reassuring network of obligations owed and favors called in at the right time?

As it turned out, Tevita benefited more than he suffered from being an only child. Instead of having to split his mother's property among many siblings, his mother's choice eight acres of taro, a gift from the Queen, came to him alone. He went every weekend with his sons to tend the root crops that fed the family well. Marriage to Filipa brought a property in town, inherited from her mother. Filipa also brought her five sisters, who all lived nearby and took a passionate interest in one another's affairs. In marrying Filipa, Tevita went from isolation, living alone with his quiet, conscientious mother, to being the patriarch of a huge and always growing brood. Through Filipa, Tevita finally was ushered into full participation in Tongan life.

Yet Tevita retained the drive of a social outcast. He had plans—big plans— which he detailed with such enthusiasm that little balls of white spit collected at the corners of his mouth.

"The aunties pick the limes and squeeze the juice," he said, "and then they ship it down to us. We put it in bottles and sell it in Nuku'alofa and make a lot of *pa'anga*. Ouch!" A spiteful smile flickered across Filipa's face as she relaxed her grip.

The deal was as good as closed.

"Good idea," I said. My voice wavered, gave me away.

Filipa's dark brown eyes softened in concern. She murmured something in Tongan to Tevita, who looked suddenly ashamed.

"We glad you are safe, Salote," Filipa said. "We watch out for you."

So that was it. All they were going to say. Well, I'd take it.

"*Malo 'aupito*," I said, "thank you very much," and finally stepped inside my cool, dark house.

It took a minute to realize that the hut was occupied by two of Filipa and Tevita's daughters. Lounging on the floor, Tupou and Heilala were making themselves at home. When my eyes adjusted, I could see the gold earrings my brother gave me glinting on Heilala's ears. Tupou had on my Kent State T-shirt and my gold pendant, a Scorpio symbol I adored.

Seeing the necklace dangle at her pudgy neck particularly galled me. It had been a parting gift from my editor and secret lover at the *Anchor-Democrat*. Yes, I'm a Scorpio, and he was, too: passionate and loyal and seduced by the dark side. He was forty-seven, divorced, smoking and drinking too much. When he got off work, he holed up in an overgrown little house in one of Laguna Beach's hippie canyons. I loved making love there, like being in the Garden of Eden under the thick ferns and pungent eucalyptus, walking around barefoot on the fragrant red-wood planks. He was under a lot of stress. I helpfully offered tantric workouts, but they weren't enough. His doctor told him he had to lose weight; he either had to eat less or quit drinking. He gave up food and turned gaunt, but he showed up every morning brilliantly clear-headed, editing our copy with a merciless blade. He had big, basset hound eyes and soft hands. Anyway, he slipped me the necklace one day just after I told him I was leaving the paper to join the Peace Corps. It was inscribed "To CT from TM, 6/76." His note said, "You gave me joy." He was one of two or three men who appealed to my heart: I might have married him if I hadn't still been so wild.

Now the pendant was the toy in a game between Tupou and me. Sometimes it would be there when I wanted it, and other times it would be resting gaily around Tupou's neck, captured from my jewelry box.

"We like your stuff," Tupou, the oldest daughter, said in precocious English as if my stuff mattered more than any dumb *palangi* murder. Maybe she thought all the *palangis* were about to get kicked out of the country, or better yet, murder one another en masse, and she wanted dibs on what would be left behind. I rubbed my still aching head and paused before responding. Was she pulling the Tongan gambit that meant I was supposed to give her whatever she admired? Well, I wasn't about to surrender these sentimental favorites. And it pissed me off that Tupou and Heilala had come in and pawed through my belongings.

"I'm glad you like them, Tupou. You can come over and try them on whenever you want to. But they are mine, and they mean a lot to me. And now I really need to be alone."

The girls stalked out, insulted, but not before dramatically throwing my jewelry on the mat.

I collapsed on my cot. An afternoon nap—now that was a concept the Tongans understood. Even the mango tree seemed to cooperate, not dropping a single fruit on the roof while I slept. For once, the air was still. I didn't wake up until Mac pulled into the driveway again, just as dark was falling, and gently knocked on the door.

CHAPTER 6

▼

Lau pe 'e he lokuá ko e moana hono taputá.
The small fish thinks his little hangout close to shore is the whole ocean.

The Coconut Club was a private establishment, a low-slung barn with cool concrete floors and push-out hurricane windows like those on my hut. Inside was a long ebony bar and, to the left through a wide arch, a snooker room. The main room was littered with worn wooden tables and rickety folding chairs. At the back of the club was an overgrown patio, where Coconut Club members hosted their wives for rare couples' nights. A little shed with squeaky swinging doors contained restrooms. Everything was airy and open, whitewashed and soaked by decades of genteel drunkenness.

Except for the rare parties, there was never any music—never anything but drinking and snooker, and snooker was a gentleman's game. That left gossip and Steinlager—with eleven percent alcohol and served in brown quart bottles at the bootleg price of fifty cents each—or whatever liquors the bartender, Viliami, could get his hands on. A pyramid of little white bags of peanuts waited on a tray at the end of the bar, and I decided to make a supper of them again tonight.

Peace Corps volunteers got memberships to the Coconut Club as an act of international generosity and capitalist ingenuity. Peace Corps women were allowed to join—the only women, other than occasional prostitutes, routinely admitted. No Peace Corps women that I knew of, myself included, had ever thought to agitate to allow all adults to join the club. We were led to believe that membership was a rare honor and that any mention of politics would put the perpetrator out on the dusty road on the wrong side of the reef. We women volunteers, philistines like all the rest, accepted the deal.

The Coconut Club membership document looked like a mortgage, clotted with rules and policies typed up in complicated Tongan phrases. I was absurdly fond of mine and kept it with me, folded up in my billfold, at all times. Sometimes it rubbed up against my legal-sized envelope containing my list of lovers. The two documents made me feel secure and happy. I was in the world, and I wasn't missing out.

On the damp tables, brown bottles piled up as volunteers congregated. They slouched over the tables and moved from one huddle to another, consoling one another, crying, drinking, and crying again.

I stood at the bar with my first two bags of peanuts and bought my first quart of Steinlager. I felt unready for a binge or for the rawness of shock and grief. I finally sat down at a table with Mac, Sam, and Jeff and nursed my beer as long as I could, avoiding conversation. After twenty minutes or so, I left my beer on the table and went back to the bar to buy a green coconut. I asked Viliami to crack the big nut open. I admired a skillful man, and Viliami didn't spill a single drop. Under his perfect white shirt, his smooth, tawny skin shone, lightly oiled the way Tongans did it. Like most Polynesians, he had no chest hair, and his strong fire dancer's muscles stood out. Curls of shiny black hair looped onto his open collar. He handed me the coconut. The flesh inside was slimy, like custard, and nutritious. And the clear milk was ambrosia.

"Any vodka on the island?"

"A treat for you, Salote. A bottle of Stoli." Ah, small vanities. I was pleased he already knew me by name.

"Stoli? Terrific. Clare will appreciate that."

"She's already here," he said. At a corner table, the widow Clare sat alone, all in black, her elegant left hand with its impossible-to-ignore diamond ring and wedding band caressing a glass of vodka. Apparently having chosen a new twist on her grief couture, she'd cloaked herself in a Tongan mourning outfit: soft black tunic and a wraparound skirt. She looked like a weary has-been actress, her face far gaunter than last night, when her late-season glow made her shine in the turquoise dress. Now she sipped lugubriously and stared at nothing.

"Man, she looks depressed," I said. "This must remind her of what happened to her husband."

"I don't know," Viliami said, looking at her sadly. "A couple of people have invited her to join them, but she keeps saying no, she'd rather be by herself."

"Poor Clare. Well, to each his own. Her own. Pour that coconut milk over a shot or two."

"That's a waste of good Russian vodka, my friend."

"Not a waste of good Tongan coconut milk?" I chugged it. "Now just pour me a little vodka over ice. Have any ice tonight?" The ice supply was iffy because the power wasn't reliable.

"Yes, it's a good day. Vodka *and* ice." He poured into a plain, straight glass. I picked the glass up and swirled it a little, savoring the clinks of real ice.

"I didn't know you were a fire dancer," I said. "You were great at the hotel last night."

"All the boys on my island learn," he said. "We're known for it."

"What island?"

"Vava'u," he said. "The most beautiful island in Tonga."

"I've heard. I want to go there."

"One bad thing, though, we fire dancers always smell like kerosene." I was tempted to lean closer to see whether it was true. He smiled at me, waiting. But I was too disheartened to flirt.

"It might be a long night around here," I said wearily.

"We're ready. We know all about it." He ran a clean white cloth down the wooden bar, as polished from leanings and confessions as an altar. He owed his flawless American accent, I'd heard, to his brief career as a Mormon. After his decision to convert—a spiritual awakening that coincided with the realization that he could not afford to get off his beautiful island—he was sent by the Mormon Church to college in Utah. He graduated with a degree in religious studies, came home to Tonga, quit the church, and took up tending bar. Someday, he often told the volunteers, he'd make a new plan.

Viliami pointed with his eyes, and I turned toward Fitzhugh Grey, a lanky, red-haired British volunteer, who had apparently been standing at the bar for several minutes and now leaned over to speak to me. I smelled him before I heard him. His bad breath, a combination of cooked onions and gin, was notorious.

"You what? Sorry?" I said. I slipped the tips of three fingers into my drink and pulled out an ice cube. I rubbed it on my forehead.

"I was saying I want to go up to Ha'apai to see the women of the crafts co-op," he exhaled. "They make the most marvelous pandanus. You should go, too, Charlotte. The ministry could pay to fly us. We could avoid the ghastly boats. You could say it was part of your orientation."

I forced my eyes to meet his. I'd been well trained as a preacher's kid. "*Look* at people when they're talking to you, Charlotte," my mother used to chide me. "Don't look at your shoes. It's rude."

Fitzhugh Grey ordered three gin and tonics at once, and when Viliami efficiently complied, Fitz lined them up in a row. He took the lime out of each and squeezed out the juice. Then, one by one, he slipped the wedge of lime into his mouth, sucked it noisily, fished it out of his mouth, and plopped it back into the drink. It was disgusting, but at least, apparently, he thought it would guarantee that nobody else would touch his cocktails. I knew I wouldn't.

"I don't know, Fitz, I haven't even reported for my first real day of work yet—that's Monday, you know. With the murder, who knows what's the right thing to do? There's something to be said for the idea of getting out of town."

Not that I'd really want to be alone with Fitzhugh Grey on a distant island. But I had to stay on his good side. Everybody tried to stay on his good side; he had the best bathroom in Tonga. Somehow the Brits had found him a house with a loo fit for a duke. A porcelain bathtub. Real tile on the floor. Hot water. Hot water. Hot water. No one liked Fitzhugh Grey, with his alcoholic bad breath and his whiny voice. But everybody buttered him up, hoping for a single afternoon in that tub, for just one hot morning shower.

But at the moment I didn't feel like cozying up to Fitz, so I left him chatting with Viliami and took my vodka back to the table. I sat down next to Mac, who for some reason didn't make room for me.

"So what do you think, Charlotte?" Jeff began. "What do you make of all of this?" It occurred to me I was the only woman in the place, except for Clare. No Bridget, no Diane. Sometimes Vic and Betty showed up, but tonight, neither one. Not even any of the *fokisis* who sometimes hung out until the old-timers made them leave.

"I don't know," I said. I pushed a chair up beside Mac, who looked the other way. "I keep thinking about what Skip said at the meeting today. Didn't anybody know Mort was behaving erratically? *Was* he behaving erratically?"

"Yeah," Mac said, "there were a couple of weird things. He had double doors on his house, and he'd painted a skull and crossbones on the upper door. We just thought he was trying to keep the kids away."

"That doesn't seem that odd to me," I said. "I was ready to call in some voodoo myself today when I got back to my hut. Tevita's daughters were in there, wearing my stuff. They'd rooted around in my jewelry and my clothes. It really pissed me off, and I kicked them out."

"There was the matter of the cat," Sam said.

"Huh?" I hadn't heard this one.

"There was a little feral kitten hanging around Melanie's place, and she'd been befriending it. One day when she got up, the cat was on her doorstep, apparently strangled."

"Judas priest, Sam, *that* sounds deliberate, aggressive," I said. "Did she think Mort did it?"

"She didn't know for sure. But there was an incident the day before when he thought she'd behaved badly in front of the other male volunteers down at Faua Wharf."

"What'd she do?"

"Oh, you know, there were a bunch of us down there hanging out, drinking on the wharf and Skip's boat, and she started saying she wanted to go skinny dipping. She was just feeling high spirited, was all. I think she'd had three or four beers."

Skip had scraped together a few extra *pa'anga* from his monthly stipend and added to it from home, and had bought a little sabot—not much more than that, really, something to tool around inside the reef lagoon, for fun. It had a little mast and its own miniature red sail, easy to recognize from the beach when he was out there enjoying himself.

"So what happened?"

"Most of us were kind of smiling and egging Melanie on, but Mort was, well, mortified. He told her she'd better not. He said something like, 'Behave yourself,' which really seemed to bug her. He shouted, 'I'm serious, Melanie, really, don't do it.' She stood up and made a big show of stripping, and then she jumped in.

"Meanwhile he's standing on the wharf, yelling, 'Get her out of the water, now. Get a towel around her.'

"But she's in the water doing flips like a dolphin, saying, 'This feels *wonderful.* You all should come in with me. That means you, Mort.' And by the way, she was beautiful."

"Were you there, Mac?" I asked.

"I was. Mort was just being an asshole," he said quietly. He finally turned my way, but looked at the floor.

"So how did it end up?"

Sam continued, "Oh, he was yelling to get her out of the water and was so upset that the rest of us told her to get out. When she finally did, cussing him out the whole time, Mort was the first to try to cover her up, but she wouldn't let him, kicking at him and pushing his hands away. Everybody just stood there, not knowing what to say. She ended up crying."

"Damn," I said, looking from one guy to another. "Didn't anybody tell him he was out of line?"

"Well," Mac said, "maybe we all felt a little bit the way Mort did."

"What do you mean?"

"Well, about half of us really wanted to see her naked. Or maybe all of us wanted to, but then again, about half of us had already seen her naked, if you know what I mean. It raised some issues."

"Yeah," I said, shifting in the hard folding chair.

"And also," Mac said, "we were afraid some Tongans might see her, and we were uneasy about that. It's one thing to do the climb through the back window secretly,"—here he deliberately avoided looking at me, I thought—"but out in the open? It's not *fakatonga*."

It occurred to me that I was somehow a party to this drama, even though I hadn't been on Faua Wharf.

"You'd think Melanie would have understood the *fakatonga* thing," I said carefully. "We all get pretty grilled in it."

"You have to understand Melanie, though," Sam said. "She was just like that. She thought swimming naked was the only way to go. She was exuberant. She didn't see anything wrong with it. "She loved her body, too, I think." The others looked at him with particular interest, and I wondered how many of them knew for sure.

"But I don't know," Mac said. "She shouldn't have done it."

"She shouldn't?" I pressed, wanting at the risk of naiveté to be the devil's defender.

"It's Tonga," Mac said. "We're volunteers. We have to think before we act. Certain things you might do at home'll get you in a lot of trouble here." He was on his third beer and it seemed the empty brown bottles on the table were lining up faster than ever.

"And we had a lot of booze," Sam said, just as I'd counted a dozen and a half empties. "Especially her."

"So what happened to Mort afterward?"

"He got on his bike and rode like a crazy man off the wharf," Mac said. "And the next morning there was a dead cat on Melanie's porch."

A bullet of anger shot through me. I looked around the table, where every man there was staring into his beer or looking at his lap. It seemed none of them wanted to face the facts.

"Did anybody tell Evelyn Henry about this?" I asked.

"None of us guys," Mac said. "It's so common for pets to go missing or show up dead around here that it would have been hard to pin it on Mort."

I knew that was true. Peace Corps volunteers were always befriending puppies and kittens and fattening them up, only to have them disappear in their prime, sometimes before major feasts. But it was not the Tongan way to be pointlessly violent. Pets in Tonga disappeared for food, not for a morality lesson.

"I know that Melanie tried to tell Evelyn," Mac said uneasily.

"She did?"

"She kind of thought he did it. She did go in to see Evelyn the next day. We heard she asked for a transfer to Ha'apai. But Evelyn, who never liked Melanie anyway, told her she had to stick by her commitment to her school and that she'd better be more concerned with her own behavior."

"Damn," I said. "So Skip was right—Evelyn knew something was wrong."

Viliamie arrived with another half dozen beers on a tray.

"Who ordered that?" I said.

"On the house," Viliami said. "Happy Hour."

"Oh lord," I said, and took a fresh beer anyway.

"But, what could she have done?" Mac said, pushing away from me slightly. "The volunteers are always wanting to be left alone to do our own thing—it's our responsibility to make things right when things go wrong."

"Wait, wait a minute," I said. "Are you saying it was Melanie's fault she got murdered last night?"

"No, I don't mean…"

"And what about Mort? Maybe leaving a dead kitten on Melanie's doorstep was a good, responsible cure for his mental illness."

"I don't mean that, Charlotte, no. I just mean…well, Melanie was a bit…flamboyant…and maybe…"

"Maybe if it hadn't been Melanie—maybe if it'd been Diane, for instance, the one volunteer who says she's still a virgin—you'd feel different?" I felt my voice get louder. The three men at my table looked aghast, along with Viliami and Fitz at the bar and three old Tongan men at the next table.

At the corner table, the wan Clare stood abruptly and walked toward the door, staring straight ahead like somebody from *Dawn of the Dead*. We stopped talking to watch her. She staggered just a tiny bit, but regained her balance and straightened up, continuing into the parking lot like the Queen of England. A middle-aged Tongan guy gently helped her into his minimoke taxi—apparently he'd been waiting—and they sped away into the darkness. A wisp of coral dust stirred up by the wheels filtered back into the club.

"Is Clare okay?" Jeff said. "Is she the next one we're going to have to worry about?"

"She'll be fine. She just wants to be left alone," Sam, the expert on everything, said. "She's in love with grief."

Mac turned back to me as if nothing had intervened.

"Look, Charlotte," he said, "I don't know what I meant. I'm sorry...I'm confused."

"There are so many of *us*," Mac sighed, sweeping his hand toward Sam and Jeff and at the next table, Greg and Dave and Tom, and even including Fitz, "and so few of *you*..." pointing at me. "It gets very confusing for us here."

"I'm not in love with grief, but I don't think I can take this scene tonight, either," I said and stood up, carrying my own empty vodka glass back up to the bar. "I'm going home."

"Might be good to get one of the guys to walk with you," Viliami said.

"Mort's in prison, Viliami," I said. "Who could harm me now?"

Resentful, I started home, the moon moving in and out of clouds so that sometimes I could see the road and sometimes I couldn't. I knew that female volunteers weren't supposed to walk alone at night, but I was exhausted and tired of being with people and determined not to need protection. The distance home was less than a mile.

There's a peculiar scraping that the wind makes in palm fronds in the tropics that isn't a comfort, not like the soft soughing of Midwest evergreens. Tonight the unreliable moonlight played havoc with my night blindness, and I had to keep peeking out of the corners of my eyes, avoiding my blind spot, to see what was there.

Even back home I'd been half-afraid of darkness. Once, camping on an island off Charlevoix during a Lake Michigan study tour, my boyfriend urged me onto a white gravel road for a late night walk. It was exciting to be away from city lights, but I clung to him. The dark spread out on either side of the road, ravenous for something, I thought. He kindly murmured, "What's wrong? Relax..." I was furious at myself. Couldn't I tell when the night was harmless? I had marched in "Take Back the Night" rallies, and this was the kind of night we dreamed of. In the mild Michigan woods, there was nothing to be afraid of.

"Humor me," I said to my nice boyfriend, and he did. We turned back, and he never made a joke.

And now I strode uneasily ahead through the busy Tongan dark. I hurried by a rundown hut with strains of kava drinking songs wafting out, that sweet and melancholy music. I strode past a little corner store, its half-front down but a dim light inside, probably somebody raiding the cigarette stash. I pounded forward furiously, my flip-flops slapping at my heels. I kept my night-blind eye out for dogs—unpredictable curs here, inbred, hungry, and mean.

What was it about Melanie?

I had always believed it was my brains, not my body, that kept my lovers engaged. I had always believed that I could trust the men who loved me because they were good men and I was a good woman. How could it be otherwise? If they were bad, what would that make me? When I think about it now, it seems extraordinary: I'd never had anything even remotely resembling a rape experience, maybe because I was so willing to say yes. Had Melanie trusted Mort, too, assuming he would never hurt her? Had she trusted herself too much? Had she trusted that the world and Mort would always love her? What was it about Melanie, that made her dead tonight, and me still alive?

When I stepped inside my dark hut and reached for the light switch, I felt something vile, crispy, and pulsing. I jerked my hand away and let out a shrieking "Fuck!" It was a flying cockroach, and I'd scared it off one of its favorite perches. When I finally got up my nerve to turn on the light again, about five other roaches, fat and purple, made a run for the dark. I furiously caught up with one and squashed it, almost relishing the sound of its shell crunching juicily under the sole of my flip-flops.

For the first time, that night, I wished I could lock my hut. But how could I even begin to keep out everything that scared me?

CHAPTER 7

▼

Longolongo e pusi kai moá. *Quiet is the cat eating the chicken.*

I probably wouldn't have slept well under any circumstance, but that night and the next the Kingdom of Tonga conspired against my intense wish to shut everything out. This time the reason was mangoes. Through July, August, and September, the Tongans had bided their time, remembering with watering mouths the yellow-green oblongs and their sweet, stringy meat. And then October came, and the fruit plumped up, and its hard skin softened. And the Tongans went mango mad.

The physical problem was the large mango tree spreading over the roof of my hut. The cultural problem was that in Tonga, theoretically, nothing belongs to anyone but the King. The fruits were anybody's game. The architectural problem was that my *fale* had a tin roof, and the sudden sound of a mango falling on tin was like a gunshot. The meteorological problem was that precipitation, increasing as the rainy season moved in, invariably brought down the fruit and brought out the mango-eaters.

First, around sunset, more people were around—little people. Both Tevita and her neighbors stationed children under the tree on rotating vigils, to grab a mango as soon as it dropped. The kids killed time by window peeping on the *palangi*, and I began to see pairs of bright eyes peering in.

Sometimes the kids brought a bamboo pole to knock down the treasures, but most of the time they simply waited. When a mango dropped, there would be squealing, running, and squabbling over who got to keep it. They ate the mangoes on the spot and dropped the yellow cores on the ground. I'd already slipped twice on the slimy leavings. And I never seemed to get a bite of mango. After dark, the kids were joined by older boys or an occasional mother who brought a flashlight to locate the fallen fruit.

The Sunday after the murder I bicycled home from Jeff's house at about ten o'clock in torrential rain, looking forward to a good sleep before my first real day of work on Monday. There, under the mango tree, was a tiny boy of no more than five or six, covered in a rain parka from head to toe. He was holding a flashlight, calmly waiting for a fruit to drop. Rustling in the shadows were two older boys, his brothers, perhaps. The kids stared at me as if I were the intruder. "Please be quiet tonight," I said wearily, and slipped inside.

Later that night I was startled awake by adult male voices as several men cheerfully knocked down mangoes. Each drop bounced noisily down the roof. I looked at my pocket alarm: 4:00 AM.

By early Monday morning, my nerves snapped. As dawn rolled in, what sounded like a dozen teenagers noisily surrounded the hut. I burst through the door, shaking my fists at the mango-eaters like a witch, yelling "*Tapuni!*"—shut up—and tried a couple of choice curses. For about two minutes, it worked. The boys insolently sauntered off, waiting for me to go back inside. They were like cats, momentarily scared away from a kill, and I figured they'd be right back. I promised myself I would ask Tevita to put out the word. I needed some peace and quiet, or I'd really start hating these people. I went back to bed, but I was unable to sleep, and I tossed and turned until full sunlight.

That was how I started my first day of work. I straggled up, bleary-eyed, filled a quart saucepan with water, lit the propane stove, and stepped into my cramped little cold-water shower. At least in October the water coming out of the rainwater tank wasn't too frigid, and I didn't mind anyway: I needed it this morning. The shower had two push-out windows, high enough to protect my decency but low enough to give me a cookie-sheet-sized view of the neighborhood. I saw Filipa walking back from the corner store with a loaf of bread under each arm and the raucous local rooster squawking crankily on a nearby fence. It would have been nerve-wracking enough to go to work for the first time anyway, but only two days after the murder, who knew what I'd encounter? For comfort, I selected my peach Tongan tunic outfit, the softest one of the three, and added a cowrie necklace I'd bought at the co-op.

I was assigned to work in the same office as Tevita. As far as I could tell, he was a bookkeeper or some kind of general assistant, who kept a lot of lists of numbers and didn't tell me what they were about. He had made it clear I was supposed to ride my own bike to work. He didn't think it would look right for me to get a ride in his old but much-beloved Zodiac Zephyr every day. So, I climbed onto my bike, holding up the skirt of my *tupenu* with one hand, and awkwardly rode two miles on the bumpy road along the lagoon to the two-story concrete block building just off the main downtown intersection. Here was where I was supposed to work from 8:00 to 5:00 as a public relations officer for the next two years. I locked my bike to a cast-iron railing, took a deep breath, checked my *tupenu* for oil stains, smoothed my tunic, and went up the stairs.

Tevita was waiting for me at the door. Since it was my first day, he said, he would introduce me around, but I shouldn't expect any special treatment after that. A few people said, "We're so sorry about the murder," but there were mostly a lot of whispering and averted eyes. They knew, like Melanie, that I was also single. They probably already knew I frequented the Coconut Club. And because I lived on Tevita's land, they might even know that I had already had a Tongan-style visitation the night of the murder. I tried to push down my anxious heartbeat and to smile as innocently as a preacher's kid could. The unfamiliar names and faces blurred, except for Fumi, the chief clerk. Tevita told me if I needed anything to talk to her.

My office was on the second floor. I had my own room, a desk and a chair, and a gray rotary dial telephone. The walls were green—lime green, as a matter of fact, making me wonder whether Tevita had picked the color. Two wide, louvered windows faced a row of palm trees, creating soft and shady light. There was nothing on the walls. It was like a cloister—trancelike to my sleep-deprived eyes.

They had promised me a typewriter, my only request, delivered in several orientation sessions during training through Wade, the Peace Corps assistant director. But I didn't see a typewriter. Thus, I had my first skirmish with Fumi.

"By the way, where is my typewriter?" I asked shyly.

"Why do you need a typewriter?" Fumi said with what I was tempted to call impudence. She wasn't tall for a Tongan, maybe five feet nine inches, but she glared at me in a way I found intimidating. She wore black mourning clothes for some nearly forgotten relative: a primly ironed tunic and a long skirt with a woven mat strapped around her from her waist to just above her knees. She piled her ebony hair high on her head like an empress and pinned it up with two iridescent abalone combs. Her makeup was disconcertingly heavy: heavy foundation, heavy lipstick, and heavy mascara.

I tried patience.

"The Peace Corps told me I would have a typewriter. I was invited here as a writer. The typewriter is one of my tools. Wade McKenzie, the Peace Corps assistant director, and I talked to Nalapu about it at our orientation meetings."

"There isn't any typewriter for you."

I tried reason.

"Wouldn't it be easier on the secretaries if my rough drafts were typed? It's also a lot faster."

"The Minister writes his drafts out in longhand," Fumi said. "So do Kitioni and Mr. Nalapu. You can do the same."

I tried insistence.

"I was promised a typewriter."

But Fumi had turned her back. My first day already felt like a bust.

I eyed my telephone. I was afraid to use it, even to call Peace Corps and ask for help. Tevita had explained that calls went through operators, but the operators spoke only Tongan, and despite little Lupe's instructions, today I didn't even trust myself to count to three.

My supervisor was Mr. Nalapu, an Indian expatriate, small and skinny as a mink, and very dark-skinned. He was the Minister's right hand man. Obviously I would have to talk with him. In the meantime, I tried to concentrate on two thick piles of papers that somebody had already left on my desk.

At ten o'clock, one of the young secretaries brought around tea and biscuits, served on good china. Tevita popped in to see how I was faring.

"What are your thoughts about Mr. Nalapu?" he asked.

"I've met him only once so far," I said, wondering where he was this Monday morning. But Tevita's question was rhetorical. Mr. Nalapu talked too fast, Tevita whispered, and had never learned Tongan. Mr. Nalapu went home for lunch every day, he murmured, avoiding Tongan food. Worst of all, Mr. Nalapu declined all invitations to feasts. Mr. Nalapu, Tevita said, shaking his head, was not the Tongan type.

"And he works too hard," Tevita concluded, taking another biscuit. "These Indians have too much energy for their own good."

"Tevita, I know this doesn't have to do with work, but I really need your help with something," I said. "I couldn't sleep last night. A bunch of people were hanging around my *fale* all night, knocking mangoes out of the tree. Could you tell them to stop?"

"The mangoes are ripe," Tevita said, picking up the last biscuit.

"I know, Tevita, but do they have to do it at night? Can't they do it during the day when I'm at work?"

"They don't want me to catch them," he said.

"I thought everything belonged to everybody here," I said, smiling.

"Well, Salote, that's true. But when the mangoes come ripe, some of us can't help thinking we own our trees, and we want them all to ourselves. That is why we are a nation of sneaks. I'll see what I can do."

Tevita wiped the crumbs from his chin and ushered me in to meet the boss, Faina, one of the country's thirty-three hereditary nobles. Wade had offered me a handful of essential facts about him. Faina was Oxford educated and urbane, and he had been a pilot for the British Royal Air Force and returned from World War II a hero. Everybody called him The Baron. He was first cousin to the King, Wade explained, and spent many hours in consultation at the Palace.

We met in Faina's office, which stretched the width of the whole building and had windows on three sides. Three men were in the room: Faina, Mr. Nalapu, and Kitioni, a beautiful, honey-skinned young man, Kitioni was supposed to be my counterpart, the Tongan to whom I was supposed to pass on all my boundless expertise. His office was next to mine, where presumably my American skills would osmose across the air.

They all stood up, and Tevita backed out. Faina was huge—at least six feet five inches and at least 300 pounds—but when he came around the desk to greet me, he moved gently in a manner that big men sometimes adopt to keep from scaring people. At this first meeting, he was a paragon of dignity. He was dressed *fakatonga* in a most sophisticated way. His straight-line, wraparound skirt looked perfectly tailored and made of linen, and later I found out that he had his *tupenus* handmade to order in Thailand.

I reached out to shake hands with each of the men. First, Faina's soft, warm hand, as large as a pitcher's mitt. When I got to Kitioni, looking at him full-face for the first time, I saw that he had startling, almost eerie green eyes, deliciously exotic. I wanted to look at him for a long time, but I forced myself to move along and to shake hands with the tight-lipped Mr. Nalapu. Then we sat down. Faina pulled out a pack of Benson and Hedges Golds and passed them around. Kitioni took one, Mr. Nalapu didn't, and I did. A gold lighter materialized from the desktop, and we lit up.

In the pause, I studied the way Kitioni smoked, the cigarette between his second and third finger, his hand flat against his face, the fingertips turned slightly outward. When he crossed his legs at the knee, I could see that he had muscular calves, elongated like a dancer's. I congratulated myself for finding a country where men wore clothes that exposed their legs. Then, with a start, I realized that I was staring and that Kitioni was not looking back.

Damn, they'd be thinking about the murder. Had I forgotten so soon? I quickly looked back at Faina, who surveyed me calmly. He flicked his last ember into a crystal ashtray and addressed me.

"First of all, we are so sorry about what happened this weekend."

I nodded. "Thank you, sir. It's very disturbing. I'm so sorry Peace Corps brought this tragedy to your country. We are all very shocked and confused."

"Well, I trust justice will be done. The young man is in jail, I understand. He will be carefully watched there. And I understand a psychologist is coming from Washington. Sad business. Sad indeed."

"Indeed," I said.

"Indeed," Nalapu and Kitioni echoed.

"You're living with Tevita Hasimoto's family, I hear?" Faina said. "There you will be safe. You must be safe."

"Yes, sir, I do feel safe," I said. "Mr. Hasimoto came and checked up on me the other night even before I knew what had happened."

The three men stared at me with interest, as if I'd said something significant. What did they know?

"This event makes it even more important for you Americans to behave respectfully," Faina said formally. "This young man, this young woman—I've been made privy to some very disturbing information. You know that Tongan culture is built upon respect. We expect this from all of you."

"Of course," I said, feeling chastised and guilty for nothing, wishing he'd offer me another cigarette. "But may I say we think this was a private problem between the two of them? May I say, there was nothing against Tongan culture in what happened? It was between them."

"There is no such thing as a private matter in Tonga," he said firmly, looking at me directly as if *I* were the one who'd jumped naked off Faua Wharf. "This reflects on us all. We already know that this is the first such murder in Peace Corps history. We are aggrieved that it happened here on this beautiful and peaceable island."

In the discomfort of the moment, I was tempted to remind him that at the craft co-op, the ladies still sold special wooden forks, reproductions of those used to eat human flesh not so long ago. The ladies found it hilarious to see how much the horrified, fascinated tourists would pay for these little tzotchkes of cannibalism.

I was also tempted to remind Faina that the Tongans had planned to slaughter Captain Cook after a feast so lavish that the British seamen, who accidentally foiled the murder plans by pulling up anchor early, forever after called the place The Friendly Islands. The Kingdom had a devious and bloody past.

"I apologize on behalf of my countrymen," I nonetheless said, feeling foolish and exposed.

"Well, we are very glad to have you here, Charlotte. May I call you Charlotte?"

I nodded, too eagerly. "Tevita, I mean, Mr. Hasimoto and his family already call me *Salote, and* if you'd like to, it would be fine with me." *Salote* was the name of the last Tongan queen, the much-beloved mother of the current king.

"Of course, *Salote*. Our queen. How nice." He never called me Salote again.

"We have many important projects underway with which you will be helping Mr. Nalapu," Faina said. "He'll keep me informed of your progress, and if you need anything, please go through him. Let's talk about some of those projects." He offered another round of cigarettes, and I gratefully puffed and listened.

There was an initiative to start a tomato juice factory. There was a coconut-button-making project. There was a small New Zealand firm interested in a soda bottling plant. Somebody wanted to manufacture soccer balls, shipping in all the supplies, of course, and taking advantage of the island's cheap labor.

My job was to write press releases about prospective ventures, seek markets for these stories at home and abroad, and arrange visits for aid officials and potential investors. The country was supposed to go metric by the King's sixtieth birthday on July 4, 1978. An Australian consultant was coming to orchestrate the changeover, and I was supposed to work with him when he arrived.

"Any questions?" Faina sat back, his big hands elegantly folded and quiet on the desk.

"Sir, I need a typewriter. It was my understanding that I'd have one."

The Baron peered at Mr. Nalapu. "There is no typewriter in Charlotte's office?"

"At the present time there isn't one yet," Mr. Nalapu said, shifting uneasily.

"Be sure Charlotte gets one, please."

The formalities were ended, and all rose. As I reached the door, the Baron added, "How nice to see you dressed in Tongan clothes."

Before afternoon tea, Tevita brought in an old, gray Royal typewriter.

I sat down and stared at it. I opened a drawer of the desk and found it empty. Wanting to avoid Fumi, I went out to Kitioni's office and asked about supplies. He gave me an inch-thick pile of legal-sized newsprint and a single pen.

I rolled a piece of newsprint into the typewriter and stared at it. Finally I typed, "Every good boy does fine." The machine worked. I went back to Kitioni's office.

"I'd like to get oriented," I said. "Do you have any reports for me to read? Annual reports, statistics on the Kingdom, that sort of thing? Anything you think I should know?"

"Can do," he answered cheerfully. He surveyed his cluttered desk, rooted around in some piles, and pulled out three or four thick files. I thanked him and carried them back to my office.

I stared at my typewriter again, and then typed:

```
Ask not what your country can do for you.
Ask what you can do for your country.
```

I paused, stared at the bare green walls, then typed:

```
I am not a crook. I am not a crook.
A crook I am not. Not a crook am I.
Am I not a crook? Crook not am I.
```

The next time Kitioni peeked in, I looked up at him only briefly and continued my important work.

But the King, through Faina, did keep me busy before long. He had the country looking for oil, and he was bringing in satellite dishes and telephones. Every other week, some foreign delegation sat at the King's table, eating suckling pig and taro leaves smothered in coconut milk. Sometimes I got to meet Aussies and Brits and Kiwis and Americans and Taiwanese who flew through with their big ideas about exporting tomatoes and orangeade and carved tikis. Everyone, everyone knew about the murder, and as another single, young American woman, I was always asked about it. How was it for me, being single? Did I feel safe?

After my first day at work, all I wanted was a good night's sleep. I settled into my cot to read *The Drifters*. Michener was always good to have on hand—such thick books, such escape. And his works were even quotable: there was one from La Rochefoucauld, "True courage is to do without witnesses everything that you are doing before all the world." Yeah, really. But that wasn't going to be the problem in Tonga. The problem in these damned Friendly Islands was to do *with* witnesses everything that I used to do without. Or to stop. Probably to stop.

A shy knock on the door. That was not the mango-eaters' style, and I didn't want to be bothered tonight. Another knock, louder. Finally, muttering unkind things under my breath, I dragged myself up and opened the door, hoping it was not the start of another noisy night.

A small boy I'd never seen before was holding out a green pandanus basket. In the dark, I could make out three ripe mangoes in it. He left the basket and dashed off without a word.

If the mango-eaters dogged my house that night, I didn't hear them. Blessed Morpheus, as my mom used to say. I slept soundly and long.

And in the morning, I ate the mangoes. They were delicious.

CHAPTER 8

▼

'Alu'alu 'i malu tau ki monu.
Sojourning with misfortune, arriving at good fortune.

The mango-eaters eventually had their fill. Melanie's body was hustled back to the States to her shocked family. The removal of her body happened without fanfare, a decision by Evelyn Henry that perplexed the Tongans and confused the volunteers. We needed a ritual but didn't get it, as if Peace Corps wanted the evidence swept away and wanted us to act as if nothing had happened.

Meanwhile, Evelyn Henry made several visits to the suspect, even taking him sandwiches in a basket bedecked with ridiculous pink bows. She probably even tucked in a mango or two. Rumor had it she read him scripture, said Protestant prayers, and tried for a jailhouse conversion. But Mort sat under twenty-four-hour guard, eating nothing, face blank as a wall, refusing to talk. Strange, well-dressed white people hurried through the Peace Corps office—attorneys from Washington, we heard, but we weren't introduced. They met with Wade and Evelyn and stayed at the Dateline Hotel, rarely surfacing, certainly not doing anything to allay our anxieties and questions.

People wondered about Gyorgy Kowalski. He, too, adopted a formal silence and wouldn't tell anyone what had happened. After only a week, he moved out of the British consulate and back to his own house, a big, airy place near the high school, and got back to the classroom. Afterward, he went to the Coconut Club and got wordlessly drunk, and Viliami took him home in the rusty Coconut Club minimoke.

Even Viliami wouldn't say a thing. We thought he knew more than he was saying, but he was a good bartender, poised and discreet.

The trial was about to begin, and Lizard Sam, intrepid LA-boy reporter, was wrestling with Evelyn about covering the proceedings. The *Tonga Chronicle* wanted him there; he wanted to file reports overseas. Evelyn Henry called him in and gave him a brief talking-to, telling him it would be better to write about copra prices and triplets born in the bush than about Mort Friedman's trial. "Wouldn't it?" she said, fluttering her fake eyelashes. "We don't really want to draw attention to this story, now do we?" She merely fueled Sam's adrenaline. At the Coconut Club, throwing back beers, he promised he'd show up at the trial every day, especially because of Evelyn.

"Doesn't she want justice?" he complained one night. "Why is Mort Friedman suddenly her best friend? Has she forgotten about Melanie?"

"Come outside for a minute," I whispered. "I want to talk to you alone."

We sidled out onto the leafy Coconut Club patio, where we almost never went because it seemed the Tongans owned that space. This time, nobody was there.

"What's up?" He ran a hand affectionately through my hair. "Anytime you want to get together again, you know I'm ready."

"Thanks, Lizard—Sam. I guess the murder hasn't affected your libido, then."

"Hell, no, and I'm counting on you to be that hippie chick I met in San Francisco."

"I don't know, Sam, it feels weird. In case you hadn't noticed, the rules are slightly different here."

"I know, but we've done okay so far."

"And they're changing even more since..." I paused. "How well do you know Mac?"

"Seems straight up to me."

"I want to tell you something. We had sex the night of the murder. He snuck in my back window."

"Congratulations."

"Listen to me. He's avoiding me, and every time I try to touch him, he jumps away."

"How *fakatonga*."

"I think he was one of Melanie's lovers."

"Charlotte, let's not be naïve. This was more than a love triangle. It was a god-damn geodesic dome."

"I feel like he's blaming me."

"For what?"

I frowned at the ground. I couldn't find the right words. Luckily, Sam tended to fill silences with very little prompting.

"He can't blame her," he said. "She's dead. And now they're making a goddess out of her. She wasn't all goddess, you know."

"But you're mad yourself at how Peace Corps is reacting."

"Whether she was a goddess or not, bubala, she was murdered. The woman had great tits. Melanie may have been a bimbo…"

"She wasn't a bimbo, Sam. I hate that word!"

"Well, not that anybody would admit it now, the way they're all making a religion of her, but the last I heard, Mort Friedman was the asshole with the dagger."

I sat down on a cast-iron love seat and made room for him next to me. He sat and put his arm around me.

"Let me tell you something—something I've never told you," Sam said. "The night Melanie died, Jeff and I were riding our bikes home from the hotel, and we had to go practically right by where she lived. Mort might have been in the house then. And when we rode by, Jeff suddenly stopped. I slowed down and looked at him, and he had this creeped-out look. He said, 'Did you just feel that?' And I said, 'What?' and he said, 'That chill. What the hell was it?' I just looked at him funny, and suddenly he hopped back on the bike and rode as fast as he could. The next day, when I found out about the murder, even I was kind of freaked out. This is a strange country."

I shivered. "Yeah, something's in the air." With a start, I felt my father's Ohio open over me like a black umbrella. But there were no words for this yet, none at least that I could come up with.

"I just keep thinking about Melanie all the time, how she died," said. "Because of sex, I keep thinking."

"Don't tell me you're giving up on that one, babe. I've got a vested interest here." I forced a weak smile to my lips. "Weren't you just the one, the other night, in the Coconut Club, saying it wasn't her fault? Just keeping telling yourself that what killed Melanie was an asshole with a knife."

"I know…but…" Some essential element was missing, but I felt confused and tongue-tied. "Well, anyway, my darling Lizard, what about Mac?"

"Let the guy alone. He's a bowlegged farm boy. Now, me; look at these pecs— and with just the flick of a finger, I can untie my *tupenu*."

I laughed but jumped off the seat, unimpressed. "I think I've lost *my* libido," I said.

"I doubt it," he called after me as I hurried back into the club. "Wait for me, and I'll buy you another round."

Sam held onto his practical outrage, asking questions no one wanted to answer and appearing with his notebook in hand every day at the trial. His persistence was all the more refreshing because of the strange, unspoken territory apparently cherished and protected by the other male volunteers. As Sam and I both noted, the Peace Corps guys were already crafting an inventory: how nurturing Melanie had been, how flawless and creamy her skin was, how much her students adored her at the Misipeka Primary School. They praised her watercolors, which she painted on a table easel in her kitchen. They noted how she grew morning glories and how the blossoms twined over her front porch. They recalled how she always asked each of them to dance at Peace Corps parties to make sure nobody felt left out. They were beatifying her. The part of her that jumped into the water that day at the wharf, the exuberant and lusty Melanie, was rarely mentioned; it was laid to rest, and shipped off to the States with the rest of her physical body. So much was left unsaid.

Sometimes when I walked into the bar, it seemed that people stopped talking and turned away. Maybe there were conversations going on among the male volunteers, but not with me. I'd never been so aware of being a woman, of being the woman who'd slept with Sam during training, who'd stepped out with Tony, who'd welcomed that midnight visit from Mac. They seemed afraid of me. They were closing me out.

It was Mac's silence that was hardest to take. Even though Sam advised me to leave him alone, I wanted to see Mac again. We had a strained date at the Coconut Club. He made it seem formal. He claimed to want to know how my job was going, and he kept asking dry questions about projects and outlines and deadlines. I said I was learning the metric system, just in case the country actually made the switch. I sat beside him, wanting to put my hand on his thigh like in the old days, or even on his shoulder, so tight and hunched. I wanted the old Mac back. I remembered our happy, playful sex, and I wanted it again. But he kept pushing his chair away, an inch at a time. As if I wouldn't notice.

I decided to grow out all my body hair. What the hell? Why risk staph infections from razor cuts? Why bother to be smooth? Why bother to be lovely? It might be best to grow a coat. The rough brush of prickly hairs came out quickly, and it pleased me.

But still I often couldn't sleep. Mac's words the day after the murder haunted me. A bloody handprint on the windowsill. A torn yellow dress. A body in ribbons.

And one sticky late afternoon after the trial began, I learned that the same images haunted someone else.

I had collapsed for a nap when I heard Filipa calling.

"Salote, wake up!" Fanning herself with a large, waxy green banana leaf, Filipa stooped to enter my hut. Her knees cracked as she fell into her customary lotus squat on the mat. She turned up the sole of her callused foot and smiled. A curl of mango skin clung to the brown sole, and she slipped her fingernail under it and picked it off.

"Delicacy," she said, probably thinking I wouldn't understand. But I'd been studying my vocabulary every night when I got tired of Michener.

I sat up groggily and wrapped a green and white *tupenu* around my waist and pulled on my Cleveland Indians T-shirt.

"Yeah, Filipa, how's it going?" I said in Tongan, yawning and running my hands through my increasingly ragged hair.

"There is someone you need to meet," Filipa began. "One of Tevita's cousins, Leota."

It was Leota, she said, who'd first found Melanie Porter after the attack.

And Leota was waiting outside.

I flicked the tip of my tongue over the point of my right canine. As always, Filipa's visit had an agenda. I realized, too, that Filipa was speaking entirely in Tongan and that I understood almost every word.

Filipa gestured to the door, and a short, doughy woman with a round, childlike face ducked inside and settled on the floor beside Filipa. As I leaped up to collect the dirty clothes scattered around the room, I found myself staring at the newcomer's bosom. Her oversized breasts had been bound inside strips of flowered cloth, and a bulge of maple skin popped out through a hole near her left armpit.

"Sorry, you caught me *mohe*," I muttered.

"See, Leota, isn't that cute how she said, 'You caught me sleep'?"

So I didn't get all my verb forms right. I offered tea and dug out some leftover cookies. Filipa made introductions. And then came the customary formal declaration of the purpose of their meeting.

"Salote, listen. I brought Leota to meet you because she has a story to tell you. She knew the poor *Pisikoa* girl who died. She saw what happened that night. You should hear this story."

I immediately stopped fussing with cookies and tea and stood still for a moment in the middle of the room. It seemed to me that the light outside suddenly shifted, a shadow moving across the room as if a large bird had just flown over. To show respect for Leota, I quickly sat down in the ladylike Tongan style, folding my legs under me the way Pulu had taught. Filipa nodded approvingly as I settled down and soberly turned to Leota.

Filipa told Leota I was getting better at Tongan, but wouldn't understand everything. She urged her to speak in simple sentences.

"What am I supposed to tell her?" Leota asked.

"Tell her everything. I think she needs to know."

Leota and her sixteen-year-old son, Pasa, lived across the street from the doomed house. Like Filipa, Leota liked having *Pisikoa* in the neighborhood, and she had made a special effort to get to know the *faka'ofa'ofa palangi* girl.

Leota was well aware of the neighborhood gossip about young Melanie's frequent visitors, the string of *Pisikoa* boys who came around, leaning their bikes on the side of the house. In one neighborhood game, people counted the shoes and sandals lined up on her doorstep and said that was how many kids Melanie would have.

Leota also knew that some of Melanie's *mafus* came to visit in the Tongan way—inconspicuously, through back windows. This was a relief to hear after the way Melanie's life kept getting bowdlerized in the Coconut Club. Leota was more bothered by the brazen appearance of the American boys through the front door than by whatever happened after dark. She wasn't sure she wanted her Pasa to emulate the public comings and goings of these *palangi* boys.

But even though they were separated by twenty years, Melanie became Leota's friend. Melanie gave her some clothes from America—so many, in fact, that Leota had to turn some down. Her neighbors knew exactly which clothes she'd received from the American and made fun of her for buttering up the *Pisikoa* girl.

Melanie showed curiosity about Tongan cooking, especially *lu*, her favorite Tongan food. Leota showed her how to make it, and they often shared their evening meals.

But Leota's favorite part of their friendship was Melanie's art supplies. In her primary school classroom, Melanie let her students finger paint, work with clay sent free of charge by Melanie's mother from the States, and try their hand at acrylics and watercolors. Leota's niece and nephew both went to Misipeka Primary School, and Melanie was their favorite teacher. They, too, loved her art classes.

Melanie had a table easel and used to do watercolor painting for relaxation. She invited Leota to try her hand at painting. It was an exciting new world for the Tongan widow. It's not that she wasn't familiar with art. Leota was a well-regarded tapa painter. The range of tapa color was beautiful, but subtle and limited: brown, dark brown, and black, applied to the beige tapa. The patterns were very traditional, and she had learned her craft from her grandmother, who'd passed it on from her grandmother, and so on, reaching back to the days long before Captain Cook.

Even before she met Melanie, Leota was an innovator. She was one of the first tapa painters to incorporate modern images into some of her designs—for example, she made stylized drawings of airplanes landing at Fua'amotu Airport. Some observers strenuously objected, and the first time she took some of her airplane swatches to the Cooperative Association store in Nuku'alofa, the store managers almost refused to take them. Tourists, it turned out, liked Leota's images, finding them unusual enough to shell out *pa'anga* for. Finally, *pa'anga,* the money, was all that counted.

Something about Melanie's clean, white paper and rainbow palette promised a great, enticing adventure. Leota had been restless for color. Melanie had her mother send a book of Gauguin prints from home, and when she looked at the rich colors—colors she recognized from the play of light on land and sea here in Tonga—she knew she'd found a soul mate.

Filipa and Leota saw each other every couple of weeks because Tevita's bush plot was near Leota's village, Ngeleia. The two women gossiped about their respective *Pisikoa* charges, and when Filipa and Tevita were offered a female volunteer, she asked Leota's opinion. Leota went directly to what she knew was Filipa's major concern. "Melanie prefers *palangis*."

"I don't have a husband to worry about," Leota said, her husband having died young of a heart attack. "But if I did, I don't think Melanie would have bothered him."

Leota had at least a passing acquaintance with both the young men in what the *Pisikoa* were calling the "love triangle." She had trouble pronouncing both their names, for they contained letters which didn't exist in Tongan. But she tried.

Leota said she had her doubts about the story she'd heard. She didn't think it was a love triangle. She'd watch her friend Melanie interact with Mort, and she didn't think the girl showed any particular ardor. Gyorgy was something different. He was always there. Melanie talked about him guardedly, perhaps, in the Tongan way, to hide her true feelings. But Leota thought Gyorgy adored Melanie.

And now, Leota was enduring one of the worst experiences of her life—testifying before the Magistrate Helu at the jury trial. She was unprepared for the way the officials grilled her and what they implied. The defense attorneys, the Americans from Washington, with their self-important Tongan translators, accused her of window peeping on her good friend. They accused her of being envious of the American's possessions and pointed out that neighbors said Leota often wore Melanie's clothes. Everybody knew that one of the best things about having *pisikoa* nearby was that you got to *kole* or borrow their interesting possessions. Melanie had made gifts to Leota of some of her clothes, but Leota couldn't prove it.

The lawyers even accused Leota of stealing. She had taken some of Melanie's art supplies from her room on the day after the murder. Leota replied that the art was the part of their friendship she loved most, and she didn't think anybody else would want the supplies. But when the police came back to question her, they accused her of tampering with evidence and made her give back the paint tubes and sketch paper and the blood-spattered easel.

Her statements had been quoted in the *Tonga Chronicle* under Lizard Sam's byline, and Leota said she hoped she never had to see her name in print again. She was done with the courtroom for now.

But in the days since, Filipa kept after Leota to come into town and talk to me, the young woman who had the same name as their late, great queen. For Melanie's sake and for the sake of her cousin Filipa whom she could not refuse, she should do it, Filipa told her.

"I told her it will be different with you," Filipa said. "I told her you need to know what she knows."

I did not know what it was that Leota knew, and my gut questioned the whole conversation. Why did Filipa think I needed to know? My stomach twisted into a brief but piercing cramp. Yet even I, with my intense and primitive desire not to know, saw that there was something important going on here. Leota needed to tell her story. She needed an American person to listen and understand. I took a breath.

"Okay," I said, "I think I understand now why you're here," though I really wasn't sure. But I would help the three of us forge on." What is it that you know, Leota?"

"I knew Melanie was at a party that night. I'd gone to bed early, unconcerned that she wasn't home. But about 2:00 AM, I sat up, suddenly overcome by an awful dread."

It was the same feeling she'd had when her husband died, she said. He worked at the abattoir where the Crown Prince was experimenting with raising and butchering beef, and her husband had fallen down dead on the job, between two cows waiting in line for the slaughter. Before anyone told her about his death, Leota knew that something had happened. Her heart constricted, and when his friends came to her door with those awful looks on their faces, she wasn't surprised. Melanie's murder was the same. Maybe Leota heard something. But all she knew was that she woke up with that same cramp in her chest.

"Then I heard a shriek," Leota said. "I heard many shrieks. They were high and jagged"—a pause as Filipa searched for the word—"a woman's voice, crying out not in any words that I could understand. It sounded like the way pigs cry when they're killed." Leota shuddered.

"What did you do?"

"At first, I couldn't move. I heard more screaming, and then I heard things banging around. I forced myself to get out of bed and try to see where the sounds were coming from. I heard footsteps, someone running. By then, the shrieking had died down, but I was horrified to see that there were lights on in Melanie's house. Then there was complete quiet. And then I saw him."

"Who?"

"Mort. Mort was in the doorway. He was holding Melanie in his arms, standing in the doorway. He didn't seem in a hurry. He just stood there. I could see her yellow dress—the one she had worn to the party—and then I almost fainted. The dress was torn and covered with blood."

"Was Melanie moving?"

"Her hands and arms were twitching," Leota said, closing her eyes against the image. I didn't understand the word "twitch" and Filipa couldn't think of the English word for it, so she demonstrated, shaking and jerking her arms and hands.

"Then what did he do?"

"He laid her down in the doorway. He walked—walked, I tell you—to his bike and got on it and rode away."

It was only after Mort rode off that Leota could move from the window, too frightened to react. In the silence, she hurried out the door, calling to her son Pasa to get up and come quickly.

When she reached Melanie, the poor girl was still breathing. It was like a nightmare, her beloved *Pisikoa* volunteer sliced up like an animal. Leota sat down next to her and tried to comfort her. In the background, she heard Pasa yelling to their neighbor to get the truck, get the truck. Leota said to Melanie, "Do you want us to take you to the hospital?" and Melanie managed to sigh, "Yes, please." She said it in English, Leota said, and when Leota got to that part, she also said it in English. Yes, please. They were Melanie's last words.

"She was such a sweet, courteous girl," Leota said, tears beginning to drop from her eyes into her lap, where she was wringing her hands.

Then Pasa arrived, she continued after a moment, and the neighbor came with the truck. They lifted Melanie into it. Melanie tried to move her body to help them get her in, but she was losing strength fast, and being lifted into the truck seemed to exhaust her. Leota got in back beside her, and the last thing Melanie did on her own was put her pale, cold hand in Leota's lap, reaching for Leota's hand.

By the time they got the truck going, Leota said, they could see that Melanie's eyes were rolling back, even though she was still breathing roughly. Leota held and stroked Melanie's bloody hand, an artist's hand, and whispered comforting things all the way to the *falemahaki*, trying not to cry in case Melanie could still hear. But Leota could see that the situation was very, very bad. When they got to the hospital, Leota and the truck bed were covered in blood.

By the end of the story, all three of us were crying. I handed tissues all around from my Peace Corps supply, and we sat, dismally wiping our eyes. Filipa blew her nose.

"It was very dark, a very dark night," Leota said.

I said, "But I remember the brilliant moon that night, and the night after."

"No," Leota said, struggling to explain. "The moon hid while it was happening. It went behind clouds. There was evil. It was an evil night." Then she repeated, "I heard footsteps. And just after the screams stopped, there was Mort, holding Melanie in the doorway." That was one scene she obviously could not forget.

"Was Melanie *mafus* to both Gyorgy and Mort?" I asked.

"I don't know, Salote. I saw the way she looked at Gyorgy, and I saw the way she looked at Mort, and there was a difference. Maybe she looked at Gyorgy like a *mafu*, but not at Mort. She treated Mort like a brother, maybe like a brother."

That choice of words confused me. Brothers and sisters were separated at puberty. If Tupou or Heilala came into my house when Mosesi was there, Mosesi had to leave because he was their brother. When boys turned twelve or thirteen, many families built a little sleeping hut somewhere on the property for the boys, to keep them as far from the girls as possible. Sisters wouldn't be caught dead treating brothers with the adoration I accorded my own brother back home. The sisters ridiculed them, insulted them, and avoided them. Brothers were rough, vulgar creatures who were to be ordered around. Filipa and Tevita hadn't gone to the extent of building their sons a separate hut, but then half the time I wasn't sure where Filipa's sons slept. I only knew that Filipa and the daughters made sure the boys stayed as far from the girls as possible.

"Melanie didn't like Mort?" I asked.

"Maybe she didn't respect him—or maybe…." Leota paused to think about it. "Maybe she just didn't see him. It was Gyorgy who had eyes for her."

I frowned again. Who had eyes for whom? Was my Tongan good enough for this?

"Gyorgy was her *mafu*, then?"

"He looked at her as if she were his angel," Leota said.

We sat together quietly, letting afternoon breezes pick up the flimsy curtains that Filipa had made for me. Outside, chickens clucked peaceably as they patrolled the pepper plants beside my hut for ripe, red treats. One late mango dropped, making us all jump.

"Mangoes," I said in English. "I love 'em. I hate 'em." Filipa quickly translated, and Leota smiled.

"Why did you want to tell me this, dear Leota?" I said, back in Tongan.

"Because you are like her," she said. "She is like your sister. Your American sister."

Her words shook me. I did not want to be like Melanie, who was, after all, dead. On the other hand, when I thought about Melanie dying that way in the back of that truck and saying, "Yes, please," I knew that even I was beginning to love her. I was beginning to love her spirit. In a strange and confusing way, I loved her tragedy. And there was something new in my gut: pure and uncontaminated hatred for the evil that had taken her. This was an evil I did not question, an evil I would not doubt.

"Thank you for loving her, Leota," I said, surprised by my emotion and by the way my voice involuntarily cracked. "Thank you for loving my sister as she died." A spark of something blue and lovely sizzled in the air, an electric déjà vu, as if Melanie, too, were sending her love.

CHAPTER 9

▼

Hange ha lupe kotone. *The pigeon eats even berries that are hard to swallow.*

The insight of that afternoon with Leota was a small epiphany for me. But this miniature first step hardly took me to the pinnacle of understanding. In fact, within days of Leota's visit, I slid back down to a state of confusion. Leota would not have recognized me, though eventually the story of what happened in Fitzhugh Grey's shower probably got back even to her. I claimed that day's debacle was because of hot water. It wasn't.

I can't remember why Fitz decided to throw a party. Maybe it had to do with the jury trial going into deliberations. We were all anxious and depressed. Lizard Sam, who stalked the proceedings, said the Peace Corps case leaned heavily on Mort's mental incompetence, the attorneys reasoning that if Mort was insane he should not be put to death.

The concept of not being guilty by reason of insanity was a new one for Tonga. If that were to be Mort's defense, sentiment among the volunteers was divided. Some wanted vengeance; bluntly, unambivalently, they wanted him dead. Others were more darkly philosophical; was it not possible that any of us could be driven to such actions? Was it not possible that this evil was within us all? One who wanted him dead was Mac Barnett, and he had stayed on an extra couple of weeks past his Peace Corps service year to await the outcome of the trial. He seemed alternately very melancholy and angrily volatile. Maybe Fitz was throwing the party for him. Under any circumstances, we feted every departing volunteer. Or maybe Fitz was just in a drinking mood. Whatever. That it was Fitz giving a party, though, with his macabre features and ludicrously luxurious bathroom, seemed strange and off-kilter. But everybody went along.

I knew him mostly from watching him suck limes and squeeze them into his gin and tonics in the Coconut Club. He did it to keep the rest of us from drinking them after he'd plunked down his *pa'anga*, his damp, colorful Tongan paper money. As if any of the rest of us would—we were happy to drink our fifty *seniti* beers. He was awkward, lanky and long-faced, with a beak nose and a high, broad forehead exaggerated by premature balding. What thin brown hair remained fell around his head like a ragged bed skirt. His bony knees and arms looked almost alarming coming out of ill-fitting khaki shorts and safari shirts. He was in his late twenties, but his bearing already suggested middle age.

A public school boy, Fitz was reputed to have descended from gentry. Yet he looked slightly askew, startled and bug-eyed. People who'd shared late drinks at the Coconut Club with him claimed to know that he was the ineffectual younger son, shipped out to the islands where he would do no harm. We presumed at home there were always maids to keep him ironed, but here, without help, he appeared pathetically unkempt.

And his months in Tonga had not improved his noxious bad breath, reeking of onions and indigestion, and when he talked, people found themselves stepping back or turning away. He must have wondered why. No one told him.

Despite all this, he lived better than any other volunteer. His house was bigger, airier, and more private than those of any of the American volunteers. Unlike mine, his house sat on its own lot, unencumbered by (or deprived of, depending on one's point of view) a sprawling Tongan family to watch his every move. Flowering bougainvillea spilled over the concrete walls and shingle roof, and he had a real patio with a wall around it. His living room was big enough for a grand piano.

His famous bathroom was the *coup de grace*. Not only was it spacious and beautifully tiled, but also it contained a huge, claw-foot bathtub, capacious enough for two. Built around the bathtub was an enormous shower and shower curtain apparatus that hung from an oval frame. A huge, real glass mirror presided over a large marble sink, and the toilet, an actual throne, was set on a raised marble platform with a shelf built in on one side for magazines or perhaps a glass of champagne. Among the volunteers, the existence of this remarkable bathroom in the Kingdom was regarded as a miracle.

Most impressive was the fact that both his bathtub faucets and the sink faucets had two handles, and in each case one of them read "hot." Most of the volunteers had running water, and most of us had showers in cubicles of cramped proportions. But no one had hot water.

I could turn around in my shower—maybe with one other person, if that happy day ever happened—but that was it. As I've noted, I could lather up in my shower while continuing to watch the neighborhood goings-on. I often saw roosters perched on a high windowsill, and it was not unusual for me to chat amiably with some old bird or other while taking a crap.

But since nobody but Fitzhugh Grey had hot water, the volunteers' showers were perfunctory affairs, functional and fast. I could get the job done in less than two minutes if the morning were cool.

At home, I'd been a bath fanatic. I used to stock six kinds of bath oil and bubbles and could take the water hot. I used to spend hours in the bathtub, for comfort and contemplation. And in my life before Tonga, I'd known several men who shared this fondness. I'd spent some drowsily erotic afternoons sudsing down some guy and being sudsed myself.

In Tonga, I was learning to live without bathtubs, but I missed hot water. It was hard to get shampoo out of my hair without it, and clothes never got completely clean.

So when volunteers went to visit Fitzhugh Grey, we invariably asked to step inside the loo. He couldn't say no, but it drove him crazy. It suited him to be held in awe for his water closet, but he couldn't stand other people using it. People had been known to disappear in there for so long that Fitz would finally knock on the door and order them out. Some male volunteers claimed to sneak their razors in and try to get their whole face done without Fitz catching them. Sometimes Fitz would be onto them, and they'd come out innocently, half-shaved, and never say a word. Some claimed they'd leave a few hairs in the sink just to get on his nerves.

One of the Melanie Porter legends was that Fitz had caught her, skirts hiked up, sitting on the tub and shaving her legs. People in the know described it as a kind of Degas moment: she was so charming, bent over her ablutions that the view struck Fitz dumb. He allowed her to finish.

In short, the chance to take a shit in Fitz's beautiful bathroom and then wash our hands and faces in frothy hot water afterward was about the only reason people went to visit him. This time he was about to set off for a three-month assignment to Vava'u, our last chance to torment him for a while.

None of us really intended Fitz's party to be a wake, but that's what happened. As bad luck would have it, on the morning of the party Fitz received a telegram saying that his grandfather died. "Pops gone stop don't come stop rites over stop Abigail stop" is what the missive from his sister said in that clipped, bygone telegraph language. In his grief, Fitz started drinking gin and tonics several hours before his guests arrived, and by the time we got there, he was well and thoroughly soused.

He greeted me at the door with a sloppy hug. He kissed me, and it wasn't dry. We had never kissed, and at that awkward moment I realized I might have unwittingly encouraged him. He was the kind of man you felt sorry for, and you'd be especially nice to him because he was pathetic, but God knows you wouldn't want to go home with him. I tasted his bad breath and repressed a shudder.

"My dear grandpapa has died," Fitz said, tears leaking out of red eyes. "Let's have a drinky."

Trapped in his grip, I looked quickly over his shoulder to see that five or six volunteers—all men—had preceded me. Sam and Tony were there, along with Skip, the long-time Peace Corps veteran. Gyorgy, the cool cat, sat in a corner quietly sizing up the scene. He seemed to be drinking iced tea; he'd been on the wagon lately, along with a chastened Tony. Jeff peeked out from the kitchen and delivered a wan smile. Oh, Lord, this wouldn't be fun. Mac was there, too.

First I had to get myself disentangled from Fitz.

"Be the last to leave," he slobbered in my ear. "I need comfort."

"First things first, dear Fitz. I need a drink."

Again, my arrival seemed to interrupt something. Was it my presence as a woman? As a woman who'd slept with several of them? Was that what made things tense? Where were my sisters, Bridget and Diane, who'd been making themselves scarce ever since the murder? For that matter, I missed my sister Melanie, who would have known exactly how to assuage this roomful of antsy men.

"Fitz might end up being a danger to himself and others tonight," Tony whispered to me. "We'll keep an eye on him." As if I might be the target.

"Thanks, Tony," I said. "I probably won't be staying long."

Just then, Jeff came out with a huge tray bearing five bottles of red wine, an exceptional find in the Kingdom.

"A gift from Viliami," Jeff said, "to help us celebrate. He wished he could be here, but he's up in Fiji, dancing at some resort in Nandi."

Jeff and Mac doled out the dark red zinfandel into a row of juice glasses. At my turn, Mac handed me a portion without making eye contact. He could have been administering communion at the rail, minus the forgiveness. What had I done?

Somebody put a tape into Fitz's machine: Marvin Gaye, "Your Precious Love."

"Let it breathe, let it breathe," Jeff warned, but nobody wanted to wait. We each took our share and called for a toast.

"*Ofa atu*," Tony began, shouting out the Tongan toast. Love to you, it roughly meant. "Bottoms up," he added, hoisting his glass so hard the deep red wine sloshed out. Apparently he was diving off the wagon.

"To Melanie." Gyorgy started it, and after everybody else said the same, we tipped our glasses back and drank. In the song, Marvin Gaye belted out to Tammi Terrell how she must have been sent from heaven above. Somebody turned the music off.

A gloomy silence. It took awhile for the party to resume. If Melanie were here, it wouldn't be like this, I thought. I wasn't up to improving the mood. I didn't have her grace. I was too self-conscious. Yet I found myself moving toward Gyorgy, making Tony move over on the rattan seat, making room for myself with Gyorgy at my side.

When I began to slip into my game of courtship, I felt a disagreeable twinge. I shook it off. I had been chaste and well behaved since Mac crawled out my bedroom window. It was just a game, and what did it matter? Gyorgy was watching—not because I was beautiful, I thought, but precisely because I wasn't. I could never be his new Melanie, but I would do what I could. Somebody turned the music back on. Damned soul music. '*Ofa atu*, love all around. Bottoms up.

I stepped into the swamp, my swamp. I did it with questions: Does he dream in Tongan? (Yes) When did it start? (After a year, and when drunk) Did he ever forget how to say things in English? (Never) When is he most lonely? (Don't know) Has being in Tonga made him think about religion? (No more than usual, why do you ask?) And, so delicately, how does he manage without…her?

The questions, his answers, twined words around me like a sari. Arrogant, silly girl, I began to believe I could dance around him, taunting and hiding, then peeking out. I moved through the Everglades, savoring the dark water.

When I asked about Melanie, he merely said, "I can't. I'm afraid I can't talk about her now." I slid imperceptibly away from the subject, and he, too, was a smooth bass, avoiding a hook. I understand, I understand, I said to myself.

"I'm night blind," I said, apropos of nothing. "I think it happened when I looked at a solar eclipse in eighth grade. I knew I wasn't supposed to, but I looked before I could stop myself."

Gyorgy turned his head toward me—not his eyes, yet, but his head.

"I was standing in the road outside one of the numerous parsonages of my youth," I prattled. "The town was named Blissfield. Misnamed Blissfield, I might add. There was one street, with houses on one side. Below it was a 'river,' if you want to call it that, named Killbuck Creek. Every spring the creek flooded the bottom part of town."

"I hope they had the foresight to build the parsonage on the high part," Gyorgy finally said. I pounced. His reserve had slipped. He was listening.

"*Au contraire, mon frere,*" I said. "The townspeople's scriptural understanding was the more you suffered, the more God loved you. That spring before the eclipse, the water came up two feet into our living room. The president of the board of trustees helped my dad move the piano up to the second floor. The president got a hernia from it, and the damn piano sounded a little squishy from then on. I used that to justify quitting piano lessons. After the water went down, of course."

"So the eclipse meant a lot to you."

"Oh, yeah. After the water went down, we were looking for stuff to be happy about. We wanted an escape. Like, our cat had three kittens—went into labor during the flood."

"When her water broke, she really did it, eh?" Ah, a small joke. He was speaking to me as if I were his little niece. But unlike a little niece, I was on my third glass of wine by then, and I would not be stopped.

"Ha. True. A kitty deluge. Anyway, you'd have thought those kittens were a litter of Messiahs, the way we took to them. We named them Ham, Shem, and Japheth, for obvious reasons."

"Of course. Did they ever come when you called?"

"Never. Obviously, you know cats, Gyorgy." I smiled.

"And love them," he said with surprising ardor. So it wasn't Gyorgy who had left that dead cat on Melanie's doorstep. Until then I didn't know I'd held him darkly responsible—for what, I wasn't sure.

"No," I said breezily, "They only came to 'kitty' and the sound of a can opener."

"What was their mother's name?"

"Well, we named her before the flood. Tigger. She came to that name."

"And the eclipse?"

"It proved to us that there was at least one good thing about living out in that god-forsaken town. We never got the flood stench out of that house, but we had a great view of the sky. We could see the Northern Lights from there, for instance. And when the eclipse happened, we knew we'd have one of the best views in the whole country. Our neighbor Cliff made a bunch of those little peep cardboards for people to look through.

"My mom even came out—she'd sort of taken to her bed during the flood and didn't much want to get up. This old woman named Mrs. Fredericks came out for it, too. She was about ninety years old and had to be propped up on her walker to look through the cardboard thing."

"How do you think you got night blind from it? Weren't you using your little cardboard peep thing?" Gyorgy asked.

"I just got excited. There weren't enough to go around, and the kids were all grabbing them from one another, and I just looked, that's all."

"When did you know something wasn't right?"

"When I couldn't get my eyes to adjust to the dark like everybody else. I can't see the Big Dipper like I used to. Or, I can see it if I look away. It's there in my vision, but not when I look at it directly. I have to look away. I think I have a blind spot. I can sometimes see Orion here, it's so bright." I suddenly remembered that the last time I'd seen it had been the night Melanie died. Time to change the direction of the conversation. "Do you remember that eclipse, by any chance?" I said, "It was in 1963, in July."

I might have wondered whether he gave a damn about talking to me. But now he was with me. He turned toward me fully, and his face was open.

"I do," he said. "My mother had married again, just a year or so before. I was ten years old. I was just getting used to my new dad—the first father figure in my life. He was an astrophysicist, and he took us to the Northwest Territory. It made him my hero."

"Wow. That's a good memory." I sat back, relaxed. I pictured myself at thirteen, ecstatically ruining my rods and cones, while Gyorgy was getting used to a new dad in the Canadian Rockies. How remarkable that we were telling each other our stories in the South Pacific. I'd had too much to drink.

"One small problem. He was a drunk," Gyorgy said. "I sometimes wonder whether it came from looking at all those stars. He was an elegant guy my mother loved, but he favored martinis— Bombay gin, olives with no pimentos. At first he'd get witty, and then wittier, and we'd all be laughing and enjoying ourselves. Then his face would darken, and he'd say something insulting to my mother. I learned there was a window of about, say, two martinis when he was really fun, a sparkling raconteur. Then it would go downhill."

"And then what?"

"He started hitting her." I flinched. "The first time was the night of that eclipse. Next day she packed us up, and we went back to Toronto without him."

I remembered the story of his childhood, how his mother had pushed him across the border in a baby carriage, running from Hungary to safety. I felt sorry for this woman.

"Did she divorce him?"

"It took her a while, but yes. I didn't want her to. I always remembered those stars, his big mirrors, his charts, his enthusiasm. I thought the three of us made a classy family. I pushed down what he did to my mother. That's how badly I wanted him to stay. I think she stayed with him much longer than she should have because of me."

The picture of Melanie, getting slashed in her hut after Gyorgy had left her that night, slid unwanted into my mind. I looked away from him, momentarily losing my appetite for the chase.

"Did she know he was a drunk beforehand?"

"She didn't know he got abusive. She'd only seen his charm—the charm between the second and third martinis. I actually moved in with him for a while when I was in college. By then he had collapsed a bit, and his body was breaking down. But he still was good company."

"Is he still alive?"

"Died the way I would have predicted, drunk in one of his astronomical journeys in the Andes. Ran a car over a cliff."

"I'm sorry," I said.

"She died of colon cancer just a few months before I applied to be a volunteer. You could say that's why I'm here."

I looked at Gyorgy's face intently. "Life is so fucked sometimes," I said. Tammi Terrell was making sweet soul promises. The sculptured lines of Gyorgy's mouth and chin almost made me cry, they were so beautiful. But I didn't care how he looked. I would have asked him to dance no matter what.

He didn't say yes or no, but simply straightened up and gathered me into his orbit. We began whirling around the room, his long legs moving against mine. He was an expert. So this was what it felt like to be in Gyorgy's sway. Headily, for a moment, twirling slow motion, I imagined that I might be Melanie, that this is what it felt like to be glamorous. I smelled him—clean, almost astringent. I felt him breathe. Jeff and Lizard Sam and Tony and Fitz watched without saying a word, sipping their wine. Maybe waiting to see whether I could be Melanie. I probably should dance with them all, I anxiously thought, if I were going to dance with anybody. Then I stepped on his foot and lost my rhythm. I'd never really learned how to ballroom dance.

"Sorry," I said.

"It's okay, really." Patiently, he pulled me in for a turn, and I knew the dance was over.

It was inevitable that I couldn't be her. The rounds of wine—and after the wine, gin—kept coming, and I lost count. I slipped off the couch and sat cross-legged next to Gyorgy on the floor. Words got scarce.

"I miss hot water," I said. "I really do."

Gyorgy looked down at me and then leaped up and walked directly into the bathroom. Was he angry with me? Fitz, arguing some rule of rugby, had his back turned. When Gyorgy reached the door, he turned around and beckoned to me.

I followed.

Almost grim with determination, we stripped and faced the gleaming tub. We scarcely looked at each other's naked bodies, though I have a sense memory of his as slim, solid, hairless, and vulnerable. We were both still holding our glasses of gin, and we clinked them together and whispered, "To hot water." Then we balanced our glasses on the wide edge of the tub.

Gyorgy turned the magic knobs and out came the water, full blast, blessed, and hot. He pulled the plastic curtain around the tub and bowed to me, welcoming me in. He climbed in behind. For a few miraculous seconds we just stood there, letting the steamy water pour over us. Then Gyorgy reached for the soap and lathered his chest and his long arms. "Damn," I think I said, "Damn, this feels good." We were poised there in a trance, our faces upturned to the wide nozzle and hot water streaming down our bodies, when Fitz ripped open the curtain.

His voice was so deep and loud he sounded like an animal.

"Take your *shower* someplace else," he shouted. "Get out of my bathroom and out of my house." He grabbed me by my wet arms and pulled me from the tub. Hot water flew everywhere. For a brief moment he tried to wrestle with Gyorgy, who was slippery with soap.

"Don't touch me, man. I'm leaving, I'm leaving." Gyorgy said.

"Don't bother to dress," Fitz shouted. "I want you both out now." In one crazy moment he was chasing us both, naked, around the living room while the others yelled and tried to get him to stop. In the chaos, I caught a look at Mac, his face twisted and miserable.

I landed on the porch, and behind me a growling Fitz gathered up my clothes and threw them at me.

"I'm sorry I told you about my grandfather," he said and spit on me. "Now get out."

Crying, I scrabbled through the pile of shoes on the steps for my flip-flops. Gyorgy was behind me, pulling on his pants and yelling at Fitz to simmer down. Two Tongan boys went by as I pulled on my T-shirt and fastened my skirt. They laughed raucously and pointed.

I got up on my feet and ran away from Fitz's house, hysteria rising.

"Wait, Charlotte, come on, wait," Gyorgy yelled.

He caught up and put his arm around me.

"It's okay, Charlotte. He's just a big, dumb guy. Come on! It'll be okay!"

"He wanted me to stay—his grandfather died."

"Let me walk you home, Charlotte. We'll talk about it tomorrow."

"I pulled a Melanie," I blubbered. "I screwed up." Drunk as I was, I knew I had trampled into unforgivable territory.

He grabbed me by the shoulders and shook me.

"Listen to me. You don't get it, do you? None of you assholes get it. *It wasn't her fault.* It wasn't my fault. It wasn't your fault. *Mort* killed her."

"But I don't get it," I stammered, crying. "I don't understand *why*."

"He was crazy, Charlotte. There *is* no why."

I pulled his hands off my shoulders, and for a moment we faced off and looked directly into each other's eyes.

"I want to forget it ever happened," I said, my voice low. Then I staggered away and got on my bike.

I circled through the coral roads, half losing my way. I ended up on Vuna Road beside the reef, slipping and sliding. The moon was waning, impotently drooping over the water, but it gave me enough light finally to find the cemetery, its ghostly burial ribbons fluttering, my signal to turn toward home.

As I wobbled back to the property, still crying and horrified with myself, something alarmed me. My door was open, and a small, pale yellow light glowed inside. Disoriented, I got off my bike twenty feet away and approached my hut as warily as a cat.

"It's just me," Mac Barnett said, his shadow filling the doorway. "Where have you been?"

"I got lost," I said. "Does Tevita know you're here?"

"He wouldn't mind if he did, Charlotte. Let me fix you a cup of tea."

He knew how to survive in Tonga better than I did. I sank onto the floor, onto my pandanus mat that could have used a good sweeping. Silence ballooned between us. Suddenly Mac jumped across the room and slammed his shoe down on something.

"What? What is it?"

His overturned shoe revealed a squashed brown centipede, a *molokau*, another of the curses of Tongan households. "Damn," he said. "That's all you need now, a *molokau* sting. Watch out for them, Charlotte. They hide under mats just like this."

"This damn country," I said. "We can't relax for a minute."

"You'll get there," he said, scrubbing the centipede corpse off his shoe with the other shoe and kicking the squishy bits out the door.

"I screwed up," I said. "I'm an idiot."

"Welcome to the human race," he said gently. "We're all tense right now. We're all confused."

When the water boiled, he poured it into one of my chipped mugs, inherited from god knows what other Peace Corps volunteer, somebody long gone, I supposed.

"I owe you an apology," he said. "I'm struggling, too."

"I know," I said.

"I'm so angry that I can barely hold it in," Mac said. "She and I were lovers a couple of times, you know."

"I thought so," I said. He sat down on the floor beside me, adjusted himself into the lotus.

"I wasn't her favorite—Gyorgy was. But she had a way of making me think I mattered. She made us believe that we all had a chance. When she died, I felt cheated. I had jokes left to tell her. I could have made her laugh. Why did some asshole have to ruin everything?"

"They looked so beautiful together, Gyorgy and her, drinking those martinis," I said absently.

"A perfect pair," Mac said. "She didn't love him just for his elegance, though. She loved him for the way he'd been hurt."

I sipped my tea, then put it down and rubbed my forehead.

"The part I don't get is Mort," I said. "I don't understand *why*. Why did he kill her? And why *her*?"

"Well, here's one theory. Didn't you ever hear about their date?" Mort said.

"I'm always the last to know," I sighed.

"He was such a naïve jerk, so determined. He had a huge crush on her, and as some weird way to deal with it, a couple of us set them up on a date. We thought if he just got a chance to be with her once, he'd be satisfied. Melanie agreed."

"Was Gyorgy part of this plan?"

"Well, he wasn't until Melanie told him it would be okay. Then he went along."

"Oh Lord, Mac, all my womanly instincts say that was a really bad idea."

"Well, it's too late now. She didn't know what else to do. They went to a movie at the HauHau, some karate flick, and then he took her home. I guess he wanted more, but she tried as gracefully as she could to tell him she just wanted to be friends. He was furious. That was a week before the party, when she was so obviously in love with Gyorgy."

"We're all so fragile," I said.

"Yeah, but most of us don't kill one another."

"I know. I know. That story doesn't make me feel better."

"It's only a theory," Mac said. "The bottom line is he killed her. She's gone forever. I don't care why he did it. I hate him for killing her." His face darkened, and his hands curled into fists. I poured him another cup of tea and gave it to him, making him open up his hands. He cradled the cup in both hands and took a long swallow. "Well, what do I know?" he said wearily. "Why does anybody do anything?

"Yeah. Like why the hell did I just get into Fitz's shower?"

"*That* I totally understand," Mac said kindly. "Gin and hot water. *That* I get. I wish everything were as easy to understand as that, Charlotte. Don't worry so much."

"It's hard not to," I said fervently, tears starting up again. "But thank you." I took his hand.

"When we 'got together' that night," I said, "You seemed so happy. You were great. I love what happened. I've been wanting to tell you."

"I did, too," he said. "But, Charlotte, everything changed when I saw Melanie's body. I have nightmares about it. I can't let it go."

He slumped a little. He was fighting back tears.

"I want to hug you," I said. He let me, and we sat there on the floor with our arms around each other tight until he let out a long breath.

"Thanks, Salote," he said as he got up, stiffly, like an old man. "Don't worry about tonight. Fitz is a jerk." And then he was gone.

When I woke in the dark from a heavy sleep to the sound of insistent pounding on my door, I didn't know at first where I was. I'd been dreaming about one of my childhood homes, a sturdy brick parsonage with Ionic columns on the front porch, a fieldstone fireplace, and a screened-in side porch where I read every Nancy Drew book one summer, slouched on the porch swing. In the dream, I was flying languidly from one room to another. It felt fabulous. I gazed lovingly and sadly at each detail in the rooms below me, knowing they were lost. My mother sat at the kitchen table, reading Hurlbut's Bible stories. She looked up when I flew near and smiled. "You're a *good* girl," my mother said. Petey, the parakeet, flapped around in his cage, which was covered with a mosquito net. "Let me out of here," he said, flapping more loudly, pounding. Then he was yelling something in Tongan.

I sat upright, alarmed. It was chilly, unusually so. The pounding continued.

"Salote, Salote, open up!" I froze. What the hell time was it? I felt for my bedside flashlight and grabbed my alarm clock: 2:14.

I didn't recognize the men's voices. There were at least three. They sounded rough and urgent. I didn't move. I heard a babble of Tongan speech. Something about the *palangi's* being afraid, and lights. Heavy footsteps running.

I had to answer. I pulled on my pink chenille bathrobe and, hoping the ruckus had scared off the cockroaches, cautiously tiptoed across the floor and opened the door.

"*Koe ha*? What?" I said, staring dazed at the three men. One of them was Oneahi, Filipa's brother-in-law.

"Salote, we need your *fale*," Oneahi said. More shouting, and I was lost, my brain refusing to work.

"Tupou, *ha'u! Tokoni*! Come on, help!" Oneahi finally cried, hailing Tevita's oldest. She came over quickly. The whole neighborhood, it seemed, was up.

"What's going on?" I was relieved to see Tupou, who explained in short sentences as if I were the village idiot.

"They need your electric," Tupou said patiently. "My uncle he died."

"Oh, I'm so sorry I didn't understand," I said. "*Fakamolemole*," I said, "please," turning to the men. "I didn't understand." They rushed in, plugging thick black cords into my two sockets, one in the living room, one in the kitchen. The cords, frayed and pieced together with duct tape, sparked and snaked from my hut and across the back of the property, through the banana patch and into the house of the deceased.

I'd never been back there as that hut faced another road. I'd sometimes seen a wrinkled old woman sitting topless in the sun there. Old women, it seemed, were allowed the old ways.

Tupou hurriedly explained that the man—it was Filipa's cousin, son of the old woman—had died suddenly. I tried to piece it together from the rush of words. He was bleeding, Tupou said, bleeding and in terrible pain. Filipa and Tevita had taken him to Vaiola Hospital at six o'clock, and he passed on just an hour ago. Somebody met Tevita and Filipa at the hospital with the truck, and they were bringing him back.

The rest of the extended family got things ready. How old was he? Tupou thought fifty-two. A bachelor, his mother's youngest child. They lived together. Tupou said "ulcer" in English. How did the kid know that word? I'd never known anyone to die from an ulcer, but anything could happen here. Polynesians, I was learning, were not the easygoing folk of legend, lounging under palm trees. They worked hard and worried hard, bound by webs of obligations to families, nobles, and clergy. The dead man could have had an ulcer.

Tupou pulled me by the arm and ordered, "You come and see the body."

"But...I'm in my bathrobe." I was shivering. I pulled the chenille belt tighter, remembering what I had on underneath: red Sears underpants and a cotton teddy.

The truck rumbled into the narrow lane behind the banana patch.

"Come now," Tupou insisted.

I let Tupou lead me in my bathrobe and flip-flops to the little hut. I had to duck down to get in. It was a traditional Tongan *fale*—oval, with a thatched roof. Several layers of mats softened the crushed coral floor. Oneahi attached light bulbs to the end of the cords and hung them from the lashed rafters. Harsh light shone on the old woman, the dead man's mother. She rocked in a corner, sighing *Oiaue, oiaue.*

Tevita and Oneahi grunted out orders and pulled the body out of the truck. Wrapped in thick cream-colored mats, it looked like a giant burrito. The image elbowed into my muddled brain. I hoped to hell I hadn't smiled. As soon as they carried him into the hut, the wailing stepped up.

About then, Filipa's sister Kalisimasi, my friend from the guesthouse, rolled onto the property in her big green car, her usually tidy grey hair disheveled, a mourning mat pulled haphazardly around her hips, and joined the other sisters in the ritual.

"*Malo e lelei,*" Kalisimasi said quietly, barely acknowledging me and choosing to speak only Tongan. This world, her first world, was a long way from the business she managed with such cosmopolitan panache. Here too, though, she had responsibilities. I was in the way.

Kalisimasi helped Filipa arrange the body. They were both crying. Gently they untied the husk twine and opened his wrappings. Inside, he was covered in another layer—fine tapa cloth—probably part of the family for generations. The women brought out an immaculate white silk sheet, embroidered in the most detailed work I'd ever seen. They slipped a silk embroidered pillow under his head. Finally, they lifted the last layer from his face, and the true wailing began. His pallid face wore creases of pain. No undertaker had censored his last anguish. The women smoothed coconut oil onto his face, and he began to look peaceful.

One of the young girls, Inglesi, motioned me to sit at the head of the deceased to begin the wake. Embarrassed by how ridiculous I must look, I tried to beg off.

"Tupou, really, I should go home. This is for family. Isn't it?" I pleaded. The old woman stopped moaning for a moment and gave me a hard look. "No, no, *ikai, ikai*," she protested. "The *palangi* should stay."

Kalisimasi stopped what she was doing. She murmured something fast to the others, and I was pretty sure she said, "Don't kowtow to the *palangi* this time." I looked beseechingly at Kalisimasi, but my friend didn't give me a bit of help. So she didn't think I deserved the place of honor, just because of where I came from. Well, I didn't want to be there either.

I finally backed out, whispering, "*Fakamolemole*, please, I'm very sorry, I'm so sorry."

Even in the half-privacy of my *fale*, it was impossible to sleep. The wailing subsided, but then somebody rang the bells on the church of Tonga, as if anybody might have missed the commotion. The *fiefekau*, the local clergyman, arrived, reciting Scripture in a dolorous drone, and the hymn singing began. It lasted all night.

I went to work the next day, but Tevita didn't. When I told Kitioni about what had happened, he confirmed I'd been offered the place of honor, pink bathrobe or no pink bathrobe, at the dead man's head. I committed a *faux pas* by begging off.

Kitioni suggested I could redeem myself by contributing to the feast. On my lunch hour I bought five chickens, had them butchered on the spot, and delivered them back to the property on my bike. I also gave Filipa fifteen *pa'anga*, an amount Kitioni thought was not too miserly and not too showy.

And despite my midnight gaffe, when I got home from work, Filipa invited me to the funeral feast. Filipa, Tevita, and all the kids and cousins were already lumbering around in mourning clothes: black dresses and *tupenus*, with huge, ragged mats tied around their waists. Filipa explained they had to wear them, even through this hottest, stickiest time of year, for several weeks. Respect, she explained, *faka'apa'apa*.

They laid out the feast in the grassy area between Filipa and Tevita's house and the banana patch. Kalisimasi appeared, again disheveled and in her most tattered mats, and refused to speak English to me. This time I thought I understood.

After the food, an hour of dancing continued the celebration. The dead man's mother took center stage. Slowly, eerily, she moved like an ancient, endangered animal, turning, turning, her bony arms and hands lifting, twisting, going through the haunting, sorrowful motions.

Her son and Filipa and Kalisimasi's cousin was buried before nightfall in the cemetery facing the lagoon on Vuna Road. Amid all the singing, feasting, and drinking, Tevita's sons collected brown beer bottles for the grave. They would push the bottles neck down around the plot as decoration, a rough rectangle of glass circles. And then they put over the grave banners of satin and chiffon, like medieval gonfalons, the brighter and more sparkly, the better.

I wish there had been a funeral like this for Melanie. On the rushed weekend of the murder, her body was crated up and shipped home by Monday, as if getting it out of the country would make the horror go away. But it didn't. I wish the Peace Corps volunteers had had a chance to grieve like the Tongans, wailing, howling, drinking, and especially dancing.

As a child I went to many funerals, whether I knew the deceased or not. Like weddings, funerals were welcome in our household—they meant extra money for the preacher, for one thing—and because a funeral required an unambiguous ritual, at which my father excelled. My mother took me because she thought children should be exposed to such things. She said she didn't want her daughter to grow up ignorant about real life.

The morticians liked me. They gave me ribbons left over from the funeral bouquets. I collected them like stuffed animals, colorful wads of what seemed, to my child's eyes, like merry final tributes. I came to think of a funeral as a ritual of subdued jollity. I would keep the bows in my room until they got dusty, and then my mother would throw them away. There was a never-ending supply.

I thought the volunteers had been deprived. We should have had Melanie's last rites in the Kingdom. The Tongans could have helped us do it right.

As Lizard Sam described it, Fitz's party fell apart after Fitz threw Gyorgy and me out. There was bad air in the room, and nobody wanted a part of it. Abandoned and angry, Fitz took out his vengeance on the only vehicle in his orbit—his bike. He rode it off Faua Wharf onto the rocks below, trashing the bike and breaking his right arm. Sam and Tony followed on their bikes but only got there in time to pull him out of the lagoon and take him to the hospital. His face and legs were cut and bruised, and he had to delay his trip to Vava'u for a week. People told me that he brandished his cast like a weapon, scaring little children.

I paid Tevita's son Mosesi fifty *seniti* to deliver a letter of apology, which I slaved over for most of one humid, rainy afternoon. Fitz never replied. I couldn't bring myself to talk to Gyorgy again for a long, long time, and he kept his distance, too. I was not to be his new Melanie.

CHAPTER 10

▼

Laku maka fai ki moana. *All the rocks you can throw will never fill up the ocean.*

When the word came in, I was at the Peace Corps office, slouched on the dilapidated couch, a garishly flowered reject left behind by a New Zealand emissary.

I was reading a letter from my mother:

Here's my latest composition. The "secret" is just what burdens me at the moment!

I have a secret
'Tis just twixt Jesus and me
He shows himself and talks with me
I'll carry you through, he says
When I can no longer go it alone.

I winced. My mother had always wanted to be a writer, but this chaotic effort was embarrassing. Worse, my mother would want to know what I thought. I couldn't tell the truth. I'd have to invent something: "Dear Mom. I'm so glad you're writing! I really like the rhyme between…" I looked at the stanza. "Between…me and me." No. "Dear Mom, I'm so glad you're writing! I really like the idea of secrets…" That could work. "I like the first two lines a lot. The word 'twixt' is charming the way you use it."

I shifted position on the couch, trying in vain to get comfortable. I pushed myself into a corner to make way for Tony, who plopped down with an offhand "Hey" to read his own letter from home. A piece of couch frame jabbed at my ribs. Lord only knows what Tony thought about the shower incident at Fitz's. I surely wasn't going to bring it up.

Your father and I went to the store for a few groceries, my mother's letter continued, *mainly milk, after church. I remember the day he wouldn't set foot in a store on*

Sundays, but he didn't try to stop me this time. He only said how many people seemed to be there, heaping their carts with processed food they probably don't even need.

Bridget wandered in and wedged herself between Tony and me, reading her mail from Indianapolis.

"Damn, Bridget, it's good to see you. How have you been?

"Good to see you, too, Charlotte. I've been up in Ha'apai on the filariasis project. It was good to be out of town."

"I missed you. We have to get caught up."

"Oh my god, my sister's getting a divorce," Tony yelled. I went back to my mother's letter.

We went to Olga Erzigeit's for a late supper of breaded eggplant and scrambled eggs. Your father hated the fare, but I kinda like her humble food. She survived a concentration camp, you know. She remembered how you used to make little drawings in church while your father preached and how you scandalized her sister once by drawing a picture of her that showed her prominent mustache. Ha ha."

"My dad got a new riding mower," Bridget mumbled. "As if the old one weren't big enough. Shit, his yard's only about thirty feet wide."

Lizard Sam burst through the door with his usual energy, yelling, "*Malo e lelei,* morons. Did you hear that Dick Clark died?"

This was news. "You're kidding! Where'd you hear that?" Bridget demanded.

"I heard it at the Coconut Club from Viliami. He heard it from one of the Mormon missionaries, who said he picked it up on his ham radio."

"Why aren't you at the courthouse, Sam?" I demanded. "Isn't the verdict supposed to come down at any time?"

"Helu's clerk is supposed to let me know," he said. "I'm going down there after this."

"I didn't even know Dick Clark was still alive," Tony said, turning back to his letter. "I always figured my sister'd come to her senses eventually. I told her and told her not to marry that asshole, but do you think she'd listen to me?"

Nobody answered.

"She probably waited till I was down here just to spite me," he said.

"What'd he die of?" I asked. I was imagining Dick Clark dancing with my mother's friend Olga, the concentration camp survivor. They were doing a slow minuet. Olga's blue hair glistened and Dick Clark's lacquered pompadour glowed. He smiled down at Olga sweetly. He put his arm around her thick waist and guided her around a shining ballroom. They were the only dancers in the room. She was so glad she'd survived, she whispered in his ear, because she got to dance with Dick Clark.

"I guess he had a rare nerve disorder that made him shake uncontrollably. It was kept a secret for years by his publicity agent. But it finally shook him to death."

Bridget, Tony, and I glared at him.

"You're joking."

"I'm serious. Ask Viliami."

Diane strolled in and checked her mailbox but shrugged when she found it empty. Sam paced the room. He did a quick karate kick toward Diane, his compact foot in its flip-flop stopping within an inch of her shoulder.

"Cut it out! It's bad enough I didn't get any mail."

"Dick Clark died," he said, grinning.

"Who the faka-fuck cares?" Diane replied, trying out her new non-innocent vocabulary. He twirled around her and delivered another fake kick at Kaseti, the Peace Corps secretary, who was walking out with a box in her arms.

"*Tapuni*, Sami," Kaseti chastised. "Who's Dick Clark?" She handed the box to Diane. "You did get mail, honey."

"Dick Clark was this beautiful man who ran a TV show that we all watched for hours every day after school, *American Bandstand*," Bridget said. "Man, I wanted to be on that show more than anything. But they didn't exactly take kids in body casts."

Diane took the box in both hands and immediately sat down in a threadbare wingback, another Kiwi reject. She ripped off the brown paper and string and lifted up the white cardboard lid.

"Cupcakes!" she squealed. "Cupcakes from home!"

The rest of us abandoned our letters and jumped up to gaze hungrily at the rows of perfect, fat beauties, nestled in a box designed for Christmas baubles. They had survived the trip remarkably: each was perfect, its round top thickly coated with white frosting and sprinkles.

"They're chocolate," Diane swooned.

The rule was nobody could touch anybody else's food from home until they were invited. Tony, Bridge, Sam, and I stood politely as Diane picked up a cupcake and took a bite. She got a little white frosting on her upper lip and slowly licked it off.

"Nothing special," she said in vain. We watched her closely, waiting. Finally, she pushed the box toward us. We each snatched one.

Everyone took a bite except Lizard Sam, who held his out to Tony.

"You can have mine if you chug it." It was a totally stupid suggestion, but so typical of Lizard.

The sad part is that Tony simply smiled and took it from him. After a dramatic pause, he crushed the cupcake into his mouth, leaving a circle of white goo around his lips. Diane instinctively retracted the box as if to protect it, but it was too late.

"Chug it," Tony said to me. "And do it right. If you don't do it right, you'll choke."

The rest of us chugged cupcakes until we had frosting in our eyebrows. Then Diane squished one into Sam's face, and he smashed one back. Bridget aimed one at Tony, but it missed. Kaseti retreated, squealing, to the back office. I grabbed another one and ate it in two bites.

Just then, as the chaos was dying down, Mac and Jeff walked in.

"Dick Clark died," Sam said, wiping white frosting off his chin.

Mac ignored him, and Jeff shot him a look. Tony wound up to fire a cupcake at them, but suddenly froze.

We heard Evelyn Henry's high heels click on the shaky steps. At the seventh stair, she had to stop to dislodge a heel tip. To our astonishment, we heard her say, "Damn it, damn it all." Sam and I exchanged wordless glances.

Evelyn Henry stood at the door in a flowered blue chiffon number, a color she would have described as periwinkle. A breeze from the lagoon picked up the ends of her teal chiffon scarf and rippled through her diaphanous skirt. I could see her lace slip underneath. For a minute, Evelyn Henry looked like a high-class ghost. She clearly did not want to come in.

"Not guilty by reason of insanity," she said. We sucked in our breath. "He's not going to get hanged. He's going home."

"Not guilty?" Mac's face stiffened, and his cheeks were splotchy red.

"Not guilty. By tomorrow at this time, he'll be back in Washington. He's agreed to check himself into a mental hospital."

"He got *off*?" Mac said in short, hot puffs. "He's going back to the States, and nothing's going to happen to him?"

"That's right. Well, he'll get treatment." She watched impassively as he paced back and forth.

"I don't believe it. I just don't believe it."

The rest of us stood as still as sheep while Mac absorbed the news, enraged, kinetic, his body trembling as he paced, his elbows cranking. It looked odd and scary. I reached for his arm. He whipped away from me as if stung by a snake. We exchanged a look of mutual horror and incomprehension.

Finally, Jeff stepped forward. "Come on, Mac, let's go somewhere. Let's go home."

"No. No, Jeff, I don't want to go anywhere with anyone. Goddamned Peace Corps. You were part of this, weren't you?" Mac glared at Evelyn Henry. "You helped get him off!" He pushed her out of the way and stormed outside, hailed one of the beat-up Nuku'alofa minimokes, and squealed off, alone.

Evelyn Henry adjusted her scarf and touched her dyed black hair.

"Well, folks, a big part of this is over," she said as if speaking to children. Even in her flouncy dress and scarf, she appeared gaunt, as if she'd lost ten pounds.

Jeff looked stricken. "I think I'll follow Mac. I'm worried about him."

The rest of us wiped off the last remnants of frosting.

Tony turned to Bridget. "A new lawn mower for your dad, eh?"

Lizard Sam headed for the door. "I can't believe Helu's clerk didn't let me know. I gotta get down there."

"Let's meet at the Coconut Club later," I said. "All you guys. We'll toast Dick Clark." Of course it turned out that he wasn't dead after all.

CHAPTER 11

▼

Matenga 'i vao kaka. *Spending oneself on work that is fruitless.*

The rainy season dug in after Mac went home. The skies clotted over day after day with thick, oppressive clouds. My wet clothes hung on a droopy rope in my bathroom. Every day I put on damp underwear, and everything, even my books—my Michener doorstops, my Tongan dictionary—began to smell mildewed. There was something wrong with the wiring in my kitchen, and each time I touched my travel iron, I got a shock.

I missed Mac.

In considering the whole situation, all I could think of were a bunch of overused sayings, and nothing clicked. Living well is the best revenge. All things turn out for good for those who love the Lord. Love conquers all. You can never be too rich or too thin—okay, not that one. Wasn't there some wisdom about losing oneself in work?

Kitioni asked me to help him write a statement to be sent, under Baron Faina's signature, to New Zealand, protesting the threatened ouster of Tongan migrant workers whose visas had run out—"overstayers," as they were called.

I drafted a strongly worded document, asserting that considering the importance of the Pacific Island work force to the New Zealand economy, considering the many pending initiatives, considering the Kiwi rhetoric of planning actions to show its support for the island economies, punitive measures toward the overstayers would be extremely ill-advised, if not hypocritical.

Kitioni loved it. He came in, sat on my desk, and read aloud some of his favorite phrases: "unconscionable overreaction!" "ill-considered blow to island relations!" "a breach of inter-Pacific amity!" I beamed back.

Then he delicately lifted the paper over the wastebasket and dropped it in.

"My dear Salote." He shook his head. "The Minister would never sign this." I could feel a flush burning on my neck.

"I'm sorry," I stammered. "I…I should have known. I should have understood this better." I wondered what exactly I meant.

He flashed me a beautiful smile that was painful to see. "My dear, I love what you've done. That's the way I'd like to write it. But the Tongan way is gentler. We'll go around the bush ten times before we say what we mean. And then," he winked, "we won't say it."

I wrestled down my pride. I wouldn't simply teach "the natives" how to do things my way. I had some things to learn. That was okay. I could do this.

"I'm a team player," I heard myself say.

Kitioni suddenly burst into shimmering laughter.

"What?" I asked timidly.

"What you just said. It reminded me of a funny story. Did you know there was a *fefine*, a Peace Corps girl, who had sex with the whole rugby team from Vava'u?"

At first I grinned, then instinctively asked, "Who?"

Kitioni pulled out a pack of the ubiquitous Golds and offered me one. I took it, and we both lit up.

"I think her name was Sylvia. Some girl from Philadelphia, I think."

"The City of Brotherly Love," I said with another grin.

"Half of them were my relatives," he said, which I doubted. "She taught at the primary school. They saw her afterward, going through sums at a blackboard under the breadfruit trees. They thought she had pretty lips."

"Did she do them all at once, or one at a time?"

"They said one at a time. It took her a couple of weeks."

The two of us considered this for a moment.

"So was she any good?"

"They said she was in a hurry."

"Probably because her Tongan father was keeping an eye on her," I said.

There was a long pause, more smoking. Several months ago, I would have found this funnier.

"Did anything bad come of it? What happened afterward?"

"Nothing bad. Well, she might have gotten some lice from some of my dirty cousins."

"Was she using birth control? Did any of the boys get jealous?"

"I have no idea, Salote. You're taking the fun out of my little story."

"She must have been a pretty stupid person," I said with surprising vehemence.

"Don't be so serious, Salote. Nothing bad happened. I promise. That's why I came in here to tell it to you."

"You came in here just to tell me *that* story?"

"No matter, Charlotte. I thought you'd appreciate it."

"I'm a little sensitive about stuff like that these days," I said. "You understand?"

"Yes, yes. Vulgar of me to push the point."

"Okay, okay. Look, Kitioni," I said, peering out the door to be sure Tevita or Fumi wasn't lurking, "when I was in California I had a lot of men." I tried to sound cynical and jaded. "But I never wanted a whole team. Maybe I should try it." My remark sounded lame.

"Only if you wanted to go home, darling. Sylvia wanted to stay another year—we thought she had her eye on the cricket team—but the Peace Corps made her go home to Philadelphia."

"Lots of teams to choose from there."

"Maybe *I* should go to Philadelphia some time," Kitioni said suggestively. He slid gracefully off the desk and out the door. I found myself watching his hips as he walked: a slight sway in the gabardine of his *tupenu* that was deliciously sexy. But he had just confessed. He was not just lovely. He was gay.

I rolled another sheet into the typewriter and tried again. I could do this.

And I continued until teatime. Just after Fefita had delivered my little tray of biscuits and thick tea, Tevita sauntered in. He hoisted himself onto my desk and took a biscuit. He chewed it slowly and noisily.

He wanted something.

"Filipa tells me you had a nice visit with Leota," he said.

"I can't forget it," I answered. "I can't get it out of my mind."

"Did it help you, Salote?"

I looked at him closely, trying to see what was behind his broad half-Japanese face.

"Help me?"

"Did it help you understand what's going on?"

What did he mean? What did everyone want me to know?

"I'm of two minds about it, Tevita," I said. "Do you know that expression?"

"Of course."

"On one hand I wish I could forget all about the murder, about Melanie, about Mort. But Leota's story, my god, Tevita, it's hard to ignore."

"You need to know," he said.

"Why? Is there something we're not being told? What do I need to know?"

"The Peace Corps cared more about the evil boy than about that poor girl."
He switched to a conspiratorial whisper: "If a Tongan boy had killed that girl,
he'd already be dead. He'd already be hanging from a rope from a breadfruit tree.
But perhaps the high-up Americans had other ideas? Who can help him now?
Who can fix his evil?" He smiled slightly and took another biscuit. A heavy afternoon cloudburst hit, rain sheeting gloomily on my open louvres. "Eventually
you'll be glad Tevita arranged that meeting for you."

"You arranged it? I thought it was Filipa."

"No, it was me. Leota didn't want to come, and I talked her into it. And anyway, I told her that if she told you her story, you would perhaps be grateful and
help me."

I knew my face fell, and I tried to catch it by smiling back. I was trapped.

"With what?" I weakly asked.

He suddenly switched from whispering to entrepreneurial bravado.

"Customers!" He was so obviously pleased with his plan that he couldn't sit
still, and he couldn't wait to begin. In fact, he said, he'd talked this all over with
Lizard Sam. Sam was going up to his aunties' island on an extended assignment—probably punishment for insisting on covering the murder trial so
avidly—and he had agreed to set up and supervise the lime squeezing.

Limes. Damn. I thought Tevita's lime project had gone the way of so many
others. But no. The idea of Sam organizing a gang of Tongan women to do anything, much less produce lime juice, seemed absurdly improbable. Yet of all people, Sam and Tevita did share a certain gusto.

"Sam thinks this is a good idea?"

"Listen to me, Salote. He started already. So!"

So. I didn't even want to know exactly how Tevita's aunties and Sam squeezed
the limes, but the lime crop on that little island yielded what at home I would
have called a shitload of juice. I grudgingly accepted my fate. Perhaps this was the
diversion I needed. Perhaps it was something I could do to contribute, to be
other than an embarrassment to others and myself. To help. To forget.

Several days after I was enlisted in the scheme, a rickety truck delivered two
fifty-gallon drums of juice to Tevita's driveway. Fifty gallons is a lot of lime juice.
One hundred gallons is more than enough for any civilized society, including one a
lot bigger and thirstier than Nuku'alofa. One hundred gallons is four hundred
quarts, which is the size the Hasimoto family and I used to market our citric largesse.

But this was *straight* lime juice, or *laimi*, as the Tongans called it. To be drink-
able, the *laimi* would have to be cut ten times with water or gin or vodka. It was
impossible simply to swill it down out of the bottle; the first swallow would burn

the whole esophagus. One quart of the stuff would last an average family, roughly, forever. There would not be a lot of return buyers for months after a sale—if there *were* any repeat sales.

Tevita bought four hundred thirty one-quart bottles cheap from the Tonga Syrup Cooperative, which made the sticky orange brew I helped market at the office. He also rented a bottler, which was a crank used by hand to fasten a lid on tight.

We soon needed more bottles because when we started the bottling process, scattered over the yard with all the dogs and chickens and Kosi the goat scampering around, we broke three bottles, two with the juice already in them. Nine-year-old Mosesi was cut by the glass, and the juice stung the cut. He shrieked and blood flew everywhere—on me, on the goat, into the vat. I hoped the *laimi* would kill whatever foreign substances made their way into Tevita's bottles. I was not looking forward to marketing the disturbingly opaque yellowish liquid.

Mosesi boasted for days of his role in the bottling process, describing his wounds in detail and even learning how to talk about them in broken English. But he and I soon had other excitement to interrupt the chaos of processing the *laimi*, and thus interposed another bloody Tongan surprise.

"*Tofua'a! Tofua'a!*" It was Mosesi, pounding at my door early one morning. Fishermen had hauled in a fifty-foot whale. The kid excitedly told me it was inside the reef lagoon across from the Catholic cemetery.

I wasn't prepared for the gore or for the sight of the giant carcass being picked apart and sold off by the pound. The whalers' sturdy craft, built for the hunt like an oversized rowboat, bobbed in the water. Chiffon streamers on the cemetery's graves across the street fluttered soundlessly, their blues and pinks and whites like dancers' arms pointing to the vanquished creature.

The whalers were busy, patiently slicing out chunks from the whale's body. People waded out with pandanus baskets through water streaked with whale blood to buy the meat. Some customers approached the whalers with awe. The fishermen had killed the whale with harpoons, and they were heroes. Tevita made sure I understood their valor. As the son of a whaler, he had special respect for them and praised them often. And he said they had treated their catch with respect because they were lucky to bring in one a year. With harpoons, it was a contest of honor whose outcome was by no means certain. The whalers battled with their wits, not sonar, and their strength, not explosives. They had to wait and listen and feel the water and smell the air. They worked hard, risked their lives, and remembered every kill.

I watched from the road, happy for a break from the *laimi* ordeal. At last I gingerly waded out to one of the men and asked whether I could have a piece of bone or a tooth. The guy smiled at me and said something to somebody next to me in the water. "No teeth," he said.

"No teeth?" I was incredulous.

He yelled up to a fisherman standing on the carcass, and the guy yelled back, "Baleen. It's a baleen whale, *fefine*, no teeth."

"Something else, then," I said. "I'll pay, of course." I watched him climb back onto the enormous hulk and disappear over it. I heard more manly yelling. I saw a hand holding a large knife swing up high and then down again. Blood splayed into the air, and I heard a crack and a crunch.

The whaler brought me back a vertebra, as big around as an elephant's foot.

"Is that the smallest thing you can find?" I shyly asked, wondering whether he was teasing me.

"The whale is big," he said flatly.

I was embarrassed once again. I had wanted something I could hide, my own little secret piece of the whale. I stared at the vertebra in frustration. How strange that in a country riddled with secrets and obsessed with discretion, there was absolutely no privacy, and everything seemed too big: big laughter, big people, big celebrations, big pigs, big bugs. Secrets, apparently, were not for the *palangi*. This was an infuriating country.

"How much do you want for it?" I finally asked, defeated.

"Twenty," the whaler said. Almost a week's pay. I took the giant spool in both arms and staggered back out of the water, the vertebra as big and awkward as a bushel basket. Mosesi laughed when he saw me and hailed a loitering minimoke driver, who carted the vertebra and me back to the property.

I couldn't take the thing inside. Still streaked with blood and with tendon and muscle still dangling, the bone needed serious cleaning. I consulted with Filipa, who barely concealed her derision. Undaunted, I moved a stack of lime juice bottles out of the way, filled a pot with water, added bleach, and applied a stiff coconut brush. My efforts drew a host of observers and an immense amount of commentary.

"What's that?" Tupou demanded.

"A bone from the whale."

"That's big! What'd you get that for?"

"I don't know, Tupou. I wanted something to remember the whale by. I've never seen a whale before, back in America."

"But why'd you get something so big?"

"I don't know. It's what the whaler gave me." The unsold lime juice bottles seemed to glare at me like spoiled brats, and I purposely avoided them.

All day people went to see the whale and buy meat and blubber and bones. The whale's carcass kept getting smaller and smaller. By dusk, its majestic ribcage arched nakedly against the horizon. By morning, even that was gone.

CHAPTER 12

▼

Limu tu'u 'i 'au. *Seaweed just flowing with the current.*

I didn't feel like selling lime juice, and for a couple of weeks, at least, nobody seemed to care. But my whale vertebra attracted attention every time anyone came to my hut, and I always found a way to be nice. After all, I was my mother's daughter, the daughter of the preacher's wife. Politeness mattered in a preacher's world because his wife and his kids were part of the profession. My mother knew how to do her job. She trained us to look at grown-ups when they spoke to us, to answer questions in a clear, deferential voice, and to be courteous at all times. As a child, I judged how I was doing by whether people liked me, especially grown-ups. That's how I knew I was fulfilling my part in the family contract and protecting my father's interests.

I hated my memories of myself as a child. I was the angel in the Christmas play, the cherub singing "How Great Thou Art" in my adorable pipsqueak voice from the balcony. I was the little doll reciting scripture for old ladies at my mother's teas. I was a very compliant dancing bear cub. Some guy in Laguna Beach told me once that I could have been a great prostitute because I was so eager to please. I was a prostitute, in a way, without the cash on the dresser. No wonder I loved saying the word "fuck" when I first left home.

One day I invited the five other women in my office to my house for lunch. Sela, Meleana, Fefita, Ana, and the infamous Fumi accepted the invitation. The two young male assistants—the Minister's driver, Peni, and a clerk, Sami—tagged along.

The hut was crowded. I fixed tuna salad and deviled eggs, prepared with a tiny jar of mayonnaise I'd found at the market. The tuna salad tasted like my mom used to make. For the hell of it, I'd bought half a dozen avocados, which were unbelievably cheap at the market, and made guacamole with fresh-squeezed lemon juice. I cut yeasty bread into thick slices and put out platters of fresh papaya and pineapple. To drink, of course, I had limeade, a twenty-to-one mix in one of Filipa's crocks.

Even though the Tongans ate a lot of tuna, they didn't like the sandwiches fixed my way, and they only nibbled on the papaya. Neither did they touch the guacamole, and I had to throw most of it out, black around the edges. Kitioni, who'd traveled the world, explained afterward that to Tongans, avocados were pig food.

"How did this get by me?" I protested, embarrassed for the third time in a week. "At home, avocadoes are a luxury!"

"Invite *me* next time," he said. "I love guacamole. It used to be my lunch, along with cheap sherry, at that international conference I went to in Mazatlan. I love it."

But his support didn't come in time to help when my seven victims sat there on the floor in my hut, politely avoiding all my food.

They looked at everything. They looked at my Chinese propaganda poster, "Feeding the Commune's Ducks," that I'd cadged from some departing volunteer. They looked at my photos from home—my father holding a giant cabbage from his little "God's Acre," that year's garden plot; my mother bending over a row of potatoes. They looked in my bedroom, at my books, my flashlight, my little stash of perfume, my portable radio and tape player, my hairdryer with its clunky transformer plugged into an outlet on the kitchen counter.

They looked at the whale bone.

But what fascinated them most was that I lived alone.

"Don't you worry about being by yourself?" Sela asked.

"I'm used to it. I lived alone in an apartment before I came here."

Sela and Meleana said they wished they could go overseas and have their own places. The other three objected that it would be awful.

"And of course, Tevita and Filipa keep a close eye on me," I said.

"Who's taking care of your parents?" Fumi demanded sourly.

"They really don't need anything. They take care of themselves quite well."

"You volunteers are funny," Peni said. "You know why all the government offices want you? All you ask for is a black bike and a little hut, and you're happy. It's very odd to us. We all want anything *but* that. We want a concrete block house and a refrigerator."

Another attack of self-consciousness. Maybe I had invited them here to prove that I could live like them, that I wanted to live like them. But after two years, I would go home to my VW bug, mothballed in my brother's garage, to endless hot water, to a refrigerator, to a TV. What kind of choice was it, really, to give that up for the short term, knowing that all that comfort and privilege would be waiting when I got home?

No wonder the Tongans had a hard time taking the Peace Corps seriously. We came here like scouts at a jamboree, having lots of fun making s'mores and burning the hotdogs. But this was the Tongans' one and only life. Sometimes, when a Peace Corps volunteer rhapsodized about experiencing the simple joys of the islands, Tongans lost their sense of humor.

"Aren't you afraid to be alone, especially after the *fakapo*?" Meleana persisted.

"It's not good for a woman to be alone," Fumi added before I had a chance to react. "This is not how we do things in Tonga."

"We've never had a woman murdered here, in my lifetime," Sela said seriously.

"It had to be a *palangi*," Fumi said. "This was a *palangi* matter, Charlotte." Like Baron Faina, she refused to call me Salote, as if my very name were an offense to the queen. "It never would have happened if that poor girl had had brothers and uncles to protect her. And if it did happen, that boy who did it never would have gotten out of Tonga alive."

I didn't care about Mort Friedman, but I was on the hot seat.

"Don't you ever have crimes of passion here?" I asked. "Doesn't a husband ever get jealous of a wife, and doesn't it ever lead to violence?"

"Oh, yes," Meleana replied with sweet unbelievability, "but his friends make him drink *kava* until his anger goes away. Then he goes home and goes to sleep. That is the Tongan way."

My lunch experiment depressed me. I didn't win any points by showing off the life of my bamboo hut. If anything, I left myself open to criticism. I believed that the lunch experiment marked me, faintly, as ludicrous.

It was not the last time I would feel that way, God knows.

"We need you to go out to the airport today," Kitioni said, rushing into my office late one afternoon. "Peni will drive you. Amin's arriving today, and I have another meeting."

Amin was a consultant on a new industrial park proposal, invited by the Minister at Nalapu's urging. The two Indians had worked together on a similar project in the Hebrides. I'd been preparing an agenda for Amin's first few days, and I'd booked him into a quiet guesthouse off the main drag. But Nalapu had made it clear that for the meaty discussions, the industrial park was too big a deal to involve me, a mere female. It wasn't the first time I'd found myself relegated to the trivial projects, where Nalapu thought I belonged.

Checking the time, I figured I had an hour's leeway and finished off a few letters. Then I hailed Peni, and we set off. I made him stop at the market, where I hoped to buy some leis to put around Amin's neck. All foreign visitors expected the gesture, after all. But it was Wednesday and late in the day, and the only ones left looked brown and sickly. I bought them anyway, ten *seniti* each.

Peni drove madly over the bumpy roads, swerving around various goats, pigs, and chickens, to the airport fifteen miles out of town. I made him slow down at the shed that declared, misspelled on its side, "Ali is the Gretest." It was one of the first written messages I saw when I myself arrived in the Kingdom months ago. Crammed into a rickety bus, a Tongan string band playing welcome songs frenetically in the back two rows, we jetlagged new volunteers noted the graffiti and wondered what on earth we had come to.

"Who do you think wrote that on there?" I shouted to Peni over the roaring engine.

"Some nut," he said. "Somebody who drank too much beer." It was never the kava that produced bad behavior. It was the *palangi* stuff that did it, he said.

"Tevita thinks kava is a health food," I said.

"Of course it is," Peni said. "Everybody knows that."

We rushed into the cool little terminal, not much bigger than a house, which was grandiosely called Fua'amotu International Airport. People filed leisurely past us, going the other way. Inside, a couple of customs agents lounged on the counters and looked at Peni and me with languid indifference.

"Plane from Suva came in an hour ago," one said.

Still gripping my pathetic leis, I looked at the big black and white clock on the wall. Kitioni had told us 16:55, which I translated as 5:55, not 4:55. Shit.

"Damn," I said, hoping my profanity would get them to take me seriously. Sometimes it worked, but not this time. "How can we find him?"

"Go talk to that guy over there in black. He'll help you find your man."

The guy in black, a security officer, took one look at me, my hair windblown from the dusty ride, my leis in hand, and said, "They sent *you* to meet him?" The word "pig" formed on my lips as it used to at home with so little provocation. "Fucking pig" felt even better. Pig. Oh, would it feel good to say that out loud. But I didn't. I was a nice preacher's daughter once again.

The guy in black advised me to write Amin's name on a piece of paper and hand it to the passport guys. I gave it to the passport guys, who peered at it casually and tucked it away.

I had cramps. I was getting my period soon.

A few tourists still filed through, and every face looked foreign and confusing. Did Indians look like Tongans? Were those brown-skinned people Fijians or Samoans? Was that man too skinny to be Tongan? Then all the people began to look alike. When they'd all disembarked and gone through customs, the guy in black yelled, "No Amin."

I looked at Peni, said, "*Ofa atu*," and threw the wilted leis around his neck. We got into the Minister's Rover and took off back to town. Amin must have found his own way in. Nalapu might be furious, but he'd also be glad. I had screwed up precisely in line with how he saw me, and he'd get off to a great start with his old buddy by skewering the American girl.

The rain, coming in heavily from the west every afternoon now, hit just as I left the office on my bike. Tongans knew how to ride and balance an umbrella at the same time, but I never got that knack, and I was drenched within the first block. I arrived home to a house full of people and had no place to change clothes in privacy. Tevita had a project underway to strip off the bamboo wall in my kitchen and to replace it with Masonite, which I hated. He sweated and grunted in the late afternoon humidity, pleased with his evolving home improvement.

Keeping Tevita company, Filipa and two of her sisters sprawled on the floor, browsing through my magazines, which were spread out around them like a bridal dress.

I tried to contain my resentment. I needed time alone. I sat down with Filipa, who was devouring every picture. She lingered on each page, especially the ones with pictures of far-off places like London and New York. She remarked on the color of people's skin and their clothes. She slowly examined and commented on each detail, sounding out the names. "Ma-ri-an-as," she said. "Oh, Marianas Islands. Yes, I've heard of that."

"Look at the dark skin on this one!" Filipa said to Finau and Isita, who seemed to be settling in for a long stretch. "Look at this beautiful red cloth! I wish we could get cloth like that here."

I stepped around them and put on a pot of tea in the kitchen, where Tevita had to move his tools aside and stop his pounding long enough for me to light the stove. I sliced some processed cheese—the only kind available, but also Ohio comfort food. I put it on a plate and served Filipa and her sisters. Isita asked for something cold to drink, and I dashed across the road to the little corner store, in the rain. They had ice and a cooler, but Lio, the guy who ran it, had unplugged the cooler for the day to save a *pa'anga* or two.

When I came back with two bottles of warm red pop (Red Dye #2 must have been dumped in Tonga), some of Filipa's children had crowded in, and Tevita was expounding his theories on how to care for the retarded. He thought tourist dollars should go into a fund for the slow-witted.

"Good idea, Tevita, since most of the tourists are slow-witted themselves," I said.

He clucked, and my joke was wasted. He was on a roll. There weren't many of these poor children, but their families sometimes abandoned them. What kind of Tongans are those? Can you imagine that anyone would abandon a child? The three sisters hardly listened, leafing from one colorful ad to another.

I squeezed into the bathroom. My period had started. I was flowing madly, and there was a spot of blood on the back of my *tupenu*. I wondered, infuriated, whether it had been there at the airport, or in front of Tevita, in front of Filipa. Stranded in the bathroom, I couldn't change my skirt without traipsing through my living room to get clean clothes and a tampon in my bedroom, which was separated by only a flimsy cotton curtain. I had no choice. I pulled the *tupenu* around so that the spot was on the side, grabbed it up in a bunch, and tiptoed back across the Hasimoto clan. The only thing clean was a shorter skirt, which exposed my now thick pelts of leg hair.

"Salote!" Filipa exclaimed when I had cleaned myself up and come back in to join my guests. "Your legs are *faka'ofa'ofa!*" I was surprised. I thought the Tongans, with their provincial racial preferences, would find me ugly. Or maybe Filipa was just teasing. I felt sorry for myself. I wanted a bubble bath.

"You should wear mini's, like in here," Filipa said, pointing to an ad in *Travel and Leisure*. Finau and Isita chimed in their assent.

"Thanks, Filipa, but I don't think so, not here in the modest Kingdom."

"No, no, you're a *palangi*. You could do it."

"No, she shouldn't," Tevita called out through a mouthful of nails. "Look what happened to that other poor girl."

"She didn't wear minis," I said, feeling compelled to point out the truth. "The guy who killed her was crazy. The last time we talked about this, you were on her side, Tevita." I felt like crying.

"But what made him crazy?" Tevita insisted.

"Not her miniskirts," I said. "Something else entirely. He was sick, Tevita, or maybe full of some kind of evil. I don't understand it, *but it wasn't her fault*. Why does everybody act like it was?" I was shouting. They had never seen me like this.

Tevita put down his hammer and came out to look at me. Filipa and her sisters stopped looking at my magazines and stared.

"We are sorry, Salote," Filipa said gently. "We are very, very sorry."

"*Oiaue*," I said, "it's so complicated. Too hard for any of us to understand."

The tea was ready. I served the women and Tevita, and finally sat down and leaned against the wall, giving up any hope of privacy or dignity. While Filipa and her sisters eventually went back to the magazines and Tevita resumed his pounding, I let my mind escape.

I'd developed the habit of reaching inside my sleeves and stroking the soft new hair in my armpits. As long as no one saw me, it was very comforting. I thought it might be nice to be at the Coconut Club or maybe at the International Dateline, relaxing on a wicker chair in the courtyard by the pool. I tried to remember what it felt like to be home, in Ohio or California, in my own rooms that people never came into unless they were invited. I could smell my own blood. The humidity enveloped me like a sticky coat that I could never get out of. Out of fear and confusion, I hadn't been laid since the night Melanie died, and there was certainly no chance it would happen any time soon. I felt as if I had been in Tonga forever.

CHAPTER 13

▼

Kai lu fa ihe tu'unga ú.
Miraculous good luck: finding a leftover "lu" in the barbecue pit.

Bottles of lime juice still waited to be sold. It seemed to be the only practical activity I had to contribute to Tonga but still I procrastinated, my entrepreneurial torpor spreading like mildew. Tevita kept prodding me. "The aunties need money."

"When the rain lets up, Tevita, I promise."

"Sam's already back in town, and he wants to know."

"I know, Tevita."

Every day I rode to work on my bike in the rain, arrived soaking wet, waited impatiently for the 10:00 AM tea to warm me up, did a bit of work, rode through the rain to the little café where I met Jeff, Tony, and Sam for a lunch of curry or boiled taro, got drenched going back, shivered until 3:00 PM tea, did a little more work, and rode to the Coconut Club.

The office dynamics were going to hell, and Fumi was at the wheel. Eventually Kitioni explained that Fumi represented a case of vintage Tongan nepotism. She was in a temporary position, covering for her older sister Anita who'd gone to Australia for six months of special training. As the second oldest daughter, he explained, all her life Fumi'd had to do Anita's bidding, and she felt very bitter. I saw the results every day. With Anita out of the picture, Fumi was a dominatrix, terrorizing the other women, making irrational demands, flying off the handle when she didn't get her way, and obstructing anyone who tried to intervene.

At first I thought of myself as an innocent bystander, but quickly realized that my very presence as an outsider made me a target of Fumi's manipulations. I posed a challenge she could not resist. For one thing, since I had no kinship connections, Fumi couldn't get to me through family pressures. I had no older sister to keep me in line. I wasn't particularly vulnerable to Fumi's role as the symbolic first in command in Anita's absence.

But *my* temporary status made me a second-class citizen. The Tongans had seen many volunteers come and go. The work we delivered ranged from mediocre to memorable, but most of us were there simply because the government got us free and invited us whether we were needed or not. The conscientious volunteers found ways to be helpful, invented projects, saw a need and figured out how to fill it.

Fumi, I gathered, thought Peace Corps volunteers were a nuisance. She thought I was redundant. She told her clerks and secretaries not to do anything I requested. She garbled translations of my writing so that it looked as if I had lost my mind. She told them to give me tea last, if there was any left.

"She'll be gone in two years anyway," Fumi said to Sela and Meleana within my pained earshot one day. "We've got bigger fish to fry."

A request from the Minister took first priority, obviously. Nalapu got work from the women because he was there for the long term, and by now he had the Minister's ear. Kitioni, Tevita explained to me, had rank and family connections, though he didn't say what. At any rate, the staff apparently couldn't afford to cross him. So I got hung out to dry.

The subject of my typewriter came up again. After weeks of the silent treatment from most of the clerical staff, I finally got Kitioni to admit that when I had asked the Minister for a typewriter, his edict came down as an order. My typewriter—the machine I hogged all day, every day—had been pulled from the clerical pool. They'd had only two to start with. Now there was one for me and one for everybody else.

"I've been set up," I said when Kitioni explained it to me.

"Oh, it's Nalapu's fault," Kitioni said. "He knew he was supposed to get you a typewriter, but he didn't agree with the request. That would have meant he'd have to find some money for it. So he just ignored it. Besides, Fumi's right. All the other professional staff write out their stuff. The secretaries think it's weird that you want to type your drafts."

For what seemed like the tenth time that day, I sighed.

"I'm going to keep it," I finally said. "I'm a writer, and I was hired to be a writer, and it was the only item I asked for." In the meantime, I resolved to try to find another machine. There had to be a way.

"Stick to your guns, Salote," Kitioni said, deliberately pronouncing it "Steek to your goons." "I love American slang," he added, trying to get me to lighten up.

"I watched every Western I could." He'd put in time at the HauHau movie house, like all self-respecting Tongan kids.

I tried talking to Tevita about my office dilemmas. He said something like "It's women's way," and I guessed that since her problems got the label of "women's troubles," they weren't worth his time. And he was always on the look-out against accusations that he favored his American tenant. "It's not my job" was one of his stress-relieving mottos.

If it wasn't for Kitioni, work would have been unbearable. He was clever and devious, unmoved by Fumi's constant nitpicking.

"Don't let Fumi touch your work," he finally advised. "I'll translate anything you need. Let's just make that a pact."

"Why did you even want me?" I asked Kitioni, cringing at how my plaintive voice squeaked out.

"Walter."

"Who the hell is Walter?"

"This PR guy from LA who worked here a couple of years ago. He made a killing in the business, retired, and came down here for the fun of it. Walter convinced us we had to have PR."

I sighed again. I was a victim of LA blue suede shoes.

"By the way," Kitioni said casually, "I've got something here for you."

He handed me a fat packet in brown paper, tied up with string.

"If that's Nalapu's latest revisions of my draft annual report, you can keep them," I said. "He keeps inserting phrases like 'inter alia' all over the place, and whenever I use the word 'envision' he changes it to 'envisage.' And he doesn't know a damned thing about journalism."

"Salote, dear, calm down. 'Envisage' is the British usage. We don't like that clipped, efficient American English in our business correspondence. Haven't you got that straight by now?"

"I still think he's a stuffed shirt. Unlike you, sweetheart."

"It's not revisions. It's something you may be interested in."

"What is it?"

"A transcript of the trial."

"Mort Friedman's trial?" My flirtiness vanished.

"The same. It was translated into English to send back to Washington, and through my many connections and thanks to the lucky accident of having a father who couldn't keep his privates in his *tupenu*, I was able to get a copy." So it was true what Filipa once confided: Kitioni was the illegitimate son of the King's youngest brother, Tuimuimoala. This was vintage Tongan power and paradox, a secret known to everyone.

I paused. "Can I ask you something?

"Certainly."

"You're not the first one who seems to want me to know more about this. What is it about this murder?"

"Salote, why wouldn't you want to know?"

"Sometimes I've just had enough," I said. "I didn't ask for this. It's something that happened. And every time I turn around, somebody has something new to pester me with."

"We don't mean to pester," he said gently. "It's just that she was as close as you have to a sister, isn't she? Isn't she, wasn't she, like you?"

"Here we go again," I said. "I barely knew her."

"But now you know a lot about her," he said, as if I had to be helped along.

"*How* am I like her?" I said, a surge of emotion taking me by surprise. "I feel her with me sometimes. I feel her spirit. I love her spirit. But if I'm like her, what does that mean?"

"Forgive us," Kitioni said kindly. "Perhaps it only looks that way to us. Perhaps we're wrong."

"Well, okay," I said, wrestling down something tearful. I tried to let it go. "Thank you for this. Is it a good translation?"

"Pretty good. My cousin, First Assistant to the Crown Prince, did it. He went to Oxford, you know, and even though he spent most of his time there dropping acid and shtupping girls on Carnaby Street, he's pretty good at the King's English."

"Shtupping? Your vocabulary never fails to delight me," I said. I took the packet. It felt heavy and dry. I looked at the title: Criminal Charge No. 1366/76, Crown v. Mr. Morton E. Friedman of the USA. Charge: Murder.

"Is this contraband?" I asked.

"Sorry? What?" he said and strolled out. I ran my finger over one of the edges of the brown paper. I could see the typed foolscap inside, but couldn't make out any complete words. I smoothed the wrapping back into place and set the packet down on my desk. It looked strangely small and helpless. I'd take it home tonight; I couldn't stand to read it here, with others watching.

I managed to make one other friend, Meleana, the young clerk who had a clubfoot. Having physical disfigurement in the Kingdom meant being treated with cruelty; Tongans made shameless fun of anyone who looked or acted different. Meleana was the only one who defied Fumi, and when it was her turn to make tea, she served me first.

"If you need any help, you come to me," Meleana said in her firm little voice.

Today at teatime, Meleana confessed that she wished she'd tried some of the guacamole at my ill-fated lunch.

"Fumi told us not to eat anything," Meleana said. "I was ashamed of myself."

"If you're game, I'll have you over again soon, just the two of us," I said. "We don't have to have avocados, though. There are lots of interesting foods to try."

A Japanese delegation came in to work with Nalapu on his big plans for the industrial park. One gloomy, drippy afternoon at an endless discussion in Baron Faina's office, one of the Japanese men, a slender, friendly fellow named Hiroshi Noguchi, passed me a note while we were having our ritual Benson and Hedges.

"Why do you stay here?" it said.

I looked at him and grinned, thinking, I'm taking him to the Coconut Club. He called me "Salote-san" a sound that pleased me. He had never been in Polynesia and was fascinated. He spoke beautiful English. Tapping my pencil on a tablet while Nalapu droned on, watching fat globules of rain slither down the Baron's louvers, I realized that Noguchi might offer the way out of my typewriter dilemma. I began to plot my gambit. After the meeting, I rushed to the phone and called Sam at the newspaper office, Tony at the health department, Jeff at the high school, and Diane at the hospital. We agreed to meet at the Coconut Club in the late afternoon as soon as all of them could get away.

Noguchi-san let me go with him in his black limo. The driver carefully installed my bike in the huge trunk for the short trip to the club.

At the first table inside the door were Fitzhugh Grey, who still hated me, and Gyorgy, who had never sought me out again. Why didn't Fitz hate Gyorgy, too? I wondered. It was Gyorgy's idea to step into that shower. British empire loyalty and some sort of gentleman's agreement seemed to trump whatever Gyorgy did. *Cherchez la femme*, I imagined Fitz saying. Fitz had just gotten the cast off his arm, and they could have been celebrating. But the two sat in lachrymose silence, as usual, an almost empty bottle of Bombay gin between them. I introduced my guests, to little effect. Fitz seemed drunk, slouching on the sway-backed table. Gyorgy, in contrast, seemed sober, leaning back elegantly and watching the room. His patrician legs stretched out, he was wearing in black denims that emphasized his long, lithe thighs. His loose, black shirt exposed his smooth chest. A fine gold chain glittered in the V of his neck. Even with what I knew about him—his alcoholic stepfather, his abused mother, and the night of the eclipse that had changed us both—Gyorgy still intimidated me.

I steered Noguchi-san to another table, where my four co-conspirators were haggling over the belongings of a volunteer who was leaving. There was a tape deck, a handheld eggbeater, and a tattered copy of *War and Peace*. The eggbeater went first, sold for a bag of peanuts. Viliami was playing an old Marvin Gaye and Tammy Terrell tape on his own boom box perched at the end of the bar. The tape was an unnerving reminder of my shower *faux pas*. But it was new fun to have music at the Coconut Club. Viliami had lately been experimenting with new twists, new drinks, much to the disgruntlement of the old school Tongan curmudgeons who also called the bar home.

"So, how're you all doing?" I asked, gazing fondly at the table of friendly faces, comforting and familiar: Sam, Jeff, Tony, Diane.

The usual responses:

"My jockey shorts are moldy."

"My armpits are moldy."

"Is green stuff on my butt anything to worry about?"

"Speaking of appetizing, I ate a piece of raw tuna the other day. Wasn't bad. Dipped it in sea water for a little salt."

"Oh yeah? My Tongan father made me suck the eyes out of a parrot fish at a feast last weekend. I took a deep breath and did it. Slimy, like tapioca pudding."

"Jeezus."

"Sam's hands are turning orange from eating papaya."

"Dick Clark didn't die."

"We knew that about ten minutes after you told us, you moron."

"And speaking of green stuff, Charlotte, you have to sell that lime juice. Tevita's getting tired of waiting," Sam said. "There's no way I can go back to Niautoputapu to see those damned aunties without money."

"I know, Sam. I have some ideas."

"The aunties don't need ideas. They need *pa'anga*."

"I said okay." The table fell silent, everybody reaching for their drinks. Noguchi-san ordered a piña colada, one of Viliami's new offerings, and sat up straight, watching us all with a big, incongruous smile.

A Tongan taxi pulled up in a puff of dust outside the door, and in walked the widow Clare, still in her Tongan blacks. She had added a woven mat around the waist, tied with a lasso of coconut twine. Her hair seemed wilder than before, Medusan. In Tongan culture, women in mourning deliberately tousled their hair, and she was going native. As always when Clare appeared, we all stopped talking and watched to see what she would do. She gave our table a faint wave and went directly to Gyorgy and Fitz's, where she gave each of them a European kiss, one on each cheek, and sat down, managing to adjust her mourning mat with grace.

"Viliami, my usual?" she said. He reached for the Russian vodka. Clare alone was keeping him busy finding Stoli.

"She speaks," Sam whispered, in awe.

"That's perfect," I said. "Clare and Gyorgy. Maybe she is the one who understands him."

"Her husband was a famous violinist," Jeff explained confidentially to Noguchi. "He had a heart attack jumping up and down on a bed, trying to get away from a mouse."

"So sad," Noguchi said, sweetly. "*So* sad."

"Yeah," we all answered, glad to have somebody new to introduce to our legends. Clare put a hand on Gyorgy's thigh, and immediately the two put their heads together, intensely talking. We were always desperate for new gossip, but we forced ourselves not to stare.

"So, did you guys hear about that guy Ned McClatchy up in Ha'apai?" Sam resumed cheerfully, as if Clare had not just made a portentous entrance.

"That redheaded guy, the one from Missouri?"

"Yeah. He's finally being sent home because Wade went up there snooping and found out Ned hadn't been doing anything but go fishing. Day in and day out."

"But did the Tongans like him?"

"They loved him. He always shared his catch. And every night he'd go to kava parties and tell dirty jokes. He was happy, and so were they. But when Wade got back, Evelyn Henry about blew a gasket. Ned was supposed to be writing a report about his model project, something to do with using fish for fertilizer. If he did any research, it was strictly by accident from him throwing fish bones out his kitchen window."

For about a minute, we mournfully pondered the decline and fall of Ned's utopia. But what the hell, the guy was history. We casually turned to Noguchi.

I told everybody about the note he'd passed me, and they laughed and tried to answer his question: why do we stay here?

Tony maintained that we had been manipulated by our respective governments, who had conspired to get us out of our home countries.

"This is a holding tank for undesirable Americans," he concluded. "They don't want our kind back there. We're just trouble." Fitz, from his table, roused at this remark and yelled that he agreed.

"These godforsaken islands are dumping grounds," Fitz said loudly. "You want second rate mackerel, cheap goddamn mutton, and second rate people? This is where you'll find it." Clare put a motherly arm around him and rubbed his back.

"You're drunk, Fitz," Gyorgy said.

Months before, I knew, Melanie would have been at that table with the Brits, a glittering ornament at Gyorgy's side. The two of them would have been the best-looking couple in the room, and everybody else would have tried to control the way their eyes slid over to look at them, to drink them in. Gyorgy might have pulled out a pack of cigarettes and tapped one out for Melanie. She would have slipped it between her lovely fingers and leaned into his light. She would have taken a long drag and let it out slowly, and all of us in the Coconut Club would have watched her, would have watched the two of them together, and then forced ourselves to look away so as not to seem like the glitz-hungry rubes we really were.

Without her, the handsome Gyorgy held a different kind of power. His isolation was luminous, his loneliness glamour-bright. We were as fascinated and intimidated by the new, tragic Gyorgy as by the old. But there was something about Clare, with him, that made sense. Perhaps she knew more than any of us what it felt like to lose a great love.

"We need more beer," Sam shouted to Viliami. "And I'm buying Noguchi-san another round."

"Buy Noguchi his favorite drink, and I'll pay you back later," I whispered to Tony, just as we had planned. Within an hour, Noguchi-san had three piña coladas lined up neatly in front of him—one from Tony, one from Diane, and one from Sam. He was having a wonderful time.

"Does your work team have a typewriter?" I asked him casually when the time was right.

"Yes. We picked one up in Suva on the way down."

"What are you going to do with it when you leave?"

"Take it back, I suppose."

Jeff and Diane jumped in, melodramatically narrating most of my sad story.

"You could help the Ministry carry on the work you've started by leaving that typewriter here," Jeff concluded.

By the time we piled the pliable consultant into his limo—a loan from the Minister—Noguchi-san had agreed to sell me his portable for a token fifteen American dollars. And to my surprise, Diane got up when Noguchi-san got up, and they went off in the limo together.

"Not that I don't appreciate it, but she didn't have to go *that* far," I said. "Isn't she still a virgin?"

"Don't be so sure," Tony said suggestively, which also shocked me. Diane was on a campaign to demolish innocence. For her, the murder simply proved that life was short and that you never knew what absurd idiocy might end it. The murder fired her up. But ever since our balcony shenanigan and the murder, I assumed Tony had been as paralyzed by guilt as I was.

"Well, anyway, thanks, you guys," I said. "That's a huge load lifted off my white *palangi* ass." I high-fived my colleagues just as Marvin and Tammy belted out from the tape player, "You're all I need to get by." I jumped up from the table and twirled around my friends. They smiled and said "*malo 'aupito*," and watched me go through my Motown paces. The only ones who didn't smile were the saturnine Brits and Clare, still hunched over their table.

"What's with them, anyway?" I whispered breathlessly to my colleagues as I settled back down for another drink.

"They're pissed off about those two Brits getting arrested," Tony said.

"What for?"

"Swimming on Sunday. They got caught at Lavengatonga Beach last weekend. The magistrate made them cool their sorry butts in jail for two days until they learned some respect for the Sunday laws." A guffaw rippled around the table.

"I'm already in a good mood, but that's frosting on the cake," I said.

"Those Brits should learn to be *fakatonga* like us PCVs," Tony said.

"Yeah, thank god for all those arcane handouts from Liz and Wade about matrilineal ancestral patterns," I said.

"And the connection between bananas and Missionary Baker."

"And the myth of the origin of kava."

"Thank god for Peace Corps, keeping us out of jail," Jeff said.

"Yeah, like Mort." Sam couldn't resist.

"Especially like Mort," I said. The others shot me a look. "If it wasn't for the Peace Corps shrink, from what I've heard, Mort never would have gotten off."

"I heard the testimony in person," Sam said, "and that's the truth."

I remembered the packet Kitioni had given me, waiting in my bicycle basket. I didn't mention it. I didn't want to think about it yet.

You've probably been wondering why I've said so little about Mort Friedman, why in all these Coconut Club gatherings and the party at Fitz's and at the Peace Corps office, we always skipped over Mort Friedman and busied ourselves worrying about lime juice or chugging cupcakes or arguing over whether Dick Clark had died. This might be the place to say it: we hated him. We hated talking about him. None of us had any answers about why he did what he did. He was our fellow American, but we didn't understand his craziness, if that's what it was. He was our fellow Peace Corps volunteer, but we didn't stop him from killing Melanie.

I suppose Mort was like us, the way one great ape is like all the rest, but we didn't want to claim him. If the Peace Corps shrink had labeled him sick, well, good for his murderous ass. He had tricked everybody. He had killed the beautiful Melanie, and that was over and done with. But he'd also stripped away our power, our confidence, and our dignity. Thinking about Mort just led us into an angry thicket, a dark maze with no way out, a terrible puzzle with no key. What he did and who he was burrowed insidiously inside all of us who were there in October 1976. We wanted him out of our lives. He was now out of the country, but what he did was still inside us, burrowing.

"Remember the last time we all went to Lavengatonga Beach?" Sam said.

"Not me. I've never been there," I said.

"We were all there—Tony, Gyorgy, Mort, Fitz, Melanie."

"I wasn't there," I said.

"We've established that," Sam said wearily. "I don't know where you were, Charlotte. We would have invited you if you were around.

"Anyway, we went down there after the last drink, and it was beautiful. There was a full moon, and Melanie said, 'What a great night.'"

"Is this another Faua Wharf story?" I said. "I'm happy now, and I don't want to lose the buzz."

"It starts the same, but has a different ending, Charlotte. Let me tell it." He paused. "She stripped off her clothes and ran into the sea."

"Mort wasn't there," Tony said.

"No, it was just the rest of us," Sam said, "and we were so happy she was there, that we were there with her. She glistened. She's out there yelling, 'Come on in, you guys, the water's great.' But none of us moved. We just wanted that moment to last forever, to watch her like that."

He sighed. "Maybe I dreamed it."

"No, I was there too," Gyorgy said from his table. "It was real. She was real." He lifted his glass of gin and said, "To Melanie," and of course we all complied with a chorus of "To Melanie."

Then we heard "To Vladimir, my lifelong love," Clare's toast, her vodka held high, the black sleeves of her tunic sliding down to reveal startlingly lovely arms.

"To Vladimir," we all dutifully responded, as if we'd known him.

"By the way," Tony said after the awkward pause, "that shrink's here now."

"What?"

"He's here at the bar."

Another long pause. I ran my hand up and down my sweating beer bottle.

"What do we care?" I said. "We don't like him."

"We hate him," Sam declared.

"God, you guys," Jeff said, "You didn't really want Mort to hang, did you?"

"Maybe," I returned.

"We didn't want him sent home for nothing," Tony said.

I squinted my eyes to get a look at Gabriel Bonner. So this was the guy. He'd spent hours with Mort in jail, and his assessment of Mort's supposed schizophrenia had had a potent effect on the Tongan jury. Now the Peace Corps was paying him to stick around, "in case anybody needs him," Evelyn Henry said.

"So, what's this guy still doing here? Is anybody, like, *seeing* him?" I said.

"He has workshops every Thursday afternoon, from three to five, when we're all pretty well worn-out," Jeff said. "He calls it the 'Be Here Now' seminar." All heads swiveled to Jeff; he was the first to admit it.

"I did my time in encounter groups in Southern Cal," I said lazily. "Great places to meet guys. I never went to one that didn't yield at least one good fuck."

As soon as I said it, I was sorry. Jeff blushed.

"She claims to be such a hippie," Tony said to Sam. "Charlotte, the word 'fuck' just doesn't become you. I know you love the word, but it doesn't sound right coming from you."

"Gabe Bonner tries to fuck our minds," Jeff said. I looked at him, startled.

"You too, Jeff," Tony said. "You can't say the word 'fuck' worth shit."

"Fuck you," Jeff retorted. "We talk a lot in the group about when we're uncomfortable and how we deal with it. He's good. He's pushing us."

"Pushing you where?" Tony demanded.

Jeff stopped talking. The others stared at him.

"Nobody *has* to go," Jeff said.

"I don't need Gabriel Bonner, fucking PhD, digging into my brain," Tony said. "I figure Washington's taken some heat about how a paranoid schizophrenic like Mort Friedman ended up here in the first place, and now they're trying to head trip us to see whether any of the rest of us are psycho."

I turned to study Gabriel Bonner. He was hunched over the bar, wearing a bright blue Hawaiian shirt and a pair of hippie muslin pants, the kind with a drawstring. Viliami was doing most of the talking, gesturing with his hands, and Bonner seemed to be listening closely and nodding as if he'd known him for years. But as soon as I looked at him, he turned and looked at me. I tried to look away, but it was too late. He put down what looked like a gin and tonic, said a word to Viliami, and approached me. When he stood all the way up, he was over six feet tall, with broad shoulders. He moved loosely, loping as if to protect worn-out knees.

He had long, disorderly hair that was prematurely, arrestingly white and pulled back in a ponytail. His skin was so pale it was almost blue. His face was too long, his cheeks had jowls too advanced for his age—I guessed mid-thirties— and his blue, deep-set eyes stared out of their caverns with exaggerated clarity. He had a thick white mustache, not quite FuManchu. He appeared to be slightly going to fat. From one angle, he was so pale that he looked vaguely like a vampire, but from another he seemed so harmless that he might look right wearing a beanie with a propeller on top.

"Hi, I'm from Maine," he said, as if that were all you had to know. For some reason I stood up. He offered his hand. When I took it, giving him my reflex Methodist handshake, I could feel the architecture of a large palm: a flexible fan of bones and the soft pad of flesh between his thumb and index finger. His hand was both masculine and feminine. I noticed that his body was covered with fine white hairs. A strange specimen.

"I'm from Ohio," I replied with what was supposed to sound like tart sarcasm but came out like an embarrassed confession.

Then Gabriel Bonner smiled. His entire face woke up, the jowls dissolved. I looked at him sharply.

"*Aha*," he said. "Five presidents and Dean Martin."

"Woody Hayes," I replied.

"James Wright," he answered.

"You know James Wright?"

"'A chicken hawk floats over/looking for home/I have wasted my life,'" Gabriel Bonner recited.

"'Suddenly I realize/that if I stepped out of my body I would break/into blossom,'" I answered.

When I looked at him again, he was staring brazenly back, smiling. It was irritating. I sat down, ruefully noting the free seat next to me at the end of the table.

"Nice dancing," he said, smiling even more broadly.

"Thanks," I said grudgingly. I hadn't been dancing for him. "My friends and I just pulled off a little victory. Had to do with a typewriter."

"What's your pleasure?"

"Lime juice. Viliami'll know to cut it with ten parts of tonic."

"An abstemious woman," Bonner said.

One of my favorite words.

He signaled my order to the bar like a regular. I stole a look at Jeff and Sam. Jeff was smiling weakly, his face a mask of innocent curiosity, and Sam, infuriatingly, gave me a thumbs up. Tony got up and wandered to the restrooms, not looking back. Viliami brought my lime juice, touching my shoulder lightly as he departed. I thought I saw him wink at Bonner. Goddamn men.

"It's not that I don't ever drink," I said. "I had a beer after I got here. But as you know, it's the rainy season, and it's dangerous to ride a bike drunk. My bike slipped in the mud a couple of times."

I didn't know why, but I swung my knee around and showed him a scab the size of two thumbs. "I haven't had scabs on my knees since I roller skated on the sidewalk in fourth grade." I was suddenly aware of my hairy legs and slid them back under the table.

He smiled and sipped from his drink.

"Beefeater?" I said.

"Water. I've had a few scabbed knees myself. I once jumped out of a third-story window when I was drunk on vodka. Landed on somebody's convertible top. Cost me a few hundred to buy 'em a new one. Seventeen years, and I haven't had a drink since."

"Why'd you do it?

"A woman. A woman who dumped me. A girl, really. We were nineteen."

"Get her back?"

"Never even saw her again. The story got back to her."

"Everybody's got a story," I said.

"My business," he said. "I'd be lost without stories."

"You'll fit in here, then, I guess."

"Do *you?*" Bonner leaned in, the question direct, arresting, irresistible. I realized with a start I'd love to listen to that voice for hours: slow and deliberate, lazy around the "r's" like Robert Frost reading his poem at JFK's inauguration.

"When they offered me Tonga," I said, "I said, 'Where the hell is that?' And then I lay in bed all night, worrying about how weird it might feel to be on an island. I thought I'd get panic attacks. I mean, if you're from the Midwest, you get used to the land going on and on, and you know you can drive your big old Chevy anywhere if you need to run away."

"But you don't have a problem?"

"I get panic attacks every Sunday afternoon. There's no flight out till Tuesday, which you probably already know."

Tony was back from the restroom and he and the others had their heads together, heatedly talking. About what? It seemed they'd decided to leave me alone with Bonner. What kind of friends were they? Bonner saw me look at my buddies and back at him. He leaned back as if he didn't care.

"I haven't had any inclination to escape," he said. "Not *yet*, at least."

"Stay long enough, you will," I said. "How long *are* you staying?"

"Somewhat open-ended," he said, "Depends on things. Probably a couple of months." A couple of months. An eternity here. A lot could happen. My spinning brain alarmed me. What did I care? Why this sudden, infernal urge to have him all to myself? But why did I also wish the others would turn around and rescue me? Why did I feel about nine years old?

"So, how do you feel about being in a country that's had a notorious Peace Corps murder?" He sat back, his gaze unflinching.

"Would you please stop staring at me?"

"I'm sorry."

I tried to decide what to say. I felt under the table for the scab on my knee and rubbed it.

"I'm lucky to have a job that keeps me busy," I finally said, "and I'm always occupied with my Tongan family when I get home. Of course, it's a bit hard at times, like when the cockroaches ate the crotches out of six of my underpants, and I had to have my mom send me a whole new batch from Sears. They took more than three weeks to get here, and I had to keep washing out the only two pairs I had left. But then they finally got here…" I trailed off in horror. What had I just said? What was *wrong* with me?

Bonner touched me lightly on the arm and said quietly, "You've never experienced anything like this. You're playful, and you like men, and you know you push the boundaries, and you have a guilty conscience, and you're mortally afraid it'll happen to you.

"And," he added with that devastating smile, "you might be mad at *me*."

I focused on the arched doorway to the snooker room. Two handsome Tongan men in black mourning shirts and scruffy mats tied around their waists leaned up against the wall. One lit the other's cigarette.

"Maybe you'd like to come to the guesthouse for a couple of rounds of Risk sometime," he said calmly. "We've had some whopper campaigns."

"World domination? Are you crazy? Well, I guess you should *know*. But, damn, there's too much testosterone around here already. Why do you guys like that game so much?"

Gabriel Bonner laughed. It really was a damned great smile.

Then Viliami shouted that the Minister of Health was ready for his snooker game, and Bonner got up and moved to the poolroom. Apparently he knew every game in the Kingdom.

The other conversations ended abruptly as soon as Bonner was gone.

"Why were you being so friendly with him?" Tony asked.

"Why are you being so crabby? Why did you leave me alone with him?" I shot back. "Maybe a joke will help. Why do Baptists make love standing up? Remember that one?"

"Come on, you guys, relax," Jeff said quickly. "We've all got island fever."

Through the push-out hurricane windows of the Coconut Club, wind rattled the palms. Outside, the light turned plummy and bruised. A musky breeze blew through the club, skimming peanut shells off the tables. The air smelled like thunder and rain. I didn't want the weather of Tonga to snare me again. Maybe I could make it home before I got caught.

I stood up and said good-bye. "*Mou nofo a, eh?*"

Tony grunted but Jeff and Sam automatically called back, "*Alu a, eh?*" The ritual comforted me—how the departing person said, "You're staying, right?" and those left behind said, "You're going, right?" In two simple phrases, the story of Polynesia. Somebody always leaving, somebody always left behind.

"Why *do* Baptists make love standing up?" Jeff called after me.

"Ask Tony," I yelled as I screeched away, fruitlessly trying to pull a wheelie.

CHAPTER 14

▼

Tala kei 'i Kapa na'a to ki Mala. *Act wisely before it's too late.*

Ma the pig bounded out of the banana patch to greet me. He was getting bigger and fatter, but no less affectionate. He rubbed against the door and looked at me soulfully, flirting with me until I scratched him under his chin and whispered sweet nothings. He tried to push inside, and I let him go ahead, just for a minute. I put down a little bowl of coconut shavings for him and watched him hungrily eat. I hoped that the coconut wouldn't attract cockroaches.

But the adorable Ma couldn't take my mind off my current concerns. Gabriel Bonner, for one: the feel of his hand and the way he looked straight at me. Damn shrink—what audacity. I'd been taught you just didn't stare at people. Who taught him manners, anyway? But. There was also the sound of his voice, touching off something primal. And the way my body wanted to turn toward his. And the way I wanted to look at him and look at him and look at him. The ping of adrenalin. The twinge in my heart when I saw him smile. Damn, I wasn't supposed to like him. I couldn't afford to like him. I was in trouble.

And two other concerns. Still in my free hand was Kitioni's copy of the trial transcript. And leaning against the door frame was a big box with my name on it. Wade must have dropped it off on his rounds, an unusual service but a helpful one because I would have found it hard to cart the box home on my bike.

I tossed the transcript onto the table, shooed Ma out, and carried the box inside. It was an early Christmas gift from my former colleagues, the crazy reporters at the *Anchor-Democrat*. This should be good. I ripped open the paper and tape.

First, a book: *Crazy Salad* by Nora Ephron. Perfect. My friends knew I'd like that. Packets of freeze-dried food, including beef stroganoff and chocolate ice cream. Freeze-dried ice cream? Could that be any good? A fragrant bundle of incense sticks for the hippie in me. And what was this? Swiss Miss powdered cocoa mix. I smiled. A letter, signed by everybody, said they hoped I was fine and wished me a Merry Christmas. I put on a kettle of water to try the hot chocolate right away.

Now there was nothing to stop me from facing the transcript. I could have started reading *Crazy Salad*, but I didn't. I could have fled to my cot for a nap, but I didn't. I could have taken a cold shower and tried to shed the fallout from Gabriel Bonner's body heat, but I didn't. I could have sat down to write in my journal, but I didn't. The transcript waited on my table, and this time I didn't turn away. I sat down, untied the string, slipped the packet out of its paper wrapping, and started to read.

There were the usual preliminaries, some of which obviously had been spoken in English: testimony by Evelyn Henry, for example, describing how she had been called to the hospital early that morning; she was told who had been killed, was led into the room, identified the body. She confirmed that Melanie Porter had been a Peace Corps volunteer for the USA.

Then testimony from Gyorgy about his movements that night with Melanie. They had gone to the Coconut Club for one last drink, but it was closed. They went to his house. They stayed an hour, and then he rode her home. Did he see anything or anyone when he left? He did not.

I moved through the testimony from Leota, Tevita's cousin, and felt my heart ache when Leota was questioned by the prosecutor about whether she was "a peeper" and a thief. I cried when Leota reported how she heard the shrieks, heard footsteps, and heard Melanie say, "Yes, please," in English.

There was testimony from Pasa, Leota's son, and Tomasi, the guy who drove the truck. Their statements were all reported flatly, the words on the page as dark and disagreeable as dead earwigs.

Then officers of the court called forward Dr. Tomasi Pelau, the Tongan Minister of Health. Because Melanie was a foreigner, an American, a Peace Corps volunteer, the police knew to get the country's top health expert, one of the thirty-three hereditary nobles and a British-trained MD, to examine her body and document her wounds.

"I saw a white girl of about twenty-five years of age lying on her back on the table. She was not aware of anything," the transcript read.

"The only signs of life from her was her attempts to breathe. She did this at thirty-seconds interval. It only lasted for about five minutes, though, and then it stopped." Kitioni's cousin should have concentrated more on grammar and less on the girls. Most of the nobles spoke beautiful English, and I didn't think Dr. Pelau would have been pleased with the awkward translation.

Dr. Pelau described the futile saline drip. He said the whites of Melanie's eyes had dried up, the eyeballs had enlarged, and the pupils did not respond to light. He attached a breathing pump for ten minutes, but it did no good, and he declared her dead.

Next he examined the body and documented her wounds.

She was one hundred sixty-eight centimeters tall and weighted about sixty-five kilograms—five feet six, 130 pounds, I quickly calculated.

He had numbered the twenty-one wounds and would describe them one by one.

Wound Number One was caused by a sharp instrument and was on the left side of the stomach, about seven centimeters above the waist. It was three centimeters in length and opened out to about one centimeter. It went into the chest through eleven rib bones. One of the fractured bones had punctured the membrane of the lung. The sharp object had also entered the left kidney and had cut the aorta. This wound, Dr. Pelau related, entered in front, then cut down, and then cut into the middle of the body.

I stopped reading, dizzy, and put the transcript into my lap. I gripped the arms of my chair until the vertigo subsided, then I continued reading. The first attack on Melanie was vicious, requiring brutal strength and rage. The doctor said Wound Number One alone was enough to kill her. But the attack hardly stopped there.

Wound Number Two also was caused by a sharp instrument and was on the neck. It cut into the muscle and sliced a large vein. The third and fourth wounds were to the right side of the face and the left jaw.

Wound Numbers Five through Eleven apparently happened as Melanie tried to defend herself. There were cuts on the backs of both wrists and both forearms, severe bruises on her arms, and a deep cut on the left thumb.

Wound Twelve was the one Mac remembered. The attacker had seemingly tried to scalp Melanie. The cut went from the front to the back of her skull on the right side. Thirteen, Fourteen, Fifteen, and Sixteen sliced open her eyebrows and punctured her mouth and cheek.

Seventeen through Twenty-one were cuts to the upper legs and knees. The attacker had continued slashing at her as she fell.

The water for tea was boiling. Dazed, I got up. I picked up one of the Swiss Miss envelopes, ripped it open, and poured the powder into a cup. The water sizzled as it landed on the powder. I picked up a spoon and stirred the mixture. And as I watched, six miniature freeze-dried marshmallows popped to the top of the cocoa and expanded. My god, how remarkable! The sweet surprise of those marshmallows! I wanted to stay there, concentrating on their trivial harmlessness and thinking about how somebody back home actually got paid to figure out how to make them, considering how my friends had dropped that packet of chocolate with its tiny marshmallows into the Christmas box without realizing how wonderful I would find them.

But the enormity of the attack dug in, sending goose bumps across my scalp. As on the day Leota first told me her story, a caul of evil descended over my mind. I could have stopped reading. But my attention was already strongly focused on the transcript. I took a breath, the cleansing breath I was taught in meditation classes. I forced my chest to open. And then I read on.

A police sergeant described finding Mort eating watermelon and holding the bloody knife. Then Gabriel Bonner was sworn in. Again I almost stopped reading at all. Did I really want to know, in black and white, how Gabriel Bonner helped get Mort Friedman off?

I did.

While making clear that he could not divulge all the specifics of their conversations, the shrink described in general terms his meetings with the accused in his jail cell and declared Friedman to be paranoid schizophrenic. After further questioning, Bonner told the court that Mort Friedman had confessed. Details that he provided confirmed the forensics evidence, which was dry, the words on the page appearing drained and gray. I tried to hear the testimony in Bonner's rich voice. Gabriel said that Mort Friedman confessed. He confessed. God. What must have the dialogue have been like in that humid jail cell, the talk between Gabriel Bonner and Mort Friedman? What must Bonner have said or done? Did Bonner touch him? Did he reach out with those beautiful hands to comfort Mort? How could he have stayed there, how could he have stood to sit still on the hard jail bench, to hear the words "I did it." I felt sickened and stunned.

Did Mort ever tell him *why* he had killed her?

I paged back to Dr. Pelau's testimony. I couldn't bear seeing those words, yet I found myself reading the paragraphs again. I sipped my cocoa, letting one spongy marshmallow after another slip down my throat. Tears started up, and I let them. I licked them away when they dripped into my mouth.

I heard night rain dinging and pinging on the tin roofs across downtown Nuku'alofa. By now I knew the way it always moved in. I knew it by sound. Now it would be at the Coconut Club. Now it would be at the Ministry of Business and Trade. Now it would be drenching the yellow brick Mormon church. Now it would be at the corner store, and now it was here, noisily pelting my own roof, making quick tide pools in the coral. I finished reading and pushed the transcript back into its paper wrapping. I pulled the strings around it and tied them tight.

I'd been so engrossed that I hadn't noticed how dim the light was becoming. I welcomed it. I pulled down the one open window so that my whole house was velvety, deep brown in all the corners. Tonight it didn't matter if I was night blind. I lit a single candle and a stick of incense: pine, not like the tropics, but like the woods back home, like Christmas in Ohio. As its fragrance wisped into the room, I stripped off my clothes and got into bed. For the first time since Tevita showed me how, I pulled down the mosquito net and tucked it tight around me to make a private nest.

In the rich, ochre candlelight I stared down at my body, the straight, healthy feet, the well-shaped legs with their down coat. I felt under my ribs—was that the kidney? I felt my neck, the coil of muscle, the reliable pulse. I touched my unscarred stomach, my good breasts, and the soft patches under each arm. I pushed one hand gently between my legs, and felt the most female parts of me. I jostled them, kneaded my fingers on them, beginning to give myself the comfort that I alone knew how to deliver. While one hand found the sweet spot, I curved a long, loving finger inside with the other, circling it around and around, until my body shuddered, and I let out a loud sigh.

No one could have heard, the way the rain kept slapping the roof. I fell asleep exhausted, certain that I, at least, was whole.

CHAPTER 15

▼

Mele Kalisimasi. *Merry Christmas.*

Christmas in Tonga was like the Fourth of July: brassy music, sweaty celebrations, done in a day. The day came and went quickly. I spent an obsessed afternoon combing the markets and meager shelves of the Nuku'alofa Burns Philp for gifts to give the family. I found perfume, cheap little bead necklaces, scarves, T-shirts, combs, socks, and kitchen utensils. I put in two packs of Pop Rocks that somebody had sent me from home. I bought a razor for Tevita. I wrapped them all in the colorful pages of magazines. I made a silly hat from newsprint, tied it with twine under my chin, and, despite the sheets of rain, delivered my basket of gifts to Filipa and Tevita's back door. The kids greeted me with squeals and cheers. "*Mele Kalisimasi*," I called out and then said it again because it was fun to say.

Tongans loved brass band music, and Christmas brought the sound of musicians strolling around the town. They played peppy Tongan folk songs and *palangi* Christmas carols, imported by generations of missionaries. I loved the scene, one of my utopias being a town with live music in the street.

But early Christmas morning, amid the rooster crows and general hubbub, I heard an ominous screech. It was Ma. I sat in my hut, the door bolted closed, in a paroxysm of rage.

The little pig was the one friend who didn't care that I was a *palangi*, I tearfully told myself, the one creature who didn't notice that I mangled my Tongan grammar, and who didn't care who came and went from my back window. He didn't know about any hijinks in Fitzhugh Grey's bathroom. He didn't know or care about any murder.

By the time the pit was opened and the dinner served, I pulled myself together, but I couldn't eat the meat. On Christmas Day, I hated Tonga.

I needed to be with *palangis*. I could have gone to the Coconut Club, which was always open, but I didn't. I knew well by then that alcohol is a depressant, and that's why I didn't want a drink. That's why, I told myself, and I went to Kalisimasi's Guest House instead. That's what I told myself. But the real reason was Gabriel Bonner.

Kalisimasi's Guest House was a lovely colonial building, built up on concrete posts to keep its civilized rooms off the damp Tongan ground. Six concrete steps, painted blue, led up to its front porch, a cool, covered portico riotous with gardenia bushes in colorful pots and bougainvillea twining up and over the roof. The porch and the steps were always scrupulously swept and scrubbed, softened with long runners of woven mats, and Kalisimasi had installed wicker rockers out there for her guests to enjoy. I climbed the beloved steps with relief. A disorderly row of *palangi* sandals and sneakers almost blocked the door. The pile of shoes that made me smile—the footwear of my Peace Corps friends.

I stepped over the shoes into the entryway. The parlor, where the notorious Risk tournaments took place, was in front, and across the hall, a dining room. I took a quick look into the parlor, where a boisterous game of Risk was underway. Kalisimasi had pulled a little potted palm tree into the parlor and had decorated it for the *palangis* with strips of sparkly cloth, a string of popcorn, some balls of aluminum foil, and gold stars cut out of Benson and Hedges boxes.

I wasn't surprised to find Sam and Gyorgy at the Risk board with Gabriel Bonner. Jeff was there, too, and Tony and Fitzhugh Grey. Guy stuff: how could they all be so addicted to a game?

"*Mele Kalisimasi, Pisikoa*," I called out. Tony muttered, "Yeah, yeah." The others ignored me. I decided to walk through the house, maybe look into my old room.

The rooms extended on either side of a narrow hallway. Bridget and Diane and I had bunked together in one of the larger ones. When I came to it, halfway down the hall, I could see that the place was a mess now—clothes, papers, and books strewn on the bed and chairs. The room smelled like pine incense, the same as my own hut had smelled recently. I spied a cone of ash collapsed on one of Kalisimasi's plates. A dozen well-used candles, fat ones and skinny, in various stages of meltdown, were lined up on the windowsill, and a large black and white yin-yang symbol was propped against the wall amid the chaos. I saw a blue Hawaiian shirt slung on a chair. Gabriel Bonner. The bastard had the whole room to himself. And he'd probably picked it so he could observe in every direction.

When I peeked into the kitchen, Kalisimasi was there, humming a Frank Sinatra song.

"*Mele Kalisimasi, Kalisimasi,*" I said with a grin. "I've been waiting months to say that."

"*Mele Kalisimasi,* Salote! I was about to take a break and have a smoke. Like to join me?"

We went out a side door and stood facing a narrow road with short date palms providing a low, pleasant overhang. Kalisimasi carried a black ashtray with "Aggie Grey's Hotel, Apia, Samoa" on the side.

"Ah, Aggie Grey's," I said, accepting a cigarette. "That was the first place I stayed in Polynesia."

"Isn't it wonderful? I understand why Peace Corps always takes the newcomers through there."

"But your place is just as good," I said. "The weeks I stayed here were some of the best in my life."

She smiled. "So, you had a rough night the other night when my cousin died, I guess."

"I couldn't figure out what I was supposed to do," I said. "I was embarrassed."

"Nobody ever died from embarrassment," Kalisimasi said. "Dignity is overrated."

"Did I do something wrong? I thought I heard you say something about me that night."

"Sometimes you *palangis* require too much maintenance," she said. "Sometimes we need to be private." It was the first time I'd ever heard a Tongan use the concept of privacy. Interesting that it had to do with leaving a *palangi* out.

"Like that infernal game in there," Kalisimasi said. "You see any Tongans at that board? We don't have a taste for it."

"What are you saying? Tongan warriors used to be all over the Pacific."

"Salote, Salote, those days are *long* gone. About the only place our mischief gets acted out now is somebody's back window."

"Filipa and Tevita killed my favorite pig for Christmas dinner," I said. "I didn't eat him. Eat it."

She put an arm around me, but didn't squeeze. "Ah, Salote, you forgot your training. You forgot and got attached."

"I don't have a taste for anything involving death these days, myself," I said. "I might give up eating meat."

"Ah, Salote, life goes on. We have to have death for life to go on. Don't forget that. And remember, there is still pleasure, even after a death."

So simple. "I want you to be my mother," I said.

"Thank you, but now I'm busy. I have to clean up this place and get to bed. Go see your friends. And be of good heart, Salote."

The Risk players didn't look up as I tiptoed in and walked around the table, watching. The board, a distorted world map, was littered with little bright-colored plastic triangles representing regiments or platoons or something.

The armchair warfare apparently had orderly rules and optimistic protocol. Each player announced when and what territory he would attack. But the exchange was not so gentlemanly. As each player took his turn, there was yelling, swearing, and a confusing movement of pieces.

"I'm taking Yakutsk from Irkutsk," Bonner announced. "I'm going to pulverize you, Gyorgy."

"Good-bye, Great Britain." Groans from Fitzhugh Grey.

"Balls to the wall, Mideast." Curses from Sam.

The dice clattering. Screaming for sixes, guaranteed success.

Not that anybody cared, but I didn't want to appear too eager to understand the game. I sat on the floor picking through a pile of tapes. Kalisimasi's guests had combined their collections for general use in the little boom box.

I turned to Jeff, who was already out of the game.

"It's so weird to see you peaceniks playing Risk."

"We can't help ourselves. Boys will be boys."

"I know. A friend of mine in California had a little boy, and she wouldn't let him play with toy guns. One day she walks into the kitchen, and he's sitting there in his high chair, saying, 'Boom, boom.' He'd made a gun out of a piece of bread, and the little bastard was pointing it at her."

"But we don't really want it," Jeff said. "War, I mean. I would have done anything to stay out of Vietnam. My eyes saved me. My blessed, ruined, scholarly eyes. I was 1-Y."

"I always thought the lottery changed everything," I said. "Broke up the unity."

Finally, the men at the table looked up.

"332," Bonner said. "I never came close. But I wouldn't have gone anyway, believe me. Before the lottery, I was ready to run to Canada."

Instead, he said, he joined the Civil Rights Movement, taking pilgrimages to the South, working on fair housing initiatives in Mississippi and Alabama. His brothers called him "the whitest of the white."

"I can see why," Sam said. "You're practically albino."

"But I'm soulful, right? Can't you see I'm not The Man?"

"No, no, no, you're The Man, all right," Sam said. "You've got The Man written all over you."

"If you'd gone to Canada, you could have stayed with me," Gyorgy said. "My ex-stepfather and I would have been happy to sponsor an underground railroad in those days. And we had lots of great booze."

Tony and Sam said they were 214 and 63, respectively. Sam came closest, but he said he'd managed to keep his education deferments fresh.

"But I'll never forget that number," he said.

"This is going to be a bloodbath," Bonner coolly announced. "I'm taking Venezuela off you, Sam." They rolled the dice. Six-four, six-one. "Get out of my way and make room for my boys."

"Hey, Charlotte, pick us some music. Something triumphant," Fitzhugh Grey called out. He was manically chewing a toothpick, and sweat oiled his upper lip. He threw his dice for God, queen, and country.

I browsed, settling on Holst's "The Planets," one of my brother's favorites. I pulled out the tape and clicked it in. A vivid memory bubbled up: my brother enthusiastically trying out his new stereo in his first apartment in Detroit. He was taking home big paychecks from what he called Generous Motors. "Sit here," he ordered, guiding me to his huge, orange easy chair. "Wait'll you hear this." He clamped giant black earphones on my head and put on "Jupiter." While I listened, he hovered, crowing, "What do you think? Isn't that *great?*" But I only saw his lips move while the majestic music pounded through my body. It was great. I could feel my own smile break wide open.

"Oh God, not *that*," Sam shouted. "Jeff's been playing that over and over every time he comes over." I quickly pulled it out.

"It makes me homesick, anyway," I said.

"For *Jupiter?*" Tony asked. They raucously laughed.

"Better than Uranus, asshole," I said.

"How about something with testosterone, something pounding?" Sam said.

"God, Sam, you're so predictable." I put on "Kiss"—didn't even notice which song. Bonner stood up to stretch while the others tried to figure out how to stop his military progress.

"Would you like some tea or coffee? Or a *niu mu'i?*" He pointed to a basket of green coconuts, and I said yes. He picked two out of the basket and called out the front door in Tongan.

"Kepu! Come open a *niu mu'i.*" Kalisimasi's little nephew darted in, smiling, proud to be asked.

By ten years old, boys in Tonga could handle the long, fierce bush knives as skillfully as a Japanese stir-fry cook wields a saikiri to chop vegetables. Kepu took the two nuts to the front porch so that the sticky juice wouldn't spill on Kalisimasi's indoor mats. I watched through the door as he expertly clunked each nut hard in a certain spot. A small cap of the shell lifted off, the piece with three dents in it that looked like a face. The boy brought the coconuts back to Bonner, who passed one to me.

"*Malo*," I said and took a swig, swallowed, wiped my mouth, and let out a long, Tongan "Ahhh…"

Bonner smiled. Suddenly he looked handsome to me. I heard my sexual Geiger counter beeping. Now I was watching every move he made.

Bonner winked at the kid. "Now I scram," Kepu said and darted away.

"I take it he learned that word from you," I said. "That's cute."

Bonner nodded. "Be flattered he tried it out on you. He's not too confident."

He took his own gulp, upending the coconut with both hands. The Risk game went on without him.

"I have something to show you," he suddenly said. "Come outside for a minute."

Dark had fallen, but from the back door of Kalisimasi's kitchen, I could make out a tripod set up on a slab of concrete. The tripod supported a telescope with a lens four inches across.

"The skies are amazing down here," Gabriel Bonner said.

"Where'd you get this?"

"Brought it with me. You need to look."

I paused on the steps, not quite ready to explain to Bonner that I was night blind.

"Back home I followed the phases of the moon on the back page of the newspaper," I said. "From being a reporter, I *know* that the full moon and bizarre behavior go together. If that puts me in league with the UFO fanatics and people who believe in JFK conspiracies, so be it."

He smiled. "Well, here you don't need any newsprint guides to the moon." He was right. Here the moon was always obvious, dangling and huge, its globe fuzzy as a ripe peach in the thick, humid nights.

I blinked into the darkness and felt my way out of the light in the building and down the concrete steps.

"I'm night blind," I told him, changing my mind, and then felt his hand, strong and warm, guiding me as if I were stepping out of a carriage. "Will I be able to see anything?"

"Try," he said.

I put one eye to the eyepiece and felt him step behind me to adjust the focus. "Can you see it now?" he asked. "Now?" His gentle arm around me felt easy and comfortable, as if he were naturally drawn to other people's bodies. Mine, I hoped.

And finally we got there, with the lens focused on the moon. I gasped. Even to my damaged eyes, the view was clear. Bonner pointed out the Sea of Tranquility and identified Tycho, the giant crater. I squinted into the eyepiece. He directed me to the Sea of Fecundity, the Sea of Cognition. I stared intensely at the crater named Copernicus.

"Now, for the *pièce de résistance*," Bonner declared. "We're doubly lucky tonight." He fiddled with the telescope, peered through, fiddled, peered again. "Look."

I saw Saturn.

"Oh, my god." I could distinctly see the rings, reddish orange, around a golden planet. I stared as long as I dared. Before I knew it, tears had welled up and blurred what I could see. "It's beautiful," I said. I pulled back and wiped my eyes with the heels of my hands. Bonner produced a handkerchief.

"I wasn't trying to make you cry," he said gently. "But I think I understand."

"Hey, Bonner, it's your turn." Sam's shout interrupted.

"Can you see your way back in?" Bonner asked. We turned toward the kitchen. The lights inside glowed softly in comparison to the moon.

"Yeah, I'm okay." But I reached for his arm anyway, holding him back just a moment. "Hey, thanks."

"My pleasure. Merry Christmas."

He disappeared back to the game, but Jeff wandered out and perched on a step. I sat down next to him, breathing in the moist air. My skin felt cool and alert where Bonner had touched me.

"My god," I said, "the moon's beautiful."

"Bonner showed you?"

I blushed. "Saturn, too."

"Beautiful sky here." We sat in silence, looking up.

I finally said, "For some reason, it makes me homesick. Are you homesick?"

"Well, I don't miss my folks yet. That's one reason I'm here, needed some distance. And remember, I was married for a year. A disaster. The worst timing, my dissertation year. And she dumped me for guess who—my dissertation advisor. It led to this whole big scandal, and I had to get a new dissertation advisor, and the whole thing was a mess. No, I don't miss that."

"I'm sorry, Jeff. I knew part of that story, but I didn't know it was your advisor. Damn."

"I miss *ease*, though," Jeff said. "I know you know what I'm talking about. I miss having a place without bugs. And of course, I miss not being reminded of death every day."

"Tevita killed my favorite pig for Christmas dinner."

"Oh, Charlotte, I'm so sorry."

"Well, life goes on. That's what Kalisimasi told me, so, now I'm wondering exactly how that's going to happen."

"I have a plan," Jeff said.

"What?"

"It goes something like this. When I get home, I'll meet the woman of my dreams. I'll take her out to a romantic, candlelit restaurant, buy us a bottle of great wine, pour us each a glass, lean over, and say, 'Dear, would you like to live down the street from me?'"

"I like that." I laughed heartily.

"You've got a great laugh," Bonner called out from the game.

CHAPTER 16

▼

Fotu e 'uluá, ngalo e tukukú. *When the big fish appears, the little fish are forgotten.*

The Royal Tonga Print Shop had mastered the fine art of engraving. His Majesty loved to give cocktail parties, garden parties, formal dinners, and receptions. And for each occasion, a little, gilt-edged card with raised golden letters was produced, delivered in a thick vellum envelope to the lucky people on the invitation list.

During the week between Christmas and New Year's, I received one of the coveted envelopes. So did all the other volunteers. New Year's Eve was the night the King welcomed foreigners—summoned us, actually. Evelyn Henry issued a communiqué on appropriate clothes and behavior: *Wear your finest, most formal clothes. Practice the special greetings for the King, but if you can't trust yourself to speak perfect Tongan, speak English. His Majesty speaks English fluently. And especially this year after what's happened, don't be boisterous. Drink moderately. We'll be on display more than ever.*

I held the card in my hand, turning it over and over. It felt like an invitation to Disneyland: an elaborate missive from a pretend king, living in his toy palace in a toy kingdom.

The invitation didn't come as a surprise. In a packet from Peace Corps I'd received before I left Ohio was a sheet describing this very night. It advised Tonga volunteers to bring something formal just for this one occasion when we would meet the King.

For someone who usually made do with peasant shirts, long flowered skirts or miniskirts, hiking boots, and skimpy halter tops, the notion of a formal gown was hard to take seriously. "A cotillion dress!" I said to my mom, and together we remembered my prom dress and the way she altered the neckline to mollify my father. That dress was still in the attic, wrapped in tissue paper, and my mother pulled it down so the two of us could have a look.

I tried it on, but I'd developed womanly curves since high school, and even tugging at it, we couldn't get it zipped.

"Oh, dang, Mom, I'm fat," I moaned.

"No, Charlotte, you're not fat," my mother said. "You're lovely."

"You're just saying that because I'm your daughter."

"No, I'm not," she said, surprising me with her assertiveness. "You're a late bloomer. It runs in the family. You're just now getting the build for having children."

"Or taking lovers." I could never resist trying to shock her.

"*Charlotte*," she said, but smiled. "What would your father think?"

"Lots of women take lovers," I said. "You should. Didn't you ever want to see what another man might be like?"

"You're talking nonsense. Your father has always been enough for me."

"Enough? What do you mean by enough?"

"He provided so well for us, Charlotte. He's such a good preacher. He has such a good way with people. And he's not bad-looking, really. Don't you think he's a handsome man, in his robes, in the pulpit?"

"He's my father, Mom. I don't really see him that way."

"Well, a lot of women think I'm very lucky to have him."

"Yeah, yeah. So does he have a good way with *you*?"

She looked at me with traces of panic and exasperation. "Charlotte, some things are between a husband and wife."

"Okay, I know, but, if you weren't happy, how would anyone know?"

"That's right, Charlotte, how would anyone know? No one's supposed to know. It's my business."

"Well, Mom, I think I know."

Her look pierced me, and I was the first to look away.

"Anyway," she said after a moment, "I'm afraid I don't have any money of my own. Otherwise I'd fly to Paris next Tuesday and woo Jean Pierre, the man of my dreams."

At last we both could smile. "It might not be too late, Mom," I said. "Jean Pierre might be waiting for you. And I bet Jean Pierre wouldn't have taken a temperance pledge in Indiana, and I bet Jean Pierre would drink sake with you," I said.

"I don't need Jean Pierre for that. I have my daughter."

"The devil you know…. Well, I'll have to buy a new dress," I said. "This one won't work."

I folded up the prom dress and tucked it back into the tissue paper. It wasn't even my mother's memory, but mine, that she was saving. After I left, she'd slip it back into its fading box, back into the dark, hot attic of her mind.

So I set out, my mother opting to stay home, as usual, to find something decent for meeting a king.

After trying on a dozen dresses in four department stores at the sprawling, upscale mall and after stopping three times to fortify myself with coffee, a greasy hotdog slathered with mustard, and two quick cigarettes from the pack I hid from my parents and never smoked at home, I found the dress I wanted. Ankle length, as the handout suggested, it had sheaths of warm ochre chiffon, a color like late afternoon sun, draped over beige satin. The top, in solid gold satin, was form-fitted to below the waist, showing off one of my best features, where it flared out dramatically. Around the neckline was an elaborate appliqué of beige lace, and the long sleeves were smooth-fitting beige lace that ended in points on the backs of my hands. The dress showed off my hourglass figure superbly.

"Oh, my god," I permitted myself to say, surveying the woman I saw in the three-way mirror. "I'm a dreamboat."

The glamorous, impractical dress had waited in its plastic bag and was carted nine thousand miles from Ohio just to be worn on New Year's Eve, 1976. Now that night had arrived.

It was to be a garden party. Hors d'oeuvres would be served, and at midnight, guests would be ushered single file into the royal residence to meet His Excellency and make a champagne toast to the New Year. Finally, there would be a formal kava ceremony.

Standing in my kitchen because it had more room than the bathroom and a counter to work on, I peered into my largest mirror—about six by ten inches—and tried to set my hair. It had grown out shaggy. My attempts to keep my bangs trimmed and straight weren't succeeding. God knows why—maybe for just this night—I had brought electric curlers and the transformer to make them work on Tonga's 220-volt current. Tevita still hadn't fixed the electrical problem, rain hadn't fallen for a day or two, and my floor and counter were dry. Just in case a curler tried to jolt me, I picked each curler off its rod as quickly as I could. Under my pink robe, I was wearing a beige slip and pantyhose that plastered down the hair on my legs. Pantyhose in the tropics—*ugh*, what was I thinking? I was already sweating. My black high heels, unworn until this night, sat at the door.

Evelyn Henry made the Peace Corps vehicles available and hired a Tongan driver to make runs back and forth to the Palace so we wouldn't have to go on our bikes. I grabbed at the offer.

Filipa and Tupou peeked in just after I'd put in the last curler, my head bristling with hot plastic and aluminum.

"Salote!" Filipa laughed. "Can you get me Radio Station A3-Zed?"

I swiveled my dome at them in mock indignation.

"Yeah, yeah, Filipa," I said. "Just remember I'm going through all this to go see *your* king in *your* country, and if I don't look nice it will be a *direct* reflection on you."

"You will look *faka'ofa'ofa*, and the King will fall in love," Filipa said.

"The Queen might have something to say about that."

"No, Salote, this is Tonga! Maybe His Majesty will creep through someone's window tonight!"

"Meaning no disrespect to His Royal Highness," I said, "there are no windows in any house in Nuku'alofa I know of big enough for His Royal Bottom to get through."

Tupou shouted, "Sa-LO-te, you are being rude!" and Filipa covered her mouth to keep from giggling.

When I reached into my little-used makeup bag, it was empty. This was the one night I wanted to put on green eye shadow, line my lids, and wear lipstick.

"Damn!" I glared at Tupou. "Did you *borrow* my makeup?"

My outburst shocked all three of us. A good Tongan never made accusations directly, especially in front of someone's mother. I had known that. I was on edge. I should have known better.

"I didn't take it! I swear!" Tupou said.

I was too hot and sweaty to argue.

Tupou stalked out. Filipa lingered uncertainly in a corner.

"Damn," I said again. I turned and looked at my face in the tiny mirror: hot, pinched, and angry.

"I'm sorry," I said to Filipa.

"It's okay," Filipa said and slinked out.

Cursing myself, I took out the curlers and put on a pair of silver earrings shaped like apples. I hadn't had them long enough for them to disappear. They had arrived late in a Christmas box from my brother, along with some fancy perfume, Chanel Number Five. I quick-sprayed some of it on myself.

Finally I put on the dress. As it slid over my body, for the first time in a long time I felt a cooling sizzle in the air: Melanie. "Things will be all right," she seemed to say, lovingly, like a sister. This would be her kind of night, and she would have known how to make the most of it. Instinctively, I looked into the highest corners of my small, dark hut. Nothing. A horn honked. I shook myself and dashed out.

There was one seat left up front for me. Gabriel Bonner was at the wheel.

"What happened to the Tongan driver?" I asked as I climbed up beside him.

"What happened to you? You're a vision," he said.

I turned and looked at all the others. I could smell the aftershave, the perfume. Bonner wore a gray linen suit and a turquoise tie on a bright white dress shirt. His shock of hair was pulled back and tied with a hank of black velvet. Jeff and Tony were there, along with Clare, Bridget, and Diane. Clare was wearing black, but a slinky cocktail dress this time, sexy as hell.

"What a bunch of goddamned beautiful *palangis*," I said, suddenly happy. "You slay me."

"Drive on, Jeeves," Clare called from the back seat. "We've got a king to meet."

There are probably a lot of words I could use to describe that night, but the one that wants to be on the page, despite my resistance, despite my fear of the cliché, is *magical*. How could I resist? The brass band, decked out in natty white uniforms, playing Cole Porter favorites under the moonlight. The amazing bowls of kingly caviar. The pile upon pile of plump, pink shrimp. The expanse of exquisitely manicured lawn and the intricate Victorian gingerbread of the palace, every cornice freshly painted. The graciousness of His Majesty himself, who took each white *palangi* hand in his soft, enormous brown hand—took it as if it were a precious commodity, and said hello and welcomed us to his Kingdom. The looming seductiveness of the deep Pacific, stretching out from that well-lighted, flawless lawn into the dark. And Gabriel Bonner.

All of us who had driven together in the white van stood in a huddle, swapping jokes and gossip. The first time a white-uniformed waiter came by with a silver tray of champagne flutes, I took one thirstily. Then the second time, and the third.

"You're drinking tonight?" Bonner said.

"I never intended to stop drinking permanently," I said. "It wasn't evangelism. Now there's a word I like, a religious word that rings like a bell. *Evangelism*."

Bonner stared. He said, "Your skin looks radiant."

"The tropics seem to agree with me—or my skin, at least," I said.

Everything paused. Sam and Bridget stared at Bonner and then at me, while Bonner and I stared at each other.

"Well, I think I'll…get some more shrimp," Bridget said. Without notice, the others drifted away, one by one.

I pulled out a cigarette and, before I looked up, he had lighted it. He lingered before he blew out the match, staring intently at me through the orange flicker. Watched me inhale. Watched me exhale.

"That gives me so much pleasure," he said.

"What?"

"Just watching you. Watching you breathe."

"Watching me breathe? Watching me...well, you will have...you'll have lots of opportunity for that...I hope...."

Then I wasn't aware of anything except his deep-set eyes, that hypnotizing smile, the way he concentrated on everything I said and did as if I were the only other person alive. His sonorous voice. I stopped averting my eyes.

I told him about losing Ma to Christmas dinner. I told him about getting instant hot chocolate from home and about the amazing freeze-dried marshmallows. I told him about the funeral, and how the deceased looked like a giant burrito.

A waiter came by with more champagne and smiled at us when we reached for fresh flutes without looking. Even Bonner took one. The band played "In the Mood." A breeze came in off the ocean, patting at the Japanese lanterns.

He told me about his life in Maine, how he spent his days driving from one mental health clinic to another, treating paranoid schizophrenics and training hospital staff. He'd been working with young adolescents, he said, the toughest heartaches, the ones whose families were just realizing the depths of the illness emerging in what were, crushingly, still kids. He told me how he'd been feeling drained and washed up, and that when the call came offering four months' work in Polynesia, he grabbed at the chance. In the jet, flying south over the equator, boarding smaller and smaller planes, flying low over atolls and the sparkling sea—the further south he got, the better he started to feel.

There was another pause.

"I told myself I wasn't going to do this," he said. "But then I caught a whiff of you. Do you know how good you smell?

"Chanel Number Five."

"Hm. No, it's something else. I don't know what. Spicy...."

I looked at him dead in the eyes. "How many moves ahead are you?"

"Would you like to play the Maine Game?" he said without blinking.

"What do you mean?"

"You know, Maine is where I'm from. It's the best part of me. I want to give you the best part of me." He waited.

"And what would that be?"

"I offer you total honesty, a cocoa butter massage, and a sunrise."

Oh, Dear Reader. Should I have turned away? Should I have trusted him? Should I have laughed? Should I have doubted?

All I can say for myself is that I wanted to play the Maine Game. Here again I'm afraid of the cliché, but what is love but one big cliché? I wanted to surrender to this man from so deep inside my body that it was an ache I'd never acknowledged, a longing I'd scarcely known was there. Yet now it leaped up like a beautiful white eagle, surged open like a giant sunflower. Wherever it was taking me was a place my whole body wanted to go.

I smiled at Gabriel Bonner. "Double sixes," I said.

I don't remember anything about the kava ceremony. Eventually Bonner got all his charges back to their various houses, and I found myself sneaking into his room, my high heels in my hand. I neatly placed them at the door like two sentries, pointed outward, while he lit a dozen candles around his thick mattress on the floor. And pulled another miracle: a bottle of red wine, a single glass, for me.

I wanted him so much that my mouth dried up with anxiety, and I had to keep swallowing and licking my lips. He sat down on a wicker chair by the bed, and I stood across from him. I took off my clothes, one steamy item at a time. Unzipped the beautiful dress and let it drop to my feet. Rolled off the hose. Peeled up the beige slip, tugging it over my head. Reached behind and unfastened the white bra. I wanted to take my time, to let him see. Left on my white bikinis. I stood in front of him while he loosened his turquoise tie, unbuttoned the bright white shirt, stood up and stepped out of his pants. And then I opened my arms.

"I can't wait to kiss you," he said. I kissed him for the first time, our lips and tongues tangling. His mustache was soft. He was delicious, like strawberries. "Are you safe?" he whispered. I explained about the Copper-7 and the little black thread, with its knot. "You can feel it if you want to be sure," I whispered back. I kissed him again and felt my body swell, flush, prepare to let him in.

"Straddle me," he commanded. I let him slip off my bikinis and pull me back into the chair. He entered me, solidly and with a sigh, and we sat that way for a long time, our chests pressed together, kissing deeply and feeling each other breathe. I felt him in my toes. My hair follicles stood up. I got goose bumps.

Later, I got my cocoa butter massage. He made me feel so good that I nearly screamed. He put his hand over my mouth. He undid his ponytail, and his hair streamed around his shoulders. His chest was surprisingly muscular and lovely. I got to know his pale belly, his fine white hairs. I nuzzled behind his ear. Kissed his eyelashes and the tops of his feet. Pressed my thumbs along his spine, feeling every bone. On the floor, he pushed into me again. I reached my legs around him and gripped, our bodies rolling and thrashing. After a few moments, exhausted, we rolled back over and almost slept, but then he reached his hand out for me again, running it across the curve of my hip.

"Come lie on me," he said, his voice so musky and gentle that my heart bucked. His eyes were liquid, dilated, and sleepy. "I need your body on mine." There was something poignant about his remark, and when I stretched myself out on his body, which was still hot and humming, I felt sad. We were covered with juices, and I wanted to warm him, to stave off a chill. I reached around the back of his neck with my hand and kissed his Adam's apple and his chin.

I was not an inexperienced woman that New Year's night. Yet because of Melanie, I was still a mess of fear and guilt. Maybe because of that—along with what was beginning to seem like my banal list of lovers, on the back of that envelope—my passion for Gabriel Bonner was about to alarm and electrify me. My body already knew this was something threatening and irresistible.

But I didn't think about any of that then. I didn't think. I just kept saying yes.

We slept and woke up again and started over. It rained, heavily. We were awake, nuzzling, when dawn light seeped through the slat blinds.

CHAPTER 17

▼

Hange ha niu afangia. *Dancing in the hurricane.*

The next day was Sunday, and although I didn't go to church, Tevita's girls came in after the service and told me all about it, chiding me for my refusal to go. I'd sneaked back home during the blessed hour when everyone was gone—I'd never been more grateful for Tongan piety. As if I'd gotten away with missing church, they brought me Sunday dinner and the weekly gossip. Today it had to do with a forty-year-old woman who was divorcing her good-for-nothing *palangi* husband to marry a twenty-seven-year-old Tongan. The girls approved and delivered a string of salacious remarks about the woman's sex life. After watching me eat, everybody fell asleep on my floor.

Between huge yawns, Tupou roused herself and offered me a gift out of nowhere. "Here, Salote," she said offhandedly, and gave me back a necklace she had borrowed again without telling me. I could hardly contain my relief. It was the gold pendant, the Scorpio symbol I'd always loved.

I put the pendant on, still warm from Tupou's body heat. Feeling it back around my own neck relaxed me, and I quickly fell into a deep sleep, just another puppy in the pile of bodies.

That was how I was when Gabriel Bonner pulled into the driveway in the Peace Corps van and tentatively knocked on the open door. Bright afternoon sunlight showed him in silhouette.

"Gabriel?" I said groggily.

Tupou, Heilala, and Inglesi woke up.

"Hi, girls," he said in English.

"Hi, Mister *Pisikoa* Man," Tupou said in smarmy, annoying English. "You want to go steady?"

"I think she's seen 'Beach Blanket Bingo' one too many times at the Hau-Hau," I said. Like rhinos in mud, the girls finally got up and squeezed through the door, mugging and giggling at him as they passed.

Gabriel had picked me up so hurriedly the night before, without really examining my house, that this was his first time to see where I lived. He sized up the lashed bamboo, the overhanging tapa ceiling, and the tiny, sparely furnished kitchen. "This house is a Peace Corps classic," he said. He picked up a sandalwood box and put it up to his nose, breathing in its spice. He delicately set it back down.

He looked at my whale vertebra, gathering dust in a corner.

"What the hell is that?"

"Piece of a baleen's spine," I said. "I saw the whale come in."

"That's a remarkable piece of furniture, Charlotte. Why'd you want a vertebra?"

"Long story. Another time," I said.

We stood three feet apart, but he was getting closer.

"Show me a corner they can't see in. I want to kiss you," he said.

"There isn't one," I said. "They see everything." He kissed me anyway. My body leaped.

"I can't do this here," I said. We kissed again, and I gently pushed him away. "But I have an idea. Do you have some time? Good. I have a delivery to make, and there's someone I'd like you to meet." I got a big box that my brother had sent me as a special request. I lifted it into the back seat of the van, and the two of us set off for Ngeleia, Melanie's village and Leota's home. On the road, we had a kind of privacy. We could touch each other, our hands slipping onto each other's thighs. I put my arm around his shoulder and reached under his ponytail to touch his sweet neck.

"Jesus, Charlotte, last night was amazing," he said.

"It was."

"I almost don't know what to say. Thank you."

"Gabriel. I love saying your name: Gabriel. Angel."

"No, hardly that, Charlotte. But I feel very emotional today. You touched me."

"I'm so glad." We fell into silence, the big van bumping along through the bush, the blue ocean appearing from time to time through rows of coconut trees and taro fields. My heart felt swollen with happiness, and if he had stopped the car any place along the way, I would have given him anything he wanted.

Leota wasn't expecting us, of course, but she welcomed me effusively. I handed her the box. "Open it!"

I somehow found my Tongan rhythm, my brain rapidly waking up, and remarkably, I could sustain the three-way conversation. Sex was apparently good for my language development.

Leota cut through the thick strapping tape and pulled out the packing. When she looked inside, she wept. The box contained art supplies, everything she needed to carry on where she had left off when Melanie died. There was a table easel just like Melanie's, tubes of acrylic paint, watercolors, multi-colored pastel chalks, all kinds of brushes, and several sketch pads.

"My brother sends this as a gift from America, with love and respect from our family," I said.

Leota wiped her eyes with a towel and asked the two of us to sit down. She called her son Pasa to get some ice from the corner store, and she served us fresh lemonade and Tongan dumplings.

I explained who Gabriel was—one of the people called in to help after the murder. She said she recognized him from the trial. He took her hand warmly and said he understood it must have been terrible to go through what she had.

Leota thanked him for his kindness. She said that she still dreamed about Melanie and about that horrible night, but that she had taken considerable comfort from the church. There was a beautiful, stone Catholic church in Ngeleia—she pointed, and we could see it from where we sat—and she went to mass there nearly every day.

"It has been hard to forgive that poor boy who did it," she said.

"You're not the only one who feels that way," I said. "A lot of the *Pisikoa* feel the same way."

"At first I wanted him to hang," she said. "I wanted to be there to see it."

"Me, too," I said. "It's hard to give up that anger. I'm still not sure I'm done with it."

"I saw her, Salote. I saw what he did to her. I heard her last words."

"I know, Leota. A terrible thing."

Gabriel took my hand and didn't interrupt. I stopped translating.

"Leota, do you believe in evil?"

"I do, Salote. I do."

"My father—he's a *fiefekau* in America, you know—he believes in evil. He spent his whole life talking about it, warning people about it. I always thought he was such a"—I stopped from respect for Leota. "It was so boring, year after year. I thought he was an old fool."

Leota smiled, and Gabriel looked at the two of us questioningly.

"I'm telling her that I used to think my dad was an old fool because he believed in evil."

"Well, he still could be an old fool, even if he's right about one or two things," Gabriel said. I loved him for saying that.

"Perhaps your father was right," Leota said in Tongan.

"Mort Friedman was sick," Gabriel said. "*That's* the evil—that such sickness is in the world. Tell her that."

I was in two conversations at once.

"My priest told me I had to forgive him," Leota said, "even if he was an evil man."

"Gabriel says he was a sick man," I translated.

"Yes, evil *is* a sickness. What else would make the pigs leap off the cliffs at Gabara, as the Holy Bible tells us?" she said.

"At least he's getting help in America," I said.

"But the evil work is already done," Leota said bleakly. "Who can bring back that sweet girl?"

"Peace Corps will make sure he gets good care," Gabriel said. "Tell her that."

"She's not too concerned about Mort," I said. "She misses Melanie."

"He won't be able to do it again," Gabriel said. "Tell her that."

"Mort won't be able to do it again," I told Leota. "Peace Corps will make sure of that."

"That's a blessing after all, then, isn't it?" she said. "Tell him that. That would be a blessing."

As we were preparing to go, something dug at me. I turned to Leota. "Do you think it would be okay if we stepped across the road to see the house?"

"No one's been keeping the house up," she said. "People think it's haunted. But go ahead."

"I want to see it," I said. I wished I'd brought some flowers, something to leave behind. On impulse, I asked to use the drawing chalks.

Leota stayed on her side of the road while Gabriel and I crossed to the other side. The house had been defaced by graffiti, and slats of plywood nailed in big exes across the blue-painted door and the windows made the house look like someone had closed off its eyes and mouth. Melanie's morning glories grew wildly, hanging in disorderly tendrils over the entrance and tangling through the plywood slats.

I stood quietly in the yard, leaning on Gabriel's shoulder. Then I walked around the house, feeling its whole presence, its dimensions. Gabriel waited at the Peace Corps van. I chose blue chalk, to match the door and the morning glories. On the wall between the doorframe and the window, about halfway up, I added my own graffiti—a foot-high peace symbol. "For Melanie," I wrote in English, "from a sister, with love."

Then I remembered my Scorpio pendant. It was a symbol of what got us both in trouble: our persistent passion. I slipped it off and hung it on a nail behind the wildest cluster of morning glories.

We were quiet on the drive back. In my mind I kept seeing visions of Melanie dancing with Gyorgy the night she died, the queen of the evening in her yellow dress. Melanie jumping into the moonlit water at Lavengatonga Beach. Then other images crowded in. Melanie taking the first savage hit. Trying to stop the blade, falling to her knees, still taking the slashes, losing energy. The moment when she knew she wouldn't get away. The moment she reached for Leota's hand, knowing she was dying thousands of miles from home. Her incredible loneliness.

I reached across the seat and took Gabriel's hand. He closed his big fingers over mine. I felt safe and not alone. I silently wept.

"I'm thinking about getting a room at the Dateline," Gabriel said the next day. "I want us to have a place where we can be alone. I need it, and you need it. I could still come and go from Kalisimasi's—could still keep my room, even. What do you think?"

Interesting now to remember: we didn't discuss our passion. We were in the middle of something big. We both knew it, no question about that. The only issue was arranging a way.

"A little Tongan love nest," I said. "Could it be on the second floor, please? So nobody'd be tempted to climb in a window?"

"I'll make sure of it."

"I know people at the Dateline, too," I said, considering. "People who would recognize me coming and going. But you're right—it's easier to come and go there, and it would be nice not to have to deal with Kalisimasi's nosy staff always watching and reporting back to Tevita and Filipa, probably."

"Okay, that's one thing settled. That feels good."

The first time I stayed with him there, the first Friday night of the year, I found the quiet of the room so narcotic that we didn't even have time for sex. I fell asleep in the middle of a sentence; when I woke up, it was broad daylight, and I didn't know where I was. I stared at the white concrete block wall, trying to make sense of it. The low hum of an air conditioner startled me.

"Boy, do you sleep soundly!" Soft voice behind my right ear, soft mustache on my neck. I remembered. I rolled over. He propped up on one arm, and I surveyed him, naked, white hair cascading across his chest. He was beautiful. I covered my mouth, afraid I had bad breath.

"No, you don't," he said. I kissed him, then flopped over on my back, trying to absorb my happiness.

"You don't know what it is to be away from the chickens and the kids," I said. "Just before I woke up, I was thinking that I was hot, but I couldn't throw off the covers because I was naked, and I didn't want the people who walked by to look in the windows and see me."

We stayed in the room all morning. He ordered up tea, toast, and strawberry jam. I took a hot shower, and we sat on the bed naked and talked, making love whenever we felt like it.

"Do you know when I first started to want you?" Gabriel asked as we lay side by side. "When you used the word 'arcane' the day I met you at the Coconut Club."

"You were eavesdropping!"

"Of course. I'm a shrink! And I wanted to make love to a woman who said 'arcane' as if it were the time of day."

"How esoteric of you," I said. "Lordy, lordy, you might be the man for me. Want to get married?"

He turned away very slightly. "Yeah," he said. "Someday."

"I didn't mean now, silly. I just met you. I'm still totting things up."

"Totting?"

"A girl has to be careful that a man has enough good qualities to make up for all the naturally bad qualities of being, well, a man," I said.

"How'm I doing so far?"

"So far, you're almost as good as a woman, but with an adorable cock." I took it in my hand, a lovely sleepy fellow at this time of the morning after doing yeoman's work. "You got my attention with the word 'abstemious,'" I said. "I love your diction."

"You're more than words," he said, running a hand over my hips.

"But I'm no bimbo," I said. "I'm no Melanie." I stiffened as soon as the words were out. "Shit," I said. "Why did I say that?"

"I don't know," he said. "Why?"

I shifted on the bed and stared at the ceiling. "I've come to *love* her, you know."

"I get that."

"She had this great spirit, this lovely earthiness. Men loved her. You know I understand that, right?"

"I do, Charlotte. Keep going."

"But, sometimes, I think that she *did* something. That she was just *too* earthy, too welcoming. Too much herself."

"Charlotte, if you're going to get hooked on the question of evil, don't let yourself forget that there is a much greater evil here."

"I'm just saying—I'm struggling now," I said. "Back in California, sex was just entertaining. I mean, it was complicated—there were always little dances about who'd be on top or how you did it—but nobody ever thought you'd die from it. Maybe I'm not making sense."

"So what? Go on."

"So the idea that Melanie got tangled in some kind of jealousy thing with Mort, somehow involving Gyorgy, who I think she really loved—and then to have it end up like that—it's just…"

I stared at the white stucco. He stroked the line of my hip.

"I'm trying to say that something isn't fair. She liked men. She loved life. She shouldn't have died, that's all. It's too much like my father said it was going to be for a woman like that."

My words came out heavy, depressing.

"I don't want to believe it," I said. "It's too much like my father said it was going to be. I'm trying to get away from all that."

"Charlotte," Gabriel said gently, "Mort was *sick*. It wasn't anything Melanie did. It wasn't her fault."

"I know."

"You know it up here," he said, touching my forehead, "but down here," touching my stomach. "You're still terrified."

"Pretty much," I said. "It eats at me."

He rubbed my belly languidly, in soft circles.

"I don't want my father to be right," I said. "But sometimes it does feel like evil is everywhere."

"Is it *here*?" he asked. I turned and looked at him, at his white halo of hair, his sweet, jowly face, his blue eyes locked on me.

"No," I said. "No, not here." I rolled into his arms.

We had something like a honeymoon, a weekend in a small, isolated resort called The Good Samaritan Inn at Kolovai, on the far west end of the island. Guests stayed in Tongan *fales*, crushed coral floors covered with beautiful mats, three out of four sides of each *fale* completely open. The bed in our *fale* was like my grandmother's. It had a huge, antique frame, an elaborately carved headboard, and crisp white sheets with lace borders and embroidery on the pillows. It seemed odd and audacious to have that bed in a Tongan hut, like bringing furniture into the back yard.

Improbably, the place had a French chef, and each night he presented elegant meals served on a bumpy table under a lean-to with a palm frond roof. He brought out an ornate candlestick, like something from Liberace's piano, and lit all six candles. The two of us and six Canadian tourists drank red wine and told jokes, and then a small band came out, and we danced barefoot in the sand until the moon went down.

The next day we ordered breakfast, ate it under the trees, and took a long walk down the beach. Gabriel presented a skinny joint, a naughty miracle.

"Where'd you get that?" I was amazed again at what he could make happen.

"Put it in the cuff of one of my shirts," he said. "In fact, several of the cuffs came here loaded."

With a pleasant buzz, we snorkeled in the lagoon. The coral off Kolovai was incredible: a forest of red, white, green, and black. Giant brain corals were anchored in a white sand bottom and sheltered dozens of rainbow-ribbed fish, darting in and out. While we drifted lazily on the surface, we were joined by a school of hundreds of small mullets. Undisturbed by our company, the fish encircled us, bobbing up and down with the current. Gabriel and I glided silently around the fish, and the fish swirled around us in response. On one side the fish were gray, but when the school flipped over, in concert, they were blue topaz, sparkling in the glittery sun shafts.

When I surfaced I was dazzled. In the protected cove, a thousand light years from Nuku'alofa's prudish scrutiny, I stripped off my suit and sunbathed topless.

I felt changed. I opened up to him, unlike any of the men on my list. I thought I might throw that list away. After him, who were they, and what did they matter? But then again, maybe they all served as preparation. My apprenticeship. For him. So that I would recognize him when he came along. So that I would know my one, true love.

We settled into a routine. Some nights I joined him at Kalisimasi's to watch the Risk games or listen to music. Occasionally I had dinner with him there, and afterward I would go out to the telescope and look at the moon or Saturn or whatever else was in the night sky.

It's not that our relationship wasn't sometimes awkward. One night when I arrived by myself at the Dateline after work, a government reception was going on in the hotel lounge, and I caught a glimpse of Evelyn Henry drinking with a couple of Australians. I did not want Evelyn Henry to know about my liaison, and I darted through the lobby before I was detected, I hoped.

Another time, a Tongan policeman, a friend of Tevita's, came up to me at the Coconut Club and said in a bullying tone, "My people are watching you, Salote. We know what happened on New Year's Eve. Just mind your step."

I was drinking with Sam, who muttered under his breath, "Tell the pig to get lost." But the cop didn't catch the comment and marched off.

Filipa's brother-in-law was the headwaiter at the Dateline, and when he greeted me enthusiastically as I was heading for the stairs one night, I blushed and assumed he knew.

Once, just as we were beginning to make love, a cleaning lady unlocked the door to our room and started to walk in.

"Do *not* come in," Gabriel yelled. "Do *not*!" The startled woman backed out instantly, mumbling apologies.

"My hero," I said as the door clicked shut.

I suspected there was talk about Gabriel and me behind our backs. Our relationship had come up in the "Be Here Now" seminars, Gabriel confessed. He said only that he'd expected it and wasn't fazed.

Two or three nights a week, I slept with him in his room. I had a heart-to-heart talk with Kalisimasi, knowing the essentials would get passed along to Tevita, who continued to feel responsible for me and my behavior, and most of all Filipa, who would be concerned about what her children saw and knew.

Kalisimasi wasn't shocked.

"I've seen a lot at the guesthouse," she said, "but it's not just that. Despite how it might appear on the surface, we Tongans are pretty tolerant about these things. Is this a good thing for you?"

"Yes," I said heartily.

"Then, *'ofa atu*," she said. "Cheers. I'm happy for you. Just be sure to observe Tongan discretion so Tevita and Filipa don't get offended."

I even managed to talk about Gabriel with Filipa. One night when I decided to stay home, Filipa ambled into my *fale* and bummed a cigarette. We sat across from each other on the floor, cross-legged, happily trying to blow smoke rings. Filipa blew beautiful rings, one after the other. I never could.

"Sex is natural," Filipa offered abruptly. I wasn't sure I'd heard her remark and said, "Say that again."

"Salote, wanting a *mafu* is natural. And if you find one, you should enjoy him."

She confided that she and Tevita had slept together before marriage. Many young people did, she said, even back then. Tevita just had to buy a little vial of pig's blood to put on the wedding sheet so that the *fiefekaus*, the preachers, and the old ladies waiting outside for the consummation were happy. She laughed. The traffic in these wedding night vials was lively even today, she said.

As Kalisimasi had predicted, Filipa liked the idea of the room at the Dateline. Better than in my hut because, inevitably, Gabriel would be seen coming and going in the Peace Corps van. Filipa preferred the discreet courtship, keeping the kids and neighbors guessing. Gradually it was dawning on me that deceptions were necessary to carve out secret space in a small and crowded culture.

"But you should sell some lime juice," Filipa reminded me. "Tevita wonders what's wrong. And he'll be happier about you and Gabriel if you do."

Damn. Everything was a tradeoff. I wished I'd never seen a lime.

Gabriel lavished me with compliments: he found me earthy and emphasized that the quality was a good and wholesome thing. He loved my earthy walk. He loved my hairy legs. He loved nuzzling the soft curls of hair under my arms. I had beautiful skin. He loved to listen to my voice. My juices tasted sweet, and my sweat smelled good. One day when we were talking, I absentmindedly pushed my bangs up off my forehead.

"Oh my god, Charlotte, do that again."

"What?"

"Push your hair off your forehead."

I did.

"That is so sexy. Your forehead is beautiful. You should let it show."

I started crying.

"What?" He rushed to my side, hugging me.

"I'm not…," I tried to say.

"You're beautiful," Gabriel told me.

"Shhh," I whispered, covering his mouth. Sometimes it was too much. I had to learn to be happy, to accept it.

I would do anything to make him laugh so that I could see his smile. I loved his sweet, round belly and his high, white forehead with its unruly wisps of hair. I loved his back and his round cheeks. I loved his stories.

"Do you know that I'm a dowser?" he said one day as we lay side by side on the Dateline bed. He was stroking my forehead, pushing back my hair, moist with lovemaking.

"You can dowse me anytime," I said.

"Seriously. I was in Putney, Vermont, for Peace Corps training. Back then they did all kinds of crazy things. They brought in some old geezer from the woods to see whether any of us had what he laconically called 'the gift.' He gave each of us a green apple bough and sent us out over this big field. Everybody was making jokes about it, pointing their forks at one another's genitals."

"Sounds like the Peace Corps I know."

"The old guy had a map of the field folded up in his pocket. We were supposed to tell him if we felt anything, if we thought we'd found water. Some people thought they did. The old guy'd walk over, chewing on a twig, and he'd take a long time to pull out his map, and then he'd shake his head and say, 'Nope.'"

"I was still laughing and wandering around, but then I got this odd sensation. My arms got tense. I felt them jerk down, almost imperceptibly."

"You're kidding."

"I'm not. I'm serious. I was fighting it the whole way! So I said to the old guy, 'There might be water here.' He came over and watched me. He opened up his map, all yellow and worn.

"He says, 'Yup. Keep goin'.' So I walked around some more, and I felt the pull three more times, and every time, he says, 'Yup.' After a few more times around the field, the old guy patted me on the back and said, 'Son, you've got the gift.'"

"Wow. How did you feel?"

"Confused. I didn't really believe it. Back then I prided myself on being jaded and rational. But this got my attention. It was like my body knew something I didn't. It was humbling. I felt chosen."

"I'm proud of you," I whispered, surprised by the way my heart suddenly clenched.

One day, after making love and nibbling on rare peanut butter and jelly sandwiches sneaked out of the Dateline kitchen, Gabriel stroked my hair off my forehead and looked at me closely. He was about to go somewhere no other man ever had.

"Charlotte, I want to ask you something."

"Shoot, babe."

"Tell me, do you like sex very much?"

"Do I like sex? I hope you'd know by now."

"But you never have an orgasm, do you?"

That was like pointing out to a guy he'd lost his hard-on. How nice it might be to crawl under the bed and hide.

"Um, no. Not usually."

"Usually?"

"Well, rarely."

"Rarely?"

"Okay, never. Well, not in the usual way."

"You mean, with another person? When you're having sex with a man?"

I nodded.

"You never fake it. I appreciate that."

"Why would I fake it?"

"But so many women do."

"I can't imagine doing that."

"I respect that about you totally, Charlotte. But, doesn't that bother you? Don't you want to?"

"Well, sure, but, well, it's too much trouble."

"Too much trouble? My sweetheart…" He took my face in his hands, gently.

"I'm not really built for it."

"What does that mean?"

"I have a high clitoris." I felt the blush come up, hot and infuriating. I'd slept with a lot of guys, damn it—I was a woman of the world who wasn't supposed to have this problem.

"A high clitoris?" We were both absurdly grinning.

"Yeah, at some women's workshop I went to once, we all looked at ourselves with mirrors, propped up on stirrups, you know, and I found out I had a high clitoris. It's too far from, well, where you go in…"

"You're embarrassed!"

"Don't make fun of me. It's hard enough that you brought it up, you bastard, and now you're trying to make me give you details!"

"Charlotte, listen to me. I'm the one who should be embarrassed. I should have figured this out by now. I want to make you happy. Keep talking. I want to know."

"So they said if I wanted to have orgasms when I was having sex, I'd probably have to go about it differently. They said it would take a lot of, um, attention."

"So why didn't you tell me?"

"I hate to call attention to it." I felt thirteen. "Besides, it was such a relief to know it wasn't something in my head—all that bullshit about the vaginal orgasm and everything, you know. I used to think I was just messed up."

"So Charlotte Thornton, the Peace Corps Jezebel…"

"Don't call me that, please, Gabe."

"I'm sorry. Charlotte Thornton, that lusty Peace Corps woman, is too shy to ask for life's rich pageant. I'll be damned."

"There were other compensations," I said primly.

"Oh, it's not about the sex, then." He cocked his head at me skeptically.

"Of course not. It's about the stories." I tried a studied ambiguity. "You're one of my best stories so far."

He smiled again, ruefully. "Thank you, I think. But, listen—you deserve to be satisfied."

"I do?"

"You do. Trust me."

Ah, yes, that was it. He kissed his way down my body. "Lie still," he whispered. "Lie still." I breathed and let him dawdle. I was on an ocean, and the waves took me out. At first I was quiet, in a boat on calm lapping seas. The kindly surf rocked me, and I let it, let the larger and larger waves carry me up and down. I stayed there, gentled by the ancient rhythm, for a long time, tasting saltwater. But then I felt my body expand and swell, and I wanted to roar. And then I *was* the ocean, creator of powerful, rolling tides. I had a shattering orgasm and the goodness of the world washed over me. I laughed out loud.

CHAPTER 18

▼

Poto hono fisifisí kae vale hono fokifokihí.
Clueless about how to roast the breadfruit but quick to eat it.

The Minister was buoyant and full of pep as he opened a fresh pack of Golds and declared the meeting of his top staff—Mr. Nalapu, Kitioni, and me—underway. After all of us but Mr. Nalapu had had our ritual cigarettes, Faina announced that he had a special project to discuss.

He said he had just returned from Vava'u, where he had met two Australians interested in solar energy. The Australians believed that Tonga was a perfect place to pursue the technology, and he himself, who had read and reread *Small is Beautiful*, was interested in environmental innovations. The three of them had spent hours talking in the parlor of the Blue Harbor Guest House. Finally, he had invited the two to Nuku'alofa, and he wanted the Ministry of Business and Trade to sponsor a conference on solar power.

"Now, we're going to need to invite the Prime Minister," Faina added. "He probably won't come, but let's make a good push to get him, anyway." The PM, the somewhat sleepy middle brother of the King, was known for his short attention span and hypothyroid vanity. But any international initiative had to have at least his nominal stamp of approval.

"These solar energy chaps have returned to Melbourne for now," Faina said, "but I told them we'd come up with dates and proposed itineraries, and would get them back here within a few weeks."

Mr. Nalapu was dispatched to begin politicking those whom Faina wanted at the meeting. Kitioni's assignment was to research sources so that a participant packet could be assembled. My job would be to help Kitioni put together the packet, write press releases for the event, and arrange the details in line with Tongan protocol.

I returned to my desk humming, happily thinking that solar power could mean hot water for everyone, not just Fitzhugh Grey. Even at the hotel, which I now knew fondly and well, the hot water supply was not reliable.

By the time Ian Redmond and Tom Beard arrived at the end of the month, the solar energy conference had been put together as tightly as a Maori drum. The environmentalists arrived two days early for individual meetings with key figures. They stayed at the Dateline, where Kitioni and I took turns picking them up and dropping them off, and I tried to keep track of which floor they were on so that Gabriel and I would not cross their path.

And, after consulting with Tevita and Filipa, I decided to have a party that weekend for some of the participants, for my Peace Corps friends, for Gabriel, for solar power, and love.

By the Friday, conference day, thirty middle- and high-level civil servants and businesspeople had signed up for the conference. Gabriel arranged for the whole Peace Corps staff to be there. Evelyn Henry gave money for refreshments, and the Peace Corps paid for copies of *Small is Beautiful* for everyone. The *Tonga Chronicle* agreed to send Sam to cover the conference. There had been no word from the Prime Minister, and while disappointed, Nalapu said it looked like the conference didn't need him—the turnout was going to be good.

Meanwhile, Tevita and I began planning our party. I felt a pleasant glow of remembered energy. At home, I liked throwing parties, and I liked the anthropology of parties. In my years in California there were always parties. I knew a lot of reporters, who loved to drink. We'd start the evening with platters of spaghetti and long, fat loaves of sourdough, and would end it awash in cheap red wine, dancing to James Brown turned up so loud that the cops would come. Most reporters I knew were lousy dancers, but they insisted on doing it anyway. Motown saved us from having to follow or lead. Given enough wine, we actually let our hips go wild. It wasn't pretty, but it was memorable.

I always hoped somebody would do something at parties that we could talk about later. Once the managing editor, a middle-aged guy in the throes of divorce, took off his jockey shorts and hurled them into a backyard bonfire. Another time, my friend Ian peeled off his clothes on a bet and streaked down Balboa Peninsula, dashing through a fancy seafood joint and hiding in a dumpster until somebody else screeched up in a VW bug with Ian's clothes in a brown paper bag. Most dramatic, in a fit of tequila-induced mass hysteria, a party of about twenty people moved in the middle of the night from an apartment barbecue in Costa Mesa to Ensenada, Mexico. After crossing the border at 3:00 AM in a noisy caravan of VW buses and beat-up Datsuns, we slept on the beach, ate lunch at Hussongs, and got home in time for the nightly news. People were always drinking too much, pairing off, beginning and ending affairs, making outrageous claims and losing stupid bets, fighting over politics and, on Monday morning, returning to their beats refreshed. Everything that happened at parties, of course, was on the record, and the people who generated the best stories were the most beloved.

It wasn't all that different in Tonga. But on the surface, social occasions demanded a formal overlay. The rituals were specific, the choreography exacting, and, compared to my past life, the ingredients exotic. Even on my Peace Corps pay, I could afford to stage a party much more lavish than I could at home.

Tevita took an interest in explaining it all. We had to hire a string band, and they had to be relatives of Filipa's, young kids who needed the money. We had to have a kava party, and I should make sure I got good stuff—from the distant island of Tofua, if possible, which grew the equivalent of Maui Wowie. I had to provide leis for everybody. I had to cook a pig, and Tevita's boys would help. There had to be too much food to give the proper impression of open-handed generosity.

Tevita warned me that we had to end the party at midnight. If we were too noisy at midnight, when the Sunday laws kicked in, the cops would come knocking, and for the sake of Tevita's reputation we couldn't have that.

I invited everybody—all the *Pisikoa* from Tonga 17, our language teacher Pulu and his brother Sione, everybody from work. I invited Kalisimasi. Nalapu seemed flustered by the invitation and begged off. Kitioni said maybe. I got up my nerve to invite the Minister, and he thanked me and said he would try, though I knew his appearance would cause a lot of bowing and scraping. The entire clerical staff buzzed about their invitations, but I predicted they wouldn't come, fearing more avocado pig food.

"I promise!" I told them. "Tevita's helping me do this *fakatonga*. We're having a pig!" They looked skeptical. I turned my attention back to the conference, hoping for the best.

The conference drew several expatriates: the American manager of the Bank of Tonga and a couple who ran a coconut button factory. It was a promising sign.

Ten minutes before blastoff, the Prime Minister threw us into chaos. His secretary called Nalapu and said he was coming after all. At the hotel where I was setting up, I got a panicky call from Nalapu, whose voice was hitting its highest registers.

I had a protocol problem to solve and not much time to do it. According to Tongan etiquette, no one's head could be higher than that of royalty. At formal occasions such as crown kava ceremonies, commoners sometimes moved around the royal personages on their knees, careful to demonstrate the proper respect. Once I saw a woman crawl toward the King on her belly. That was old-fashioned abasement, Kitioni assured me afterward, but a practice that persisted. Since I didn't want any sprained backs or belly-sliding at the solar energy conference, I had to work fast. Faina's blue-blooded head would be safely elevated on the dais with Redmond and Beard. But we would need another raised platform—at least a foot higher than the regular dais—to accommodate the PM. If it wasn't for Filipa's brother, who'd been promoted to event manager, we would never have made it work.

I sat between Gabriel and Kitioni, body heat rolling off them both. On my right, under the table, Gabriel kept sneaking his hand onto my thigh. Once he whispered, "You look so beautiful, I can't wait to get you alone."

On my left, Kitioni kept poking at my other thigh. At first I tried not to notice, but finally he poked me so hard that I jumped.

"Don't say anything, you dummy," he hissed out of a corner of his mouth. "Just take it." Under the table, he passed me a little packet wrapped in lavender tissue. "Put it in your bag for later," he said. "It'll keep you happy for hours."

Later, safely hidden in a stall in the ladies' room, I unfolded the packet, uncovering three efficiently rolled joints.

"You've got *cojones*, chump," I whispered to him when I got back. I knew he knew every word, in every language, for the male anatomy. "But thanks. Come to the party tomorrow night, and we'll try it."

"Kitioni gave me a gift," I whispered to Gabriel. "I'll tell you later."

At the end of the conference, for entertainment during dinner, I'd arranged for Jeff to come back to play ragtime. He played and played, waiting for the nobles to eat and leave so that the rest could follow. But the PM was having so much fun that he kept asking for one more song and kept forgetting to eat. The regular Tongans refused to eat while he was still there; from respect, we *palangis*, our mouths drooling at the trays of mango and shrimp, held off, too. Finally Jeff gave up and stopped playing. It was what the PM needed to be reminded to eat and, finally, to leave.

Jeff came by our table. "I thought I'd have to play all afternoon," he said, shaking out his fingers.

"I'm glad South America didn't get you. Did you ever dream you'd be playing ragtime for solar energy?" I hugged him. "Come to my party tomorrow night!"

Despite the trouble he'd caused, the PM had been transformed. He wanted to be a strong advocate for solar power, he said. He wanted information about how to do it and how much it would cost. Evelyn Henry offered to supply volunteers with solar panels. Maybe Fitzhugh Grey and his successors would not be the only ones to have hot water. Maybe anyone, including Tevita and Filipa, would have hot water one day.

Kitioni and I carted platters of uneaten food back to Business and Trade, where the rest of the staff hungrily divvied it up. I made sure Tevita took a heaping portion for Filipa and the kids. Then I ran home to work on my own party. I told Gabriel that he would have the night off.

Tevita let me use his minimoke, which, amazingly, was running that weekend, and did my errands, including dickering for a pig at the market. Early Saturday morning, I paid twenty *pa'anga*, a sixth of my monthly pay, for an anonymous pig. I tried not to think about Ma and avoided eye contact with the victim. I brought it home, live and squealing in a burlap bag, to Tevita's sons. Touliki, the oldest, proudly told me he'd do the killing. He used an ice pick, thrust quickly and cleanly into the throat. It took several seconds for the pig's shrieks to subside. I felt faint, but Touliki removed the ice pick with a flourish. For the rest of the day he wore streaks of the pig's blood on his cheeks, the sign of heroism.

Killing the pig was the worst part. The other preparation, dealing with a bushel of yams, taro, and cassava, was a comfort, piling the root crops on banana leaves to be later tucked underground in the baking pit. All afternoon, I sat cross-legged in the yard between our two houses with Filipa, Tupou, and Heilala, peeling and wrapping the vegetables in leaves, making Tongan dumplings and coconut cream.

I bought a case of Steinlager from the Coconut Club and had it delivered. I got Peni, the Minister's driver, to go on a kava hunt. Amazingly, he found me some, though not from Tofua. Filipa pulled out the family's volcanic rocks to pound the kava, and best of all, offered their huge wooden kava bowl, which had been in the family for three generations.

"This will be your time to make the kava," Filipa said.

"I'm not graceful enough," I protested. "It would be better if Tupou did it." I didn't want to press the point, but kava was supposed to be made by a virgin. Or, on major occasions, by the highest ranking woman, like Kalisimasi.

"Tupou will help, but it wouldn't be right for anyone else to do it," Filipa insisted, smiling. "It's your party."

By midday, Tevita's sons had dug the underground oven, lined it with rocks that would hold the intense heat, and filled it with bright red chunks of burning charcoal. Ceremoniously, the boys lifted in the pig—its body cavity filled with rocks and flavorful grape leaves, its body swaddled in banana leaves like a green mummy—and circled it with yams and packets of *lu*. The boys piled on more banana leaves, tamped them down, and then shoveled back the dirt. They wouldn't open the pit for six hours. The whole property smelled of tangy burning leaves and barbecuing pork.

We were ready.

Bridget and Diane showed up first. Both wore Tongan clothes, Bridget in a twirl of brown and beige that complemented her beautiful eyes, and Diane in a blue-green combination that accented her peachy skin. Each sported a fragrant lei of frangipani.

"When did you two go *fakatonga*?" I exclaimed, delighted. "You look great!"

"As much as I adore bugs, I got tired of having them crawl up my legs uninvited," Bridget said.

"I'm just trying to find a way to hide my Wisconsin fat," Diane said.

"It's not fat! You're Rubenesque!" I said. Diane struck a vampish pose. Her outfit did bring out her natural curves. She was much more lovely than she realized.

"By the way, Diane, I appreciate what you did with Noguchi to help me get a typewriter. You didn't have to go that far."

"The further I can get from Wisconsin, the better," she said.

"I know the feeling."

At about six, with the sky threatening rain again, Lizard Sam, Jeff, and Tony arrived together, doing wheelies on their bikes, wearing their most beautiful Tongan wraparound skirts, and exposing garish American boxer shorts underneath. Betty and Vic came, their guitars at the ready in case folk singing broke out.

Sam nuzzled up to me and whispered, "*Laimi*, Charlotte. This is the night to sell the *laimi*!"

"Damn," I said, "Of course! Why didn't I think of it?" The perfect night to market the moldering lime juice, piled up in bottles behind my hut. Together we went back there and filled our arms with bottles, declaring them the gift of the sun. Bridget and Diane said they wanted some, but asked me to deliver them later because it was hard carting them home by bike. We were finally making a start.

Where was Gabriel? He said he'd come.

Instead, a black taxi rolled up, bearing Fitzhugh Grey, Gyorgy, and the widow Clare. The handsome Tongan at the wheel also got out and joined the other three. He wasn't the taxi driver, but Clare's…date? But what about Gyorgy? Tonight she was back to wearing her Tongan blacks along with a bulky, tattered mourning mat, but she was smiling and bright.

"Who's this adorable man?" I asked, smiling broadly as the fellow offered Clare a Steinlager.

"My friend Matthew," Clare said formally. "He's a music teacher at the high school."

I recognized the way they looked at each other, trying not to show that they were a little hungry. Matthew bowed slightly to me and said in sober, flawless English, "It is my pleasure to meet you." His exaggerated formality, I thought, gave them away: he was trying to hide. Clare, faithfully wearing black in public and practically in menopause, was the first among us to take a Tongan lover.

I steered her into a quiet corner. "I'm sorry I don't have any Stoli for you," I said, watching her take a hearty swig of beer.

"No problem, Charlotte. It's not the thirteenth."

"How about some lime juice?"

She smiled. "Sell some to Matthew. Under the circumstances, he'll probably say yes to anything."

"So, congratulations. That man is gorgeous. But I thought maybe you and Gyorgy…?"

She smiled. "Yes, me and Gyorgy. I love that sad and needy guy. He's had so much loss. He doesn't know which he needs more, a mother or a lover, and until he knows that…that calls for a lot of tenderness. But most of all, he's not done mourning. Believe me, I know."

"But you're still wearing black yourself."

"We all find our own ways to move on," she said. "Vladimir is still with me, and I want the world to remember. But now he's cheering me on, Charlotte, playing beautiful music in the background. I hear strains of his violin almost every day."

"Clare, I want to tell you something." I realized I had never told anyone, not even Gabriel. "I sometimes hear or feel or sense…Melanie," I said. "I don't know why she picked me, but I know she's around."

"That means something, Charlotte. Gyorgy might like to know. He's had a couple of intense moments when he believes he's seen her. Maybe you should tell him. Tonga's a good place for ghosts." Clare smiled. "Vladimir likes it here. Maybe I'll never leave."

I gave her a hug and said, "How is *he*?" nodding toward her Tongan man.

"Considerate," she said with a serene smile. "Fantastic." I put a lei around her neck and watched happily as she walked back to Matthew, who was already chatting with Betty and examining Vic's guitar.

Soon a tangle of black bikes leaned against my house. The party outgrew my small digs, and we moved outside and sat on logs, waiting for the opening of the pit. The string band arrived, dressed in matching orange shirts, white flowers poked behind their left ears. They didn't want to set up in one spot and stay there all night. They were happier strolling where the music took them, they explained, mixing with the guests. I sold them each a bottle of juice.

Where was Gabriel? He said he'd be there long before dark. I kept watching the road for dust trails that we could sometimes see before a vehicle appeared on the road.

Kalisimasi drove up at the wheel of her large green Buick, one of the best cars on the island not owned by a noble, with Isita and Finau sitting regally up front and a slew of Filipa and Tevita's nieces and nephews in the back seat. Isita and Finau lived only a block away, but Kalisimasi had picked them up anyway so they could arrive in style.

A black minimoke was next, and I recognized Kitioni at the wheel. He looked stunning in tight black jeans with silver studs down the seams, high-heeled black boots, a black silk shirt, a silver pendant, and three silver rings. I detected a faint line of eye makeup around his green eyes.

But Kitioni wasn't the main event. Out of the car, like Jayne Mansfield arriving at the Oscars, stepped Liki, the island's most famous drag queen. He wore false eyelashes and lavender eye shadow. His gold lame top, cut low over his oiled chest, expanded outward to baggy sleeves gathered in at the wrists. He was wearing a lavender miniskirt and turquoise platform shoes. One huge earring, a pile of costume pearls and crystals, adorned one ear, and a gardenia was tucked behind the other. A silver bracelet glittered on his ankle. He did moves with his hips that I could only dream of.

"To the sun!" he declared, throwing his arms up, a perfect vogue.

Liz, Wade, Vic, and Betty dropped their guitar picks in the middle of the third verse of "If I Had a Hammer."

"Mama-mia," Lizard Sam said.

"Hoo-boy," Tony added.

"It's about time somebody acknowledged the reason for my party. Somebody get that gorgeous queen a drink," I called out.

Cross-dressing and homosexuality were common in the Kingdom. Liki and his compatriots found safe haven and good business by hanging around the Dateline Hotel and plying their trade on the wharf when cruise ships bearing hundreds of foreigners pulled into the harbor once a month. The Peace Corps volunteers loved the cross-dressers and invited them to every party. The cross-dressers had the best tapes and kept up with all the Hollywood gossip.

But Liki's presence set off a disagreeable stir among the Tongans. No sooner did they spot him prancing onto the property than a gaggle of little boys formed behind him in a precocious parade, making kissing sounds and imitating his walk. I hadn't been sure about Tevita. "All man," I imagined him saying of himself. Child of a whaler, son of the King's cook. Now I could see his face darken.

This called for bold action. I strode up to Kitioni and Liki and hugged them both warmly. Liki smelled like Emeraude.

Tevita cut off his conversation with Gyorgy and Fitzhugh Grey, turned toward them, and greeted Kitioni stiffly. "*Malo e laumaulie*," he said, using the special greeting for nobles. For once I was glad for Tonga's class system; even if Kitioni was a bastard, the system forced Tevita to be civil in spite of his instincts.

Filipa and her daughters and sisters giggled loudly in the shadows like naughty little girls, huddling, staring, and pointing. They annoyed me.

"The like-a-lady man is here," Filipa twittered in a sing-song voice. "Maybe your boss Kitioni likes him?" The other women twittered back. I could see Kalisimasi barreling in from across the yard to stop their chatter, but I wanted to beat her to it.

"I'm *glad* he's here," I told them. "Everybody's welcome at my party. Now who wants some lime juice?"

I went back to Kitioni and Liki. Kalisimasi joined us.

"You know Tevita's a horse's ass about these things," Kalisimasi said to Kitioni. "And my sisters, well, you know there's no stopping them."

"*We're* glad we're here," Kitioni reassured us.

"And doesn't Salote look wonderful this evening?" Kalisimasi said, giving me a warm, motherly hug. "And putting on such a *fakatonga* party—my dear, you've learned well."

"You look lovely, darling," Liki cooed at me.

I smiled. "Why do drag queens the world over call everybody 'darling,' Liki?"

"It's in our rule book, darling." He turned to Vic. "Know any show tunes, darling?"

"You betcha," Vic answered and plunged into "I Gotta Wash That Man Right Out of My Hair." Before they could be stopped, Liki, Vic, and Betty had started singing "There is Nothing Like a Dame" and followed with the inevitable "Bali Hai."

That was when the Minister himself arrived in a black government sedan, along with the solar energy experts, Redmond and Beard. Faina, in a black linen *tupenu*, white shirt, and silk tie, gracefully extricated himself from the driver's seat, the two Aussies in tow, both dressed as oddly as usual in Bermuda shorts and knee socks.

Tevita practically trampled me to get to the Minister first. While he was welcoming the PM, Faina called me over and handed me a bundle. "Some kava from Tofua," he said. "If this is going to be a real Tongan party, I'm sure we'll have some kava soon, and it should be the best."

He spotted Kalisimasi and shyly grinned. "Kalisimasi could make the kava," I quickly said, beginning to wonder something.

"No," Faina said. "You'll be the one to make it. Kalisimasi can help."

Tevita and Filipa scrambled to find a chair for the noble that would place him higher than the rest of us.

"Please, don't worry about that tonight," he said, melting my heart and shocking them both. "Tonight, let's all be friends together."

Finally, out of the corner of my eye, I saw Gabriel. He was walking, sort of shambling. He'd probably had to park down the road. He was in the same endearing drawstring pants and blue Hawaiian shirt he'd worn the first time I met him at the Coconut Club.

He found me and threw an indiscreet arm around me, then drew it back to greet Faina, who appraised us both. "Dr. Bonner," Faina said. "Minister," Gabriel said.

It took a few minutes for me to get him alone. "Where were you?"

"Trouble at home," he said. "I was at Cable and Wireless trying to get through."

"What kind of trouble?" We'd talked so little about his life. He said he wanted it that way. Be here now, he always said.

"I don't want to go into it now," he said.

"But Gabriel, if there's anything wrong I…"

"I promise, sweetheart, I'll explain everything later. I promise."

Tevita rescued us by announcing that it was time to open the pit. I never figured out how they knew the right moment, but I never ate an undone pig. Opening the pit was high drama. The boys, muscles shining with sweat, shoveled off the dirt, then lifted off the scalding layers of leaves one by one, the steam and fragrant smoke billowing in great puffs around them. Filipa and the other women stood by to pile the blackened yams and packets of *lu* into baskets and then laid them out on a grassy spot covered with mats. At last, Tevita's boys lifted out the pig. They gently placed it on a long table and peeled off its leaf coating until, with one last flourish, the golden brown carcass was unveiled, perfectly crisp on the outside, dripping clear juice. The guests cheered, with special "*malie's*" for Touliki, who still bore the blood sign.

With Gabriel at my side, I watched my friends devour the feast. I relaxed enough to eat, especially my favorites, the chewy white manioc and intricately celled breadfruit. The string band stopped and ate. Once when I looked up, Liki appeared to be flirting with Gyorgy, Tevita was discussing auto repair with Vic, and Liz and Wade were talking with Tony and Pulu about being Catholic.

"It's not too late for me to find a husband," I heard Kalisimasi assert to Clare, and I swore that Faina's ears perked up like a big St. Bernard's. "And it's not too late for you. We're just getting to the point where we really appreciate a man warming our backsides, are we not?" Kalisimasi elaborately winked at Matthew, Clare's shy escort. Kalisimasi had probably helped arrange the whole thing.

Happily full of roast pig, the band swung into an old Tongan tune, and Kalisimasi popped up and began a *ta'olunga*. The way she did it, with an almost poker face, was totally lewd and inviting. Tevita, in the flush of a few beers, was pushed up out of the crowd to leap around his sister-in-law. Faina got up with surprising agility and pressed a *pa'anga* onto Kalisimasi's formidable *ngako*, that sexy part of a woman's thigh that she bawdily showed off to huge cheers from the crowd. Filipa, Finau, and Isita shouted insults at Tevita, but the rest of the crowd screamed its approval, and I thought Kalisimasi was spectacular. I took Gabriel's hand and looked at him. He was smiling broadly, too.

"I'm so glad you're with me, here, now," I said.

"I love you," Gabriel said. First time. Everything, as they say, momentarily stopped. I drank in his blue eyes, how his whole face, focused intensely on me, grabbed my heart.

"I love you, too," I said.

Then, from the shadows, came much rustling and whispering, followed by the rattle of a biscuit-tin drum. People stopped talking, and the drum rhythm picked up. Then we saw a flickering torch, and, with a shout, a fire dancer leaped into the circle of light and announced that the dance would begin. It was Viliami.

We could have been in a cave three thousand years before, lost in a celebration of fire. We could have been celebrating a kill. We could have been mourning a death. Yes, that was it, that was the spirit of Viliami's dance—glorious, pounding, angry, full of grief. He twisted the fiery batons so close to his face that I thought he'd immolate himself. He took chances, his strong feet flying and furiously landing back on earth. He threw the balls of fire into the darkness and dared them to fight back. His chanting shouts stilled every other noise. "To the sun," he bellowed. Finally, the drum stopped, and Viliami disappeared with a rustle, back into the bush.

Just then rain came in, torrentially, and the whole crowd burst into chaos.

"We'll go to our house," Filipa shouted. The food, the mats, the beer, and the bodies somehow all got piled into Filipa and Tevita's living room.

The rain continued pelting the roof as serious darkness set in, and I officiated at my first kava ceremony, the *faikava*. Faina sat regally in the lotus position on Tevita and Filipa's best mat, across from the huge kava bowl, with Gabriel at his side: they were the two highest-ranking men. Viliami reappeared to pound the kava on the old stones at my back. At my right, Kalisimasi gave instructions on how to move my hands through the cool water in the deep, wide bowl. On my left, Kitioni prepared to call the servings. When the kava was ready, the color of swirled cappuccino, Kitioni cried, "*Kava kuoheka!*" *The kava is ready!* I enlisted Bridget and Diane, lovely in their Tongan garb, to take one coconut shell at a time from the bowl as I scooped it full for them. Then they offered each shell, with both hands around it, to a drinker. The first cup to Faina, then to Gabriel, then to Tevita, and on around the circle. "*Kava kuoheka,*" Kitioni called out again and again, a mantra, a joy. I let my arms accept their own grace, and then the heartbreaking singing began. I caught Kalisimasi's eye, and the older woman smiled, then mouthed "*Malie*, Salote."

At midnight, Tevita said, "Let's not stop, good friends. If the police come, I'll send them away."

"*I'll* send them away," Faina said genteelly. Then he emphatically downed another cup of kava.

We sang, and I swirled my hands in the cool kava, scooping out round after round for my friends. Kitioni closed his eyes as he called out each round, ecstatic. Gabriel watched me, silent, accepting every cup he was offered. One by one, people got up and quietly went home. As Liki disappeared into the car, a flock of the girls pressed around to see him off, asking where he got the Emeraude. He had won them. And he'd bought two bottles of *laimi*.

Redmond and Beard, each with a bottle of juice under his arm, declared it was the best party they'd ever been to as Faina helped them totter to his noble black car. When Faina deliberately didn't say good-bye to Kalisimasi, I knew something was up between them. I was going to treasure that tidbit.

By two o'clock, everyone was gone except Gabriel. I was exhausted and knew this was a night I needed to stay home in my Tongan home. He walked me back to the door of my hut and kissed me for the first time that night.

"What kind of trouble at home?"

"I'll tell you all about it later, I promise. Everything's okay."

"Say you love me again," I said.

"I love you," he said.

And then he left. The whole property was quiet except for a soft breeze in the mango trees. I fell into bed and slept.

CHAPTER 19

▼

Kuma si'i toe vela hono ikú.
The little mouse burns his own tail, making an already bad situation worse.

"CheezWhiz and Joan Baez."

Another lazy afternoon in the Coconut Club with sultry hours to kill. Gabriel was gone to Vava'u on Peace Corps business. Jeff was bemoaning his latest package from home.

"So where is it? I could use a shot of CheezWhiz about now to give me reason to live." I swigged my third Steinlager, idly munched the Coconut Club's peanuts, which tasted stale. "God, these nuts are awful."

"The CheezWhiz exploded," he said. "When I opened the box, there was a mess of metal shrapnel and hardened melted cheese. The tape's ruined."

"Well, get a load of this letter from home," I said. "This'll cheer you up." From my string bag, I pulled out the latest epistle from my mother and unfolded the feminine blue stationery.

June McDowell gave me a lot of Swiss chard on Saturday,
I read.

I cooked some today, also some beet tops including their tiny little beets. They need to be thinned. Dad doesn't especially like such leafy greens but he'll eat them. I like them very much, and they facilitate my elimination!

"Gripping."

"There's more."

Iris came to Cleveland bringing Vernon to the hospital for treatment following a heart attack. She took him home on Wednesday, but she slept here two nights. I enjoyed having her here. She's no sponger! She contributed foodstuffs—a half gallon of ice cream, two quarts of her vegetable soup, and Prell shampoo to fill my bottle.

"Your mom uses Prell shampoo, too?"

"Yeah, don't all these women from the Depression? They all smell the same. I wonder why they like it so much."

"Cheap?"

"Green?" We smiled and drank beer and thought about our mothers. Jeff ordered another round.

"Okay, so I can't take it any more," he said. "Tell me about Gabriel."

"Does everybody know?"

"Pretty much, love. Worst kept secret in town now."

"He is so *sensual*," I said, realizing I'd been craving a chance to tell someone.

"Is it okay to talk about this?"

"I'm thinking…I'm thinking." He leaned onto the table, his hand on his chin like a shrink himself. "Okay, yes, I really want to know. Charlotte, he's amazing in the 'Be Here Now' seminar. I'm not surprised he's got, well, charisma in bed."

"One day, for instance, Clare was…"

"Wait, Clare's going to the seminars, too?"

"Yeah, didn't you know?"

"Who'd tell me? Certainly not Gabriel. It's personal."

"Well, I hope I'm not revealing something I'm not supposed to, but, anyway, this day, Clare was trying to talk about her grief over Vladimir, and she got to a point where she wanted to say she was angry at him for abandoning her. All of a sudden she got really cold and analytical and stopped herself entirely. The rest of us clammed up and felt helpless.

"Well, Gabriel stood up and walked over to her without a word. He knelt down in front of her and put his arms on her shoulders. He looked into her eyes and said, 'Clare, let it go.' There was this pregnant pause, with him keeping his arms on her shoulders, and then she burst into tears and cried for almost ten minutes. He was completely there for her."

"Wow." I'd experienced some of the same intense attention. I tried to imagine what the moment was like.

"He told me he was the chess champion at Harvard," I said.

"Actually, yes, he's somewhat of a legend there. I'd heard of him before I met him. He supposedly won an Austin-Healey in a chess bet against the professor he hated most."

"He thinks about twenty moves ahead."

"He *is* about twenty moves ahead."

"Exciting, is it?"

"And a bit scary."

We sat in silence.

"To the intuitive bastard," Jeff raised his glass.

"To the intuitive bastard," I echoed.

"If anybody can handle him, it's you, Salote."

"To me, then," I grinned.

"To me. Oh, I mean, you."

Finally, in Gabriel's absence, I seriously tackled the lime juice. We'd sold a dozen bottles at the party, but that left roughly 388 to be dealt with, and even some of the ones I'd sold still had to be delivered.

"Tupou, get in the minimoke," I said one day when Tupou was hanging around, getting into my jewelry, covetously fingering my clothes. I had to distract her. "We're gonna sell some of this liquid gold."

Tupou reluctantly pulled herself away from my stuff. For three hours we made the rounds. We started with Peace Corps volunteers, pulling the noisy moke into every school compound, hospital apartment, and even the electrification project eight miles out of town.

I made the pitch, hoping the Peace Corps ethos would squeeze the price of fifty cents a quart out of every buyer. Tupou, wearing a huge mourning mat in observance of some death I didn't even know about, wrote out a receipt for each sale. But she'd forgotten her *kefa*, the coconut strand rope that held the mat around her waist, so she had to keep holding it on with one hand while writing out the figures with the other.

We bumped along back roads and sold bottles to Evelyn Henry, the bartender at the Dateline Hotel, and people who'd been softened up by the Sun party: Liz and Wade, Gyorgy, and Vic and Betty. At Diane's we stopped in for a quick cup of tea.

"Charlotte!" Diane seemed delighted to see me, though we'd had few real conversations over the months. Her apartment was on the second floor of a whitewashed compound, and everything appeared clean and Spartan.

"You look great," I said sincerely. The Peace Corps' most innocent volunteer looked less so—more womanly, as if she'd lost weight and been exercising.

"Thanks. I just got back from Ha'apai, and I had a wonderful time. I went to about a dozen islands, handing out filariasis pills and giving little classes. It's beautiful up there."

"Did you see the unfortunate Ned?"

"Oh, Ned, the lovely Ned. Yes. I stayed at his house, as a matter of fact, and helped him pack up to go home. He came back on the same boat I did. He just left for the States a couple of days ago. The Tongans really loved him. Too bad Evelyn Henry was such a tight-ass."

"He was lovely?" I raised a mischievous eyebrow.

"Very lovely."

"How lovely?"

"Very, very, very lovely."

"Diane, you rascal. Congratulations."

"But now he's gone, of course. I guess I'm okay with it. Or will be."

"Maybe you guys can get back together in the States."

"That's interesting to think of. Hard to imagine, really. But who knows?"

"And I never heard you use the word 'tight-ass,' Diane."

We smiled at each other.

"As a recovering tight-ass, I can spot 'em," Diane said. "Now, I understand that you, too, you naughty girl, have been having some fun down there in the city. Tell me something about it."

Tupou was tugging at my sleeve and threatening to explore Diane's dresser drawers, but I wanted to accept the invitation. "Do you have any sweet stuff from home—cupcakes like the last time, say, that Lizard Sam didn't make us all chug?"

"I do, as a matter of fact," she said. "Ever since that day, Kaseti in the Peace Corps office gives me secret little notes when I get my mom's baked goods. That way I can sneak them out of the office before anybody else sees them. It takes planning."

"That day was so weird. The day the verdict came in. I'll always remember it. I think we were all pretty tightly wound."

She pulled out a platter, and on it were frosted brownies, moist and thick.

"Tupou, want some dessert?" I knew that would keep her busy for a while, and I was right. She immediately abandoned her scavenging and sat down at Diane's kitchen table, poring over a magazine she'd found, just like her mother, oblivious to anything we'd say.

"Yes, he's something else. It's different from anything I've ever experienced."

"Be careful, though," Diane said with precocious new wisdom, "you know how it is down here. The moon comes up, and you get a whiff of sea water, and the palm trees start to dance around, and before you know it, you don't care who the guy is. You want him."

"I know, I know, but...this is different," I said. I looked at Tupou and decided she was safely in a brownie-induced trance.

"Can I tell you something really intimate?"

"The more intimate the better," Diane said. "Don't you get me yet?"

I smiled. "Okay. Here it is. He's uncircumcised."

"*Really*...!" She put down her cup of tea. "So...damn...what's that like? Do you like it?"

"I gotta tell you, Diane, it's the first time for me. It's so damned sexy. It's like a secret thing, a secret waiting to be revealed."

"That is so cool," she said. "You didn't find it ugly? Or scary?"

"Not in the least. It's like he's in a little sleeping bag, waiting to be seduced out."

"I never could figure out why we do that to boys, anyway," she said.

"I know. I think it denies them pleasure. Not to mention women. I think there's a difference."

"Hmm," she said, picking up a brownie. "Those are going fast—better get one," she said, as Tupou dug into her third.

"I'll tell you, too, Diane," I said. "It makes him more feminine, in a way—that he's got a secret on his body, like women do."

"A man with secrets. That can be fun, but also trouble."

"I mean secrets on his body, is all," I said. "He's promised me total honesty."

"Yeah, we heard that line at the King's party," she said. "And a cocoa butter massage. How was it?"

"You heard that? Dang!"

"Why do you think we all suddenly left you alone?"

"Well, it was great. Came with a sunrise, at Kalisimasi's Guest House. Right in our old room."

"I salute you," Diane said. "You're my idol."

At the mention of Kalisimasi, Tupou seemed to rouse and said she was really ready to go. While my nerve was sharp, I took us to Fitzhugh Grey's luxurious abode.

I hadn't been there since the shower disaster.

"What the hell?" Grey growled, pulling his silk bathrobe tighter around him when he answered the door.

"Want to buy some lime juice, fresh from Niuatopatapu?"

"Huh?" He took a bottle from me and peered at it as if it were a urine sample. "I heard you going on about this at your party. Not a bad party, by the way."

"I hope solar energy makes it so everybody gets hot water," I said, feeling reckless and brave. "Maybe then nobody'll ever bother you again."

"Oh, pishtosh," he said. "I've already forgiven you." He looked impatient and, behind me, I could feel the hyperactive Tupou rustling her mourning mat.

"Well, anyway, drink a glass of this a day, and you'll never catch cold," I said weakly. "Great with gin."

"You've got to be joking," he sputtered. But bought one anyway.

"Why he wear that bathrobe at 2:00 PM?" Tupou asked when we clambered back into the moke.

"Maybe he just got up," I said.

"His legs were skinny-looking," Tupou observed as we bumped back to the main road.

"That's because…he never goes out in the bush or digs up taro or…for Christ's sake, Tupou, don't ask me to explain *palangis*."

"So, does it have to be refrigerated?" Bridget asked when we got to the teachers' compound where, even though she was an entomologist, they'd put her up. Jeff and Tony were next door. I'd never considered the refrigeration question, but I just wanted to sell some more. Shameless, I quickly decided.

"Do you have a refrigerator here?" I said.

"No."

"It'll be fine," I said. "The bottling process, combined with the natural acidity of the juice, should take care of whatever might be a problem. Like vinegar," I said, pleased with myself. "Not that it tastes like vinegar."

She handed over a couple of crumpled *pa'anga* for her order of three bottles from the party. She said Jeff and Tony wanted two bottles each, and paid for those. They were out jogging, she said. She asked whether I was going to join Jeff's jogging club.

"Haven't heard about it," I said, with the tiniest wince of jealousy. "I was just drinking with him, and he didn't say a thing."

"Well, maybe he forgot. He wants to run the Honolulu Marathon next year, and he's looking for people to help him train."

"Twenty-six miles?"

"Nothing better to do," Bridget said.

Again, Tupou pulled at my arm.

"All right, Tupou. I haven't seen my friend to talk to her for weeks."

But I was already getting dragged out the door, and I had to yell good-bye from the third step down the landing.

And finally, we went to Kalisimasi's Guest House, where Tupou immediately sat down at the kitchen table and began wolfing down half a chicken as if there had been no brownies, as if free food from her aunt were the only reason to be there.

"Lime juice, Kalisimasi?"

"Is this another of Tevita's schemes?" Kalisimasi said, looking severely at Tupou. "That kid is so spoiled she's never going to find a husband."

"You didn't find a husband, and you seem to be doing fine."

"If I didn't think you were the best student in the last training, I'd throw you out," Kalisimasi said. "Tupou, that whole chicken is not for you," she snapped in Tongan. "Save some for my guests."

"Well," I persisted, "Maybe if you bought some lime juice, it would bring you luck, and a beautiful man will walk through the guesthouse door, and it'll be your husband." I carefully chose not to mention my suspicions about Faina.

"Two things," Kalisimasi said, picking up one of the bottles as if to throw it. "First, who would want a husband getting in the way around here, probably spouting a lot of useless opinions? And second, I've been through about ten of Tevita's brilliant ideas, and none of them ever works out."

"Come on, Kalisimasi, it's to help your own family, your own sister!"

"You think you're the expert in the Tongan way, do you?"

"I've been through Peace Corps training. Of course I am."

"Well, I pity you for getting trapped by Tevita. That's the only reason I'm buying two bottles."

"How about four for the price of three?"

"How about three for the price of two?"

Kalisimasi won that one. Tupou wiped her greasy fingers on her *tupenu,* and we climbed into the minimoke and sped home.

When we got back, we still had two dozen bottles left in the back seat. Tupou handed over twelve dollars, minus two for gas, to her dad.

"Don't worry, don't worry, good start," he said.

The island's thirst for *laimi,* or "that damned *laimi*" as it came to be called in expatriate circles, was slaked rather faster than the supply receded. I made up flyers at work—strictly a no-no, since this was an independent project—and posted them everywhere: in the Peace Corps office, at the Dateline Hotel, at the Coconut Club. "Be scurvy free for life!" one of them declared. "Lime Juice: Mother Nature's Perfect Food" another trumpeted. I had no basis for either claim, of course.

I made up recipes, most involving alcohol, and put them in the Peace Corps newsletter. My biggest coup was a sale of twenty quarts to the bartender at the Dateline. For a couple of weeks, every drink that featured lime juice was a house specialty, although the cook's experiment with lime soup was a bust with tourists. At the Coconut Club, Viliami offered Steinlager with a side of lime juice by the shot, cut with a little Grenadine. He thought it might appeal as a kind of masculine strut, like a strong man ordeal. But it didn't go over. When people drank Steinlager, they cast aside self-respect. That was the point.

The day after Gabriel got back, a huge Paradise Pacific cruise ship pulled into the Nuku'alofa harbor. It docked at Queen Salote Wharf, the biggest of the four along the waterfront, the only one deep enough for the big boats.

Normally I hated cruise ship days and tried to avoid the hullabaloo they caused. The main road along the waterfront would be clogged with sunburned tourists, and the last thing any volunteer wanted was to be connected with these overfed, badly dressed *palangis* who paid too much for cheap crafts and made the Tongans lose all dignity as they ran around trying to milk the Americans for every dollar they could.

But a cruise ship visit had its rewards. It could yield American cigarettes very cheap, or prized items like tampons and film. With the right connections, volunteers could sometimes sneak on board. We'd dig into our mildewed suitcases and find clothes we hadn't worn since training: Bermuda shorts, a Banlon shirt. We'd hang a camera around our neck and, most important if we could find one, plop on an oversized porkpie hat or straw boater to hide the face. Then we'd just walk brazenly on board and hope to hell no Tongan who knew us would be hanging around the wharf.

Or it could be done legally by getting an invitation from one of the passengers, for instance, somebody's mother's great aunt or somebody's high school civics teacher, somebody from the old life whom nobody really wanted to see. Sometimes the Tongan Tourist Bureau got invitations and passed them around as favors. Evelyn Henry had a proper invitation for this docking and offered it to her Peace Corps staff. Liz and Wade begged off, but Gabriel said he'd take it, and thus it happened that he and I went onboard.

At about three o'clock, dressed in American clothes I'd found abandoned in my suitcase under the bed—a red A-line jumper and a demure, white cotton blouse—I strode on board the Paradise Pacific on the arm of my man.

Wandering around the huge, immaculate halls, strolling through what seemed to be twelve or fourteen lounges, I felt unsteady on my feet. My body was brimming, oscillating with lust for Gabriel Bonner. It was all I could do to keep my hands off him. Aggravating my vertigo, everywhere I turned was another clean, well-lit room full of white strangers speaking American.

"There's so much furniture," I observed.

Gabriel laughed. I wanted him to laugh again and again.

The air conditioning seemed strange, making my skin feel dry and oddly prickly. Nobody stared at me, or at Gabriel and me. Nobody knew who we were, and nobody cared. It felt great.

"Let's go to the bar," I said.

"Which one?"

On the third deck, we found the Trusty Anchor Lounge. Its broad windows looked out over Nuku'alofa. From there, the little town looked raggedy and insignificant. All that stood out was the crisp white bric-a-brac of the Palace with its red roof and the Norfolk Island pines that framed it. We could make out a few bicyclists coursing along Vuna Road as if in slow motion, and we watched minimokes decorated with palm branches and red hibiscus flowers come and go with loads of tourists.

"Would you rather look out at the ocean?" Gabriel asked.

"Too intimidating," I answered.

Seated at a varnished wood table by the window, we surveyed our choices. The first treat was foil packets of honey-roasted peanuts, not dry, unsalted, and stale like those at the Coconut Club. I ate three packets on the spot and, feeling like Heidi, put several in my purse for later.

Gabriel ordered me an Absolut Bloody Mary, which came spicy, frosty, and garnished with dill pickles. We reached our hands across the table like newlyweds.

"I missed you when you were gone," I said.

"I missed you, too."

"I sold some lime juice. We're up to about fifty dollars. Not exactly a fortune."

"You're doing your best to help Tevita, though. I know he appreciates it."

I pulled out the pickle and nibbled off an inch or two. I sipped the drink.

"We call these *Mele Toto* when we order them at the hotel," I said. "Tongan for Bloody Mary."

"I like that. It's fun to say. *Mele Toto.*"

Then I asked what I didn't want to know. "How long do we have, anyway?"

"About three hours, unless we want to stow away to Tahiti. Which isn't such a bad idea."

I looked at him. That wasn't what I meant, and he knew it.

"March first, I'm gone," he said. "My wife's expecting a baby."

My heart lurched. I reached for a cigarette.

"Your *wife?*"

"You didn't know, then." He watched my face carefully.

"A *baby?*" I felt my insides cramp. I lit my own cigarette.

Clashing started up inside me. Cymbals, tympani. Bagpipes screeching. Accordions. The noise wasn't just in my head. My whole body was a pounding, obnoxious percussion section.

This felt bad, real bad. I remembered his three-part offer. I put them in the order I'd heard them: *total honesty*, a cocoa butter massage, and a sunrise.

I'd been had.

"That was why you were late for my party. You were talking to her at home."

"She was spotting and cramping," he said. "But her mother got her to the hospital, and it turned out all right."

"How far along is she?" This conversation felt surreal.

"Five months. Due in April. We're having it at home with a midwife. Kalisimasi's getting some relative of hers out in the bush to weave the baby a crib. Like Moses."

"So Kalisimasi knows you're married?"

"I thought everybody knew I was married."

I wished I could play the game as adroitly as the man across from me, watching the moods race across my face.

"I just want to tell you a couple of things," he said. "She's my second wife. She's twenty-two. It's her first child, my second. We have an open marriage."

"You have another child?"

"A daughter. She's six. With my first wife."

"Will your wife—your wives—know about us?" I suddenly visualized the two wives drinking tea together at a big oak table in a folksy Maine cottage, the little girl drawing a picture of a house on the floor, a house with lots of doors.

"I don't know yet." He squirmed. I watched him back.

"One of those *open* marriages." I felt my lip curl. I imagined that my face looked twisted.

"Charlotte, this is not a problem for me. What I feel for you came as a huge and wonderful surprise. I believe in being open to the world. I believe in experiencing all there is to experience. I feel that openness in you."

I stubbed out my cigarette.

"I have to go to the bathroom," I said.

"Charlotte, I—"

"Excuse me."

I kept going, and he didn't follow. I tried to walk slowly, with conscious dignity, out of the Trusty Anchor Lounge. But when I was out of his sightline, I walked faster and faster until I was almost running down a long and unfamiliar hallway, everything too clean, too bright. At an intersection with doors marked "Buoys" and "Gulls," I took Gulls. I rushed in and threw up.

In the pristine, all-American ladies room, washing my face and rinsing my mouth, I stopped just to stare—at the white expanse of porcelain, the spacious stalls, and most of all, the huge, clear mirror. I hadn't seen this much of myself for months.

Was that the person I thought I was? I moved in closer, examining the face, the straight brown hair, the mouth. I appeared to be all in one piece, though the forehead looked knotted. I didn't choose the precious hot water. I needed cold. I pulled out a long skein of paper towel from a shiny holder, wet it with cold water, and rubbed at my ribbed forehead. I turned the knob on the large brass faucet and doused my face again. Slapped it, slapped it, until the skin was red.

I finally stopped and stood up straight, facing my reflection.

So I'd had my magical night, my New Year's Eve, my Polynesian courtship. My innocence almost reclaimed. After all the men I'd bedded, this man felt like The One. I should have known.

I couldn't go back to the Trusty Anchor Lounge. I took one last look at myself in that bright mirror and walked out, down the long halls, out of the cruise ship, down the wobbly ramp, and back into the dusty Kingdom.

CHAPTER 20

▼

Kai lalo hakalo. *The bird that'll do anything for easy food.*

Sitting in a beat-up easy chair in the Peace Corps office, I opened the new letter from home. Gabriel not in evidence, to my relief; the sting still fresh, raw, and unresolved. Inside the thick airmail envelope, three onionskin pages filled with my mother's orderly, feminine script. On top of the first page, in delicate blue ink: "*Entre Nous*," something so personal she couldn't even write it in English.

One day, looking for a box of staples, she wrote, she opened a drawer in my father's desk, and found a letter, folded up, stuffed at the back. She said she shouldn't have picked it up, unfolded it, and read it, but she did. The letter was from a woman my mother knew well, a parishioner, begging for more time together with my father. Clearly, they were having an affair. Clearly, they had been having an affair for years.

Loretta D., she wrote, the period after the "D" firm and black on the page. I knew who this was: Loretta D., curvy, manicured, unlike my mother. A rich man's wife. She loved furs and girdles and carried little gold compacts filled with perfumed powder. Unlike my mother.

"*It's been going on ever since you were a child,*" my mother wrote. "*I suspected it from time to time, but until I found this letter, I had no proof.*"

The bastard.

I picked up the flimsy pages and went out to the porch overlooking the lagoon. The mangroves looked even more desperate and droopy than usual, their black stilts tangled in the dark water like veins around a heart. What makes a woman begin to doubt her man? What makes her deny the truth she knows in her heart? And then, what cracks, what tremors of the soul make her open up to truth, even knowing there will be pain? How can she give up the dream?

"I won't leave him…what can I do?" my mother wrote. *"He has asked me for forgiveness. He has said he'll give her up. I have no one to talk to but you. I want you to know because I've been unhappy and I know you notice. Now I'm beginning to understand why he was the way he was. But he's the father of my children."*

"He's sixty-nine years old," I found myself muttering. "The bastard."

Once again, the Coconut Club. I rode my bike straight there, even though it was 3 PM and I was supposed to be back at work. Viliami seemed to be off. I ordered a Steinlager from Teti, the part-timer, and sat at a table by myself, reading and rereading the letter.

Bad news from home: the bane of a volunteer's life. Sometimes people had to pick up and fly home to deal with something—family troubles, a sick brother, death. Sometimes, if there was nothing they could do, they'd plead island fever and fly off to Fiji or Samoa until they got over it. Sometimes they'd just sit in their mildewy huts, in the steamy afternoon heat, and brood. Now it was my turn.

I hadn't seen Gabriel since the cruise ship, a week ago. The bastard.

If only I were there for my mother now. We would go out to dinner somewhere, where we could say everything we had always wanted to say. I could let my mother run away and be with me, and let my father try to fix his own goddamned dinner and fold his own goddamned clothes.

The bastard.

Once, when I was about ten, relatives were visiting, and I had to sleep on a cot in my parents' bedroom. I heard them making love, almost silently, except at the end. My mother said, in a weary voice, "Are you finished?" and he said, "I don't think I'll ever be finished making love to you." Even then, I sensed a sorrowful gap between them—my mother's isolation, my father's mysterious yearning.

At ten, what did I know? Maybe that one night meant nothing to them. Maybe it was a fluke, one night out of hundreds of nights of sleeping together, one night when she was tired and he wanted her more than she wanted him. Yet I always remembered what she said, "Are you finished?" so unromantic, so businesslike, and what he said, so forthright, so vulnerable. Did she want him?

Who can understand a couple's inner life, even the man and the woman themselves?

But I didn't want to empathize with him, not yet. The bastard.

I was about thirteen, wanting to know, and got up my nerve to ask my mother about orgasms. I didn't know then there was a word for my own fingering, fumbling pleasure, my secret treat that made a cloud of fishy steam under the covers.

I thought "orgasm" was something else, something you had to have a husband for. What is it, anyway, I asked. What is it like?

My mother got up and walked into another room. She called back over her shoulder, "It's like a sneeze. It's a relief."

"A sneeze?" My fledgling sense of romance cracked.

"Well, then, it's like a game of tennis," my mother trilled. The mother who'd never played tennis in her life. "Good exercise," she said. I assumed—I *prayed*—my mother was speaking out of ignorance. Real sex was something else. *Had to be.*

Was there something about her that I needed to know? Some way that she and my father had never connected? Who taught her about sex? Him? And most of all, what role did love play between them?

Eavesdropping, I heard my parents argue about underwear. He thought she bought cheap *brassieres*, as he self-consciously called them. He wanted her to get the expensive kind, maybe like Loretta Young wore, that would make her stand out. But my mother hated shopping, especially the painful kind where you had to deal with women clerks and stare at your discouraging body under those bright lights in the three-way mirrors. To avoid it, my mother accepted hand-me-down bras from her sister, who didn't even wear the same size.

Why didn't she like herself? Why didn't he like her the way she was?

How hard it must have been for them both.

The bastard.

Only once did my mother expose her own desire. "I wish your father and I knew how to dance," she confided, before my prom. "Just once, I'd like to know what it's like to sweep across the floor in your husband's arms."

He had an advantage. Every Sunday he got to put on his black robes and stand up in front of 300 people and say whatever he wanted to say for twenty minutes. Everybody sat there and pretended, at least, to listen; the women, in their shiny Stern and Mann suits and silk blouses, their solid, shapely bosoms heaving with "amens." And my mother, in the front row; back straight, in her little lavender hat with its black net, elbows covered, high neckline, exactly who and where my father expected her to be.

The bastard.

I didn't know what to do. It would be hard to send my mother a telegram without my father knowing. They were almost always together—except, it now became clear, during those long afternoons of "pastoral visits." Damn. My mother had always been at his side.

Jeff came in just as I was ordering my second Steinlager.

"Want company?"

"You're about the only man I could stand to see now."

He got his own beer and sat down. I was suddenly aware of why I liked him: he didn't always need to talk.

"I'm not in a very good mood," I said. "I have to warn you."

He took off his glasses and rubbed his eyes. "Pleasant people are really irritating, don't you agree?"

I managed a smile.

"Man. It's humid out today. I had my kids outside performing *Romeo and Juliet,* and we finally had to pack it in. They were wilting."

"Do they like the play?"

"Teen sex and violence? What's not to like?"

I gulped the beer.

"I just found out my dad's having an affair."

"Dad the pastor?"

"That dad. My mother says it's been going on since I was a kid. I know the woman."

"Yikes." He sipped his beer. "Want some peanuts?"

I nodded absently, picked up the blue pages of the letter, looked at them again, and laid them back down on the table.

"I guess the acorn doesn't fall far from the tree," I said. "You'd think if I understood anybody, it'd be my fucking father."

"Huh," he said.

"And his wife is *pregnant,* for God's sake," I added. "Did you know?"

"We all knew, Charlotte. We thought you did, too. We thought you were just being bold."

"I'm not bold, Jeff. I was never bold. How could I not know? How did everybody else know? Where was my head? Damn it. And now I want him and I can't have him, and now he's going to fly home, and there'll be all these women and babies and midwives. And they'll all love him, and there's no room for me. Nothing's turning out right. And you guys are all jogging without me!"

That last comment just popped out of nowhere. I started crying, and it was one of those times I knew that I wasn't going to stop.

Jeff sat in silence a while and let me cry. After a minute he asked, "You want to jog with us?"

"Yes," I sniffed, blowing my nose into a damp bar napkin.

"We didn't think you'd be interested. You've been sort of occupied. But we'd love to have you. We meet three days a week at a quarter 'til six."

"Why so early?"

"Because you'd never get up in time," he chided. "Seriously, come join us."

I sniffled some more, dabbed at my eyes, and unsuccessfully fought off another wave of tears.

"It'll get better," he said. "It will."

I took his hand in mine and kissed it, my tears dripping on the soft skin, on the blue veins standing up. I loved him.

"Should I go home—back to Ohio, I mean?"

"You know what you should do? Go to Cable and Wireless and use one of those free test calls. Talk to your mother. Or talk to them both. But then I'd leave your parents alone. They have a lot of work to do on their own before they can deal with you."

Jeff sat there with me until the sobbing, the tears, the undignified snot all subsided, and then he drove me home and got me in the house before making a compassionate, quick departure.

So I decided to call home. Riding my bike along Vuna Road, I forced myself to breathe, breathe, breathe with the ticking of my wheels through the coral. None of this would be easy.

Cable and Wireless' new satellite dish loomed like a giant kava bowl at the Telephone and Telegraph Office near the downtown reef lagoon. The dish was supposed to improve long-distance phone calls, and to test the system, C&W offered free calls, one per person, for one week. I had four minutes.

"Who's there? Who's there?"

"Dad? Hello, Dad?" Of course, he'd answer the phone. My heart sank, and yet, I felt a new, small dagger of empathy.

"Well, I'll…" (scratchy static)…

"Can you hear me? It's Charlotte…"

"Well, I'll…it's Charlotte!" he called to my mother.

"I just wanted to call and say hello. And I want to talk to Mom. Can you hear me?"

"Yes, we love you!" They both always said "we love you" as if they were Siamese twins. I wished one of them would break rank, just once, and take individual responsibility.

"Can you hear?" The new line sounded perilously weak.

"Yes, yes, it's fine. What time is it there?" My father was fascinated by the time difference. He found it the most interesting news.

"It's 10:00 AM Saturday here!"

"What?"

"It's 10:00 AM Saturday. It's yesterday here!"

"What?"

"Never mind. Can I speak to Mom? Can you hear me?"

"Yes, but not like when you used to call from California!"

"Dad, are you there?"

"Yes, we love you very much."

"Can I speak to Mom?"

"It's just so good to hear your voice!" Perhaps my call had broken up a long silence between them. Perhaps my call would distract them.

"Let me talk to Mom. Dad? Are you there?"

"Yes, here's Mom."

"Mom, can you hear me?"

"Yes, Charlotte. Your voice sounds shaky!"

"Mom, I got your letter. I love you. He's a jerk, Mom. I wish I could be there to help you. Are you okay?"

"What?"

"Dad's a jerk. You should leave him. Come down to Polynesia and be with me. You must be hurting so badly, Mom. I love you…" I was babbling.

"Thank you, Charlotte. We love you, too," my mother said. A pause. She continued. "Uncle Emmett visited. He listened to your tape. We finally got a recorder that works."

Another long pause, static.

"Your father fixed the roof…"

"Good. He should fix everything, the sucker. He owes you."

"And we're getting your camera fixed!"

"Don't worry about it. No hurry!"

"I made blackberry pie for dessert."

Holy shit.

"He doesn't deserve it, Mom. He's a jerk."

"But, but…" There was another long pause. What was she feeling? What was she thinking? "I picked the berries myself," she said, her voice quavering, "at Isa's blackberry patch."

It was hard going for blackberries. The bugs would torment you in the swampy spots that the berries favored, and there'd be prickles and thorns on everything. Once my mother got poked in the eye in a blackberry thicket and had to have the butt end of a thistle painfully removed.

"It's not your fault, Mom. It's his problem. Right?" I didn't know whether any of it was getting through.

"That's fine, dear," my mother said, weakly. He must have been leaning over her, trying to hear.

"I have to go," I said. "I'm so sorry about what happened. Thank you for telling me. I love you."

"We pray for you every day."

The static sizzled up again. I couldn't tell whether we were still connected. Then I heard, as if from the Twilight Zone, a small distant gasp, a haunted cough. Was it my mother?

The operator said, "I think she's crying."

"Mom, don't cry!"

"I'm not crying!"

"I love you!"

"I love you too!"

Tears welled up. She'd heard me.

"Good-bye!"

Outside Telephone and Telegraph, a soft wind blew. I got back on my bike absently, tears drying. My face felt hot. And the first person I met along the road was Liki, Kitioni's *fakalaite* friend, the fabulous drag queen. He was in dowdy drag today, though, one of the ladies from *Mayberry RFD*. I hadn't seen him since the party.

"Hell-oooh, Salote!" he sang out, his quilted velvet handbag swinging.

"Eh, Liki, how're you doing? I just called my parents in America," I said in Tongan. I didn't want to speak in my mother tongue just then. Neither, it seemed, did he.

"Ooohh, I really like your hairstyle," Liki answered in English.

"Thanks, Liki. Sorry, I've been crying," Still in Tongan.

"Your hair is so straight You look just like Helen Reddy!" Still, stubbornly, in English.

I surrendered, finally switching to English. "Thank you, Liki. I wish I could sing like her. Maybe then I wouldn't be just a poor Peace Corps volunteer."

Liki went happily traipsing off, and I went straight to the Dateline Hotel and treated myself to a *Mele Toto*, the first of many. I decided never to drink Steinlager again: too murky. I needed something vivid and biting.

Maybe Liki came back, and maybe I bought him a couple of drinks. Maybe I told dirty jokes with a bunch of Kiwis. Maybe I told them everything, and their eyes glazed over, and they felt sorry for me. Maybe I looked around, furtively and angrily, for Gabriel. Maybe I stood up, swaggering, and cursed Gabriel and cursed my father with an empty, red-streaked *Mele Toto* glass. I didn't know whether Gabriel still had the room at the Dateline. I didn't want to know. Maybe I told the cringing Kiwis that. Maybe I shouted that I didn't want to remember what it was like, the sweet pleasure and peace of that white room.

Maybe somebody called me a taxi and helped me get my bike into the back. I don't remember getting home, but when I woke up the next morning in my own Tongan cot, I felt jolted and clear, and I wanted to see him again.

CHAPTER 21

▼

Pala 'a kahokaho. *Even the best yam is rotten.*

In the morning, I made sure the door of my *fale* was closed and latched. I filled my iron tub to the brim, pouring in boiling water from the stove to make it bearable, and shaved my legs.

I sat butt-down in the tub, reaching my legs up in the air one by one, to scrape off my pelts, and I thought.

In Southern California I had a friend who was involved with a married man. Everybody felt sorry for her and thought she was a bit stupid about the whole thing. In the first place, if Marcy wanted sex, there was plenty to go around. Southern California was a great place to be single. But Marcy had to have this guy—this particular guy—and I recall thinking, "What a dope."

Shit. Now I began to understand.

For all the times I'd chased some guy or been chased, for all the games I'd played and all the motel rooms and bedrooms and living rooms I'd fucked in, for all the times I'd licked and kissed and been licked and kissed and all the times I'd petted and massaged and eaten and drunk by candlelight and broken up and made up and broken up again, I always had one rule: no married men.

That was my ethos. One rule.

If my parents had pressed me—I sometimes fantasized this conversation, with my father especially—I could say with confidence, "You don't think so, but I do have morals. I don't mess with another woman's man."

Shit.

He had promised me total honesty. What, exactly, was the nature of that honesty? Clearly not the facts.

Maybe it was a kind of physical, or maybe chemical, honesty. His desire for me was unambiguous. His body, at least, wasn't lying.

I winced. I'd nicked my shin bone, and a fat drip of blood squeezed out. Shit. I wiped it clear and surveyed the damage. Not bad, just a little nick.

But *my* body, *my* body. That was the thing. It was my body that wanted *him*. My body arching up against him, wanting him in me totally, wanting him to touch all my flesh, wanting him to fill me up. Which he did. Again and again and again. Two into one into two, he said. An end to loneliness. At the peak moments, pure love, as overwhelming as those first orgasms he'd given me, pure love in the orgasms, pure love in the sweetness that came after, when I twined my leg over the curve of his body and pressed my breasts against his chest, and when I looked at him, tears sliding down my cheeks. I always cried. I loved how he smiled and didn't try to stop me. It meant I was happy. *We* made me happy together. He said he was happy. He said I made him happy.

To be happy with a man was a miracle. A snippet remembered, as my razor rounded the difficult backside of the knees: Ann Bradstreet's endearing seventeenth century poem from college: "If ever wife was happy in a man, compare with me, ye women, if you can." Simple, heartfelt, rare. I never thought that would happen to me. But I felt it. I hadn't been gypped by life. I was happy in a man. He was the one I wanted. That recognition was so clear, my body so sure that I yielded to him, again and again, reveling in my union, at last, with my real soul mate.

I remembered my father showing me how to pet a cat, how he explained you should pet it from head to tail, not ruffling its fur backward. Plowing his treasured "back forty," a plot of less than a quarter-acre that he planted in vegetables every year, he felt terrible when he accidentally sliced a garter snake in two. He worried about the baby snakes that he might have orphaned.

In my heart, I always believed that he didn't want to hurt anybody. I always believed he had religion, and because of that, life was plain and simple for him, not like it was for me, so full of questions and doubts, arguments and complications. He was supposed to be a man without doubt. Even in the middle of our worst fights, I presumed he was, at least, consistent. I'd always counted on that.

But he wasn't. Gabriel wasn't. Neither was I.

Hairless and smooth for the first time in months, I stepped out of the tub and poured out the gray water. Sad little flecks of suds circled counterclockwise down the drain on the concrete floor. I smoothed coconut oil over my silky legs. They weren't bad, really. I hadn't seen this much of them since Melanie died.

"Shit," I said audibly, and then "Shit" again when the white van screeched into the driveway and Gabriel got out.

"Mort Friedman left the hospital and walked away," he said.

"You're shitting me."

Gabriel had put his hair into its usual ponytail, but he didn't catch it all, and long strands of it swirled around his face. He was hunched, his shoulders tense. He looked as if he hadn't slept, his eyes dark, the skin under them sallow and slack.

"And the worst thing is, it didn't just happen. He walked away about three days after he got home, and they've been keeping it a secret ever since. I cannot believe it. The Peace Corps shrink back there, the idiot, didn't think Mort was a danger to himself or others. They ignored my recommendations. They ignored my warnings. They signed him in voluntarily. That means they couldn't keep him."

"Damn." I said. "Let me fix you a cup of tea."

"I'd rather go someplace," Gabriel said. "I need to drive. Would you come with me?" He looked at me so pleadingly, so intensely, that I said yes without blinking. We headed out of town. I let Gabriel decide where.

"How'd you find out?" I said.

"Mac Barnett, that volunteer who left last fall, tried to go to see him at the hospital in DC. They said he'd been discharged months ago. Mac was outraged, and he's been calling Peace Corps Washington and writing his Congressman ever since. He got a call through to Evelyn Henry, and that's how I found out."

"Mac Barnett? Weird. I knew him pretty well," I said, shifting in my seat. "I'm surprised he went to see Mort. He was very angry about the verdict."

"Well, that's an interesting angle," Gabriel said. "For Mac's sake, it's a good thing Mort wasn't there."

"What do you mean?"

"When he found out Mort wasn't there, he got so angry that the security guard had to be called in, and they found a weapon on him."

"A weapon? A weapon? What kind of weapon?"

"A short wooden club. From here."

"What the hell was he doing carrying a wooden club?"

"I think he wanted to kill Mort."

"Mac Barnett? He's the most easygoing guy I know. I can't imagine." I sat back in my seat, shaking my head. What was Mac Barnett doing in Washington DC, anyway? What happened to hydrology school? What had happened to Mac?

"I know exactly what it was, I bet," I said. "I bet it was a tapa pounding mallet." All the volunteers bought them. We loved the heavy ironwood, solid in the hand, instrument of the rhythmic sounds that so often woke us up.

"So what happened to Mac?"

"They tried to talk him down, and since he hadn't done anything, they let him go. They confiscated the mallet, I guess. I don't know where he is now."

"How about Mort? Where is he?"

"Somebody probably knows, but nobody at Peace Corps seems to know."

"Dammit, Gabriel. Do Melanie's parents know?"

"I don't know who knows. I'm not sure whether there's anything anybody can do."

"Somebody should tell them."

"I know. Dammit," he said.

"Oh, Lord, Gabriel, the volunteers…it's going to upset a lot of people."

"I know, I know."

"And what about Leota? The thought of Mort getting help was all she had to cling to."

"I know."

"I can't believe Mort's walking around free," I said. "The whole thing, how we felt about the whole thing, this makes it so much harder to take."

"I want you to know: I can't work for the Peace Corps anymore," he said. "I can't deal with this. I'm quitting."

We bumped along in stunned silence. Mac Barnett running around with a Tongan mallet, Mort Friedman free…and Gabriel, of course, Gabriel—it was too much to take. Tears started to spill down my face.

"That wasn't the only reason I came to get you," he said. "I want to talk."

I wiped the tears off my face with the back of my hand. I wished he couldn't see me crying. "Okay," I said.

"Let's go back out to Kolovai," he said. Ah, site of our honeymoon, where we swam with the glittering, beautiful fish. Our big bed, its legs anchored in a coral floor so sharply crunchy that we'd yelp every time we put down our feet. "This is great," he had said at the time. "To be safe, we'd better stay in bed."

I fixed my eyes on the scrappy villages along the way, watching for the "Ali is the Gretest" graffiti, preparing to warn Gabriel about pigs and dogs and kids dashing out. Mac Barnett going after Mort, Mort Friedman walking around free. Unbelievable. Gabriel married…too depressing. What could he possibly have to say?

We threaded our way down to the sea, where the bed and breakfast appeared deserted. We parked and walked along little shell-lined paths to a shady gazebo, the sea roaring beyond us.

There was a picnic table. We sat side by side on its bench facing the beach, the table edge jutting into our backs.

"I shaved my legs," I said. I opened the bottom of my *tupenu* a crack and showed him. The nick on my shin looked angry.

"Oh, Charlotte," he said. "I'm sorry." He reached down to touch me, but I wouldn't let him.

"It's just a little nick," I said, "It's not that bad."

"No, I'm sorry you shaved. I loved…" he trailed off. He paused. "I feel like a failure," he said.

"You're not a failure," I said.

"Whatever. But I want to ask to be the first to speak about *us*," he said. I wouldn't let him take my hand. He turned to face me.

"I want you to hear this. What's happened between us…I didn't…I never expected it. I didn't want to fall in love with anyone. When I got here to Tonga, I was already in love. With my wife. I've loved only two women in my life. My wife and you. That's it."

I couldn't bring my eyes up to his. I examined my cuticles, the moons on my nails, my fingertips.

"How, I ask myself again and again, how did this happen? How could I be in love with two women at once?"

My fingers curled into fists. I stood up and felt the blood rise. All my frustrated anger—at him, at Mort, at Peace Corps, all my conflicts and confusion and even my love for stupid Mac and what he tried to do—all of it exploded like a storm front inside me. Gabriel pulled back, his face pale, seeing it coming. But not in time. I hit him as hard as I could on the soft part of his chest, just below the heart.

"How could you? How *could* you?"

He doubled into himself and coughed, muttered, "Fuck." I ran, stumbled down a messy dune of sand and rocks and into the water. Put my whole body into it, wet from head to toe. Fell down and stayed there, the water crashing over me, cooling me.

He followed me. Came into the water and sat down in it with me.

"I'm sorry I didn't tell you I was married," he said.

"You bastard," I said, my face in my hands, little waves assaulting us. "You bastard."

"Charlotte, I always believed I should be open to life. That's the only way I know how to live," he said. "To be in the present, to take life as it comes. To embrace it. I wasn't prepared for this…this confusion. But now I have to own what I've done, what I feel."

"You were *the one*," I said. "I knew it."

"Charlotte, look at me." He shook off a wave and took my face in his hands. "The time wasn't right for us to be together forever, and I think you know it, too. I have to go home."

"I know," I said.

"I don't regret what happened between us," he said. "Not one second of it."

I took my time to think that one through.

"I don't either," I finally said. But I wanted the whole ocean to wash over me, to erase my rising loneliness.

"I need you to know one thing. This is the truth of me. It's the most important thing I'm going to say. I've loved you since the first time I heard your voice. I love you now. And I will always love you."

I stared at the vast Pacific. Just over the top of a rocky bluff, the surf forced huge geysers through ancient cavities in the rocks.

"But I can't have you, can I?" I said, in a bubbling whoosh between explosions. I was facing away from him, and at first I thought he couldn't hear me over the crashing surf.

"Not now," he said, and I let him hug me, the water deluging us both.

We were still soaked with water and salt spray by the time we got back into the van and headed back to town. Whose idea was it, on that melancholy, dusty ride? Mine, I think, as the truth of him and the truth of myself caked onto my skin like sea salt. We decided to take one last trip together before he went home to Maine. I didn't care that he was married. I didn't care how many other women were waiting for him. I wanted more.

CHAPTER 22

▼

Manako maka fai ki Tofua. *Craving something difficult to get.*

Word of Mort's walk to freedom and Mac Barnett's shocking visit quaked through the *Pisikoa*. Gabriel Bonner's resignation registered a powerful third tremor on the gossip Richter scale. For days nobody heard from Mac, and we drove ourselves crazy with worry. As far as we knew, Peace Corps didn't know where Mort was, either. It would have been easy for him to slip away and disappear, back in our mother country, not like little Tonga, where nobody could hide.

Lizard Sam tried to get news through press sources, tried to get the story both in and out, but met resistance at every turn. Peace Corps seemed determined to be mum. Bureaucrats promised that they were contacting Melanie's parents. But was Mort dangerous? Would he even care? Why would he go to see her parents? From what we'd heard, her father would probably kill him. And who could blame him? Or how would they protect themselves, anyway? What would they look for? A crazy guy in the bushes, with another crazy guy following him with a tapa-pounding mallet?

Mac Barnett was our hero, taking an outlaw stab at justice, making the USA safe from Mort Friedman before we got home. We loved him for what he had done. We knew he was a *mensch*, and we didn't want him getting hurt. So when the word came down, eventually, that Mac was back in Cedar Rapids, supposedly seeing a therapist and quietly re-enrolled in grad school, we all heaved a sigh of relief. There were stories we needed to know, but we suspected that Mac's particular story would take time to play out.

Gabriel's resignation earned him some respect. People said that his scorching letter, sent to the top of the chain of command, might get a couple of people in Washington fired. It didn't make Evelyn Henry look good, either. On top of everything, rumors of her affair with the regional director kept surfacing. She took another of her sojourns to Singapore.

It was a good time to leave town. My head was full of unfinished stories, and I would take them with me, add them to the one I was working on: my own story with Gabriel.

We picked Tofua, a volcanic island a hundred miles north of Nuku'alofa, the source of the kava that Faina had offered at my Sun party. Perhaps that was the connection that disposed me toward it: the sun party was a happy night, the night I made kava for the first time. The first time Gabriel said he loved me.

But Tofua also suffered under a *palangi* curse, with its dark history of an eighteenth century murder: John Norton of the *Bounty*, who'd been stoned to death by the island's natives. Nuku'alofans drank Tofuan kava whenever they could get it and had robustly strong opinions about the Tofuans. Some celebrated them as heroes, like Mac Barnett, and others feared them. Some bemoaned the way the stupid stoning by the Tofuans' great-great-great granddaddies had hurt Tonga's image all these years.

Gabriel and I didn't care. We were pushing our luck anyway. I wanted more memories. Specifically, I wanted our *bodies* to have more memories because, as Gabriel put it, it is the body that learns trust first, before the head, even before the heart. I wanted some trust. A memory of trust like a tattoo. I already hurt. But I was obsessed by my desire for him, and I wanted it to leave a mark.

Tofua had one tiny village, Hokula, and a single guesthouse. Gabriel would write his final report. He wanted to watch the stars. I would rest and read, maybe take photos for the Ministry of Business and Trade.

Tevita and Filipa offered to take us in Tevita's old Zodiac Zephyr to Faua Wharf, where the rickety vessel named the Ongoha'angana bobbed at its mooring. Filipa insisted on sitting in the back seat with Lupe and Heilala, who begged a ride. I sat in the front, wedged between Tevita and Gabriel. In the trunk was Gabriel's telescope, packed in a series of tubes and tied up in mats.

At the wharf, Filipa gave me a lunch for the trip—a pandanus basket packed with two *lu*'s, a roast chicken, a pound of crunchy white manioc, and two green coconuts. The gesture touched me, and I gave Filipa a hug—our first, after all the months I'd known her. I planted a kiss on Lupe's fat check, and the baby shyly waved good-bye. Tevita offered Gabriel a handshake as if we were leaving for a year, not a week. The Tongans respected the ocean and what it could do.

"Don't forget your Tongan mommy," Filipa called out warmly as Gabriel and I stepped aboard. When I looked back at Tevita and Filipa waving good-bye, they looked for all the world like my own parents, standing worriedly in their Ohio driveway when I'd left for college. I was surprised by the stab of homesickness for my parents as the Ongoha'angana pulled away from the dock.

The Ongoha'angana edged away from the wharf into the lagoon, flat as bathwater, and the passengers staked out spots on deck, unrolled their mats, and settled in. Five pigs, caged in boxes with wooden slats, snorted and squealed. This was the pigs' last trip. I had a pang of pity, remembering Ma.

"It's good to be getting out of Dodge," I said as I pulled out the first of Filipa's *lu*'s. "What did Evelyn Henry say when you told her you were quitting?"

"Before or after our shouting match?" Gabriel said. "She's scared of me and tired of me and glad to see me go."

"She deserves all the heat she gets."

"But it wasn't just her," he said, "I can't believe how the other people in Washington screwed up. I've always loved the Peace Corps. But I can't stand this. I can't stand what has happened."

"No news about Mort yet?"

"Nothing. My instinct is that he'll disappear and live quietly the rest of his life."

"You don't think he'll hurt anybody again?"

"I don't know. He has powerful reason not to. Powerful reason to control his impulses, if they're still there."

"Not a serial killer?"

"I didn't think so. But I'm not too confident in my own judgment these days."

"Mac's supposedly settled down," I said.

"I hope he's getting treatment," Gabe said. "Mort should be seriously thinking, wherever he is. A lot of people are going to come home and be very unhappy that he's free."

"This has made a lot of people crazy," I said.

"It could happen to anybody."

We munched Filipa's food and leaned against each other, taking in the sea air.

"Sometimes things end badly," I said.

"Yeah, like Robert Frost said, 'Dear Lord, if you'll forgive my little jokes on thee, I'll forgive thy great big joke on me.'"

"Good old curmudgeon."

"So Evelyn Henry got in a swipe or two at me. Told me she wasn't the only one who demonstrated bad judgment. Told me she'd reported our little indiscretion to Washington."

"Oh, shit, Gabriel."

"It won't hurt you, Charlotte. And it probably won't hurt me, since I already told them I'm quitting."

"I wish you'd told me. I wish I'd known. But it's our business, not theirs. Damn. It's not some tawdry thing."

"I know," he said.

The boat slipped through the reef and into the deep Tongan sea, always capricious and dramatic. The water changed from benign turquoise to somber blue-black, and in minutes we understood that the Ongoha'angana didn't handle seagoing well. It sat too high in the water. We felt every ripple. The ship didn't just pitch forward and back. It lurched crazily from left to right. We unrolled our mats and wedged the telescope, still in its own cushioning mats, between us. We were the only *palangis* on board.

"The name of this boat sounds like vomit," I said, feeling my stomach churn. "It sounds like somebody getting seasick. I bet there's a reason for that."

"Look out to sea," Gabriel instructed. "Concentrate on the horizon, and you'll be okay."

He went to the rail and stood next to three bent, corpulent old women in black, their tattered mourning mats making their bodies look even broader. Beside them, Gabriel looked upright and exotic. The wind picked up his white ponytail and whipped it out behind him. I remembered how he'd looked to me the first time I saw him in the Coconut Club and how I didn't find him handsome.

And then I changed my opinion as I grew to know his body's sweet niches. His eccentricity made him a better lover. I knew he'd learned that it wasn't the way his body looked that mattered, but what he did with it. I knew what it could do, what he could do. He loved me inventively, imaginatively. He paid attention. He was grateful. I was beginning to forgive him.

The boat bucked, and I took one last, wistful look back at Nuku'alofa. But Gabriel faced north, toward our destination.

Finally, the little ship plunged into what the Tongans called the *moana*, the mammoth, deepest sea. The vessel rolled more now, waves coming at the tipsy craft from all directions, so that we couldn't anticipate the waves and brace for them.

We forged on between the two Hunga islands, eerie, uninhabited cliffs of rock that rose reefless out of the wild sea. Hundreds of sea birds, mostly brown boobies, screamed and dived around us, then veered back to their desolate sanctuary.

One of the old ladies pointed out a row of palm trees at the peak of the western Hunga. She seemed to think that Gabriel would want to know about them, but he couldn't understand her. He hailed me. She explained they'd been planted by another *palangi*, a Danish hermit, who had lived there alone for years. I'd heard of him: Vigo. He was probably in his fifties by now. Feeling his age, we heard, he had moved to Tofua. I was hoping to meet him.

"*Peaua! Toka kovi*," the old woman muttered, now that she'd broken the ice. It meant a wavy, bad sea. Whitecaps stabbed off the top of every wave. Swells bigger than a house careened at us, and the boat rode them crazily. Between the assaults, we tried to relax.

Then the pigs started vomiting.

Something about the plight of the poor, caged animals triggered Gabriel's anxiety. He puked over the rail, desperately hanging onto it, and the old women looked on gleefully.

"Are you okay?" I lunged up to the rail, where Gabriel, green-faced, miserably wiped his mouth with a spray of salt water. I massaged his back, trying to calm him.

"Look at that *palangi* spew," one of the old women cackled.

"They're weak people, no doubt about it," another one croaked. I tried to stare them down, but they won, their raucous half-toothed grins mocking us both. Something about Tongan old ladies: they had to comment on everything, especially when *palangis* were losing their dignity.

But soon the ocean got revenge on all of them, and the Tongan crones abandoned their ridicule and crawled to the rail.

"Ha ha," I couldn't resist crowing to Gabriel, still wordless with nausea. "It's a wonder the Tongans ever made it to Fiji. Lousy sailors." But then I lost my own bearings and threw up over the rail at Gabriel's side. Mass vomiting—the great social equalizer.

The sea's violence and our nausea went on for two hours, and then the sea calmed down. We staggered to our mats and collapsed, bloated and sleepy, and snuggled into one another. The weak sun felt good.

Then somebody yelled, "Dolphins!" And we leaped back to the rail. Less than a hundred yards off the port side, a dozen lithe creatures hurtled out of the sea, their bodies' shiny curves exploding in overlapping half circles in the air. They dove back in so seamlessly that the water barely splashed. They did it again and again, playfully circling the Ongoha'angana. Gabriel and I hugged.

"I'm so glad we did this," he said, nuzzling me. "This moment is ours."

On the other side of the boat, a rich female voice started singing, "*Matangi ake, matangi hifo, o fepaki tu'u i hoku loto.*"

"Listen, listen, Gabriel," I said. "I recognize that song from training. Queen Salote wrote it herself. It means something like 'The storm comes up, the storm subsides, and everything is crashing in my heart.'"

"It's great," he said. "I like the music here." He fell asleep to it, lying in my arms.

Slowly the sun set, and a brilliant bowl of stars came up, along with a waning orange moon, pendulous and indolent. I gently woke Gabriel to see it, and as my night-blind eyes adjusted, he helped me pick out the belt of Orion and Sirius, the brightest star in the sky. We sat up and drank in gulps of fresh air.

"That sky's incredible," he said, his head intently upturned. "Can you believe people have been looking at these stars for all of human history?"

He told me that Sirius came from the Greek for "scorcher." That star played a role in the life of the ancient Egyptians, he said. "Supposedly the Nile overflowed its banks at the time of year that Sirius rose at dawn," he said. "That meant the delta would be re-fertilized, so the Egyptians looked at it as the start of the New Year."

"I love that you know this," I said. "What else do you know?"

"They even connected it with resurrection," he said. "The return of the mummified god Osiris."

I squinted into the blackness. "I'm hoping for my own rebirth," I whispered.

"You're not dead, Charlotte," he said, his arm tightening around me. "You're so alive. You're going to have a wonderful life."

"I'm missing you already," I said, my voice cracking.

"No, don't," he said. "Be here now."

The little ship's engine puttered along, laying down an insignificant wake through the black *moana*, the deepest sea, and soon even the doomed pigs were snoring. Under the vast sky, we fell asleep again with all our clothes on, Gabriel nestled at my back, his arm flung over me.

When I woke up, the engine was silent, and the ship was bobbing in darkness. I heard someone whispering roughly. Somebody bumped into me. I sat up. Gabriel was gone. "Is anybody there? Gabriel? Are you there somewhere?"

A shadow sat up a couple of bodies away. And then another.

The engine's dead, I whispered to myself. This can't be right.

I heard Gabriel before I saw him, feeling his way toward me. "Just got back from the captain's lookout. Engine trouble."

"Shit. Where are we?"

"Six hours south of Tofua."

"Do they have a radio?"

"In Tonga? What's that?"

Sharp goose bumps popped up along my arms.

"Damn, we're alone out here," I said. The ship rolled and creaked. I reached for Gabriel's hand. We heard clanking and a Tongan curse from below the deck. I felt a crazy, fearful desire. I put my arm around Gabriel and pulled his ear to my mouth.

"I don't want to die out here," I said.

"You won't," he said. "We won't." But his ear, his face, his hands were cold against mine.

The pilot came on deck and called to Gabriel. He asked him to pass out life jackets. But there weren't enough to go around. He gave them to the oldest women and the kids, and when all of the life jackets were handed out, neither of us had one. There were no lifeboats.

"You should have saved one for yourself," I said urgently. "You're a father, dammit."

"I have to do something," he said, shrugging. "I'm going to go see if there's anything I can do." He left. I waited and waited, listening to the clanking and pounding and Tongan curses. Then I heard Gabriel's voice: "Goddamned cock-sucking son of a bitch."

And then one of the old women started speaking rhythmically. Oh, my god, I muttered to myself, she's praying. As her pleas to the Almighty picked up steam, a chorus of "*Oiaue, oiaue!*" echoed along the boat's damp planks.

We waited longer, longer, the formerly majestic cap of starlight seeming to be more and more unfeeling. I invoked my own childhood prayer: "What time I am afraid, I will trust in thee." The old mantra calmed me, but I was glad that the inky night kept the others from seeing my lips move. "What time I am afraid, I will trust in thee, what time I am afraid, I will…"

And then my anxiety ran out of steam, and when the engine still wouldn't start, I just sat there.

The boat tossed silently in the sea for two hours while Gabriel and the Tongan sailors toiled below deck. Finally, with a shudder, the engine sputtered out a series of sharp clacks, and then another one, and then a series of sputters until the sounds merged into one loud, ratcheting hum. The passengers cheered, but then I held my breath. Slowly, ploddingly, the ship moved. I smelled fuel and welcomed the burst of fumes into my lungs.

When Gabriel came back up, appearing as a silhouette behind a flickering flashlight, his voice was shaky.

"What was wrong?"

"I have no idea," he said. "I don't know a damn thing about boats. They wanted me down there just because I'm the only white man on board. But I couldn't help them. Some kid from Vava'u finally figured it out."

I don't think any passenger slept for a minute the rest of the night. It was midday by the time the unreliable, unsteady Ongoha'angana plowed into the channel between Kao, the grand cone volcano, and Tofua, our flat-topped destination. A sulphur vent on the west tip of the crater sent up a spooky, intermittent column of steam, like cryptic smoke signals. We were the only passengers to disembark, as the rest were going further north to Vava'u.

This was the channel where Fletcher Christian tossed Captain Bligh off the Bounty in 1789, along with his eighteen loyal crewmen. It was the channel where John Norton died, stoned by the fearful Tofuans. As our boat neared the rocky shore and a few men came into view, scrambling down to meet us, I felt a shiver of foreboding.

Our host, Filimone, was an unsmiling, bony man with a startling gold front tooth and white hair shaved almost down to his skull. He led us from the landing to our accommodations. We trudged up a steep, worn path, Gabriel struggling with the bulky telescope. In Nuku'alofa, I thought, there'd be a kid offering to carry it for a couple of seniti. Nobody here offered. In fact, there seemed to be nobody to offer. Even the men who'd met us at the landing had disappeared.

In the noon stillness, the sun boiled. Blue skinks skittered across our path. Sweat dripped down my back. Finally we pushed through a dense fan of foliage and into town.

Ten oval houses with thatched roofs and lashed bamboo walls were arranged on either side of a packed dirt street. Two skinny dogs approached, heads down, and sniffed us. An old woman, the only person in sight, paused to stare, gripping her stiff coconut spine broom.

Besides the little clutch of fales were a Church of Tonga and the guesthouse. The guesthouse had been built on a concrete block foundation several feet above the ground, and in contrast to the low-slung fales, its dimensions suggested a shrine. Or maybe a pyre.

I was prepared to tell Filimone that we were married, but the question never came up. He seemed singularly incurious. Our room was empty except for the usual mats layered on the floor like a pile of tortillas and a high wooden bed with a foot-thick kapok mattress. An incongruous, dainty step stool waited by the bed, its cushioned top needle pointed "Ofa mo e melino," love and peace. The essentials. No door, only a flimsy, flowered cotton curtain. Unscreened windows on three side of the room offered unobstructed views inside at the eye level of an average man. Out one window we could see the shower shed and toilet, and out another, the central meetinghouse, open on all sides.

"We'll have a *faikava* for you tonight," Filimone announced mournfully. "It's been a long time since having *palangis* on Tofua. Except Vigo, who never comes to see us. The best kava in Tonga, Tofua kava."

We put down our gear. Filimone stood in the room, silently watching us. "Ten *pa'anga*," he said. "Forty for the whole time."

Gabriel fished into his pocket and produced the money, damp with Ongoha'angana saltwater. Filimone took it and slunk away without another word.

"Friendly sort," Gabriel said as we stared at each other. "What I really like about him is his *joi de vivre*." We started to giggle.

"We'll have a *faikava* for you tonight, for your *funeral*," I said.

"Ten *pa'anga*, forty for the whole *fabulous* time you're going to have at our luxury resort," Gabriel said.

I hadn't laughed for a long time. We fell onto the tall bed and sank into the kapok so deep that we were in separate, sweaty valleys.

"It's too hot to touch you," Gabriel said. "But I still love you."

"I love you, too." Automatically, without thought. We fell asleep, not hearing the footsteps under our windows, not seeing the eyes. We roused to Filimone's call. The feast in our honor was ready.

I wrestled myself into my black-and-white Tongan outfit, the tunic crazily wrinkled from the trip, and Gabriel put on khaki shorts and a red Hawaiian shirt. His white hair stood out dramatically. I risked kissing him in our steamy half-privacy. "You look like the Prophet Isaiah," I said. "A prophet in Bermuda shorts. On you, a good look." I smoothed down his collar, the way a wife might. He caught me and smiled. "That's nice," he said. My hand dropped away, and I fought off a stab of sadness.

"After the *faikava* I'm going to set up the telescope," he added with forced heartiness. "It'll be beautiful, you'll see. These skies will be totally dark."

A feast like every other. Mountainous piles of *lu* and lobster. A suckling pig, gold-encrusted and shiny in its skin, at Gabriel's place. Platters of gray taro, white manioc, yellow cassava. Packets of sweet Tongan dumplings. Sticky orange drink to wash it all down. Cigarettes tied with ribbons on the ends of bamboo sticks, gathered into bouquets for later. The excess made me a little sick.

As we took our first bites, an old man appeared carrying a live baby pig with a horrid deformity: a huge bulb above its nose. The Tofuans screamed with laughter. The man put the pig down on the ground, and four skinny dogs darted at it.

For one awful moment I thought that was it—they would all sit there and watch the poor animal be torn to bits.

"Stop it," Gabriel said in English. "Stop that now."

I reached a hand toward him, to shush him. He pushed my hand away.

"I'm serious," he warned. He turned to Filimone, who regarded him flatly. "Tell that man to call off the dogs."

Filimone muttered something, and the man resentfully yelled at the dogs and lobbed a couple of stones. The pig escaped into the bush. His chin set, Gabriel turned back to the pile of food and methodically cut me a chunk of taro. We pointedly avoided the suckling pig.

We dragged back to our room after eating, hoping for a moment of calm. I pulled out two cigarettes from the feast, and we tried to sit side by side on the mattress to smoke. Our behinds sank into the kapok. But the bed was so high that our feet dangled like little kids' on grown-up chairs.

"This is a very odd place," I said.

"No shit, Sherlock," Gabriel replied. We smoked, little puffs seeping like thought balloons out of the bed. The air gave up some of its sadistic humidity, and the combined fragrances of burnt coconut husks from the feast and frangipani blossoms improved our mood. The sun finally slouched onto the horizon, coloring everything ochre.

Our brief respite ended with quick calls from outside—two boys running, a shout. Finally, Filimone again, at our door—what passed for a door.

"Vigo came for the *faikava*," he said. "Come now." He scurried off.

We struggled out of our dents on the bed and hustled to the meetinghouse, where a circle of men was already assembled. At the far end was a small, gaunt white man in a black *tupenu*. His stringy gray hair limped greasily on his neck, down to his collar bone. His beard extended in irregular wisps onto his chest. It appeared that his only concession to the occasion was a clean but holey white T-shirt, three sizes too big. It showed a giant pea pod and read, "Give peas a chance."

I saw that he was used to sitting cross-legged; both his skinny legs were pretzeled flat to the ground. The toes on his bare feet splayed out like palm fronds as if he'd never worn shoes. His eyes sparkled, and he peered energetically at us.

We shook his hand and said hello before taking our places.

"We're very glad and honored to meet you, Vigo," Gabriel said.

"Many Peace Corps have come to try to find me!" he said so loudly that I wondered whether he was deaf. "I have something they seem to want!"

"You'll help us understand the conversation tonight, perhaps," I said. I'd been having trouble following the Tofuans' conversation. It had a dialect, an unfamiliar rhythm.

"Oh, I don't speak Tongan!" Vigo said. "I'd rather not."

I was dumbstruck. Vigo seemed to hear others' voices just fine although he shouted every comment.

"I get along fine!" he said. "I get what I need!" Perhaps in all his years of silence, he had forgotten how to modulate. I wished he had a volume knob. Even the Tofuans seemed to draw back.

At the head of the circle, a young girl swished the *foa*, a coconut husk, into the bowl—a more difficult method than the way I'd been taught. A boy behind her poured in water. The soothing ritual began. Maybe if I could hear an hour or two of kava singing, I would be all right.

But just as the first song began, Vigo shouted, "What matters is that you know what you need and what you want and the difference between the two!"

The Tofuans stopped singing, mid-measure, and waited for someone to translate. They looked at Gabriel. They looked at me. I shrugged and offered simplistic phrases that probably made Vigo sound like a village idiot. Which maybe he was.

"What a man needs is food, shelter, and clothes, and nothing more," Vigo yelled. "What keeps humans from feeling that there's any difference between living and dying is helping others!"

Filimone whispered what might have been a rough translation to the others. A few murmured assent.

"That's certainly true," Gabriel said. "I think you must have come by this wisdom the hard way."

I stared at Gabriel. Was he kidding? Did he really admire this cliché-ridden little man? Then again, it was a night to be gracious. Be here nice, be here nice, be here nice.

Vigo sat quietly for a moment, and the young woman at the bowl resumed serving. Again, I held my breath, thinking the singing was about to begin. Again, the men started. Again, they made it through the first four bars.

"Once on Hunga I almost felt like dying!" Vigo yelled. "Until one day someone shipwrecked on my island! I saved him! Suddenly, I realized my life had meaning! I had made a difference!"

The Tofuans gave up. They sat in silence, except for the splash of kava being scooped into bowls.

Maybe it was just the exhaustion of the trip and the day's searing heat, but finally Vigo's story touched me. How lonely he must have been. How he must have sometimes questioned the hard choices he had made. On the desolate Hunga, he had come face to face with the human condition.

"You see that I don't have many muscles!" Vigo continued, and this time, everybody jumped when he resumed. "But I don't need them! I'd rather have a healthy liver and pancreas! And so I eat accordingly! Papaya, my friends, papaya is the godly food!"

Gabriel stroked his chin and nodded soberly. The Tofuans waited. I tried to readjust my legs, which were getting numb.

"That makes sense. You've found a way to eat that is also very kind to the natural world," Gabriel said.

"The important thing is to see things as they really are!" Vigo bellowed. "The truth—the truth will change you!"

Again, awkward silence descended. The Tofuans seemed unwilling to risk another song. I accepted a second bowl of kava and reminded myself I was not responsible. For anything. For this strange old man. For Gabriel. For Mort going free. For Mac and his crazy gesture. For this impossibly remote place. For the deepening darkness. But maybe, I was responsible for taking up the truth, whatever there was of it, in what the little hermit said.

Filimone hand-carried a bowl of kava to Vigo, who took it and downed it in one gulp.

"You have a telescope," Vigo said, suddenly calmer, to Gabriel.

At last. On this point, I could thoroughly understand the loquacious Gandhi look-alike. I remembered the night of the Risk game, how much I'd wanted to see the moon.

"Yes, I want to set it up tonight."

"I will come back," Vigo said, and with that, he unpretzeled his legs and nimbly stood up. Filimone handed him his unnecessary walking stick, and without another word the hermit vanished into the bush.

But when we got back to the guesthouse, the telescope was gone.

For three days, Gabriel tried to find it—tried to get Filimone to locate the culprit. He offered money. He swore there would be no blame. He begged me to try my best Tongan on old women, on children. He tried to send word to Vigo, but nobody seemed to know where he was. He asked to see the village preacher, but the *fiefekau* was off the island getting a hemorrhoid repaired. We never saw Vigo or the telescope again.

The heat badgered us by day, but at night, cool breezes came in from the sea. We sank into the kapok with relief, its poofy cushion a kind of privacy. We made love, sometimes letting our moans explode defiantly, sometimes as quietly as parents.

Gabriel was inconsolable about the telescope.

The last night, wiping at my own tears, I saw that he was crying, too.

"You can get another one when you get home," I said.

"It's not that. I wanted to leave it with you. I wanted you to be able to see the stars after I'm gone."

I cried again, and then he cried again, and we both fell asleep that way, our tears soaking into the pillow that read, "Peace and Love."

We came back to Nuku'alofa by plane, the one that had brought the preacher home, gripping his blow-up ass pillow. Gabriel explained about the telescope, and the good preacher promised to try. Gabriel told him if he found it to send the telescope to me.

Back in Nuku'alofa, an urgent message awaited Gabriel. His wife was having complications. He left instructions for mailing the cradle he'd had made in the bush for the baby that everyone knew about but me, and he caught the next plane home.

CHAPTER 23

▼

Hulu pe ka na'e muka. *Now she's unhappy, but once she rode the crest of good fortune.*

At work, I was distracted and miserable. I sat at my desk, shuffling drafts of press releases, my mind drifting. To my mother. To Gabriel's pregnant wife. To Gabriel's telescope. To Gabriel. He was lodged in my heart like a bullet, deep enough to hurt but not enough to kill me. He was in there, throbbing with every beat.

I arranged an itinerary for a Taiwanese sugar expert. There was some excitement about increasing the small Tongan sugarcane crop, and Faina hoped the Taiwanese might be interested.

I was supposed to order a black limousine from the Prime Minister's office to pick the guy up. A half hour late, the driver picked me up at the office, and I sat, wordless, in the enormous back seat while he drove madly, silently through the bush to the airport. When we got there, two Chinese diplomats from the embassy in Nuku'alofa were already there in their own black limousine to pick up the visitor. As usual, there'd been a mix-up. The PM's driver, at least, had the prized key to the VIP lounge, so I opened it and served weak orange soda to Mr. Lee. I presented Mr. Lee with his itinerary and the perfunctory lei, and then the Chinese hustled Mr. Lee into their limousine, leaving his luggage for me.

"Sorry I made you come all the way out here just to haul somebody's bags," I said in Tongan to the PM's driver. He seemed surprised that I spoke Tongan, and I caught him smiling at me in the rearview mirror. He answered, in a faultless David Niven accent, "Good riddance."

Faina asked me to stand in for him at a dinner for Mr. Lee at the Taiwanese embassy with Mr. Nalapu. Seated at a large, round table for twelve, the other guests and I had quail eggs and sea cucumber, oxtail soup, squid, tofu and rice pudding, and little thimbles of rice wine. Every bite was delicious, and it was so different from the heavy Tongan cuisine that I felt energized. I wanted to fit in with these calm, tidy people. But the Taiwanese were taciturn and formal, and I felt gawky and awkward, every inch Ohio.

Faina emphasized that Mr. Nalapu and I, like winos waiting out the sermon at the Rescue Mission, had to stay for The Movies, apparently part of every dinner party at the embassy. Faithful team members, we did as we were told. The first film was about Taiwan's National Day, October 10, 1976. Just four days before Melanie's murder. What was the world like then? I couldn't quite remember. Did the Taiwanese know? Did they care? The movie was a treatise on "Freedom and Prosperity," and it featured endless air shows, a motorboat navy, tanks, jets, and row upon row of uniforms. It concluded with the exhortation, "Give Us Back Our Land." A second thriller, "Social Welfare," showed children in orphanages, scrupulously clean and uniformed, a couple receiving a TV from their employers, girls going happily home from work to a factory dormitory—eight to a room— and patients being x-rayed. Throughout, a sound track blared, "These Are a Few of My Favorite Things."

On the ride home, Mr. Nalapu, who endeavored never to eat anything but his wife's Indian food, groused, "I think they'd eat anything unless they could make a missile out of it." I confessed that I loved the food, but it was the propaganda I couldn't take.

"No wonder they admire the Tongans," he said, and I nodded. "Never taken over by anybody."

Nothing in my life, my job, the Coconut Club, the ocean, my books, even the Taiwanese oxtail soup—none of it seemed to help me forget that Mort had walked away free or that Mac had gone after him. Nothing helped me forget my mother's unhappiness, or my father's infidelity, or Gabriel, or my own stupidity.

One hot, damp day, taking photos with an antique, clunky, three-and-a-quarter-inch camera at the craft cooperative, I saw a baby crib just like the one Gabriel had shipped home. Viciously, I snapped shots of it, then burst into tears. The sweet woman from the co-op rushed over, murmuring comfort, but I ran outside and rode my bike recklessly back to the office, furious with myself. That night at the Coconut Club, I told Jeff and Lizard Sam that I didn't care about Gabriel at all.

"It was too much hassle," I said, swilling my second quart of beer. "It was a royal pain in the ass, trying to 'relate,' for God's sake."

Jeff and Sam exchanged glances.

"And another thing," I said. "I don't need any damn future in my damn relationships. The present is good enough, thank you very much."

Sam said, "You miss the fucker, kid."

"I don't need any damn fucker, kid," I blubbered. "All I need is you guys. You're still here, you guys, and I love you guys. You're the guys I love. Here's to Mac Barnett, that crazy guy. He's another guy I love." Sam and Jeff tolerantly toasted to the heroic Mac, as we'd all been doing for weeks.

And then they escorted me home, one on each side, their two black bikes as upright as judges as I swayed, swerved, and giggled miserably on mine, failing to miss every second pothole.

Dear Reader, I fell apart. Maybe I was changing, but believe me, it wasn't in a straight line. Before the end of the rainy season, angry and despairing, I slept with five more men.

I slept with a Hawaiian poet. At the Coconut Club one Tuesday night, I found myself sitting next to him, a half-Tongan on a visiting lectureship at the swampy local college, Kalileo Academy. "I am very drunk and very aggressive," he warned me. "I am not an anthropologist like these other damn foreigners always strutting in and out of here. I cannot talk to you and write down everything you say in a little notebook. I am a poet, but my wife says to me, 'You are a shit.'" He took my hand and laughed. "I need reassurance. This is not a sexual gesture." But it was.

Viliami gently said, "Can I help you get home, Lolo?" and Lolo called him a bloody bastard and told him to leave him alone. He asked me to drive him in his Land Rover to his office at Kalileo, and after I helped him inside, we made love on his desk. He wasn't very good because he was drunk. He wanted me to spank him. I did. He hissed, "Don't worry, I won't tell anybody." I walked home in the mist of early morning.

I slept with a visiting American, the brother of an expatriate banker. I was invited to a dinner of excellent gin and tonics, steak, and pumpkin pie in the expatriate's ranch-style house. We were served by a Tongan maid whom they barely acknowledged. When I spoke to her in Tongan, the expats gave me sharp looks, and the maid disappeared. After dinner we played charades: *The Great Gatsby, Seven Year Itch, Rear Window*. In his room at the guesthouse on Vuna Road—mercifully not Kalisimasi's—while the rain battered the corrugated roof, I gave him a blow job he would never forget. And I wished I could.

I slept with a young Australian yachtie crewing on a boat headed for Tahiti. He told me I was his third lover and that he had a special place in his heart for older women. "I'm only twenty-six," I moaned. He came fast and fell asleep immediately. I considered biting him and leaving a scar. Luckily, he left the next day.

I slept with a water engineer who was in town to fix a bilge pump at the harbor. He smelled bad, called me a "fuckin' wench" and wanted to spank *me*. I sent him packing.

And finally, I slept with Lizard Sam for the first time in a long time. He took me to a party at Tony's where everybody was drinking home brew. Diane was the only other woman there, back from another work trip on the outer islands. We hugged, and I stayed close to her. Tony was nastily, vilely drunk. Every time he wanted to talk he stood up, swaying, as if he were giving a speech, and shouted lustily that he missed his Tongan girlfriend, To'e Tu'u. A dirty joke, bordering on blasphemy. It was Tongan, literally, for stand up again—also, it meant the resurrection.

"Thank god you're here," Diane murmured as we arrived. "Before you came, there were a bunch of *fokisis* here. Finally they made the *fokisis* leave, but then the girls stood outside the windows, and the guys kept passing them cigarettes through the louvres. It was depressing."

"Does Tony even have a Tongan girlfriend?" I watched him sway and fall.

"Not that I know of. God, who'd have him? Well, except me, that time. But that was enough."

"Once was enough for me, too," I whispered.

"You too?"

"Bad scene. The first month we were here. On a balcony."

"I'm glad to know I'm not the only one with bad judgment," Diane said.

"Confucius say, the way to wisdom is experience, and the way to experience is bad judgment," I said.

"I must be getting very wise, then."

"But not innocent," I said. "Think of it that way."

"Be careful what you want," she said.

The guys were wasted, sitting and leaning on one another in a ragged circle on the mat-covered floor. Tony had stripped off his shirt. His chest and flat belly were streaked with sweat, and his ribs showed through. He looked pale and underfed. I thought he had been running too much, getting ready for the Honolulu Marathon with Jeff. He was agitating a group of Tongan guys to sing kava songs. There was no kava, no kava circle; the atmosphere was all wrong for kava songs, and the Tongans weren't in the mood. When they didn't perform on command, Tony started yelling Tongan curses.

"You Tongans," he howled. "What good are you? If you can't eat it or fuck it, you break it." A tiresome saying, repeated surreptitiously at volunteers' most frustrated, racist moments.

"Stop it," Diane said, "Shut up." But he persisted, and some of the other volunteers joined in, as if to parade their *kapekape*, the slang of sex and blasphemy. One of the Tongans stood up and yelled, "You *palangis* need to show more respect. Maybe you should back to the *lotu*, the church." Somebody else shouted him down, and, crestfallen, he sidestepped out the door.

"Diane, com'ere," Tony loudly slurred. "Com'ere, Di, or you'll die. Di-dee," he shouted. "Do you know what sex is like? Sex, Di-dee, sex is like taking a shit. Just ask your slutty friend there, Charlotte, and she'll explain."

Sam swung into action and grabbed Tony by the collar, pulling him up and slamming him against the wall.

"You're going to stop this now," Sam said. "Stop drinking and shut your goddamn mouth."

"Oh, shut your kike piehole, too, asshole."

Sam slammed him in the belly and then left him collapsed on the floor, gasping for breath.

Diane and Sam and I fled outside, where three Tongan boys asked me my name four times. Sam said, "It's Mele, leave her alone." Tony reeled to the door to piss, and the Tongan boys threw rocks and curses. We agreed to follow Diane home, and when we rode away, the Americans were still howling like dogs—literally howling at the moon.

"Why is Tony so angry?" Diane said. "It's gotten worse, not better, since he got here."

"There must be things we don't know," I said.

"Under the circumstances, somebody should talk to him," Sam said.

"But none of us like him enough to care," Diane said.

"Jeff always cares," I said. "Let's get him. But not tonight."

Sam came in when he dropped me off. "Well, that was nice," I said, despair pulling at the hair on the back of my neck. He put a Temptations tape on my boom box, and we slowly danced. I clung to him, and he guided me straight to bed. He pulled down the mosquito net around us. "I hate this place," I mumbled into his ear.

"I know. Me, too. I'm going back up to Niuatoputapu to get away for a while." He stroked my forehead. It felt like the way Gabriel used to do it, and I started to cry. I was a lousy lover for him, and I was asleep before he left.

I got several voluminous letters from Gabriel, one fourteen pages long. He was passionate, fervent. He begged me to write back in kind. I didn't. I didn't write back at all. Eventually, I got a letter saying that his wife had had her baby, a boy. He enclosed a newspaper article featuring him as a father who helped the midwife with a home delivery. There was a picture of him in a dark turtleneck, his white hair pulled back and tied with a strip of something that looked Guatemalan. He was cradling and nuzzling the baby, whose little squirmy face peeked out from a papoose of blankets. Gabriel looked like a goddamned male Madonna. In the background was the Tongan crib. No sign of the wife.

Regardless of how emotional the mail from Gabriel made me, I showed up at the Peace Corps office twice a week. Hoping for something. What, I could not have said.

Not long after the baby photo, a single letter from my mom. I plopped onto the tired old couch.

I signed up for a class. Your father wanted me to take something 'crafty,' like decoupage. But I picked Women's Literature. My teacher's name is Dr. Johnson. She wears sensible shoes exactly like mine. We read a strange thing called 'As I Stand Here Ironing.' Lord knows I've done that enough.

God. I'd read that Tillie Olsen piece myself at Kent State. It was about a mother and a daughter. The mother mourns the daughter's difficult childhood and a wall that seems to have grown up between them. The girl, despite her sickliness and awkwardness, has won a talent show and suddenly is in demand, impatient with the mother. But the mother keeps on ironing, the two still failing to connect. "You think because I am her mother I have a key?" the mother says.

I felt momentarily dizzy. I read on to see whether my mother had something to say, something, anything, about mothers and daughters.

Anyway,

my mother continued,

the other day, your father was out on his riding mower, and he accidentally ran over a garter snake. Again. He felt so bad. He came back in the house right away. He said if he'd just seen it in time, he would have gone around it. He was down in the dumps all day. There is goodness in him.

I let the letter drop into my lap, and I stared out to the lagoon, familiar and comforting, where the late afternoon sun laid spoons of orange on the ripples. After a moment I didn't exactly see the lagoon. I saw my parents walking side by side after supper around their lot, commenting on everything—how the new Winesap apple trees were coming along, that goldfinch there in the raspberries. They were old, a little hunched over as they strolled their path through the rye grass, noting everything they'd made together. Was this why my mother would forgive him? Is it why I would, too?

Anyway, we were out driving to the fish supper at Faith Baptist, and we came upon a dead duck in the road, my mother wrote.

For some reason, your father stopped the car. In the bushes a couple of feet away, we saw the duck's mate, honking sadly. I think she was keeping vigil.

I tried to imagine my parents standing there in the scudding autumn leaves, the clean red Mustang humming on idle.

It would have been so much easier if my mother were angry, if we could be angry together. But I could begin to understand. She loved him. God. I put the letter down and wearily rubbed my eyes, then let my hands drop to my lap, my fingers finally drumming on my thighs, a pang in my heart for them both.

An arrow of empathy and understanding grabbed me unexpectedly. I felt something crack, as if it were about to sprout. Or end. If I forgave Gabriel, would I have to forgive my parents, too?

I picked up the letter again and read the postscript.

How is your elimination, dear? Can you get prunes there? I just couldn't get along without them. Remember, good elimination is what keeps your constitution in good condition. Dried apricots also work. Be good.

I was smiling as I folded up the dainty letter, when Evelyn Henry swooshed outside in a pink suit that looked alarmingly like what Jackie Kennedy was wearing the day of the assassination.

"Charlotte, darling, come in and say hello to me for a while."

It was much more fun when Liki called me darling. When Evelyn Henry said it, I bristled. I slunk inside behind her cloud of talcum and Je Reviens.

"How can I help you?" she said, crossing her ankles the way women were supposed to about a hundred years ago. Evelyn Henry's lipstick was on a little bit crooked, on the lower left lip.

"Sorry?"

"Well, I've been hearing that you might be…having some *problems.*"

"I'm fine, Evelyn, really."

"Charlotte, *I know.* I know more than you think."

Oh, shit. I knew she knew. But I didn't want her to say so. I tried crossing my ankles like hers, then uncrossed them. I resolved to say nothing, but the angry lipstick frightened me into talking.

"Gabriel Bonner and I were just friends, but now we're not, and anyway, he's gone, long gone," I blurted.

"Oh, Charlotte, Charlotte," said Evelyn Henry. "We need you now, more than ever, to *behave.* We really do."

That was, apparently, the extent of her comfort, solace, and advice. I forced myself to stand up and take the fistful of knuckles and rings extended to me.

"You know, if you really want to look at somebody who's struggling, you should talk to Tony," I said. "He's in a lot worse shape than me, and I don't know why."

It felt odd to say anything about another volunteer out loud, especially Tony, whom I'd never spoken with privately since that one weird night on the balcony. I didn't really know a thing about him. I didn't know why he was so angry or why Tonga seemed to be making his bitterness grow. The only thing I understood was the guilt that oozed out of him like sweat, contaminating everything else. That I recognized.

"You should check Tony out," I said, backing away from Evelyn Henry, backing out of the office. I practically slid down the splintery banister getting out of there and rode recklessly away. I was sure that as soon as I left, Evelyn Henry would fill out a report in triplicate.

Instead of going to the Coconut Club, I made myself ride along Vuna Road, where I could get lungfuls of fresh air and a little exercise. I stopped for a breather at Faua Wharf, where a clutch of wiry boys were diving off the pier, running and sailing over the edge in wild pirouettes. The water smelled richly stagnant, but it didn't seem to stop the boys from jumping in. I sat on the breakwall, feeling weighed down and remote from their exuberant childhood.

Not that childhood was all that great. Childhood really was overrated.

Be Good. Behave. I'd been an expert at it, but no matter how often I sang "How Great Thou Art" for the congregation in my little pinafore or recited that boring Longfellow poem, "The Psalm of Life." Nothing worked. *Tell me not in mournful numbers, life is but an empty dream.* Not even my best performances at Missionary Society teas, nothing ever seemed to lift my mother's melancholy.

Except for one vivid moment of pure happiness. A summer Sunday morning, the Ohio sun silvery white. My mother, in a soft, flowery, go-to-church dress, took me by the hand.

"Let's find flowers for our dresses," my mother said, her voice for once rich and resonant with calm. We walked through the bright, new grass. I remembered dewdrops glistening on my patent leather shoes. "Don't worry," my mother said, "It'll dry and leave a little magic dust."

Ah, that part of her, that made something okay. And magical. I remembered that part of her now. Maybe it was why she loved to read Bible stories to put me to sleep: in those stories, anything could happen.

"*Then* what will happen?" I remember saying, examining the dew dust.

"Then you'll go anywhere your heart desires. You'll get to go anywhere you want. Up here, of course." She smiled at me and delicately touched one finger, her index finger, to my temple. "Try it."

I shut my eyes for a few seconds and found out I could still picture my mother, standing there. The pure sun. Her flowered dress. I opened my eyes, and my mother was still there. I drank her in.

"You'll find out," my mother said.

We tiptoed together through the misty lawn, and the sun was just warm enough to leave a little sheen of heat on our cheeks. In an overgrown hedge, my mother found a cluster of tiny rosebuds.

"These are so beautiful," my mother said, so happy, so happy in the morning light.

"Oh, smell it," she said, bending a bud down to my nose. *She wants me to be happy too*, I remember my new little mind thinking. Rosebud: the smell of luxury, of love. My mother bent over to clip off two buds, one for each of us, and I breathed in her Sunday morning scent of soap and sweet face powder. Just the two of us, squinting in the sun, one Sunday before church.

"You'll find out," my mother said again. "It'll be wonderful."

That one moment.

I slid down from the breakwall into the sand and stretched out, taking warmth from the late afternoon sun. I absently began to fan my arms up and down, and when I got up, I left a big, floppy, open-armed angel on the beach.

Then I got sick. I went to bed with a rampaging sore throat and fever. I lay there for hours, then days, sticky and miserable, while last gasps of the rainy season poured down. In the early morning, I began to hear the tapa pounders, a sign that the hot weather was ending, and the soothing, hypnotic rhythm worked its way into my feverish dreams. Mac was in there somewhere, pounding away on Mort. Gabriel came and went in my dreams: Sometimes he was back, and I got to have him. Most often I didn't. I'd just be saying good-bye to him again and again. I was at the side of the road, and there was a duck, bleating for its lost mate. My mother and father were there, holding hands and crying. I dreamed of tidal waves. Huge swells coming at me. I could see them, enormous and gunmetal gray. Sometimes I woke up before they got to me. Other times they crashed over me, and I'd wake up bathed in sweat, my heart wildly pumping.

I didn't want to see anyone and didn't want to talk to anyone, but Filipa wouldn't let me alone and made me drink foul-smelling bush remedies. She offered me a good, hot *lu*, but I couldn't keep it down. When I didn't come around, Filipa got Clark, the Peace Corps doctor, to come. The first time, I thought he was St. Francis of Assisi and told him, I heard later, that I was a broken bird. Eventually I recognized him and looked forward to his daily doses of pills and comfort.

There was a mouse family in the house, and they scrabbled noisily across the floor mats and played in my sandals. At first I thought I was seeing things.

"I think the house has mice," I told Filipa wearily from my cot one day.

"It wouldn't surprise me, Salote," she said. "You haven't been up enough making noise yourself to scare them away."

"I like them," I said. "They're cute."

"I'll put out a trap," she said, as if she hadn't heard me. "I'll put it in your bathroom. They like it there." She had a soft side, but not for rodents. "Go back to sleep."

I watched little blue-green skinks come and go, crawling busily in and out of the lashed bamboo walls. They soothed me, and I would have even welcomed them crawling onto my hot skin because they ate bugs and seemed so playful. But they never got that close.

Then whatever damned tropical virus had hold of me turned into diarrhea. I'm surprised I didn't set the mousetrap off myself, stumbling to the john. In an awkward secret talk, Filipa suggested I might be drinking the milk from too many green coconuts, about the only liquid I wanted. One day Filipa sent Tupou over with another glass of vile-looking liquid, unidentified leaves mushed up into a thick brew, a viscous film on top.

"Filipa said to drink this before I leave," Tupou said sternly.

I stared suspiciously at the potion.

"Tupou, you have the soul of a despot. Do you know what that means? Hitler? Mussolini? You're too young to be so frightening."

"Drink it," she ordered.

"How about if I drink half of it now and half of it later?"

"*Mahalo pe*," Tupou said, surprisingly softening. "Maybe, maybe that's okay, but don't tell Filipa."

Just then the mousetrap in the bathroom snapped.

"You'll have to get it, would you, Tupou? You're the type that probably likes getting rid of a dead mouse, and it's probably Timmie, and I don't want to see him dead."

"Timmie?" She disappeared into the shower.

"Okay, so I named one of them. Does he have a white spot on his little butt? Don't let me see. I don't want to see him."

"*Io*, Salote, it's 'Timmie.'" She looked at me with something approaching pity—not that she had much to work with in her repertoire. I hadn't thought fast enough to hide the disgusting potion. "Drink it," she said, holding the trap behind her large backside. "Drink it, or I'll make you look at Timmie."

I held my nose and downed one large swallow. It tasted disgusting, like rotten cauliflower. As soon as Tupou left, I muttered a toast to the bygone Timmie and tossed the rest of the medicine out the back window.

Clark agreed with Filipa about the coconuts. He also advised me to stay off Steinlager, as if I'd been tempted lately. He said to drink hot cocoa and a bit of caffeine, saying it would give me relief. And restoring my faith in American quick fixes, he gave me another vial of pills.

But the pills seized me up like a block of concrete, and I had the opposite problem. Clark suggested I stop eating red meat, as he thought I might have picked up bacteria. He ordered plenty of liquids—not coconut milk, he repeated—and emphasized no Steinlager, no other booze. He said that I might have to weather it and wait for it to run its course.

A huge brown spider planted itself in my bathroom, convenient entertainment for the room where I was spending so much time. I declared it a female and decided she was a good omen. She built a large, lacy web in a moist corner and stayed there, seemingly content with her digs, catching and patiently eating flies and mosquitoes. I drew a picture of the spider and put it in my diary: her head was a half-inch across, the circumference of her legs the width of my fist. One day, the spider captured a cockroach, itself two inches long. It took the spider three days to devour it. Sweet revenge, I said to her again and again, practically singing, look who's getting it now.

I kept my doors and windows closed, craving privacy more than light and air. I got Clark to bring me a pile of books from the Peace Corps library and dived in, not caring what they were about. I read by candlelight, enjoying the cozy glow, the soft, false, tapa ceiling like a parachute.

One Thursday night as I sat in my favorite chair, a breeze blew my cheap curtains into the candle. They caught on fire.

I jumped up screaming, ran for water, yelled for Filipa. Before I could put it out, the flame shot into the tapa cloth ceiling. Then Filipa and Tupou were there, and the three of us managed to beat it out. In the smoky remains was a burn hole three feet across.

The room was a mess, wet and coated with bits of ash. I was embarrassed and told Filipa so. She understood, and hugged me sweetly. I was shaking, and I surrendered to a good cry. I was exhausted.

"It's okay," Filipa assured me lovingly. "Don't be afraid. Everything will be okay, Salote dear."

The next day, before I'd even managed to get out of bed, Filipa carted a ladder into my living room and, busily humming a Tongan hymn, replaced the burned tapa. By the time I'd woozily arisen, Filipa was gone, but there was a bouquet of flowers on the kitchen table and a small, carved sandalwood figure—a kava drinker with a big belly, one of my favorite Tongan designs.

I liked the way Filipa never said another word about the fire. As the miniature tragedy receded in time, only she and I could see the seams in the tapa cloth. I gave up reading by candlelight, that romantic idea, but I was also experiencing a small, quiet peace. I was slowly getting back my strength.

I watched the spider a lot. It takes a long time to digest something big, doesn't it, I murmured to her one day. I wanted her to train me—me, a difficult and restless student—in the diligence needed to satisfy continual hunger.

CHAPTER 24

▼

Kaka tu'u ofi. *Settling for what is close at hand.*

One day, still too weak to get around, I heard the scratch of bike wheels on the coral outside my hut. I had a visitor. I didn't answer the knock, but the person wouldn't go away.

"Charlotte, it's me, Jeff. I'm worried about you. Let me come in. Please."

I let him in. "I've always been glad to see you, darling Jeff," I said. "But I look like shit," I'd been wearing my pink bathrobe for about three days straight. I pulled it tighter around me and ran a hand through my hair.

"Don't apologize. You've been very sick. Look, I brought something."

He held out a pack of Japanese green tea and a circle of cheese wrapped in foil. "I've been to Fiji for a vacation since you've been sick. Do you realize you can get almost anything you want there? At least compared to here. Want some?"

"Is that Brie? And real crackers, not hardtack. Wow. I'd love some. I haven't had an appetite for weeks. Suddenly, this all looks good. You're adorable."

He moved with gentle confidence into the kitchen and bustled around, finding everything he needed. He brought the cups, the pot, and a little dish with a knife.

"Are you okay?"

"Getting better. Slowly. I guess the Ministry is wondering what happened to me, even though Tevita's probably giving them daily updates."

"I'm sure they don't mind, Charlotte. You need to get better. We miss you at the Club."

"The thought of a Steinlager now about makes me gag," I said. "This could be the best thing that's ever happened to me in Tonga, come to think of it."

We sipped our tea.

"Has anybody heard anything about Mort? Or Mac?"

"Mort, no, not that I know of."

"That's unbelievable. Unbelievably creepy. Can you believe that guy is walking around at home?"

"I know. Some people are afraid to go home—afraid he'll stalk them or something."

"I don't blame them. Does anybody understand what's going on with this guy? What he might do? Who's in charge of this madness?"

"Not Gabriel Bonner anymore, I guess," Jeff said, avoiding eye contact.

"Yeah, he ducked out pretty neatly."

"Gained some honor by quitting, though," Jeff said. "I don't know what to think."

"I'm trying not to think," I said.

We nibbled at the Brie.

"Well, as for Mac, I guess Sam got a letter from him," Jeff said. "He's okay, but angry, angry as hell."

"It's justifiable," I said. "Some anger is good anger."

"Yeah, but you can't go around waving a tapa mallet," Jeff said. "That could hurt somebody."

"A tapa mallet. I swear. What was he thinking?"

"I guess he had it in the waistband of his pants, like a gun or something. Awfully hard to hide."

"Oh, god, like, is that a tapa mallet in your pants or are you glad to see me?" I said. "Mac. Jeezus. What a putz." We smiled.

"Are you okay?" he said again.

I smiled. "Yeah, I'm getting there. Tough patch, recently. Pretty shitty times."

"Things fall apart, my friend. Doesn't make it any better when you're nine thousand miles away from home."

"You know Chinua Achebe was quoting Yeats when he named that book, don't you?" I said.

"Of course I know that. Do you think I could have gotten a doctorate in literature and missed that?" We scooped Brie onto crackers and slowly munched.

"Our old life seems far away," I said. "Did you ever think you'd be eating Brie with your slutty friend Charlotte in a little hut in Polynesia?"

"No, I didn't, and you're not slutty," he said. "You're…energetic. You're resourceful. Imaginative."

"Okay, okay, thank you, Jeff. Tony was the one who called me slutty. The last time I know of, anyway. How's that old fart doing?"

"Oh, I forgot to tell you. He's going home."

"Home? Dropping out?"

"There *was* a story there, one he didn't want to tell anybody. He finally told me before he told Evelyn. I guess his father was beating his mother. After Tony left to come here, it got worse. He just found out it happened again. She's in the hospital, and the father's in jail."

"Damn, that's terrible, Jeff. I knew something was wrong. When's he leaving?"

"This week, I guess, as soon as he can get out. The weird thing is, he's been going around buying up Tongan crafts like a madman. He's saying he wants to start some kind of a sales deal from home, import/export, that kind of thing, with the Tongans."

"That is so weird. He never acted like he liked anything here."

"Maybe it's the hustler in him," Jeff said. "Lots of energy. And by the way, since he's going home, we're looking for another jogging partner. Want to get in on this Peace Corps fitness revolution?"

"Look at me," I said, pointing to my messy hair and sloppy bathrobe. "Who do I look like, Wilma Rudolph?"

"You're getting better," he said. "It'd be great for you. Bridget and Diane and I would love to have you."

"I don't think I can run one mile, not to mention five," I said.

"Well, you can drop out anywhere along the route and really not be far from home," he said. "Let us come by here and take you out one day, just to give you a taste of it."

It sounded good.

And they did come by, about a week later, at 5:45 in the morning and knocked on my door. Bridget said they half expected me to cuss them out and send them away, but I said it was a boring Thursday, and I'd been bored silly for days. Clark had told me I could go back to work the next Monday, and I figured I'd better get my lazy body going.

I was so glad to see the three of them, in fact, that I hugged them all around, the four of us whispering in the dark.

"Hey, why are we whispering?" I suddenly said, loudly. "Do you realize how often my neighbors have waked me up around here? Let's make a lot of noise."

But we didn't, out of respect for one of the quietest times of day.

"I like your outfits," I said to Bridget and Diane. They were in T-shirts and short, flowered *tupenus* over shorts, along with their jogging shoes and socks. I had to dig under my bed for my jogging shoes. I almost hadn't brought them, but somebody said something about maybe having to climb around coral and lava.

"Watch out for centipedes under there," Bridget said. "The last thing you need, now that you're getting better, is to get stung. And check your shoes before you put them on, for god's sake. I hate those things."

"I feel much more comfortable knowing that there's one bug the resident entomologist doesn't like," I said.

"I got stung on one of my trips out in Ha'apai," Bridget said. "It hurt like hell for about three days."

"Damn, babe, there's so much I don't know about what's happened to you," I said. "It's been too long."

"Same here," she said. "It seems like yesterday we were sitting around that table at the hotel, watching Melanie dance."

No getting around it. We all remembered. We dated time by how long it'd been since the tragedy we'd shared.

"It does. But a lot's happened," I said. "We're hardly unscathed."

They showed me how to stretch in slow, languorous bends, hands and arms pressed against the side of my hut. "I have to tell you, Charlotte," Bridget said, "running here is one of the best things I've ever done. I feel so free. I never thought I could do it."

"Me, either," Diane said. "And look at me—thinner, thinner. I wouldn't mind going home lithe."

"You're great coaches, you two," I said. "You're making me want to."

I made a slow mile the first time out. Then two, then three. They ordered me to run flat-footed, not on my toes. They insisted I stretch before and after. We stopped for water halfway. They had the routes, the water stops, already mapped out. I found a pair of baggy shorts to go under my *tupenu,* just like Bridget and Diane. We were an odd-looking quartet, but we were getting in shape.

Like theirs, my body responded. Finally I could do the whole route, five miles, and be home by breakfast, three times a week. It felt amazing.

We took turns meeting at the high school teachers' compound where they all lived and at my place on the other side of town. At first I dreaded the times I had to ride to them through town before dawn. I'd never conquered my fear of the Tongan dark. My flashlight in hand, I kept an eye out for the occasional surly dog, but if one ran out at me, teeth bared and growling as always, I would stop immediately, jump off my bike, and bark out a Tongan curse. I learned where all the bad dogs lived, and once past them, I could cycle peacefully by the biscuit factory, breathing in the yeasty fragrance of new bread. An ancient man swept the street outside almost every day with a stiff coconut rib broom. I'd murmur a greeting, my blood pressure returning to normal. He would pause and look up, as if glad for a reason to unbend. "*Lelei*," he'd say back, "mornin'."

Jeff convinced us that jogging was about endurance, not speed, and said if we couldn't keep talking as we went along, we were going too fast. Before the first streaks of light showed up behind the wharf, we'd be gabbing about everything: how poor Tony kept his anguish to himself all those months, where we thought Mort might be hanging out, how we loved Mac, how we loved to hate Evelyn Henry. We swapped tales about various feasts we'd survived, about having to sit still and listen to interminable speeches that we couldn't understand, about having to fart and trying to hold it. I told them about my weird visit to Tofua, about Vigo, and how he shouted his weird sayings. Diane talked about Ned, the slothful Ned of the fishing utopia in Ha'apai, and how she loved him. She said she might look him up in the States when she got back. She said it was Ned to whom she had gleefully abandoned her virginity, and she would never forget it: on a Polynesian island on the beach under a full moon.

One day Jeff told us he'd gotten an upsetting letter from home. It was from his ex-wife.

"The professor dumped her," he reported. Bridget, Diane, and I hooted. "What she deserved," Bridget snorted.

But we forget the intensity of his unrequited love. Touchy moment.

"I feel bad for her," he said defensively. "She must be lonely."

"So what'd she want?" I asked.

"She wants to get back together. She wants to come down and see me."

"Oh my god!" Repeated three times. "Do you want to?"

He made us jog about a quarter mile before he said anything.

"Come on, Jeff, what are you going to say?" I finally blurted.

"I told her *no*," he said. "I still love her, but it's over. She hurt me too much. I'd never trust her again."

"Makes sense," I said. "Trust, once broken, is gone forever."

We all jogged on in respectful silence.

"I'm so sorry," Bridget finally said. She put an arm around his back, even while they were moving down the coral road. Diane and I trotted along behind.

No accident. "I think they're falling in love," Diane said, nodding at the two of them. "I think he's crazy about her. And vicey versy."

"How did I not know this?" I said. "I'm always the last to know."

"No, you were the one with the top secret love affair that went on forever and that everybody knew about, Charlotte. And then you were sick, sick, sick. You can't expect to know everything."

"Oh, but I do expect to, I do."

We caught up at the water stop.

"Got a poem," Jeff said. We settled on a stone bench and waited.

"It's for Bridget," he said, "but you two can listen in."

"Thank you very much," I said.

"*Had we but world enough, and time,*" he began,

"*This coyness, lady, were no crime.*
We would sit down, and think which way
To walk, and pass our long love's day.
Thou by the Indian Ganges' side
Shouldst rubies find; I by the tide
Of Humber would complain. I would
Love you ten years before the flood...

Bridget's face was pink, and I saw the beginnings of tears. Jeff smiled at her and resumed:

"*Now, therefore, while the youthful hue*
Sits on thy skin like morning dew,
And while thy willing soul transpires
At every pore with instant fires,
Now let us sport us while we may,
And now, like amorous birds of prey,
Rather at once our time devour
Than languish in his slow-chapped power.
Let us roll all our strength and all
Our sweetness up into one ball,
And tear our pleasures with rough strife
Thorough the iron gates of life:
Thus, though we cannot make our sun
Stand still, yet we will make him run."

We cheered. Jeff bowed, and Bridget gave him a hug. But art never seemed to last long in Tonga. Before we even finished clapping, a kid darted out of the bush, making lewd faces and yelling, "Hey, *palangi* ladies! Are you fuck? Are you fuck?"

We groaned in unison.

Jeff ran at him, yelling "*Tapuni, faka'apa'apa*" and the kid disappeared, only to reappear and try to jog behind us when we started up again.

"Possibly a future student of yours," Diane yelled up at Jeff, who was already jogging companionably up ahead with Bridget.

"Yeah, well, if Jeff is his teacher, he'll learn better grammar," Bridget called back.

And that's how I found out, jogging breathlessly into the sunrise, that Jeff and Bridget were in love. I was happy for them. I was glad it wasn't me, slipping afresh into all that risky territory, all that potential to be hurt. I was glad Jeff was just my friend.

C H A P T E R 25

▼

Teka 'a ma momoko. *Only that inconspicuous person can bring us bread.*

Sam kept going back and forth to Niuatopatapu on the creaky little boat that took days each way, or on an unsteady plane if he could afford it, pursuing stories that never seemed to make it into the *Tonga Chronicle*. Trying to get the story of Melanie, Mort, and Mac some attention exhausted him, and nobody wanted to listen. Nobody wanted to know. I thought going up north was therapy, where he'd go when he couldn't take it any more. He was an honest journalist, stuck, in a way, in both heaven and hell.

After one such agonizing hop to the faraway island, he called me at work, saying he wanted to collect the lime juice take. The Hasimoto clan and I had sold only 200 quarts and had an entire fifty-gallon vat untouched.

His request triggered a wave of guilt, but I invited him to dinner. He was getting a reputation for being the most *fakatonga* volunteer, so I planned my best version of Tongan fare. I was fueled by curiosity: what was happening to my cynical LA friend?

The dinner was part business—I invited Tevita and Filipa—but also part pleasure. I scripted the dinner deliberately, hoping, with just a sliver of shy hope, that maybe Sam and I...Sam and I...to be honest, I wanted to get laid. My increasingly fit body was asking to be used. And I wanted to make up for the last time with Sam, when I'd been drunk and pitiable.

Within the first ten minutes, when Filipa and Tevita had barely settled into the comfortable lotus postures that meant they'd be there a while, Tevita gave Sam eighty *pa'anga*, the entire return minus gas for the moke. That meant Tevita got nothing. I knew Tevita did it out of guilt, for he wasn't a generous man. But Sam wasn't happy.

"Don't you realize how long it took to squeeze this juice?" he said mournfully.

Then he made us listen, each of us grappling with our own cringing consciences, while he described how a crew of about ten people—mostly, as promised, Tevita's aunts and cousins—sat in a hut using coconut scrapers and old tin juicers to maul out the limes, one at a time. People scraped their knuckles, and the juice stung. When they got tired, they'd wipe their eyes, and the juice would get in their eyes and hurt like hell. After a while their forearms would ache, and at night they'd get cramps and have to massage one another's hands and arms back to life for the next arduous day. But they kept at it, day after day, heroically, because of the money they were going to get, the gold teeth they might be able to have implanted, the new radios they might be able to buy. Now he was the one who'd have to divide up the cash among Tevita's aunties, and there wouldn't be a lot to go around. He didn't know, he said sadly, how he was going to handle it.

Tevita, Filipa, and I lugubriously munched my baked *manioc* and my beautiful *lu* with the coconut juice squishing out of the tender green leaves. We avoided looking at our unhappy business partner. But we kept eating. It was really good food. I could tell Tevita liked it because he kept on taking big gulps, like the man he was, trying to hide his problematic happiness with the free food on the solemn occasion. There wasn't much we could say.

"Well, anyway, I'll do the best I can," Sam said. We swallowed in unison, as if he'd given us permission.

"And the thing is," he continued, "there's a family up there with two beautiful daughters." Tevita slapped him on the back. He knew the ones, exactly.

"One of them is eighteen, and the other is twenty. At first I thought I was in love with two women," (here, the ever-blunt Sam looked at me) "not that that's not possible, I know, but in my case, I realize it's the older one I really love. We're getting married."

I nearly dropped my plate of dumplings. "Married?"

"Yes, Salote, she stole my heart. I can't explain it."

There was much huzzahing, exuberance, and unintelligible cheering from Filipa and Tevita. They shouted out to the kids, enviously circling my *fale* and sniffing my good food: "Sami's getting married! Sami's marrying a Tongan girl!"

Sure that my honor and theirs was safe with Sam happily betrothed to a Tongan girl, Tevita and Filipa left us alone together.

"Here's the really wild part," Sam said. "Her name is—well, it's Melenia."

"She's named Melanie? Wow."

"We're getting married up there next month. Traditional Tongan stuff for her and her family, of course, and then eventually we'll go back to LA."

"You're taking a twenty-year-old girl from Niuatopatapu to Los Angeles?"

"She's dying to go, Charlotte. She can't wait. And you know there are a lot of Tongans there. She's even got an auntie or somebody who lives in Torrance. They have feasts and Tongan dances and *faikavas*. They're in the *LA Times*. But she wants to see Hollywood."

"How does she know about Hollywood, anyway?"

"Everybody knows about Hollywood, Charlotte. They hang a sheet up on a clothesline and show movies. She's seen every movie that's been in Nuku'alofa."

"Hmm. I'm happy for you, Sam, even though I'm also shocked, I have to say. I'm really shocked." I was cleaning up the dishes, standing at the sink. He came up behind me and folded his arms around me.

In my ear he said, "I really love having sex with you. I'll always have great memories of you."

"I will of you, too, Sam," I said.

"I'd even entertain the thought of having sex with you tonight, just for old times' sake." He nuzzled his nose into the most vulnerable part of my neck, and I felt goose bumps rise along my arm.

It had been my plan all along to tumble into bed with Lizard Sam again. I'd dabbed extra dashes of Chanel Number Five at all the right places, just in case. But now I had a strange impulse. I thought about that innocent girl waiting for Sam to come back, waiting to begin her exciting new life, and I felt for her and what she was about to go through, and I said no.

"I love you, Sam. But." I turned around and hugged him affectionately, face to face. "I don't want to tread onto young Melanie's territory. You're hers, now, sweetheart. Keep yourself for her."

"I still say you're the best lay in Peace Corps," Sam said, gracious as always. "Even if you start saying no."

"Thank you, Lizard. What an honor, and please keep that delightful secret between us."

The next week Tevita threw a kava party for Sam, probably spending another twenty or thirty dollars on the best kava he could find, just to make a point. He chipped in another ten, and so did I, so that Sam could go back to Niuatoputapu with an even hundred. I lost track of the other fifty-gallon drum. Probably, I suspected, the *laimi* ate through the metal and trickled back into the earth, where it would have killed every organism known to island botany.

I went to see Kalisimasi at the Guest House. I stopped on the way to pick up a pack of Rothman's, Kalisimasi's favorite cigarettes. I needed the comforting scents of Kalisimasi's kitchen, the cosmopolitan hubbub, and the exquisite order.

The older woman, sitting at her desk at work on the books, smiled at once and pushed back a strand of errant hair. She immediately called into the kitchen for a pot of tea.

"Did you hear? Sam's getting married, to a girl from Niautoputapu," I began, stripping open the fresh pack and offering one to Kalisimasi. She lit it with a wooden match.

"I heard. I hope he understands about culture shock if he takes that girl to Los Angeles. I hope she understands."

"She won't, of course," I said. "But if they love each other…who knows?"

"Were you surprised?" Kalisimasi watched my face closely for clues.

"Dumbfounded. Sam and I've been close since the first plane to Tonga, and I never thought, never. But, you know, he's got a big, generous heart."

"That he does. He really got into the *laimi* trade, Tevita told me."

"Yeah, that was practically a bust, but not because of him."

"And you're looking a little pale, Salote, and you've lost weight. I heard you were sick. Have you been taking care of yourself?"

"Filipa helped. I'm okay. I'm coming back around. I've started jogging, with Jeff and Bridget and Diane—remember them? It feels pretty great."

"So why are you smoking now?"

"Because I love smoking with you, Kalisimasi. Moderation is my motto.

"So how's business?"

"Thanks to the U.S. Peace Corps, very fine indeed," Kalisimasi said. "And we have a few other tourists here as well, a kayaker and an anthropologist and two strange Swiss people who seem excessively exhilarated by our little kingdom."

We smoked quietly for a minute, a gentle pacing I had first learned from Faina.

"Faina says hello," I said. I was reaching. Kitioni gave me almost daily updates about Faina making up reasons to drop by the guesthouse. Kitioni said he was there almost every night.

Kalisimasi whacked me on the back of the head. "Don't be nosy," she said. "A single pack of Rothman's will get you no secrets from me. You were a star student in your Peace Corps training, even if you did slip away a little too often with— who? Mr. Sam, I believe. You know the Tongan way."

"But he's such a nice man, and you're such a wonderful woman, and wouldn't you like somebody to warm your backside once in a while?"

"Salote!"

"You said it first—I heard you—at my sun party."

"I deny everything." Kalisimasi's mellifluous voice was like a good massage. The tea arrived, and Kalisimasi stared at me intensely over her bifocals, a trick that only a pro hostess could manage.

"Kalisimasi, I need a woman's perspective."

"You are still brokenhearted over your friend," she began.

"I can't keep a secret from you, even if you keep your secrets from me. You knew all about it, I guess."

"I'm your elder, and I have that right. Besides, I can see through you, and you have a long way to go to see through me."

"Oh, Kalisimasi, I am trying…"

"And what else?"

"Trouble at home. Bad news at home."

She deeply sighed. "You *palangis* all live for your blessed mail, but half the time it brings you nothing but grief."

"My father's been having an affair with another woman. My father, the minister. I know who she is. I've known her since I was a child. My mother found a letter."

"Oh, Salote, she must be so hurt."

"I don't know. I don't know. I called her, but I couldn't tell much. She saw a duck holding vigil over its dead mate, and she decided to be loyal. She signed up for some class."

"That sounds encouraging, actually." We sipped our tea.

"And you must be very angry," Kalisimasi said.

"Well, who am I to judge? I'm hardly the one to lord it over anybody."

"Salote." Kalisimasi put a hand on mine, on the desk. "This is going to sound like a strange thing to say, but there was a time when I wanted a moped more than anything in the world. I think I wanted it for two years of my life, two years I could not afford to waste on wanting something so much. By the time I stopped wanting it, I could have afforded it.

"Then I wanted a set of encyclopedias, and there they are." She swept her hand toward the bookshelves.

"When I was a kid, we traded for everything, Filipa and Isita and me and all the rest. We were champions at getting soap for our mommy or finding clams in the lagoon that we could trade for money to go to the movies at the HauHau. But now my fellow Tongans seem to be crazy for things that only money can buy: gold teeth and gold watches."

I nodded. I'd seen it. We lit two more cigarettes.

"And sometimes I wanted a man," Kalisimasi said. "I've got my heart broken once or twice. We all want something."

"I wish all I wanted was a gold watch," I said.

"You want what you want. I will tell you that I disagree with the Buddhists. When you stop wanting, you stop living."

"It's not pretty in my case."

"Salote, dear, when is it ever? You try to ignore your rumbling stomach, but does it make you less hungry? You try to ignore your heart, and does it make you any more serene?"

Kalisimasi looked at me closely, as if examining a sty in my eye.

"This is not easy, Salote."

"I...I think I just want some peace of mind."

"Salote, you're too young for that."

CHAPTER 26

▼

'Auto e manu ki Toku. *Finally, going back.*

The night Viliami came to call, I didn't even know for over an hour that he'd come to see *me*. When a battered old truck that he and his buddies probably borrowed from somebody at the Coconut Club pulled in, spewing blue clouds of oil, I peeked out my louvres but didn't recognize anybody and didn't think anything of it. Tevita was always getting visits from various cronies and partners in his schemes. But as Filipa explained later, Viliami came with a band of brothers and reported in respectfully to her and Tevita, who invited them in. There Viliami and his four buddies sat and chewed the fat and munched from a platter of dumplings as if I had nothing to do with it.

Eventually Viliami told Filipa that he had something important to give me. And, he casually added, they wanted to have a *faikava* and wondered whether I would entertain. So Filipa, having been shown the proper deference and always hungry for a little gossip, finally led the parade to my doorstep. She stopped before coming in and elaborately pointed to the crew behind her.

"Salote, do you want a visit from these good-for-nothings?" she asked. I barely made out Viliami, lurking behind Lopini, Siuela, Funaki Ofa, and Siokiatame, part-time bartenders and roustabouts from the Coconut Club.

"Maybe," I said, playing out my role. "Did they bring me anything to eat?"

There was jostling near the back of the pack, and somebody produced a couple of papayas. "Okay, then, I guess they can come in."

Filipa marched in first and took a spot on the floor in everybody's way, settling down cross-legged, as crabby and interfering as possible. Everybody but Viliami came in and settled down on the floor in a ragged circle around her.

And finally, Viliami came in, his arms holding up something wrapped in a fat mat held together with coconut twine. He set it down, pushing the others aside to make room, and untied it, the mat finally dropping away.

It was Gabriel's telescope.

Viliami smiled at me brilliantly. "There you go, Salote."

"Oh, my god. Viliami. Where did you get it?"

"It's a mystery. Somebody brought it into the Club but couldn't remember Gabriel's name. Since he was a *palangi*, they figured if it went to the Club, we'd find him. And it *was* the right place, because Gabriel told me before he left that if we ever found his telescope, I should give it to you."

"But who was it? What happened? Was it Vigo the Hermit?"

"No, a Tongan, some Tofuan. Filimone, maybe, was his name?"

"The saddest innkeeper I've ever met," I said, smiling. "He knew how upset Gabriel was to lose it. God. You don't know how much this means to me." I couldn't keep my hands off it, touching it like a ransomed child. It looked shiny, undamaged. I looked at its lens, which was miraculously uncracked. "Where has this thing been, anyway, I wonder. Viliami, you're my hero."

We had a kava party to celebrate. Lopini pulled out a packet of kava root, Filipa brought in the family bowl and rocks, Viliami pounded the root, and I mixed the brew, my hands as happy as my heart every time I looked at the telescope. The Tongans wanted gossip. They wanted to know how Mort could have been freed. They wanted to know all about Mac Barnett and his brave and crazy actions in America, and there was much appreciative laughter and admiration when they found out that Mac's weapon of choice was a tapa mallet.

"It could hurt somebody," Lopini said. "My granny used to chase me all over the place with hers when I acted up."

"Maybe we should give them to all the *polisi*," Funaki Ofa said. "Maki Barnett had a good idea."

They'd all heard gossip about Evelyn Henry, who they agreed was extremely attractive, and they wondered who her *mafu* really was. And whether she'd get fired. I kept looking at the telescope where it leaned in the corner. Its sturdy tripod and its orderly tube and glass and mirrors were reminders of reason and order and far away planets and the mystery of the universe. And a gift from my lost love.

I asked them just to sing. I wanted kava songs. It's so rare to get what you want, and I got it, a couple of hours of the most beautiful music in the world.

And then, in a sublime act of trust even more touching than when they left me alone with Sam, Tevita and Filipa left me alone with Viliami's crew, and then Viliami's crew left me alone with Viliami.

Apparently my evolution was incomplete, my vulnerability unresolved. Maybe I wanted him to be Gabriel that night. I wanted to make love and remember the rings of Saturn, the craters of the moon. Maybe I'd always wanted to seduce the fire dancer, to say I *had*. Whatever, I surrendered when Viliami quietly came to me.

"You need something," he said. "Tonight, I think you need me." I knew he meant *tonight*, probably tonight only.

I pulled out soft mats, and we sprawled out on them and made love without saying a word. I could faintly smell kerosene, his occupational hazard, and in the heat of us both I briefly wondered whether we might spontaneously combust. But he was as smooth and elegant as a leopard. People call women feline, but men can also move like cats. He stretched across my body, self-assured, kissing my neck and shoulders, pushing my arms straight out and holding me down with his, our hands clutching. I pointed my toes and tried to make my body as long as his, wanting to meet him everywhere. We kissed and kissed. I felt for his cock, which was fat like Gabriel's. I slid him into me, and I took him in until we both moaned. I wanted to let go, but Gabriel was in my head somewhere, and I didn't come. I didn't care.

"You're delicious," I murmured.

"You needed me," he repeated when we were resting, finally, smoking cigarettes, our sweat evaporating into the dark. "You needed love." I noticed the past tense. Already.

He knew a lot about me. Too much. "Don't feel sorry for me, Viliami. Leave me some dignity. Everybody needs love."

"Ah, yes. But you, Salote, *you*…are a special case." His ember flared up orange, the only light in the room. He could see much more in the dark, I imagined, than I, with my night-blind eyes. Well, he would see what he would see, and I would get by.

"I'm about as happy as anybody else," I said.

"You should stay in Tonga and marry a good man and have babies," he said quietly. "You'd like it." He stroked my belly, the place that would expand with child. The skin and muscles rippled under his touch, as if trying to say yes. Damn the logic of the body.

"You might be right," I said.

"I've been other places. I've been to the United States. But I'm so happy to come home."

"The trouble is, Viliami, this isn't my home."

"It could be, if you found love."

"I suppose you're right." I lay back, my useless, wide-open pupils gazing into the dark, which was like a velvety cocoon. "I'm not sure, but I think I have to go back to my home, whatever that is. Wherever I might find it, at least."

"I know," he said. "And I know something else. Your sadness betrays you. You're not just looking for your home, Salote. You're looking for the great love. Perhaps you already found him. I could love you, but it isn't me. I think you are mourning the loss of your great love."

To hide my embarrassing tears, I led him into my cramped, cool bathroom, with the push-out windows down to keep out prying midnight eyes. We ducked under the cold spray, our bodies necessarily squashed together, lathered and taut.

He dried me off gently and said, "Thank you, Salote."

He lit a match so I could see my way out of the shower, then lit a single candle, safely on the floor, away from my drapes. I sank back onto the mats and drank in his body in the burnished light as he got dressed.

"Don't give up on your great love," Viliami said. "The telescope came back."

"Thank you, Viliami." And then he kissed me tenderly and ducked out my back window, just like Mac Barnett so many months before.

I fell into a blessed sleep. I didn't know where I was when the rumbling woke me up. My eyes popped open, seeing nothing but dense black. Even though I didn't grasp what was happening at first, my heart was already beating hard, alarmed. Then the cot jumped and dumped me out onto the floor, and then the cot leaped over and landed on me. That was when electrical pops and explosions started, and I realized I was in the middle of a fucking huge earthquake.

The bucking and rumbling got worse. Pots and pans and books and bottles fell off the shelves, and then the shelves themselves crashed over on the telescope, and in seconds I heard screams and an infernal, metallic banging.

With the strength of adrenaline I pushed the cot off me and got up. The earthquake threw me down, and I banged my head on the corner of a shelf. Three times I got up and tried to make it to the door, and three times the earthquake threw me down. The fourth time I made it, screaming, into Tevita's yard. Spilled into the coral driveway on my knees, I vomited with fear. Reliable physics gone, palm trees swayed wildly, and, to my horror, I saw the ground rolling toward me in waves. Concrete cracked and glass broke. I couldn't stand up. Dogs howled.

I was going to die nine thousand miles away from home. My heart was pounding so hard I could feel it in my stomach, my eyeballs, my lips.

I was going to die, and my father would never know that I forgave him, and my mother would never know how much I hated her unhappiness, and Gabriel Bonner would never know I'd loved him up to my last breath. I was going to die instead of making up for Melanie. I wasn't supposed to die. I was the one who *lived*. This was all wrong.

Damn it, damn it, damn it. I thought I was yelling, but nothing came out.

The incessant banging on metal clanged on, as terrifying as the quake itself. Somewhere in the distance I heard Filipa's voice. "Salote, are you there? Are you there?"

And then it was over, and the trees settled down, and the ground stopped rolling, and I was still alive. I was shivering and couldn't stop. A huge palm tree lay cracked and collapsed on Filipa's cooking porch, the concrete blocks in a jumble underneath. Kids yelling "*Mofoike*! Earthquake!" So weird, their yelling almost happy, as if they'd been on a roller coaster. Tevita and Filipa were at my side, helping me up. Rare hugs, which I hungrily returned.

"Are you okay? Are you okay?" Everybody was out in the road, and Tevita and the teenage boys were running back and forth, checking on all the aunties. Filipa called out to the kids by name, and they came immediately, for once. No one was hurt.

"What the hell was that banging?" I finally managed to ask, my teeth chattering, my body still shaking out of control. "Tupou, hang on to Salote," Filipa ordered, and my nemesis grabbed me and held me up.

"Now you know that the old religion lives," Filipa said. "When the god of the underworld shakes us, we bang on metal to scare him away."

"Jesus Christ, Filipa, it scared the hell out of me."

"That's the point." Tupou gripped me tighter because I was about to fall down.

"Salote needs to sit down," she told Filipa. Tupou guided me to the nearest stump. But it wasn't a stump. It was my whale vertebra, tossed from the hut. She eased me down on it. Somebody produced a blanket, and Tupou tucked it around me.

"I just realized that I love you," I told her.

"*Tapuni*, Salote," she said. "Don't talk crazy."

"I mean it. I love your mean cruel self. I'm crazy about you." And she smiled at me, a lovely sight.

After sweeping up the worst of the broken glass and tucking some pots and pans back onto their shelves, Filipa and Tevita clustered with the kids and wouldn't let me out of their sight.

"You shouldn't sleep alone tonight," Tevita said. "You sleep here."

I didn't have the will to disagree. But first I had to check inside my jumbled house. Taking a deep breath, I ventured over the threshold. The telescope. Damn. I lifted off a pyramid of books and there it was, nestled in the mats from last night where Viliami and I had lolled. I pushed off the books and stood the telescope up on its tripod. It seemed okay. Then I shambled back to Tevita's house and sought my shelter for the rest of the night. The kids brought out piles of mats and tapa cloth, and I slept as soundly as I'd ever slept in Tonga, cushioned by a pile of small bodies as warm and innocent as puppies.

A few mild aftershocks rumbled across the island the next morning, none damaging, and after only a few hours off the air, Radio Station A3Zed crackled back to life. A calm voice said that only one person died, even though the quake had registered 7.2 on the Richter scale and lasted an incredible forty-five seconds. The country was making international news. Would my parents hear that I was safe?

Mosesi came back from bicycle reconnoitering, excited. The Virgin Mary had toppled off a steeple at the Catholic church by the cemetery on Vuna Road. "Bad, bad omen," Filipa groaned. A couple of government buildings, brick and plaster in rigid colonial designs, had cracked down the middle. Electricity was out on most of the island. But Tongan houses, with their flexible lashed beams, held up.

Padding around the chaos in my *fale*, I felt raw and greatly exposed. The day was brilliant, the sunlight mockingly cheerful, as if the little turmoils of the people of earth were nothing much. But I was still alive.

I went to my row of amulets: stones, shells, a piece of driftwood, the kava drinker, the sandalwood box. They'd all been tossed off the windowsill. Some had fallen out the window into the bushes. I reached down and got them. I touched each one and put it back. Living in Tonga, I had the fewest possessions of my life: enough plates for three or four, a saucepan, a spaghetti pot, a frying pan. But in the morning's bleached light, what I had seemed like far too much. I felt so tired that picking up a single dish threatened to exhaust me. But I was still alive.

There was something I needed to do. In the afternoon, after resting all day, I gathered up enough strength to pick up the whale vertebra and stuff it into my bike basket. I rode to the end of Faua Wharf, which seemed to be untouched and blessedly deserted. The sun was glimmering and hot, as if there'd never been a quake, never a murder, never a painful love. I wrapped my arms around the vertebra, lifted it, and threw it off the end of the wharf. "Peace," I cried. It splashed into the green water where it belonged and immediately sank. When it was out of sight and the ripples had disappeared, I lay down on the biggest boulder I could find and forced myself to breathe. But when I took deep breaths, I started to cry. My head hurt from where I'd hit the shelf last night. My body hurt. My neck muscles felt sprained. Shock pulsed through my nerves. I felt uneasy in my body. But I was still alive.

After I cried, I lay back and let the sun bake me, the green water soothe me as the small reef-waves lapped on the rocks, until I fell fitfully asleep. When I woke up, the sun had fallen into the horizon and I had goose bumps on my arms. I rode back fast to the inland warmth.

There was a dinner party that night. Incredibly, Evelyn Henry had decided to try to make up with her disgruntled volunteers. She scheduled a bunch of soirees to which everyone went resentfully, only because of the free food and booze. She was probably going to leave soon; people said Peace Corps Washington had just about had enough. But all that didn't matter, because she was still here, and it was my turn. Wade came by in the Peace Corps van, Gabriel's white Peace Corps van, I would forever think, to see whether I was okay. I was. He told me that all our parents were getting telegrams. And the dinner's still on, he said. It'll be good for you, he said.

Somehow Evelyn Henry's two cooks—not Evelyn Henry, of course, but the husband and wife who fed her and lived out back in a small, traditional hut—managed to bring to the table a six-course dinner featuring Beef Wellington, without electricity and less than twenty-four hours after the biggest earthquake in the country's history.

I thought that not enough was made of this feat. The cooks didn't even appear; Evelyn, strangely muted and sedate, gray roots showing and no dervish scarf hiding deep lines on her neck, scooped up compliments for them. And there was Faina, my boss, and there was my place next to him, and there was Clare and at her side, there was Gyorgy. And we were all alive, and the food was good. Of course we all swapped chatter about how we had survived, about how the banging on metal had unnerved us—except Faina, of course, who smiled. "It's good for you *palangis* to come face to face with the primal," he said, "Or is it the primeval?" We agreed that it was both. I described how I'd been unable to stand up and how I'd slept in a comforting heap with Tevita's kids. The others had similar stories, and the half dozen bottles of red wine Evelyn had managed to scavenge from somewhere were blessedly unbroken in the earthquake. We quaffed wine like water, toasting our survival again and again.

Maybe it was the earthquake, or maybe it had been going on under my nose all along and I simply hadn't noticed, but this time it seemed that Clare and

Gyorgy must have figured out the whole "my mother/my lover" thing because they seemed totally affectionate and in each other's adoring orbit. I didn't ask what had happened to Matthew, but these things happen, the ups and downs, the infatuations, so many hellos and good-byes.

At any rate, Clare and Gyorgy were starting something. Not just their June-October romance, maybe, but also something else. Now that I knew what it felt like to be in love—the darting glances, an eagerness to touch the beloved—I saw that they had the look. Watching them, listening to them, was almost too much. I felt wizened and weary, but I drank wine and listened anyway.

"So try this on for size: we want to start an arts program for the kids of Tonga," Clare declared. "We want you all to help. My late husband, Vladimir, left me a lot of money, and Gyorgy has some, too, from his stepfather. We're calling it Melanie's House, and it will be in Ngeleia, where Melanie used to live."

Gyorgy smiled and threw his elegant arm around Clare. He said they were going to tear down the house where Melanie had been murdered and start all over, making something new and beautiful and full of love. It would be a kind of exorcism, a redemption beginning with architecture.

Leave it to new lovers to have the naïve energy, the gumption, for a big project, I thought, fighting down tears. I forced myself to breathe. I would have liked to lose myself in something with Gabriel—a grand enterprise, a love child. But without him, I still could dip my toes into Clare and Gyorgy's project. I'd never been much of an altruist, but it wouldn't kill me. I'd mostly seen its boring twin, self-righteousness, but maybe I would take another look.

"We'll have tapa painting and other painting, too. And music." Clare was happily babbling. I found myself smiling.

"Melanie's House. I like the sound of that," I said. "I bet Leota would teach painting, and Viliami could fire dance."

Faina said Melanie's House would fit in perfectly with ideas he had for the Ministry of Business and Trade. He was thinking of sponsoring a folklore conference, and he'd been talking to Kalisimasi about some of the possibilities. I figured I could be involved, if I stayed, and if I made it through the rest of my last year. I was such a backslider, feeling guilty and shy as my old enthusiasm for doing the right thing bubbled up. Gabriel, I realized, had left me with one concrete item to offer.

"I got a gift last night, a miracle, actually," I said, "and it survived the earthquake without a scratch. It's a telescope. Do you think your kids would like the inspiration of the moon and the stars?"

Gyorgy gave me a look that said, "You are one of us."

"Yes," he said. "We'd love a telescope. I remember, Charlotte. I remember that you and I have something in common—that solar eclipse." He kindly didn't mention our drunken dash into Fitzhugh Grey's hot shower, though tonight that affair suddenly didn't seem so bad, just one of those things that happened on a night when we all missed Melanie. "The children of Tonga should have a chance to see the planets, the moon," Gyorgy said, "like you and I once did."

"The first time I ever saw the rings of Saturn was here in Tonga," I said, turning significantly to Evelyn Henry, who kept her cryptic silence. Maybe she'd already resigned or had gotten the boot. "I saw Saturn through that very telescope. Gabriel Bonner showed me, and I think he helped me change my life." Evelyn Henry smiled and smiled. I didn't care what she thought.

I needed to tie up one loose end. I picked a Sunday morning for it, the time when the Tongans would be in church, and I could ride my bike along the roads to Ngeleia with almost no dust, and when I got there I could have the place to myself—my small, sorrowful chapel. I wanted to see it again before it was gone.

I found Melanie's house collapsed, imploded on itself, the twining morning glories tangled up in swatches of torn thatch and ragged accordions of lashed bamboo. The Masonite and plaster walls with their graffiti were broken up, and small palm seedlings already sprouted in the debris. I could make out a fragment of my peace symbol on one of the larger pieces.

It was good to be there, in the brilliant light, even though I didn't know exactly why I was there. Melanie, or what I'd always believed was Melanie, hadn't come to visit me for months, and I thought that perhaps her ghost was finding some sort of peace. Sweat rolled down my back as I circled the place, wanting it to tell me something, wanting the sun to glint significantly through the cracks of the ruins like Stonehenge at the solstice.

But all that happened was that itchy grasses scissored against my shaved legs and flies pestered around my hairline. A skinny black dog sniveled out from behind Leota's house and sniffed toward me. Was he supposed to be some kind of messenger? I wasn't in the mood for symbols; if he insisted, he would get a piece of my resistance. I picked up a chunk of coral and sailed it at the dog's ass. It connected, and he yelped and slunk away.

So, evil would always be there. Sometimes it would lurk in the dark, but sometimes it would come out into the sunlight and make a big show of itself. Somewhere Mort was living free, wrestling with torments he could never escape. Somewhere Mac Barnett was studying for an exam, keeping an eye on the tapa mallet he'd never use again, even to pound in a single pushpin on a piece of cork.

Somewhere Melanie's parents were grieving, touching old photographs and writing letters to bureaucrats, the cruelty and injustice still painfully raw. Somewhere, my father and my mother were walking a well-worn path in the woods, talking about this year's strawberry crop, salvaging something tentative and delicate and good.

Somewhere, I wanted to believe, Gabriel Bonner was looking up at his beloved sky after putting the kid to bed, wondering whether he'd ever see me again.

The beefy sun caught on a bit of debris. Following the gleam, I found the source in a shard of plaster: my Scorpio pendant.

I bent over, and when I reached into the weeds toward it, I saw that the pendant rested in a florid bloom of thistles. I stood up and smiled. "That figures," I said to the dog, who sat on his bony haunches at a safe distance, eying me warily. "What the hell," I said. I was ready to have it back. To have my past with no regrets. To be simply me.

So I reached for real this time and pulled it out. The thistles bit at my hand, and two small bubbles of blood popped up, like a snakebite, on my palm. I wiped the blood on my *tupenu*, my fist wrapped around the pendant. I fiddled with the clasp, got it open, fumbled behind my head and put it around my neck. It felt good on my body again.

There'd be salve and a band aid in my first aid kit for the little stigmata. It wasn't serious, and I wasn't in a hurry. I would take my time saying good-bye to Melanie. And then I would take my time riding back into the dusty town. I'd ride back knowing that I wasn't sure about anything except that I had been changed by love and death and that on this one shimmering day, I was still alive, and that was something.

Informal Glossary of Tongan Terms and Places in Night Blind

Alu a, eh?: good-bye, farewell—literally, "You're going, eh?" Depends on the circumstances—paired with *"Mou nofo a, eh?"*—literally, "You're staying, eh?"

faifekau: preacher or pastor.

faikava: kava party.

faka'apa'apa: respect.

fakafiefia: to make happy; enjoyable.

fakakata: to amuse; to make somebody laugh.

fakalaiti: colloquial Tonganization for gay—lit. "like a lady."

fakamolemole: please.

faka'ofa'ofa: beautiful.

fakapo: murder.

fakatonga: in the Tongan way.

fale: house; by itself, usually a small hut in the traditional Tongan design.

falelotu: church (house of holiness).

falemahaki: hospital—lit. house of disease.

fefine: girl.

foa: coconut husk used to swirl and mix the kava in the kava bowl.

fokisi: Tonganized "fox," colloquial for prostitute.

Fua'amotu Airport: the main airport on Tongatapu.

Ha'apai: the middle of Tonga's three island groups.

ha'u: come here.

'io: yes.

'ikai: no.

Kalisimasi: Tonganized word for Christmas.

kapekape: dirty words, slang, esp. regarding sex or blasphemy.

kava: mildly narcotic beverage made from the ground roots of the *piper methysticum* plant; it plays a central role in Tongan social life and rituals.

Kava kuoheka!: The kava is ready! Called out as each cup of kava is served at a kava ceremony.

kefa: coconut strand rope that holds a mourning mat around a mourner's waist.

koe ha?: What? What's happening? Who's there?

kole: borrow.

kosi: to cut. Also, a goat.

Kao and Tofua: volcanic islands in the Ha'apai Group. The channel between them was the site of the mutiny on the *Bounty* in 1789, and where fearful Tofuans stoned one of Captain Bligh's loyalists, John Norton, to death.

laimi: lime juice.

lu: Tongan dish made with meat or fish and coconut milk wrapped and baked in taro leaves.

ma: bread.

mafu: heart; also, colloquially, sweetheart.

mahalo (or *mahalo pe*): maybe.

malie: common shout of praise; bravo; three cheers!

malo: thank you.

malo 'aupito: thank you very much.

malo e laumalie: greeting for a noble.

malo e lelei: most common greeting—thanks for being well.

ma'ulu'ulu: a traditional sitting dance, usually performed by large groups of women.

Mele Toto: Tonganized term for Bloody Mary.

moana: one of many terms for the ocean. Deep part of the ocean outside the reef.

mofoike: earthquake.

mohe: sleep.

molokau: stinging brown centipede.

Mou nofo a, eh?: good-bye, farewell—lit. "You're staying, eh?" Paired with *"Alu a, eh?"* or "you're going, eh?"

ngako: 1. The "cracklin'" or tasty, crispy layer of top skin on a roast pig—considered a delicacy and often offered to a guest of honor.

   2. Colloquially, the sexiest part of a woman's anatomy—the two or three inches just above her knee.

niu: coconut.

niu mu'i: green coconut.

Niuatoputapu: by far, the northernmost island in Tonga—closer to Samoa than the rest of the Tonga islands.

nika: Tonganization, painfully, of "nigger"; reputedly picked up from American soldiers in World War II.

Nuku'alofa: capital city of Tonga, on the southern island of Tongatapu.

'ofa: love.

'ofa atu: common Tongan toast. It means "love to you" or, generally, here's to you.

'ofa moe melino: love and peace.

oiaue: all-purpose interjection of surprise, amazement, enthusiasm, frustration, sorrow, pity, or anguish.

pa'anga: Tongan unit of currency. A dollar.

palangi: foreigner. Usually specifically a white person.

Pisikoa: Tonganized version of Peace Corps.

Salote: Charlotte's Tongan name. Also the name of the late great Queen of Tonga, mother of the King Taufa'ahau Tupou Fa.

taha, ua, tolu: one, two, three.

ta'olunga: traditional "standing dance" performed solo by a woman.

tapa: papyrus-like cloth made by pounding and gluing strips of bark and painting them in intricate brown and black designs.

tapuni: shut; shut up.

Toe tu'u: 1. Tongan word for Easter—lit. to stand up again or resurrection. 2. Vulgar sexual allusion.

toka kovi: bad sea, rough sea.

Tofua: see Kao and Tofua. Reputedly source of the best and most prized kava in Tonga.

tofua'a: whale.

Tongatapu: largest island in Tonga, situated in the southern group; home of Nuku'alofa, the capital city. Means "sacred land" or "sacred south."

tupenu: wraparound skirt knotted at the waist, worn by both men and women.

Vava'u: the northernmost of Tonga's three island groups. Its largest town is the beautiful Neiafu.

ABOUT THE AUTHOR

Jan Worth is a poet, essayist, fiction writer, and writing teacher at the University of Michigan—Flint. Her work has appeared widely, including in *Blaze, Contemporary Michigan Poetry, Controlled Burn,* the *Detroit Free Press,* the *Drexel Online Journal, Drought, Fourth Genre,* the *Los Angeles Times,* the *MacGuffin, Marlboro Review, Passages North, Witness,* and many others. An Ohio native, she was a Peace Corps volunteer in the Kingdom of Tonga from 1976–78. She has been a newspaper reporter and social worker. She holds an MSW from the University of Michigan and an MFA from Warren Wilson College. She and her husband, Ted Nelson, commute between Michigan and Los Angeles.

978-0-595-39977-2
0-595-39977-0

CPSIA information can be obtained at www.ICGtesting.com
Printed in the USA
270031BV00001B/7/A